Richard D. Blackmore

Perlycross

A Tale of the Western Hills

Richard D. Blackmore

Perlycross
A Tale of the Western Hills

ISBN/EAN: 9783337080211

Printed in Europe, USA, Canada, Australia, Japan

Cover: Foto ©Andreas Hilbeck / pixelio.de

More available books at **www.hansebooks.com**

PERLYCROSS

A TALE OF THE WESTERN HILLS

BY

R. D. BLACKMORE

AUTHOR OF "LORNA DOONE," "SPRINGHAVEN," ETC.

THIRTEENTH THOUSAND

LONDON

SAMPSON LOW, MARSTON, & COMPANY

LIMITED

St. Dunstan's House

FETTER LANE, FLEET STREET, E.C.

1894.

LONDON:

PRINTED BY WILLIAM CLOWES AND SONS, LIMITED,
STAMFORD STREET AND CHARING CROSS.

CONTENTS.

b

iv

CONTENTS.

PERLYCROSS.

CHAPTER I.

THE LAP OF PEACE.

In the year 1835, the Rev. Philip Penniloe was Curate-in-charge of Perlycross, a village in a valley of the Black-down Range. It was true that the Rector, the Rev. John Chevithorne, M.A., came twice every year to attend to his tithes; but otherwise he never thought of interfering, and would rather keep his distance from spiritual things. Mr. Penniloe had been his College-tutor, and still was his guide upon any points of duty less cardinal than discipline of dogs and horses.

The title of "Curate-in-charge" as yet was not invented generally; but far more Curates held that position than hold it in these stricter times. And the shifting of Curates from parish to parish was not so frequent as it is now; theological views having less range and rage, and Curates less divinity. Moreover it cost much more to move.

But the Curate of Perlycross was not of a lax or careless nature. He would do what his conscience required, at the cost of his last penny; and he thought and acted as if this world were only the way to a better one. In this respect he differed widely from all the people of his parish, as well as from most of his Clerical brethren. And it is no little thing to say of him, that he was beloved in spite of his piety.

B

Especially was he loved and valued by a man who had known him from early days, and was now the Squire, and chief landowner, in the parish of Perlycross. Sir Thomas Waldron, of Walderscourt, had battled as bravely with the sword of steel, as the Churchman had with the spiritual weapon, receiving damages more substantial than the latter can inflict. Although by no means invalided, perhaps he had been pleased at first to fall into the easy lap of peace. After eight years of constant hardship, frequent wounds, and famishing, he had struck his last blow at Waterloo, and then settled down in the English home, with its comforting cares, and mild delights.

Now, in his fiftieth year, he seemed more likely to stand on the battlements of life than many a lad of twenty. Straight and tall, robust and ruddy, clear of skin, and sound of foot, he was even cited by the doctors of the time, as a proof of the benefit that flows from bleeding freely. Few men living had shed more blood (from their own veins at any rate) for the good of their native land, and none had made less fuss about it; so that his Country, with any sense of gratitude, must now put substance into him. Yet he was by no means over fat; simply in good case, and form. In a word, you might search the whole county, and find no finer specimen of a man, and a gentleman too, than Colonel Sir Thomas Waldron.

All this Mr. Penniloe knew well; and having been a small boy, when the Colonel was a big one, at the best school in the west of England, he owed him many a good turn for the times when the body rules the roost, and the mind is a little chick, that can't say—"Cockadoodle." In those fine days, education was a truly rational process; creating a void in the juvenile system by hunger, and filling it up with thumps. Scientific research has now satisfied itself that the mind and the body are the selfsame thing; but this was not understood as yet, and the one ministered to the other. For example, the big Tom Waldron supplied the little Phil Penniloe with dumps and penny-puddings, and with fists ever ready for his defence; while the quicker mind sat upon the broad arch of chest sprawling along the old oak bench, and construed the lessons for it, or supplied the sad hexameter. When such a pair meet again in later life, sweet memories arise, and fine goodwill.

This veteran friendship even now was enduring a test too severe, in general, for even the most sterling affection. But a conscientious man must strive, when bound by Holy Orders, to make every member of his parish discharge his duty to the best advantage. And if there be a duty which our beloved Church—even in her snoring period—has endeavoured to impress, the candid layman must confess that it is the duty of alms-giving. Here Mr. Penniloe was strong—far in advance of the times he lived in, though still behind those we have the privilege to pay for. For as yet it was the faith of the general parishioner, that he had a strong parochial right to come to church for nothing; and if he chose to exercise it, thereby added largely to the welfare of the Parson, and earned a handsome reference. And as yet he could scarcely reconcile it with his abstract views of religion, to find a plate poked into his waistcoat pocket, not for increase, but depletion thereof.

Acknowledging the soundness of these views, we may well infer that Perlycross was a parish in which a well-ordered Parson could do anything reasonable. More than one substantial farmer was good enough to be pleased at first, and try to make his wife take it so, at these opportunities of grace. What that expression meant was more than he could for the life of him make out; but he always connected it with something black, and people who stretched out their hands under cocoa-nuts bigger than their heads, while "come over and help us," issued from their mouths. If a shilling was any good to them, bless their woolly heads, it only cost a quarter of a pound of wool!

Happy farmer, able still to find a shilling in his Sunday small-clothes, and think of the guineas in a nest beneath the thatch! For wheat was golden still in England, and the good ox owned his silver side. The fair outlook over hill and valley, rustling field and quiet meadow, was not yet a forlorn view, a sight that is cut short in sigh, a prospect narrowing into a lane that plods downhill to workhouse. For as yet it was no mockery to cast the fat grain among the clods, or trickle it into the glistening drill,

to clear the sleek blade from the noisome weed, to watch
the soft waves of silky tassels dimple and darken to the
breeze of June, and then the lush heads with their own
weight bowing to the stillness of the August sun, thrilling
the eyes with innumerable throng, glowing with impene-
trable depth of gold. Alas, that this beauty should be of
the past, and ground into gritty foreign flour !

But in the current year of grace, these good sons of our
native land had no dream of the treason, which should sell
our homes and landscapes to the sneering foreigner. Their
trouble, though heavy, was not of British madness, but
inflicted from without; and therefore could be met and
cured by men of strong purpose and generous act.

That grand old church of Perlycross (standing forth in
gray power of life, as against the black ruins of the Abbey)
had suddenly been found wanting—wanting foundation,
and broad buttress, solid wall, and sound-timbered roof,
and even deeper hold on earth for the high soar of the
tower. This tower was famous among its friends, not only
for substance, and height, and proportion, and piercings,
and sweet content of bells; but also for its bold uplifting
of the green against the blue. To-wit, for a time much
longer than any human memory, a sturdy yew-tree had
been standing on the topmost stringing-course, in a
sheltering niche of the southern face, with its head over-
topping the battlements, and scraping the scroll of the
south-east vane. Backed as it was by solid stone, no storm
had succeeded in tugging its tough roots out of the meshes
of mortar ; and there it stood and meant to stand, a puzzle
to gardeners, a pleasure to jackdaws, and the pride of all
Perlycrucians. Even Mr. Penniloe, that great improver,
could not get a penny towards his grand designs, until he
had signed a document with both Churchwardens, that
happen what might, not a hair of the head of the sacred
yew-tree should perish.

Many a penny would be wanted now, and who was to
provide them? The parish, though large and comprising
some of the best land in East Devon, had few resources of
commerce, and not many of manufacture. The bright
Perle running from east to west clove it in twain ; and the
northern part, which was by far the larger, belonged to the

Waldrons ; while the southern (including the church and greater part of village) was of divers owners, the chiefest being the Dean and Chapter of Exeter. It is needless to say that this sacred body never came nigh the place, and felt no obligation towards it, at the manhood of this century.

" What is to be done ? " cried the only man who could enter into the grief of it, when Richard Horner of Pumpington, architect, land-agent, and surveyor, appeared before the Clergyman and Churchwardens, with the report required by them.

" One of two things," answered Mr. Horner, a man of authority and brevity ; " either let it crumble, or make up your minds to spend a thousand pounds upon it."

" We should be prepared to spend that sum, if we had only got it ; " Mr. Penniloe said, with that gentle smile which made his people fond of him.

" We han't got a thousand, nor a hundred nayther You talk a bit too big, Dick. You always did have a big mouth, you know."

The architect looked at his cousin, Farmer John (the senior Churchwarden of Perlycross, and chief tenant of the Capitular estates), and if his own mouth was large, so was that of his kinsman, as he addressed him thus.

" John Horner, we know well enough, what you be. It wouldn't make much of a hole in you, to put down your hundred pounds—to begin with."

" Well," said his colleague, Frank Farrant, while the elder was in labour of amazement ; " if John will put down his hundred pounds, you may trust me to find fifty."

" And fifty to you is a good bit more than a thousand to him, I reckon. Book it, Mr. Penniloe, before they run back ; and me for another five and twenty."

" I never said it ; I never said a word of it"—Farmer John began to gasp, while cousin and colleague were patting him on the back, crying,

" Don't go back from your word, John."

" Now, did I say it, Parson Penniloe ? " he appealed, as soon as they would let him speak ; " come now, I'll go by what you say of it."

" No, Mr. Horner ; I wish you had. You never said anything of the kind."

"Parson, you are a gentleman. I do like a man as tells the truth. But as for them fellows, I'll just show them what's what. Whether I said it, or no—I'll do it."

Mr. Penniloe smiled, but not with pleasure only. Simple and charitable as he was, he could scarcely believe that the glory of God was the motive power in the mind of Farmer John.

CHAPTER II.

FAIRY FAITH.

AT the beginning of July, work was proceeding steadily, though not quite so merrily perhaps, as some of the workmen might have wished; because Mr. Penniloe had forbidden the presence of beer-cans in consecrated ground. A large firm of builders at Exeter (Messrs. Peveril, Gibbs & Co.) had taken the contract according to Mr. Horner's specifications; and had sent a strong staff of workmen down, under an active junior partner, Mr. Robson Adney. There are very few noises that cannot find some ear to which they are congenial; and the clink of the mason's trowel is a delight to many good people. But that pleasant sound is replaced, too often, by one of sadder harmony— the chink of coin that says adieu, with all the regret behind it.

Perlycross had started well on this, its greatest enterprise; every man was astonished at his neighbour's generosity, and with still better reason at his own. Mr. Penniloe's spirit rose above the solid necessity of repairs, and aspired to richer embellishment. That hideous gallery at the western end, which spoiled the tower entrance and obscured a fine window, should go into the fire at last; the noble arch of the chancel (which had been shored with timber braces) should be restored and reopened, and the blocked-up windows should again display their lovely carving. In the handsomest manner, Sir Thomas Waldron had sent him a cheque for five hundred pounds; which after all was only just, because the vaults of the Waldron race lay at the bottom of half the lapse. The Dean and Chapter of Exeter had contributed a hundred pounds ; and the Rector another hundred ; and the Curate's own father —an ancient clergyman in the north of Devon, with a tidy living and a plump estate—had gone as far as twenty pounds, for the honour of the family.

With this money in hand, and much more in hope, all present designs might well be compassed. But alas, a new temptation rose, very charming, and very costly. The Curate had long suspected that his favourite church had been endowed (like its smaller sister at Perlycombe) with a fair rood-screen ; perhaps a fine one, worthy of the days, when men could carve. And now, when the heavy wooden gallery of Queen Anne's time had been removed, it happened that Sergeant Jakes, the schoolmaster, who had seen a great deal of old work in Spain, was minded to enquire into the bearings of the great bressemer at the back. He put his foot into a hole beneath it, where solid brickwork was supposed to be ; but down went his foot into a lot of crumbling stuff, and being no more than a one-armed man, Mr. Jakes had a narrow escape of his neck. Luckily he clung with his one hand to a crossbeam still in position, and being of a very wiry frame—as all the school-children knew too well—was enabled to support himself, until a ladder was clapped to. Even then it was no easy thing to extricate his foot, wedged between two trefoils of sharply cut stone ; and for more than a week it was beyond his power to bring any fugitive boy to justice. The Parson was sent for at once, and discovered the finest stone-screen in the diocese, removed from its place by a barbarous age, and plastered up in the great western wall.

There was little of that hot contention then, which rages now over every stock and stone appertaining to the Church. As the beauty of design, and the skill of execution, grew more and more manifest to his delighted eyes, Mr. Penniloe was troubled with no misgivings as to " graven images." He might do what he liked with this grand piece of work, if the money were forthcoming. And the parish suspected no Popery in it, when after much council with all concerned, and holding the needful faculty, he proposed to set up this magnificent screen as a reredos beneath the great

Chancel window, and behind the stone Communion-table, generally called the Altar now.

Yet brave as he was and of ardent faith, some little dismay was natural, when the builders assured him that this could not be done, with all needful repairs and proper finish, for less than three hundred and fifty pounds, and they would not even bind themselves to that; for the original was of the best Beere stone, difficult to match, and hard to work. Mr. Penniloe went to the quarries, and found that this was no exaggeration; and having some faith in mankind—as all who have much in their Maker must have—he empowered the firm to undertake the task, while he cast about zealously for the cash.

With filial confidence he made sure that his reverend father must rejoice in another opportunity for glorifying God; and to that effect he addressed him. But when the postman wound his horn at the bottom of the village, and the Parson hurried down from the churchyard to meet him, at the expense of eightpence he received the following dry epistle.

"SON PHILIP,—We are much surprised and pained by your extraordinary letter. You speak very largely of 'duty to God,' which ought to be done, without talking of it; while you think lightly of your duty to your parents, the commandment that carries the blessing. If you had not abandoned your Fellowship, by marrying and having a family, it might have been more in your power to think of Church-windows, and stone-carving. We did not expect to be treated like this, after our very handsome gift, of not more than three months agone. Look for no more money; but for that which a good son values more, and earns by keeping within his income—the love of his affectionate parents,

"ISAAC, AND JOAN PENNILOE."

"Ah! ah! Well, well, I dare say I was wrong. But I thought that he could afford it;" said the Curate in his simple way: "'tis a sad day for me altogether. But I will not be cast down, for the Lord knoweth best."

For on this very day, a year ago, he had lost the happiness of his life, and the one love of his manhood.

His fair wife (a loyal and tender helpmate, the mother of his three children, and the skilful steward of his small means) had been found lying dead at the foot of the " Horseshoe Pitch," beneath Hagdon Hill. While her husband was obliged to remain in the village, waiting for a funeral, she had set forth, with none but her younger boy Michael, to visit an old woman on the outskirts of the parish, very far advanced in years, but still a very backward Christian.

The old woman was living at the present moment, but could throw no light upon her visitor's sad fate, and indeed denied that she had seen her on that day. And the poor child who must have beheld what happened, though hitherto a very quick and clever little fellow, could never be brought to say a word about it. Having scarcely recovered from a sharp attack of measles, he had lost his wits through terror, and ran all the way home at the top of his speed, shouting " Rabbits ! Rabbits ! Rabbits ! "

From the child's sad condition, and a strict search of the " Horseshoe," it appeared that he had leaped after his poor mother, but had been saved from death by a ledge of brambles and furze which had broken his fall. Even now, though all trace of his bruises was gone, and his blue eyes were as bright as ever, the tender young brain was so dazed and daunted, by the fall, and the fright, and agony, that the children of the village changed his nickname from " Merry Michael," to " Mazed Mikey."

Mr. Penniloe had been fighting bravely against the sad memories of this day. To a deeply religious mind like his, despondency was of the nature of doubt, and sorrow long indulged grew into sin. But now a cloud of darkness fell around him ; the waves of the flood went over his soul, his heart was afflicted, and in sore trouble ; and there was none to deliver him.

All men have their times of depression ; but few feel such agonies of dejection, as the firm believer and lover of his faith, when harrowing doubts assail him. The Rector of Perlycross, Mr. Chevithorne, though by no means a man of vast piety, had a short way of dealing with such attacks, which he always found successful. To his certain knowledge, all debility of faith sprang directly from " lowness of

the system ; " and his remedy against all such complaints
was a glass of hot brandy and water. But his Curate's
religion was a less robust, because a far more active power ;
and his keener mind was not content to repel all such
sallies, as temptations of the Devil.

Sensitive, diffident, and soft-hearted, he was apt to feel
too acutely any wound to his affections ; and of all the
world now left to him, the dearest one was his mother.
Or at any rate, he thought so for the present ; though a
certain little tender claim was creeping closer and closer
into the inmost cell of love.

" Can mother have forgotten what day it would be,
when I should receive these cruel words ? " he said to
himself, as he went sadly up the hill towards his white-
washed dwelling-place, having no heart left for the finest
of stone-carvings. " If she did, it was not like her ; and if
she remembered, it seems still worse. Surely he would not
have dared to sign her name, without her knowledge. But
whenever he thinks of that Fellowship—well, perhaps it
was wrong on my part to attempt so much. It is high
time to look more closely into ways and means."

That was the proper thing to do beyond a doubt, and he
hastened inside to do it. But when he sat in his lonely
bookroom, with the evening shadows of the dark ilex
slowly creeping over him, his mind went back into the
past, and a mighty sadness conquered him. Instead of the
list of subscriptions for the church he had drawn from the
long portfolio (which his wife had given him on the last
wedding-day they should ever keep together) a copy of a
sad despondent hymn, which he had written in the newness
of his grief. As he read the forgotten lines, once more
their deep gloom encompassed him ; even the twinkle of
hope, in which they ended, seemed a mockery.

" Will it ever be so, or is it all a dream, inspired by our
longings, and our self-conceit ? Whatever is pleasant, or
good, or precious, is snatched from our grasp ; and we call
it a trial, and live on, in the belief that we are punished
for our good, and shall be rewarded tenfold. If so, it can
be for those alone who are able to believe always ; who
can dismiss every shadow of doubt, and live with their
Maker face to face. Oh that I could do so. But I

cannot; my shallow mind is vexed by every breeze.
When I was a young man, I felt pity, and even contempt
for Gowler's unfaith—a man of far superior powers. He
gave up his Fellowship, like a conscientious man; while I
preach to others, and am myself a castaway. Oh, Ruth,
Ruth, if you could only see me!"

This man of holy life, and of pure devotion to his sacred
office, bent his head low in the agony of the moment, and
clasped his hands over his whitening hair. How far he
was out of his proper mind was shown by his sitting in the
sacred chair,* the old "dropping-chair" of the parish,
which had been sent back that morning. Of this, and of
all around, he took no heed; for the tide of his life was at
the lowest ebb, and his feeble heart was fluttering, like a
weed in shallow water.

But his comfort was not far to seek. After sundry soft
taps, and a shuffle of the handle, the door was opened
quietly, and a little girl came dancing in, bringing a gleam
of summer sunshine in a cloud of golden hair. The gloom
of the cold room fled, as if it had no business near her, and
a thrush outside (who knew her well) broke forth into a
gratitude of song. For this was little Faith Penniloe, seven
years old last Tuesday, the prettiest and the liveliest soul
in all the parish of Perlycross; and Faith being too substantial perhaps, everybody called her "Fay," or "Fairy."
Nothing ever troubled her, except the letter *r*, and even
that only when it wanted to come first.

"Father, fathery, how much colder is the tea to get?"
she cried; "I call it very yude of you, to do what you like,
because you happen to be older."

As the little girl ran, with her arms stretched forth, and
a smile on her lips that was surety for a kiss—a sudden
amazement stopped her. The father of her love and trust
and worship, was not even looking at her; his face was
cold and turned away; his arms were not spread for a
jump and a scream. He might as well have no child at all,
or none to whom he was all in all. For a moment her

---

* In country parishes an easy-chair, for the use of the sick and
elderly, was provided from the Communion offerings, and lent to those
most in need of it. When not so required, it was kept under cover,
and regarded with some reverence, from its origin and use.

simple heart was daunted, her dimpled hands fell on her
pinafore, and the sparkle of her blue eyes became a gleam
of tears.

Then she gathered up her courage, which had never
known repulse, and came and stood between her father's
knees, and looked up at him very tenderly, as if she had
grieved him, and yearned to be forgiven.

"Child, you have taught me the secret of faith," he cried,
with a sudden light shed on him ; "I will go as a little one
to my Father, without a word, and look up at Him."

Then, as he lifted her into his lap, and she threw her
arms around his neck, he felt that he was not alone in the
world, and the warmth of his heart returned to him.

CHAPTER III.

THE LYCH-GATE.

THE old church, standing on a bluff above the river, is
well placed for looking up and down the fertile valley.
Flashes of the water on its westward course may be caught
from this point of vantage, amidst the tranquillity of
ancient trees and sunny breadths of pasture. For there
the land has smoothed itself into a smiling plain, casting
off the wrinkles of hills and gullies, and the frown of
shaggy brows of heather. The rigour of the long flinty
range is past, and a flower can stand without a bush to
back it, and the wind has ceased from shuddering.

But the Perle has not come to these pleasures yet, as it
flows on the north of the churchyard, and some hundred feet
beneath it. The broad shallow channel is strewn with flint,
and the little stream cannot fill it, except in times of heavy
flood ; for the main of its water has been diverted to work the
woollen factory, and rejoins the natural course at the bridge
two or three hundred yards below. On the further side,
the land rises to the barren height of Beacon Hill, which
shelters Sir Thomas Waldron's house, and is by its conical
form distinct from other extremities of the Black-down
Chain. For the southern barrier of the valley (which is
about three miles wide at its mouth) is formed by the long

dark chine of Hagdon Hill, which ends abruptly in a steep descent ; and seeing that all this part of the vale, and the hills which shape it, are comprised in the parish of Perly-cross, it will become clear that a single Parson, if he attempts to go through all his work, must have a very fine pair of legs, and a sound constitution to quicken them.

Mr. Penniloe, now well advanced in the fifth decade, was of very spare habit and active frame, remarkable also for his springy gait, except at those periods of dark depression, with which he was afflicted now and then. But the leading fault of his character was inattention to his victuals, not from any want of common sense, or crude delight in fasting, but rather through self-neglect, and the loss of the one who used to attend to him. To see to that bodily welfare, about which he cared so little, there was no one left, except a careful active and devoted servant, Thyatira Muggridge. Thyatira had been in his employment ever since his marriage, and was now the cook, housekeeper, and general manager at the rectory. But though in the thirty-fifth year of her age, and as steady as a pyramid, she felt herself still too young to urge sound dietary advice upon her master, as she longed to do. The women of the parish blamed her sadly, as they watched his want of fattening ; but she could only sigh, and try to tempt him with her simple skill, and zeal.

On the morrow of that sad anniversary which had caused him such distress, the Curate was blest with his usual vigour of faith and courage and philanthropy. An affectionate letter from his mother, enclosing a bank-order for ten pounds, had proved that she was no willing partner in the father's harshness. The day was very bright, his three pupils had left him for their summer holidays, and there happened to be no urgent call for any parochial visits. There was nothing to stop him from a good turn to-day among trowel and chisel and callipers ; he would see that every man was at his work, and that every stroke of work was truthful.

Having slurred his early dinner with his usual zest, he was hastening down the passage for his hat and stick, when Thyatira Muggridge came upon him from the pantry, with a jug of toast-and-water in her hand.

"Do'e give me just a minute, sir," she whispered, with a
glance at the door of the dining-room where the children
had been left; and he followed her into the narrow back-
parlour, the head-quarters of his absent pupils.

Mr. Penniloe thought very highly of his housekeeper's
judgment and discretion, and the more so perhaps because
she had been converted, by a stroke of his own readiness,
from the doctrines of the "Antipædo-Baptists"—as they
used to call themselves—to those of the Church of England.
Her father, moreover, was one of the chief tenants on
the North Devon property of Mr. Penniloe the elder; and
simplicity, shrewdness, and honesty were established in
that family. So her master was patient with her, though
his hat and stick were urgent.

"Would you please to mind, sir,"—began Thyatira, with
her thick red arms moving over her apron, like rolling-pins
upon pie-crust—"if little Master Mike was to sleep with
me a bit, till his brother Master Harry cometh back from
school?"

"I dare say you have some good reason for asking;
but what is it, Mrs. Muggeridge?" The housekeeper was
a spinster, but had received brevet-rank from the village.

"Only that he is so lonesome, sir, in that end hattick, by
his little self. You know how he hath been, ever since his
great scare; and now some brutes of boys in the village
have been telling him a lot of stuff about Spring-heel Jack.
They say he is coming into this part now, with his bloody
heart and dark lantern. And the poor little lamb hath a
window that looks right away over the churchyard. Last
night he were sobbing so in his sleep, enough to break his
little heart. The sound came all across the lumber-room,
till I went and fetched him into my bed, and then he were
as happy as an Angel."

"Poor little man! I should have thought of it, since
he became so nervous. But I have always tried to make
my children feel that the Lord is ever near them."

"He compasseth the righteous round about," Mrs.
Muggeridge replied with a curtsey, as a pious woman
quoting Holy Writ; "but for all that, you can't call Him
company, sir; and that's what these little one's lacks of.
Master Harry is as brave as a lion, because he is so much

older. But hoping no offence, his own dear mother would never have left that little soul all by himself."

"You are right, and I was wrong ; " replied the master, concealing the pain her words had caused. "Take him to your room ; it is very kind of you. But where will you put Susanna ? "

"That will be easy enough, sir. I will make up a bed in the lumber-room, if you have no objection. Less time for her at the looking-glass, I reckon."

Mr. Penniloe smiled gravely—for that grievance was a classic—and had once more possessed himself of his hat and stick, when the earnest housekeeper detained him once again.

"If you please, sir, you don't believe, do you now, in all that they says about that Spring-heeled Jack ? It scarcely seemeth reasonable to a Christian mind. And yet when I questioned Mr. Jakes about it, he was not for denying that there might be such a thing—and him the very bravest man in all this parish ! "

"Mrs. Muggeridge, it is nonsense. Mr. Jakes knows better. He must have been trying to terrify you. A man who has been through the Peninsular campaign ! I hope I may remember to reprove him."

"Oh no, I would beg you, sir, not to do that. It was only said—as one might express it, promiscuous, and in a manner of speaking. I would never have mentioned it, if I had thought——"

Knowing that her face was very red, her master refrained from looking at it, and went his way at last, after promising to let the gallant Jakes escape. It was not much more than a hundred yards, along the chief street of the village, from the rectory to the southern and chief entrance of the churchyard ; opposite to which, at a corner of the road and partly in front of the ruined Abbey, stood an old-fashioned Inn, the *Ivy-bush*. This, though a very well conducted house, and quiet enough (except at Fair-time), was not in the Parson's opinion a pleasing induction to the lych-gate ; but there it had stood for generations, and the landlord, Walter Haddon, held sound Church-views, for his wife had been a daughter of Channing the clerk, and his premises belonged to the Dean and Chapter.

Mr. Penniloe glanced at the yellow porch, with his usual

regret but no ill-will, when a flash of bright colour caught his eye. In the outer corner he described a long scarlet fishing-rod propped against the wall, with the collar and three flies fluttering. All was so bright and spick and span, that a trout's admiration would be quite safe; and the clergyman (having been a skilful angler, till his strict views of duty deprived him of that joy) indulged in a smile of sagacity, as he opened his double eye-glass, and scrutinised this fine object.

"Examining my flies, are you, Reverend? Well, I hope you are satisfied with them."

The gentleman who spoke in this short way came out of the porch, with a pipe in his hand and a large fishing-creel swinging under his left arm.

"I beg your pardon, Dr. Gronow, for the liberty I am taking. Yes, they are very fine flies indeed. I hope you have had good sport with them."

"Pretty fair, sir; pretty fair"—the owner answered cheerfully—"one must not expect much in this weather. But I have had at least three rises."

"It is much to your credit, so far as I can judge, under the circumstances. And you have not had time to know our water yet. You will find it pretty fishing, when you get accustomed to it."

The angler, a tall thin man of sixty, with a keen grave face and wiry gray hair, regarded the Parson steadfastly. This was but the second time they had met, although Dr. Gronow had been for some while an important parishioner of Perlycross, having bought a ·fair estate at Priestwell, a hamlet little more than a mile from the village. People, who pretended to know all about him, said that he had retired suddenly, for some unknown reason, from long and large medical practice at Bath. There he had been, as they declared, the first authority in all cases of difficulty and danger, but not at all a favourite in the world of fashion, because of his rough and con-temptuous manners, and sad want of sympathy with petty ailments. Some pious old lady of rank had called him, in a passionate moment, "the Godless Gronow;" and whether he deserved the description or not, it had cleaved to him like a sand-leech. But the Doctor only smiled, and went his way; the good will of the poor was sweeter to him than the good word of the wealthy.

"Let me say a word to you, Mr. Penniloe," he began, as the Curate was turning away; "I have had it in my mind for some short time. I believe you are much attached to Sir Thomas Waldron."

"He is one of my oldest and most valued friends. I have the highest possible regard for him."

"He is a valuable man in the parish, I suppose—comes to church regularly—sets a good example?"

"If all my parishioners were like him, it would be a comfort to me, and—and a benefit to them."

"Well said—according to your point of view. I like a straightforward man, sir. But I want you to be a little crooked now. You have an old friend, Harrison Gowler."

"Yes,"—Mr. Penniloe replied with some surprise, "I was very fond of Gowler at Oxford, and admired him very greatly. But I have not seen him for some years."

"He is now the first man in London in his special line. Could you get him to visit you for a day or two, and see Sir Thomas Waldron, without letting him know why?"

"You astonish me, Dr. Gronow. There is nothing amiss with Sir Thomas, except a little trouble now and then, caused by an ancient wound, I believe."

"Ah, so you think; and so perhaps does he. But I suppose you can keep a thing to yourself. If I tell you something, will you give me your word that it shall go no further?"

The two gentlemen were standing in the shadow of the lych-gate, as a shelter from the July sun, while the clergyman gazed with much alarm at the other, and gave the required promise. Dr. Gronow looked round, and then said in a low voice—

"Sir Thomas is a strong and temperate man, and has great powers of endurance. I hope most heartily that I may be wrong. But I am convinced that within three months, he will be lying upon this stone; while you with your surplice on are standing in that porch, waiting for the bearers to advance."

"Good God!" cried the Parson, with tears rushing to his eyes; then he lifted his hat, and bowed reverently.

C

"May He forgive me for using His holy name. But the shock is too terrible to think of. It would certainly break poor Nicie's heart. What right have you to speak of such a dreadful thing?"

"Is it such a dreadful thing to go to heaven? That of course you guarantee for your good friends. But the point is—how to put off that catastrophe of bliss."

"Flippancy is not the way to meet it, Dr. Gronow. We have every right to try to keep a valuable life, and a life dear to all that have the sense to feel its value. Even a scornful man—such as you appear to be, unable to perceive the childish littleness of scorn—must admire valour, sense of duty, and simplicity; though they may not be his own leading qualities. And once more I ask you to explain what you have said."

"You know Jemmy Fox pretty well, I think?" Dr. Gronow took a seat upon the coffin-stone, and spoke as if he liked the Parson's vigour—"Jemmy is a very clever fellow in his way, though of course he has no experience yet. We old stagers are always glad to help a young member of our Profession, who has a proper love for it, and is modest, and hard-working. But not until he asks us, you must clearly understand. You see we are not so meddlesome as you Reverends are. Well, from the account young Fox gives me, there can, I fear, be little doubt about the nature of the case. It is not at all a common one; and so far as we know yet, there is but one remedy—a very difficult operation."

Mr. Penniloe was liable to a kind of nervous quivering, when anything happened to excite him, and some of his very best sermons had been spoiled by this visitation.

"I am troubled more than I can tell you,—I am grieved beyond description,"—he began with an utterance which trembled more and more; "and you think that Gowler is the only man, to—to——"

"To know the proper course, and to afford him the last chance. Gowler is not a surgeon, as I need not tell you. And at present such a case could be dealt with best in Paris, although we have young men rising now, who will make it otherwise before very long. Sir Thomas will listen to nothing, I fear, from a young practitioner like Fox. He has been so knocked about himself, and so close to death's door more than once, that he looks upon this as a fuss about nothing. But I know better, Mr. Penniloe."

"You are too likely to be right. Fox has told me of several cases of your wonderful penetration. That young man thinks so much of you. Oh, Dr. Gronow, I implore you as a man—whatever your own opinions are—say nothing to unsettle that young fellow's mind. You know not the misery you may cause, and you cannot produce any happiness. I speak—I speak with the strongest feelings. You will think that I should not have spoken at all—and I dare say it is unusual. But you will forgive me, when you remember it is my duty as a clergyman."

"Surely you are responsible for me as well"—replied the doctor with a kinder tone ; "but perhaps you regard me as beyond all cure. Well, I will promise what you ask, good sir. Your sheep, or your foxes, shall not stray through me. Will you do what I suggest about Gowler ?"

"I will try to get him down. But from all that I hear, he is one of the busiest men in London. And I dislike procuring his opinion on the sly. Excuse me—I know how well you meant it. But perhaps, through Lady Waldron, he may be brought down in the regular course, and have the whole case laid before him."

"That would be the best thing, if it could be managed. Good-bye! I go a-fishing, as your prototypes expressed it."

CHAPTER IV.

NICIE.

IN the bright summer sunshine the old church looked like a ship that had been shattered by the waves, and was hoisted in a dry dock for repairs. To an ignorant eye it appeared to be in peril of foundering and plunging into the depths below, so frequent and large were the rifts and chasms yawning in the ancient frame-work. Especially was there one long gap in the footings of the south chancel wall, where three broad arches were being turned, and a solid buttress rising, to make good the weakness of the Waldron vault.

Sacks of lime, and piles of sand, coils of cord and blocks of stone, scaffold-poles and timber-baulks, wheel-barrows grovelling upside-down, shovels and hods and planks and ladders, hats upon tombstones, and jackets on graves, sacred niches garnished with tobacco-pipes, and pious memories enlivened by "Jim Crow"—so cheerful was the British workman, before he was educated.

"Parson coming," was whispered round, while pewter pots jumped under slabs, and jugs had coats thrown over them, for Mr. Penniloe would have none of their drinking in the churchyard, and was loth to believe that they could do it, with all the sad examples beneath them. But now his mind was filled with deeper troubles; and even the purpose of his visit had faded from his memory.

"Just in time, sir. I was waiting for you"—said Mr. Robson Adney, standing in front of the shored-up screen, on the southern side of the tower,—" if it bears the strain of this new plinth, the rest is a matter of detail. Your idea of the brace was capital, and the dovetail will never show at all. Now, Charlie, steady there—not too heavy. Five minutes will show whether we are men or muffs. But don't stand quite so close, sir, I think we have got it all right; but if there should happen to be a bit of cross-grain stone—bear to the left, you lubber there ! Beg your pardon, sir—but I never said—' damn.'"

"I hope not, I hope not, Mr. Adney. You remember where you are, too well for that. Though I trust that you would say it nowhere. Ah, it is a little on the warp, I fear."

"No, sir, no. Go to the end, and look along. It is only the bevel that makes it look so. Could hardly be better if the Lord Himself had made it. Trust Peveril, Gibbs; & Co. for knowing their work. Holloa ! not so hard—ease her, ease her ! Stand clear for your lives, men ! Down she comes."

They were none too quick, for the great stone screen, after bulging and sagging and shaking like a cobweb throughout its massive tracery, parted in the middle and fell mightily.

"Any one hurt ? Then you haven't got what you ought "—shouted Adney, with his foot upon a pinnacle— "old Peter made a saint of ? Get a roller, and fetch him

out. None the worse, old chap, are you now? Take him
to the *Ivy-bush*, and get a drop of brandy."

Sudden as the crash had been, no life was lost, no limb
broken, and scarcely a bruise received, except by an
elderly workman, and he was little the worse, being safely
enshrined in the niche where some good saint had stood.
Being set upon his feet, he rubbed his elbows, and then
swore a little; therefore naturally enough he was known
as "St. Peter," for the residue of his life among us.

But no sooner did Mr. Adney see that no one was hurt
seriously than he began to swear anything but a little,
instead of thanking Providence.

"A pretty job—a fine job, by the holy poker!" he kept
on exclaiming, as he danced among the ruins; "why,
they'll laugh at us all over Devonshire. And that's not
the worst of it. By the Lord, I wish it was. Three or
four hundred pounds out of our pockets. A nice set of
—— fellows you are, aren't you? I wish I might go this
very moment——"

"Is this all your gratitude, Robson Adney, for the
goodness of the Lord to you?" Mr. Penniloe had been
outside the crash, as he happened to be watching from one
end the adjustment of the piece inserted. "What are
a few bits of broken stone, compared with the life of a
human being—cut off perhaps with an oath upon his lips,
close to the very house of God? In truth, this is a
merciful deliverance. Down upon your knees, my friends,
and follow me in a few simple words of acknowledgment
to the Giver of all good. Truly He hath been gracious
to us."

"Don't want much more of that sort of grace. *Coup de
grace* I call it"—muttered Mr. Adney. Nevertheless he
knelt down, with the dust upon his forehead; and the
workmen did the like; for here was another month's good
wages.

Mr. Penniloe always spoke well and readily, when his
heart was urgent; and now as he knelt between two
lowly graves, the men were wondering at him. "Never
thought a' could have dooed it, without his gown!"
"Why, a' put up his two hands, as if 'twor money in his
pockets!" "Blest if I don't send for he, when my time

cometh !" "Faix, sor, but the Almighty must be proud
of you to spake for Him !" Thus they received it; and
the senior Churchwarden coming in to see the rights of the
matter, told every one (when he recovered his wits) that
he had never felt so proud of the parish minister before.
Even the Parson felt warmly in his heart that he had gone
up in their opinions; which made him more diffident in
his own.

"Don't 'e be cast down, sir," said one fine fellow, whom
the heavy architrave had missed by about an inch, saving
a young widow and seven little orphans. "We will put it
all to rights, in next to no time. You do put up with it,
uncommon fine. Though the Lord may have laboured to
tempt 'e, like Job. But I han't heard a single curse come
out of your lips—not but what it might, without my
knowing. But here coom'th a young man in bright clothes
with news for 'e."

Mr. Penniloe turned, and behold it was Bob Cornish,
one of his best Sunday-school boys last year, patient and
humble in a suit of corduroy; but now gay and lordly in
the livery of the Waldrons, buff with blue edgings, and
buttons of bright gold. His father sold rushlights at the
bottom of the village, but his mother spent her time in
thinking.

"From Sir Thomas?" asked the Curate, as the lad with
some attempt at a soldier's salute produced a note, folded
like a cocked hat, and not easy to undo.

"No, sir, from my lady "—answered Robert, falling
back.

Mr. Penniloe was happy enough to believe that all things
are ordered and guided for us by supreme goodness and
wisdom. But nature insisted that his hands should tremble
at anything of gravity to any one he loved ; and now after
Dr. Gronow's warning, his double eyeglass rattled in its
tortoiseshell frame, as he turned it upon the following
words.

"DEAR SIR,—I am in great uncertainty to trouble you
with this, and beg you to accept apologies. But my
husband is in pain of the most violent again, and none the
less of misery that he conceals it from me. In this country

I have no one now from whom to seek good counsel, and the young Dr. Fox is too juvenile to trust in. My husband has so much value for your wise opinion. I therefore take the liberty of imploring you to come, but with discretion not to speak the cause to Sir Thomas Waldron, for he will not permit conversation about it. Sincerely yours,
"ISABEL WALDRON."

Mr. Penniloe read these words again, and then closed his eyeglass with a heavy sigh. Trusted and beloved friend as he was of the veteran Sir Thomas, he had never been regarded with much favour by the lady of the house. By birth and by blood on the father's side, this lady was a Spaniard ; and although she spoke English fluently—much better indeed than she wrote it—the country and people were not to her liking, and she cared not to make herself popular. Hence her fine qualities, and generous nature, were misprised and undervalued, until less and less was seen of them. Without deserving it, she thus obtained the repute of a haughty cold-hearted person, without affection, sympathy, or loving-kindness. Even Mr. Penniloe, the most charitable of men, was inclined to hold this opinion of her.

Therefore he was all the more alarmed by this letter of the stately lady. Leaving Mr. Adney to do his best, he set off at once for Walderscourt, by way of the plank-bridge over the Perle, at no great distance above the church ; and then across the meadows and the sloping cornland, with the round Beacon-hill in front of him. This path, saving nearly half a mile of twisting lanes, would lead him to the house almost as soon as the messenger's horse would be there.

To any one acquainted with the Parson it would prove how much his mind was disturbed that none of the fair sights around him were heeded. The tall wheat reared upon its jointed stalk, with the buff pollen shed, and the triple awns sheltering the infancy of grain, the delicate bells of sky-blue flax quivering on lanced foliage, the glistening cones of teasels pliant yet as tasselled silk, and the burly foxglove in the hedgerow turning back its spotted cuffs—at none of these did he care to glance, nor linger for a moment at the treddled stile, from which the broad valley he had left was shown, studded with brown farm and white cottage, and looped with glittering water.

Neither did he throw his stick into his left hand, and stretch forth the right—as his custom was in the lonely walks of a Saturday—to invigorate a hit he would deliver the next day, at Divine service in the schoolroom.

"What is to become of them? What can be done to help it? Why should such a loving child have such a frightful trial? How shall we let him know his danger, without risk of doubling it? How long will it take, to get Gowler down, and can he do any good, if he comes?"— These and other such questions drove from his mind both sermon and scenery, as he hastened to the home of the Waldrons.

Walderscourt was not so grand as to look uncomfortable, nor yet on the other hand so lowly as to seem insignificant. But a large old-fashioned house, built of stone, with depth and variety of light and shade, sobered and toned by the lapse of time, yet cheerful on the whole, as is a well-spent life. For by reason of the trees, and the wavering of the air—flowing gently from hill to valley—the sun seemed to linger in various visits, rather than to plant himself for one long stare. The pleasure-grounds, moreover, and the lawns were large, gifted with surprising little ups and downs, and blest with pretty corners where a man might sit and think, and perhaps espy an old-fashioned flower unseen since he was five years old.

Some of the many philosophers who understand our ways, and can account for everything, declare that we of the human race become of such and such a vein, and turn, and tone of character, according to the flow, and bend, and tinge of early circumstance. If there be any truth in this, it will help to account for a few of the many delightful features and loveable traits in the character of Nicie Waldron. That young lady, the only daughter of the veteran Colonel, had obtained her present Christian name by her own merits, as asserted by herself. Unlike her mother she had taken kindly to this English air and soil, as behoves a native; and her childish lips finding *Inez* hard had softened it into *Nicie*. That name appeared so apt to all who had the pleasure of seeing her toddle, that it quite superseded the grander form, with all except her mother. "*Nicie* indeed!" Lady Waldron used to say, until she found it useless—"I will feel much obliged to you, if you shall call my daughter Inez by her proper name, sir." But her ladyship could no more subdue the universal usage, than master the English *wills* and *shalls*.

And though she was now a full-grown maiden, lively, tall, and self-possessed, Nicie had not lost as yet the gentle and confiding manner, with the playful smile, and pleasant glance, which had earned, by offering them, good-will and tender interest. Pity moreover had some share in her general popularity, inasmuch as her mother was known to be sometimes harsh, and nearly always cold and distant to her. Women, who should know best, declared that this was the result of jealousy, because Sir Thomas made such an idol of his loving daughter. On the other hand the Spanish lady had her idol also—her only son, despatched of late with his regiment towards India ; his father always called him *Tom*, and his mother *Rodrigo*.

Mr. Penniloe had a very soft place in his heart for this young lady ; but now, for the first time in his life, he was vexed to see her white chip hat, and pink summer-frock between the trees. She was sitting on a bench, with a book upon her lap, while the sunlight, broken by the gentle play of leafage, wavered and flickered in her rich brown hair. Corkscrew ringlets were the fashion of the time ; but Nicie would have none of them, with the bashful knowledge of the rose, that Nature had done enough for her.

And here came her father to take her part, with his usual decision ; daring even to pronounce, in presence of the noblest fashion, that his pet should do what he chose, and nothing else. At this the pet smiled very sweetly, the words being put into his lips by hers, and dutifully obeyed her own behest ; sweeping back the flowing curves into a graceful coronet, in the manner of a Laconian maid.

Now the sly Penniloe made endeavour to pass her with a friendly smile and bow ; but her little pug *Pixie* would not hear of such a slight. This was a thorough busybody, not always quite right in his mind, according to some good authorities, though not easily outwitted. Having scarcely attained much obesity yet, in spite of never-flagging efforts, he could run at a good pace, though not so very far; and sometimes, at sight of any highly valued friend, he would chase himself at full gallop round a giddy circle, with his reasoning powers lost in rapture.

Even now he indulged in this expression of good-will, for he dearly loved Mr. Penniloe; and then he ran up, with such antics of delight, that the rudest of mankind could not well have passed unheeding. And behind him came his fair young mistress, smiling pleasantly at his tricks, although her gentle eyes were glistening with a shower scarcely blown away.

"Uncle Penniloe," she began, having thus entitled him in early days, and doing so still at coaxing times; "you will not think me a sly girl, will you? But I found out that mother had sent for you; and as nothing would make her tell me why, I made up my mind to come and ask you myself, if I could only catch you here. I was sure you could never refuse me."

"Nice assurance indeed, and nice manners, to try to steal a march upon your mother!" The Parson did his utmost to look stern; but his eyes meeting hers failed to carry it out.

"Oh, but you know better, you could never fancy that! And your trying to turn it off like that, only frightens me ten times more. I am sure it is something about my father. You had better tell me all. I must know all. I am too old now, to be treated like a child. Who can have half the right I have, to know all about my darling dad? Is he very ill? Is his precious life in danger? Don't look at me like that. I know more than you imagine. Is he going to die? I will never believe it. God could never do such a cruel wicked thing."

"My dear, what would your dear father say, to hear you talk like that? A man so humble, and brave, and pious——"

"As humble and brave as you please, Uncle Penniloe. But I don't want him to be pious for a long time yet. He swore a little yesterday,—that is one comfort,—when he had no idea I was near him. And he would not have done that, if there had been any—oh, don't go away so!

I won't let you go, until you have answered my question. Why were you sent for in such haste?"

"How can I tell you, my dear child, until I have had time to ask about it? You know there is to be the cricket-match on Tuesday, the north against the south side of the valley, and even the sides are not quite settled yet; because Mr. Jakes will not play against his Colonel, though quite ready to play against his Parson."

"Will you give me your word, Uncle Penniloe, that you really believe you were sent for about that?"

The clergyman saw that there was no escape, and as he looked into her beseeching eyes, it was all that he could do to refrain his own from tears.

"I will not cry—or at least not if I can help it," she whispered, as he led her to the seat, and sat by her.

"My darling Nicie," he began in a low voice, and as tenderly as if he were her father; "it has pleased the Lord to visit us with a very sad trial; but we may hope that it will yet pass away. Your dear father is seriously ill; and the worst of it is that, with his wonderful courage and spirit, he makes light of it, and will not be persuaded. He could scarcely be induced to say a word to Dr. Fox, although he is so fond of him; and nobody knows what the malady is, except that it is painful and wearing. My object to-day is to do my very utmost to get your dear father to listen to us, and see a medical man of very large experience and very great ability. And much as it has grieved me to tell you this, perhaps it is better upon the whole; for now you will do all you can, to help us."

"Sometimes father will listen to me," Miss Waldron answered between her sobs; "when he won't—when he won't let anybody else—because I never argue with him. But I thought Dr. Fox was exceedingly clever."

"So he is, my dear; but he is so young, and this is a case of great perplexity. I have reason to believe that he wishes just as we do. So now with God's help let us all do our best."

She tried to look cheerful; but when he was gone, a cold terror fell upon her. Little *Pixie* tugged at her frock unheeded, and made himself a whirligig in chase of his own tail.

CHAPTER V.

A FAIR BARGAIN.

THE Parson had a little shake in his system ; and his faith in Higher Providence was weaker in his friend's case than in his own, which is contrary perhaps to the general rule. As he passed through the large gloomy hall, his hat was quivering in his hand, like a leaf that has caught the syringe ; and when he stood face to face with Lady Waldron, he would have given up a small subscription, to be as calm as she was.

But her self-possession was the style of pride and habit, rather than the gift of nature. No one could look into her very handsome face, or watch her dark eyes as she spoke, without perceiving that her nature was strong, and warm, and generous. Pride of birth taught her to control her temper ; but education had been insufficient to complete the mastery. And so she remained in a foreign country, vehement, prejudiced, and indifferent to things too large for her to understand, jealous, exacting, and quick to take offence ; but at the same time a lover of justice, truthful, free-handed, and loyal to friends, kind to those in trouble, and devoted to her husband. Her father had been of Spanish, and her mother of Irish birth, and her early memories were of tumult, war, distress, and anarchy.

All English clergymen were to her as heretics and usurpers ; and being intensely patriotic, she disliked the English nation for its services to her country. Mr. Penniloe had felt himself kept throughout at a very well measured distance ; but like a large-hearted, and humble man, had concerned himself little about such trifles ; though his wife had been very indignant. And he met the lady now, as he had always done, with a pleasant look, and a gentle smile. But she was a little annoyed at her own confession of his influence.

" It is good of you to come so soon," she said, " and to break your very nice engagements. But I have been so anxious, so consumed with great anxiety. And every-

thing grows worse and worse. What can I do? There is
none to help me. The only one I could trust entirely, my
dear brother, is far away."

"There are many who would do their best to help you,"
the Curate answered with a faltering voice, for her strange
humility surprised him. "You know without any words
of mine——"

"Is it that you really love Sir Thomas, or only that you
find him useful? Pardon me; I put not the question
rudely. But all are so selfish in this England."

"I hope not. I think not," he answered very gently,
having learned to allow for the petulance of grief. "Your
dear husband is not of that nature, Lady Waldron; and
he does not suppose that his friends are so."

"No. It is true he makes the best of everybody.
Even of that young Dr. Fox, who is ill-treating him.
That is the very thing I come to speak of. If he had a
good physician—but he is so resolute."

"But you will persuade him. It is a thing he owes to
you. And in one little way I can help you perhaps a
little. He fancies, I dare say, that to call in a man of
larger experience would be unkind to Fox, and might
even seem a sort of slur upon him. But I think I can
get Fox himself to propose it, and even to insist upon
it for his own sake. I believe that he has been thinking
of it."

"What is he, that his opinions should be consulted?
He cannot see. But I see things that agitate me—oh
darker, darker—I cannot discover any consolation anywhere. And my husband will not hear a word! It is so
—this reason one day, and then some other, to excuse that
he is not better; and his strong hands going, and his
shoulders growing round, and his great knees beginning
to quiver, and his face—so what you call cheerful, lively,
jolly, turning to whiter than mine, and blue with cups,
and cords, and channels in it—oh, I will not have my
husband long; and where shall I be without him?"

As she turned away her face, and waved her hand for
the visitor to leave her, Mr. Penniloe discovered one more
reason for doubting his own judgment.

"I will go and see him. He is always glad to see me;"

he said, as if talking to himself alone. "The hand of the Lord is over us, and His mercy is on the righteous."

The old soldier was not the man to stay indoors, or dwell upon his ailments. As long as he had leg to move, or foot at all to carry him, no easy-chair or study-lounge held any temptation for him. The open air, and the breezy fields, or sunny breadth of garden full of ever-changing incident, the hill-top, or the river-side, were his delight, while his steps were strong ; and even now, when-ever bodily pain relaxed.

Mr. Penniloe found him in his kitchen-garden, walking slowly, as behoves a man of large frame and great stature, and leaning on a staff of twisted Spanish oak, which had stood him in good stead, some five and twenty years ago. Following every uncertain step, with her nose as close as if she had been a spur upon either boot, and yet escaping contact as a dog alone can do, was his favourite little black spaniel *Jess*, as loving a creature as ever lived.

"What makes you look at me in that way, Jumps ?" the Colonel enquired, while shaking hands. "I hope your are not setting up for a doctor too. One is quite enough for the parish."

"Talking about doctors," replied the Parson, who thought it no scorn when his old schoolmate revived the nickname of early days (conferred perhaps by some young observer, in recognition of his springy step)—"talking about doctors, I think it very likely that my old friend Gowler—you have heard me speak of him—will pay me a little visit, perhaps next week."

"Gowler ? Was he at Peter's, after my time ? It scarcely sounds like a West country name. No, I re-member now. It was at Oxford you fell in with him."

"Yes. He got his Fellowship two years after I got mine. The cleverest man in the College, and one of the best scholars I ever met with. I was nowhere with him, though I read so much harder."

"Come now, Jumps—don't tell me that ! " Sir Thomas exclaimed, looking down with admiration at the laureate of his boyhood ; "why, you knew everything as pat as butter, when you were no more than a hop o' my thumb ! I remember arguing with Gus Browne, that it must be

because you were small enough to jump into the skulls of
those old codgers, Homer, and Horace, and the rest of
them. But how you must have grown since then, my
friend! I suppose they gave you more to eat at Oxford.
But I don't believe in any man alive being a finer scholar
than you are."

"Gowler was, I tell you, Tom; and many, many others;
as I soon discovered in the larger world. He had a much
keener and deeper mind, far more enquiring and penetrating, more subtle and logical, and comprehensive, together
with a smaller share perhaps of—of——"

"Humility—that's the word you mean; although you
don't like to say it."

"No, that is not what I mean exactly. What I mean
is docility, ductility, sequacity—if there is any such word.
The acceptance of what has been discovered, or at any rate
acknowledged, by the highest human intellect. Gowler
would be content with nothing, because it had satisfied the
highest human intellect. It must satisfy his own, or be
rejected."

"I am very sorry for him," said Sir Thomas Waldron;
"such a man must be drummed out of any useful regiment."

"Well, and he was drummed out of Oxford; or at any
rate would follow no drum there. He threw up his Fellowship, rather than take orders, and for some years we heard
nothing of him. But he was making his way in London,
and winning reputation in minute anatomy. He became
the first authority in what is called *histology*, a comparatively new branch of medical science——"

"Don't Phil, I beg of you. You make me creep. I
think of Burke, and Hare, and all those wretches. Fellows
who disturb a man's last rest! I have a deep respect for
an honest wholesome surgeon; and wonderful things I have
seen them do. But the best of them are gone. It was the
war that made them; and, thank God, we have no occasion
for such carvers now."

"Come and sit down, Tom. You look—at least, I mean,
I have been upon my legs many hours to-day, and there is
nothing like the jump in them of thirty years ago. Well,
you are a kind man, the kindest of the kind, to allow your
kitchen-gardeners such a comfortable bench."

"You know what I think," replied Sir Thomas, as he made believe to walk with great steadiness and vigour, " that we don't behave half well enough to those who do all the work for us. And I am quite sure that we Tories feel it, ay and try to better it, ten times as much as all those spouting radical reformers do. Why, who is at the bottom of all these shocking riots, and rick-burnings? The man who puts iron, and boiling water, to rob a poor fellow of his bread and bacon. You'll see none of that on any land of mine. But if anything happens to me, who knows?"

" My dear friend," Mr. Penniloe began, while the hand which he laid upon his friend's was shaking, "may I say a word to you, as an ancient chum? You know that I would not intrude, I am sure."

" I am sure that you would not do anything which a gentleman would not do, Phil."

"It is simply this—we are most anxious about you. You are not in good health, and you will not confess it. This is not at all fair to those who love you. Courage, and carelessness about oneself, are very fine things, but may be carried too far. In a case like yours they are sinful, Tom. Your life is of very great importance, and you have no right to neglect it. And can you not see that it is down-right cruelty to your wife and children, if you allow your-self to get worse and worse, while their anxiety increases, and you do nothing, and won't listen to advice, and fling bottles of medicine into the bonfire? I saw one just now, as we came down the walk—as full as when Fox put the cork in. Is that even fair to a young practitioner?"

" Well, I never thought of that. That's a new light altogether. You can see well enough, it seems, when it is not wanted. But don't tell Jemmy, about that bottle. Mind, you are upon your honour. But oh, Phil, if you only knew the taste of that stuff! I give you my word——"

"You shall not laugh it off. You may say what you like, but you know in your heart that you are not acting kindly, or even fairly, by us. Would you like your wife, or daughter, to feel seriously ill, and hide it as if it was no concern of yours? I put aside higher considerations, Tom I speak to you simply as an old and true friend."

It was not the power of his words, so much as the trembling of his voice, and the softness of his eyes, that vanquished the tough old soldier.

"I don't want to make any fuss about it, Phil," Sir Thomas answered quietly; "and I would rather have kept it to myself, a little longer. But the simple truth is, that I am dying."

There was no sign of fear, or of sorrow, in his gaze; and he smiled very cheerfully while offering his hand, as if to be forgiven for the past concealment. Mr. Penniloe could not speak, but fell back on the bench, and feared to look at him.

"My dear friend, I see that I was wrong to tell you," the sick man continued in a feebler tone; "but you must have found it out very shortly; and I know that Jemmy Fox is well aware of it. But not a word, of course, to my wife or daughter, until—until it can't be helped. Poor things —what a blow it will be to them! The thought of that makes me rebel sometimes. But it is in your power to help me greatly, to help me, as no other man on earth can do. It has long been in my thoughts, but I scarcely dared to ask you. Perhaps that was partly why I told you this. But you are too good and kind, to call me selfish."

"Whatever it is, I will do it for you readily, if God gives me power, and ordains it so."

"Never make rash promises. What was it you used to construe to me in the *Delectus?* This is a long and a troublesome job, and will place you in a delicate position. It is no less a trouble than to undertake, for a time at least, the management of my affairs, and see to the interests of my Nicie."

"But surely your wife—surely Lady Waldron—so resolute, ready, and capable——"

"Yes, she is all that, and a great deal more—honourable, upright, warm, and loving. She is not at all valued . as she should be here, because she cannot come to like our country, or our people. But that would be no obstacle; the obstacle is this—she has a twin-brother, a certain Count de Varcas, whom she loves ardently, and I will not speak against him; but he must have no chance of interfering here. My son Tom—*Rodrigo* his mother calls him,

D

after her beloved brother—is barely of age, as you know,
and sent off with his regiment to India; a very fine fellow
in many ways, but as for business—excuse me a moment,
Phil; I will finish, when this is over."

With one broad hand upon the bench, he contrived to
rise, and to steady himself upon his staff, and stood for a
little while thus, with his head thrown back, and his
forehead like a block of stone. No groan from the chest,
or contortion of the face, was allowed to show his agony;
though every drawn muscle, and wan hollow, told what he
was enduring. And the blue scar of some ancient wound
grew vivid upon his strong countenance, from the left
cheek-bone to the corner of the mouth, with the pallid
damp on either side. Little *Jess* came and watched him,
with wistful eyes, and a soft interrogative tremble of tail;
while the clergyman rose to support him; but he would
have no assistance.

"Thank God, it is over. I am all right now, for another
three hours, I dare say. What a coward you must think
me, Phil! I have been through a good deal of pain, in my
time. But this beats me, I must confess. The worst of it
is, when it comes at night, to keep it from poor Isabel.
Sit down again now, and let me go on with my story."

"Not now, Tom. Not just yet, I implore you," cried
the Parson, himself more overcome than the sufferer of
all that anguish. "Wait till you find yourself a little
stronger."

"No. That may never be. If you could only know the
relief it will be to me. I have not a great mind. I cannot leave things to the Lord, except as concerns my own
old self. Now that I have broken the matter to you, I must
go through with it. I cannot die, until my mind is easy
about poor Nicie. Her mother would be good to her, of
course. But—well, Tom is her idol; and there is that
blessed Count. Tom is very simple, just as I was, at his
age. I have many old friends; but all easy-going fellows,
who would leave everything to their lawyers—none at all
to trust, like you. And I know how fond you are of
Nicie."

"To be sure I am. How could I help it? But remember that I am not at all a man of business."

"What does that matter? You are very clear-headed, and prudent—at any rate for other people. And you will have Webber, a careful and clever Solicitor, to back you up. And mind, I am not asking you to supersede my wife, or take what should be her position. She is quite unacquainted with English ways, she does not think as an Englishwoman would. She must have an Englishman to act with her, in the trusts that will arise upon my death; and when we were married in Spain, as you know, there was no chance of any marriage-settlement. In fact there was nothing to settle as yet, for I was not even heir to this property, until poor Jack was killed at Quatrebras. And as for herself, all the family affairs were at sixes and sevens, as you may suppose, during the French occupation. Her father had been a very wealthy man and the head of an ancient race, which claimed descent from the old Carthaginian Barcas, of whom you know more than I do. But he had been too patriotic, and advanced immense sums to the State without security, and in other ways dipped his fine property, so that it would not recover for a generation. At any rate nothing came to her then, though she ought to have had a good sum afterwards. But whatever there may have been, her noble twin-brother took good care that none of it came this way. And I was glad to get her without a *peseta;* and what is more, I have never repented of it; for a nobler and more affectionate woman never trod the earth."

As the sick man passed his hand before his eyes, in sad recollection of the bygone bliss, Mr. Penniloe thought of his own dear wife—a far sweeter woman in his mild opinion; and, if less noble, none the worse for that.

"But the point of it is this, Tom," the clergyman said firmly, for he began to feel already like a man of business, however sad and mournful the business must become; "does Lady Waldron consent to receive me, as—as co-trustee, or whatever it is called, if, if—which God forbid—it should ever prove to be necessary?"

"My dear friend, I spoke to her about it yesterday, in such a way as not to cause anxiety or alarm: and she made no objection, but left everything to me. So you have only to agree ; and all is settled."

"In that case, Tom," said Mr. Penniloe arising, and offering both hands to his friend, "I will not shirk my duty to a man I love so much. May the Lord be with me, for I am not a man of business—or at least, I have not attained that reputation yet! But I will do my best, and your Nicie's interests shall be as sacred to me, as my own child's. Is there anything you would like to say about her?"

"Yes, Phil, one thing most important. She is a very loving girl; and I trust that she will marry a good man, who will value her. I have fancied, more than once, that Jemmy Fox is very fond of her. He is a manly straightforward fellow, and of a very good old family, quite equal to ours, so far as that goes. He has not much of this world's goods at present; and her mother would naturally look higher. But when a man is in my condition, he takes truer views of life. If Jemmy loves her, and she comes to love him, I believe that they would have a very happy life. He is very cheerful, and of the sweetest temper—the first of all things in married life—and he is as upright as yourself. In a few years he will be very well off. I could wish no better fortune for her—supposing that she gives her heart to him."

"He is a great favourite of mine as well;" the Curate replied, though surprised not a little. "But as I have agreed to all that you wish, Tom, you must yield a little to my most earnest wish, and at the same time discharge a simple duty. I cannot help hoping that your fears—or I will not call them that, for you fear nothing—but your views of your own case are all wrong. You must promise to take the highest medical opinion. If I bring Gowler over, with Fox's full approval, will you allow him to examine you?"

"You are too bad, Phil. But you have caught me there. If you let me put you into the hands of lawyers, it is tit for tat that you should drive me into those of doctors."

CHAPTER VI.

DOCTORS THREE.

PUBLIC opinion at Perlycross was stirred, as with a many-bladed egg-whisk, by the sudden arrival of Dr. Gowler. A man, who cared nothing about the crops, and never touched bacon, or clotted cream, nor even replied to the salutation of the largest farmer, but glided along with his eyes on the ground, and a broad hat whelmed down upon his hairless white face ; yet seemed to know every lane and footpath, as if he had been born among them—no wonder that in that unsettled time, when frightful tales hung about the eaves of every cottage, and every leathern latch-thong was drawn inside at nightfall, very strange suspicions were in the air about him. Even the friendship of the well-beloved Parson, and the frank admiration of Dr. Fox, could not stem the current against him. The children of the village ran away at his shadow, and the mothers in the doorway turned their babies' faces from him.

Every one who loved Sir Thomas Waldron, and that meant everybody in the parish, shuddered at hearing that this strange man had paid two visits at Walderscourt, and had even remained there a great part of one night. And when it was known that the yearly cricket-match, between the north side of the Perle and the south, had been quenched by this doctor's stern decree, the wrath of the younger men was rebuked by the sorrow of the elder. Jakes the schoolmaster, that veteran sergeant (known as " High Jarks," from the lofty flourish of his one remaining arm, and thus distinct from his younger brother, " Low Jarks," a good but not extraordinary butcher), firm as he was, and inured to fields of death, found himself unable to refuse his iron cheeks the drop, that he was better fitted to produce on others.

Now that brave descendant of Mars, and Minerva, feared one thing, and one alone, in all this wicked world ; and that was holy wedlock. It was rumoured that something had befallen him in Spain, or some other foreign outlands, of a nature to make a good Christian doubt whether woman

was meant as a helpmate for him, under the New Covenant.
The Sergeant was not given to much talking, but rigid, and
resolute, and self-contained; more apt to point, and be, the
moral of his vast experience, than to adorn it with long
tales. Many people said that having heard so much of the
roar of cannon and the roll of drums, he could never come
to care again for any toast-and-butter; while others believed
that he felt it his duty to maintain the stern silence, which
he imposed in school.

There was however one person in the parish, with whom
he indulged in brief colloquy sometimes; and strange to
say, that was a woman.   Mrs. Muggridge, the Curate's
housekeeper, felt more indignation than she could express,
if anybody whispered that she was fond of gossip.   But
according to her own account, she smiled at such a charge,
coming as it only could from the lowest quarters, because
she was bound for her master's sake, to have some acquaintance with her neighbours' doings; for they found it too
easy to impose on him.   And too often little Fay would
run, with the best part of his dinner to some widow,
mourning deeply over an empty pot of beer.   For that
mighty police-force of charity, the district-visitors, were
not established then.

Thyatira, though not perhaps unduly nervous—for the
times were sadly out of joint—was lacking to some extent
in that very quality, which the Sergeant possessed in such
remarkable degree.   And ever since that shocking day,
when her dear mistress had been brought home from the
cliff, stone-dead, the housekeeper had realised the perils
of this life, even more deeply than its daily blessings.
Susanna, the maid, was of a very timid nature, and when
piously rebuked for her want of faith in Providence, had a
knack of justifying her distrust by a course of very creepy
narratives.   Mrs. Muggridge would sternly command her
to leave off, and yet contrive to extract every horror, down
to its dying whisper.

Moreover the rectory, a long and rambling house, was
not a cheerful place to sit alone in after dark.   Although
the high, and whitewashed, back abutted on the village
street, there was no door there, and no window looking
outwards in the basement; and the walls being very thick,

you might almost as well be fifty miles from any company. Worst of all, and even cruel on the ancient builder's part, the only access to the kitchen and the rooms adjoining it was through a narrow and dark passage, arched with rough flints set in mortar, which ran like a tunnel beneath the first-floor rooms, from one end of the building to the other. The front of the house was on a higher level, facing southwards upon a grass-plat and flower-garden, and as pretty as the back was ugly.

Even the stoutest heart in Perlycross might flutter a little in the groping process, for the tunnel was pitch-dark at night, before emerging into the candlelight twinkling in the paved yard beside the kitchen-door. While the servants themselves would have thought it a crime, if the butcher, or baker, or anyone coming for them (except the Postman) had kept the front way up the open gravel walk, and ventured to knock at the front door itself. There was no bell outside to call them, and the green-baize door at the end of the passage, leading to the kitchen stairs, deadened the sound of the knocker so much, that sometimes a visitor might thunder away for a quarter of an hour, with intervals for conscientious study of his own temper, unless little Fay's quick ears were reached, and her pink little palms and chest began to struggle with the mighty knob.

So it happened, one evening in the first week of August, when Mr. Penniloe was engaged in a distant part of the parish, somebody or other came and knocked—it was never known how many times or how long,—at the upper-folk door of the rectory.

There was not any deafness about Thyatira; and as for Susanna, she could hear too much; neither was little Fay to blame, although the rest were rather fond of leaving things to her. If the pupils had returned, it could not have happened so; for although they made quite enough noise of their own in the little back-parlour allotted to them, they never failed to hear any other person's noise, and to complain of it next morning, when they did not know their lessons.

But the present case was, that the whole live force of the rectory, now on the premises, was established quite happily

in the kitchen yard ; with a high wall between it and the
village street, and a higher wall topped with shrubs between
it and the garden.   Master Harry, now at home for his
holidays (a tiger by day, but a lion at night, for protection of the household), was away with his father, and
sleeping soundly through a Bible-lecture.   And so it came
to pass that the tall dark man knocked, and knocked ; and
at last departed, muttering uncourteous expressions through
his beard.

Even that might never have been known inside, without
the good offices of Mrs. Channing, the wife of the baker,
whose premises adjoined the rectory garden, and the drive
from the front gate.

" 'Twas nort but them Gelany fowls," she explained,
before she had her breakfast, because her husband was the
son of old Channing, the clerk, and sexton ; " them Gelany
birds of ours, as drew my notice to it.   They kept up such
a screeching in the big linhay just at dusk, instead of
sticking their heads inside their wings, that I thought they
must be worriting about a dog, or cat.   And so out of
house I runs ; but I couldn't see nort, till I heers a girt
knocking at Passon's front-door.   Thinks I—'What's up
now ?'   For I knowed a' wurn't at home, but away to they
Bible-readings.   So I claps the little barn-steps again your
big wall, and takes the liberty of peeping over, just between
the lilac bush and old holly.   You must understand, Mrs.
Muggridge, that the light wurn't very clear ; but I could
make out a big tall man a-standing, with a long furrin
cloak, atwixt the pillars of your porch.

" 'Passon's not at home,' says I; 'can us give any
message ?'

" Then a' turns round sudden like, and stands just like
a pictur', with the postesses to either side of him, and his
beard falling down the same as Aaron's.   But if a' said ort,
'twaz beyond my comprehension.

" 'Did you please to be looking for the Doctor, sir ?' I
said—'the Doctor as is biding now with Mr. Penniloe ?
I did hear that he was 'gone to Squire Waldron's house.'
For I thought that he was more the sort to belong to that
old Gowler.

" But he only shook his head, and turned away ; and

presently, off he walks most majestic, like the image of a man the same as I have seen to Exeter. I felt myself in that alarm, that go away I couldn't, until I heard your gate fall to behind him. Then I thought to come and tell you, but I hadn't got the nerves to face your black passage, after what had come across me. For to my mind it must have been the Evil One himself. May the Lord save us from his roarings and devourings!"

When Mrs. Muggridge heard this tale, she thought that it had better go no further, and she saw no occasion to repeat it to her master; because no message had been left, and he might imagine that she had not attended to her duty very well.

For it had chanced, that at the very moment when somebody wanted to disturb them, the housekeeper was giving a most pleasant tea-party to the two little dears, Master Michael, and Miss Fay.

And by accident, of course, Sergeant Jakes had just dropped in. No black passage could be anything but a joke to a man of his valour; and no rapping at the door could have passed unchallenged, if it reached such ears. But the hospitable Thyatira offered such a distraction of good things, far beyond the largest larder-dreams of a dry-tongued lonely bachelor, that the coarser, and seldom desirable, gift of the ears lay in deep abeyance. For the Sergeant had felt quite enough of hardship to know a good time, when he tasted it.

"Now, my precious little dears," Thyatira had whispered with a sigh, when the veteran would be helped no more; "there is light enough still for a game of hop-scotch, down at the bottom of the yard. Susanna will mark out the bed for you. You will find the chalk under the knife-board."

Away ran the children; and their merry voices rang sweetly to the dancing of their golden hair.

"Sergeant Schoolmaster," continued the lady, for she knew that he liked this combination of honours, "how pleasant it is, when the shadows are falling, to see the little innocents delighting in their games? It seems to be no more than yesterday, when I was as full of play as any of them."

"A good many yesterdays have passed since that," Mr. Jakes thought as he looked at her; but he was far too gallant and polite to say so. "In your case, ma'am, it is so," he replied: "yesterday, only yesterday! The last time I was here, I was saying to myself that you ladies have the command of time. You make it pass for us so quickly, while it is standing still with you!"

"What a fine thing it is to have been abroad! You do learn such things from the gift of tongues. But it do seem a pity you should have to say them so much to yourself, Mr. Sergeant."

"Ma'am," replied the veteran, in some fear of becoming too complimentary; "I take it that some of us are meant to live apart, and to work for the good of others. But have you heard how the Colonel is to-day? Ah, he is a man indeed!"

"There are doctors enough to kill him now. And they are going to do it, this very night." Mrs. Muggridge spoke rather sharply, for she was a little put out with her visitor.

"What?" cried the man of sword and ferule. "To operate, ma'am, and I not there—I, who know all about operations!"

"No, Mr. Sergeant; but to hold a council. And in this very house, I believe; the room is to be ready at ten o'clock. Dr. Fox, Dr. Gronow, and Dr. Gowler. It is more than I can understand. But not a word about it to any one. For Sir Thomas would be very angry. To frighten his people, and make such a fuss—they durst not propose it at his own house. And Gronow has never been called in, as you know. But Dr. Jemmy made a favour of it, for he thinks very highly of that man; and the gentleman from London did not object. Only he said that if it must be so, and everything was to be out of proper form, he would like my master to be present with them."

"Three doctors, and a parson to sit upon him! The Lord have mercy on the Colonel's soul! There is no hope left for his poor body. I will tell you, ma'am, what I saw once at Turry Vardoes—but no, it is not fit for you to hear. Well, my heart is like a lump of lead. I would sooner have lost my other arm, than heard such a thing of the Colonel. Good night, ma'am ; and thanking you for all your kindness, I'm no fit company for any one, no longer."

He was gone in a moment. His many-angled form sank into the darkness of the flinty tunnel, as swiftly as ever a schoolboy vanished, when that form became too conspicuous. Thyatira heaved a deep sigh, and sat down in the many-railed beechen chair at the head of her cruelly vacant table. She began to count the empty dishes, and with less than her usual charity mused upon the voracity of man. But her heart was kind, and the tear she wiped away was not wholly of selfish tincture.

"The hand of the Lord is upon us now. My master will lose the best friend he has got," she was thinking, as the darkness gathered ; "faithful as he is, it will try him hard again ; for Satan has prevailed against us. And this will be a worse snare than any he has laid. To have in Parsonage house a man, as chooseth not to come to prayers ; or at any rate standeth up at mantel-piece, with his back turned on the kneelers ; till my master told him, like the Christian he is, that he would not desire him, as his guest, to go contrairy to his principles,—and pretty principles they must be, I reckon,—but would beg him to walk in the garden, rather than set such example to his household ! Alas the day that such a man came here, to the house of a holy minister ! No blessing can ever attend his medicine. Ah, the times are not as they was ! No wonder that Spring-heeled Jack is allowed to carry on, when such a heathen is encouraged in the land. It would not go out of my grains, if he was Spring-heeled Jack himself ! "

Much against her liking, and with a trembling hand, this excellent woman brought in the candles, and prepared the sitting-room, for the consultation of unholy science.

But the first to arrive was a favourite of hers, and indeed of all the parish, a young man of very cheerful aspect, and of brisk and ready speech. No man had ever known Jemmy Fox despair of anything he undertook ; and there were few things he would not undertake ; only he must tackle them in his own way. A square-built, thick-set, resolute young fellow, of no great stature, but good

frame and fibre, and as nimble as a pea in a frying-pan.
There was nothing very wonderful about his face; and at
first sight a woman would have called him plain, for his
nose was too short, and his chin too square, and his mouth
too wide for elegance. But the more he was looked at, the
better he was liked by any honest person; for he was
never on the watch for fault in others, as haters of humbug
are too apt to be.

And yet without intending, or knowing it at all, this
son of Chiron had given deep offence to many of his
brethren around Perlycross, and it told upon him sadly
afterwards. For he loved his Profession, and looked upon
it as the highest and noblest in the world, and had worked
at it too thoroughly not to have learned how often it is
mere profession. By choice he would have dropped all
general practice, and become a surgeon only; but this was
impossible except in some large place, and cities were not
to his liking. As the only son of a wealthy banker he
might have led an idle life, if he pleased; but that he
could not bear, and resolved to keep himself; for the old
man was often too exacting, and the younger had some
little income of his own. Perlycross suited him well, and
he had taken a long and rambling house, which had
formerly been a barn, about half a mile from the village.

"Seen anything of Spring-heeled Jack, the last night or
two, Mrs. Muggridge?" he enquired too lightly, as he flung
down his hat in similar style at a corner. "Have you
heard the last thing that has come to light about him?"

"No, sir, no! But I hope it is no harm," replied the
palpitating Thyatira.

"Well, that depends upon how you take it. We have
discovered for certain, that he is a medical man from a
country parish, not such a very long way from here, who
found his practice too small for the slaughter on the
wholesale style he delights in. And so he turned his
instruments into patent jumpers, tore the heart out of his
last patient—he was obliged to choose a poor one, or it
would have been too small—then he fitted a Bude-light to
his biggest dark lantern. And you know better than I do
what he shows you at the window, exactly as the Church-
clock strikes twelve."

"Oh, Dr. Jemmy, how you do make one creep! Then after all he is not, as everybody says, even a dissolute nobleman?"

"No. That is where the disappointment lies. He set that story afoot no doubt, to comfort the relatives of the folk he kills. By the by, what a place this old house would be for him! He likes a broad window-sill, just like yours, and the weather is the very thing for him."

"I shall nail up a green baize every night. Oh, Dr. Jemmy, there is a knock at the door! Would you mind seeing who it is—that's a dear?"

Dr. Fox, with a pleasant smile, admitted Dr. Gronow, on his very first visit to the rectory.

"Others not come yet?" asked the elder gentleman, as the trembling housekeeper offered him a chair; "his Reverence would hardly like a pipe here, I suppose. Well, Jemmy, what is your opinion of all this strange affair?"

Mrs. Muggridge had hurried off, with a shiver and a prayer.

"I am mum, before my betters," the young man replied. "The case is gone out of my hands altogether."

"And a good thing for you. I am glad of it for your sake. But we must not anticipate Gowler. I have no business here, except as what the lawyers call *Amicus curiæ*. By the by, I suppose you have never seen the smallest ground for suspicion of foul play?"

"Never. I should have come to you first, if I had. There could be no possible motive, to begin with; and everybody loves him like a father."

"A man is too fatherly sometimes. One never can understand those foreign women. But you know the family, and I do not. Excuse me for a horrible suggestion. But I have had some very dark experiences."

"And so, no doubt, has Gowler. The idea crossed his brain; but was scattered immediately, when he knew the facts. Hush, here they come! Let us think no more of that."

Mr. Penniloe was tired, and in very low spirits; for he looked upon this meeting as the fatal crisis. After seeing to his visitors, and offering refreshment—which none of them accepted—he took a chair apart, being present as a listener only.

Thereupon Dr. Gowler in very few words gave his view of the case, premising only that he spoke with some doubt, and might well be mistaken, for the symptoms were perplexing, and the malady was one which had not as yet been studied at all exhaustively. His conclusion agreed in the main with that of his young and sagacious coadjutor, though he was enabled, by longer experience, to be perhaps a little more definite. He spoke very well, and with a diffidence which particularly impressed the others, on the part of a man whose judgment was of the very highest authority.

Dr. Gronow immediately confirmed his view, so far as the details at second hand could warrant, and gave his own account of a similar case, where the injury was caused by the handle of a barrow, and continued latent for several years. The unanimous decision was that no hope remained; unless the poor patient would submit to a surgical operation of great difficulty and danger, in the then condition of medical science; and for which it was advisable to have recourse to Paris.

"I know him too well. He will never consent," Mr. Penniloe came forward, and sought from face to face for some gleam of encouragement; "surely there must be some other course, something at least to alleviate——"

"There may be: but we do not know it yet, and I fear that we never shall do so. And for this very sufficient reason"—here Dr. Gowler took a glove from his pocket, and presented a most simple and convincing explanation of the mischief that had happened, and the consequence that must of necessity ensue, without surgical redress. Even that he admitted was of very doubtful issue, in plain English—"either kill, or cure."

The Parson sighed heavily, and even Dr. Fox was too much affected to say a word; but the elder physicians seemed to think it right and natural, and a credit to their science, that they knew so much about it. Gowler and Gronow were becoming mighty friends—so far as two men of the world care to indulge—and the great London doctor accepted with pleasure the offer of a day's fly-fishing.

"I have not thrown a fly, since I was quite a boy," he said.

"And I never threw a fly, till I was an old man," said the other; and their host knew well which would have the better chance, though he felt a little vexed at their light arrangements.

"It is not for the sake of the fishing, my dear fellow," Dr. Gowler assured him, when the other two were gone; "I was to have left you in the morning, as you know; and I have not had such a holiday for seven years. I positively needed it, and shall be twice the man. But I felt that I ought to stay one day longer, to give you one more chance of persuading poor Sir Thomas. See how handsomely he has behaved—I mean, according to country notions; though I often make more in one day, in Town. He slipped this into my hand, sealed up; and I did not refuse it, for fear of a fuss. But you will return it, when I am in the coach, and explain, with my kind regards, that it is against my rule to take any fee, upon a visit to a friend. I came to renew our old friendship only, and from my great regard for you. We do not think alike, upon the greatest of all matters. Perhaps that is better for your happiness than mine. But after all my knowledge of the world, I do believe that the best friends are those, who are like you."

Mr. Penniloe took the cheque for fifty guineas, and placed it in his desk, without a word; for he knew his friend's character too well to argue. Then he shook him very warmly by the hand, and said "Good night."

But as he sank back in his chair to reflect, and examine himself of the bygone day, he hoped that his ears had deceived him that night, in a matter which had shocked him sadly. Unless they had erred, Dr. Gronow had said—"In a case of this kind, for the advance of knowledge, autopsy should be compulsory." And Harrison Gowler had replied —"Exactly so; but in this benighted part, I suppose it is impossible."

CHAPTER VII.

R. I. P.

"Oh, Mr. Sergeant, how you did alarm me!" cried a very pretty damsel one fine October evening, as she almost fell upon the breast of "High Jarks," from some narrow stone steps at the corner of a lane. She was coming by the nearest way to the upper village, from the side-entrance to Walderscourt, a picturesque way but a rough one. For the lane was overhung, and even overwhelmed, with every kind of hindrance to the proper course of trade. Out of the sides, and especially at corners, where the right of way should have been most sacred, jutted forth obstacles most inconsiderate, or even of set purpose, malicious. If a great stool of fern could be treated as nothing, even with its jagged saws quivering, or a flexible ash could be shoved aside lightly, with the cowardly knowledge that it had no thorns; yet in ambush with their spears couched, would be the files of furze, the barbed brigade of holly, or the stiff picket of blackthorn. And any man, engaged with these deliveries of the moment, might thank his stars (when visible through the tangle overhead) if by any chance he missed a blinding thump in both his eyes.

Alas, it would have been indeed a blessing, as well as a just correction, for the well-seasoned master of the youth of Perlycross, if a benevolent switch from the hedgerow had taken him sharply in the eyes, that had so long descried nothing but motes in more tender orbs. As the young maid drew back from the warlike arm, which had been quite obliged to encircle her, one flash of her eyes entered those of Mr. Jakes; and he never saw again as he had seen before.

But his usual composure was not gone yet. A true schoolmaster is well assured, whatever the circumstance may be, that he is in the right, and all others in the wrong.

"I beg you will offer no apologies, Miss," he began with a very gracious smile, as he rubbed up the nap of his old velvet coat where a wicked boy had tallow-candled it: "I take it that you are a stranger here, and not quite familiar with our kind of road. The roads about here have a manner of showing that they know not in what direction they are going?"

"But, Mr. Sergeant, don't you know me? Not so very long ago, I ran up this very lane, over the plank-bridge, and up to this heling, because of the temper you were in. It was my brother Watty you wanted to catch: but you flourished your cane so, that the girls ran too. But you would not have beaten poor me, Mr. Sergeant?"

She skipped back a step or two, as if still afraid, and curtsied to show her pretty figure, and managed to let her bright hair fall down over the blush of her soft round cheeks. Then she lifted her eyes with the sweetest appeal; for the fair Tamar Haddon was a born coquette.

"Why, Tamar, my dear, can it possibly be you? I could never have supposed that you would come to this. You were always the prettiest child among the girls. But, as you know, I had nothing to do with them. My business has always been with the boys."

"And quite right, Mr. Sergeant—they are so much better, so much quicker to learn, as well as better-looking, and more interesting!"

"That depends upon who it may be," said Mr. Jakes judicially; "some girls are much better at round-hand, as well as arithmetic. But why have I lost sight of you all these years? And why have you grown such a—well, such a size?"

"Oh, you *are* rude! I am not a size at all. I thought that you always learned politeness in the wars. I am only seventeen round the waist—but you shan't see. No, no, stick you to the boys, Mr. Sergeant. I must be off. I didn't come out for pleasure. Good evening, sir; good evening to you!"

"Don't be in such a hurry, Miss Haddon. Don't you know when I used to give you sugar-plums out of this horn box? And if I may say it without offence, you are much too pretty to be in this dark place, without somebody to take care of you."

"Ah, now you are more like the Army again. There is nothing like a warrior, in my opinion. Oh, what a

E

plague these brambles are! Would you mind just holding my hat for a moment? I mustn't go into the village, such a fright, or everybody will stare at me. My hair is such a trouble, I have half a mind sometimes to cut off every snip of it. No, no, you can't help me; men are much too clumsy."

Mr. Jakes was lost in deep admiration, and Tamar Haddon knew it well, and turned away to smile, as she sat upon a bank of moss, drawing her long tresses through the supple play of fingers and the rosy curve of palms; while her cherry lips were pouting and her brown eyes sparkling, in and out the golden shower from her saucy forehead. The schoolmaster held her little hat, and watched every movement of her hands and eyes, and wondered; for the gaiety of girlhood, and the blushes and the glances were as the opening of a new world to him.

"I know what you are thinking now, it's no good to deny it," she cried as she jumped up, and snatched her hat away; "you are saying to yourself—'What a poor vain creature! Servants' hats are not allowed in well-conducted households.' But you must understand that I am not a common servant. I am a private lady's-maid to her ladyship, the Countess; and she has none of your old-fashioned English ways about her. She likes to see me look—well, perhaps you would not call it 'pretty,' for that depends upon the wearer, and I have no pretension to it—but tidy, and decent, and tolerably nice——"

"Wonderfully nice, and as lovely as a rose."

"Oh, Mr. Sergeant, you who must know so much better! But I have no time for such compliments, and they would turn my little head, from such a learned man as you are. How can I think of myself for a moment, when things are so dreadful? Poor Sir Thomas—you know how ill he is; he is longing for something, and I am sent to fetch it on the sly, so that Dr. Fox should have no idea, but her ladyship says that it can do no harm, now."

"What, the poor Colonel waiting, Miss, and I have kept you all this time? I was just on my way to enquire for him, when—when I happened to meet you. I can scarcely believe in any doctor conquering him."

"They are though—they are doing it. He is very low to-day. They seem to have brought him down to a flat .

knock-under, just as you do with the schoolboys. I can't hardly think of it, without crying."

The fair Tamar dropped her eyes, and hung her head a little, and then looked softly at the veteran, to plead for his warmest sympathy.

"There, I declare to you, I have cried so much that I can't cry no more," she continued with a sigh; "but it is a calf's sweetbread that I be bound to get; and where from, I'd like to know, unless it is to Mr. Robert's."

A pang shot through the heart of Mr. Jakes, and if his cane had been at hand he would have grasped it. For Mr. Robert was his own brother, the only butcher in the village, a man of festive nature (as a butcher ought to be), of no habitual dignity—and therefore known as "Low Jarks"— a favourite with the fair sex, and worst of all, some twenty years the junior of "High Jarks."

"What, young Bobby!" cried the Sergeant, striking out, "there is nothing that he knows worth speaking of. And what is more to the purpose, he never will know nothing. I mean to say 'anything.' Sometimes I go back from all my instructions all over the world, to the way—to the way you talk, in this part of the world."

"But, Mr. Sergeant, that is only natural; considering that you belong to this part of the world. Now, you do— don't you? However learned you may be."

"Well, I will not deny that it comes up sometimes. A man of my years—I mean, a young man by age, and yet one who has partaken in great motions, feels himself so very much above butchers' shops, and the like of them. And all the women—or as they call themselves now—all the ladies of the neighbourhood, have now been so well educated, that they think a great deal of the difference."

"To be sure," said Tamar Haddon, "I can quite see that. But how could they get their meat, without the butchers' shops? Some people are too learned, Mr. Sergeant."

"I know it, Miss. But I am very particular, not to let any one say it of me. I could quote Latin, if I chose: but who would put a spill to my pipe afterwards? One must never indulge in all one knows."

"Well, it does seem a pity, after spending years about it. But here we are, come to the river-side at last. You mustn't think of coming across the plank with me. It would never do to have you drownded; and you know what Betty Cork is. Why, all the boys to Perlycross would be making mouths to-morrow? And I shall go home along the turnpike-road."

The schoolmaster saw the discretion of this. Charmed as he was with this gay young maid, he must never forget what was thought of him.

For she was the daughter of Walter Haddon, the landlord of the *Ivy-bush*, a highly respectable place, and therefore jealous of the parish reputation. Moreover the handrail of the footbridge was now on the side of his empty sleeve; and the plank being very light and tremulous, he feared to recross it without stepping backward, which was better done without spectators. So he stayed where he was, while she tripped across, without even touching the handrail; and the dark gleam of the limpid Perle, in the twilight of gray branches, fluttered with her passing shadow.

Just as she turned on the opposite bank, where cart-ruts ridged the water's brink, and was kissing her hand to the ancient soldier, with a gay "Good evening!"—the deep boom of a big bell rang, and quivered throughout the valley. Cattle in the meadows ceased from browsing, and looked up as if they were called, birds made wing for the distant wood, and sere leaves in the stillness rustled, as the solemn thrill trembled in the darkening air.

"For God's sake, count," the old soldier cried, raising the hat from his grizzled head, and mounting a hillock clear of bushes; "it is the big bell tolling!"

But the frolicsome maiden had disappeared, and he was left to count alone.

At intervals of a minute, while the fall of night grew heavier, the burden of the passing-bell was laid on mortal ears and hearts.

> "Time is over for one more,"

was graven on the front of it, and was borne along the valley; while the echo of the hills brought home the lesson of the reverse—

> "Soon shall thy own life be o'er."

Keeping throbbing count, the listener spread the fingers of his one hand upon his threadbare waistcoat; and they trembled more and more, as the number grew towards the fatal forty-nine. When the forty-ninth stroke ceased to ring, and the last pulsation died away, he stood as if his own life depended on the number fifty. But the knell was finished; the years it told of were but forty-nine—gone by, like the minutes between the strokes.

"Old Channing perhaps is looking at the tower-clock. Hark! In a moment, he will strike another stroke." But old Channing knew his arithmetic too well.

"Now God forgive me for a sinful man—or worse than a man, an ungrateful beast!" cried the Sergeant, falling upon his knees, with sorrow embittered by the shameful thought, that while his old chief was at the latest gasp, himself had been flirting merrily with a handmaid of the house, and sniggering like a raw recruit. He wiped his eyes with the back of his hand, and the lesson of the bell fell on him.

It had fallen at the same time upon ears more heedful, and less needful of it. Mr. Penniloe, on his homeward road, received the mournful message, and met the groom who had ridden so hard to save the angelical hour. And truly, if there be any value in the ancient saying—

> "Happy is the soul
> That hath a speedy toll,"

the flight of Sir Thomas Waldron's spirit was in the right direction.

The clergyman turned from his homeward path, and hastened to the house of mourning. He scarcely expected that any one as yet would care to come down, or speak to him; but the least he could do was to offer his help. In the hush of the dusk, he was shown through the hall, and into a little sitting-room favoured by the ladies. Believing that he was quite alone, for no one moved, and the light was nearly spent, he took a seat by the curtained window, and sank into a train of sombre thoughts. But presently a lapping sound aroused him, and going to the sofa, there he found his favourite Nicie overcome with sorrow, her head drooping back, like a wind-tossed flower; while *Pixie*, with a piteous gaze, was nestling to her side, and offering every now and then the silent comfort of his tongue.

" What is it, my dear ? " The Parson asked, as if he did not know too well. But who knows what to say sometimes ? Then, shocked at himself, he said—" Don't, my dear." But she went on sobbing, as if he had not spoken ; and he thought of his little Fay, when she lost her mother.

He was too kind to try any consolations, or press the sense of duty yet ; but he put on his glasses, and took little *Pixie*, and began to stroke his wrinkled brow.

" This dear little thing is crying too," he whispered ; and certainly there were tears, his own or another's, on the velvet nose. Then Nicie rose slowly, and put back her hair, and tried to look bravely at both of them.

" If mother could only cry," she said ; " but she has not moved once, and she will not come away. There is one thing she ought to do, but she cannot ; and I am afraid that I should never do it right. Oh, will you do it, Uncle Penniloe ? It would be an excuse to get her out of the room ; and then we might make her lie down, and be better. My father is gone ; and will mother go too ? "

Speaking as steadily as she could, but breaking down every now and then, she told him, that there was a certain old ring, of no great value, but very curious, which her father had said many years ago he would like to have buried with him. He seemed to have forgotten it, throughout his long illness ; but his wife had remembered it suddenly, and had told them where to find it. It was found by a trusty servant now ; and she was present, while Mr. Penniloe placed it on the icy finger, and dropped a tear on the forehead of his friend, holy now in the last repose.

On his homeward path that night, the Curate saw through the gloom of lonely sorrow many a storm impending. Who was there now to hold the parish in the bonds of amity, to reconcile the farmers' feuds, to help the struggling tradesman, to bury the aged cripple, to do any of those countless deeds of good-will and humanity, which are less than the discount of the interest of the debt, due from the wealthy to the poor ?

And who would cheer him now with bold decision, and
kind deference, in all those difficulties which beset the
country clergyman, who hates to strain his duty, yet is
fearful of relaxing it? Such difficulties must arise; and
though there certainly was in those days, a great deal more
fair give-and-take than can be now expected, there was
less of settled rule and guidance for a peaceful parson.
Moreover, he felt the important charge which he had
undertaken, as co-trustee of large estates, as well as a
nervous dread of being involved in heavy outlay, with no
rich friend to back him now, concerning the repairs, and
in some measure the rebuilding, of the large and noble
parish church.

But all these personal troubles vanished, in the memories
of true friendship, and in holy confidence, when he per-
formed that last sad duty in the dismantled church, and
then in the eastern nook of the long graveyard. He had
dreaded this trial not a little, but knew what his dear
friend would have wished; and the needful strength was
given him.

It has been said, and is true too often (through our
present usages) that one funeral makes many. A strong
east wind of unwonted bitterness at this time of year—
it was now the last day of October—whistled through the
crowd of mourners, fluttered scarf, and crape, and veil, and
set old Channing's last tooth raging, and tossed the
minister's whitening locks, and the leaves of the Office for
the Dead. So cold was the air, that people of real pity
and good feeling, if they had no friends in the village,
hied to the Ivy-bush, when all was over, and called for hot
brandy and water.

But among them was not Mr. Jakes, though he needed
a stimulus as much as any. He lingered in the churchyard, till the banking up was done, and every one else had
quitted it. When all alone, he scooped a hole at the head
of the grave, and filled it with a bunch of white chrysan-
themums, imbedded firmly to defy the wind. Then he
returned to the sombre school-room, at the west end of the
churchyard, and with one window looking into it. There,
although he had flint and tinder, he did not even light a
dip, but sat for hours in his chair of office, with his head

laid on the old oak desk. Rough, and sad, and tumbled
memories passed before his gray-thatched eyes, and stirred
the recesses of his rugged heart.

Suddenly a shadow fell across his desk. He rose from
his dream of the past, and turning saw the half-moon
quivering aslant, through the diamond panes of the lattice.
For a minute he listened, but there was nothing to be
heard, except a long low melancholy wail. Then he
buttoned his coat, his best Sunday black, and was ashamed
to find the empty cuff wet, as the bib of an infant, but
with the tears of motherless old age.

After his manner—when no boys were nigh—he condemned himself for an ancient fool, and was about to strike
a light, when the sad low sound fell again upon his ears.
Determined to know what the meaning of it was, he groped
for his hat, and stout oak staff, and entered the churchyard by the little iron gate, the private way from the
school premises.

The silence was as deep as the stillness of the dead ; but,
by the light of the westering moon, he made his way
among the white tombstones, and the rubbish of the
builders, to the eastern corner where Sir Thomas Waldron
lay. His old chief's grave was fair and smooth, and the
crisp earth glistened in the moonlight, for the wind had
fallen, and a frost was setting in ; but a small black figure
lay on the crown, close to the bunch of flowers. A low
growl met him ; and then a dismal wail of anguish, beyond
any power of words or tears, trembled along the wan
alleys of the dead, and lingered in the shadowy recesses of
the church.

"Good little *Jess*, thou art truer than mankind," said
the Sergeant, and marched away to his lonely bed.

CHAPTER VIII.

THE POTATO-FIELD.

Live who may, and die who must, the work of the world shall be carried on. Of all these works, the one that can never be long in arrears is eating; and of all British victuals, next to bread, the potato claims perhaps the foremost place. Where the soil is light towards Hagdon Hill, on the property of the Dean and Chapter, potatoes, meet for any dignitary of the Church, could be dug by the ton, in those days. In these democratic and epidemic times, it is hard to find a good potato; and the reason is too near to seek. The finer the quality of fruit or root, the fiercer are they that fall on it; and the nemesis of excellence already was impending. But the fatal blow had not fallen yet; the ripe leaves strewed the earth with vivid gold, instead of reeking weltering smut; and the berries were sound, for boys and girls to pelt one another across the field; while at the lift of the glistening fork across the crumbling ridges, up sprang a cluster of rosy globes, clean as a codlin, and chubby as a cherub.

Farmer John Horner, the senior Churchwarden, and the largest ratepayer on the south side of the Perle, would never have got on as he did, without some knowledge of the weather. The bitter east wind of the previous night, and the keen frost of the morning, had made up his mind that it was high time to lift his best field of potatoes. He had two large butts to receive the filled sacks—assorted into ware and chats—and every working man on the farm, as well as his wife and children, had been ordered to stick at this job, and clear this four-acre field before nightfall. The field was a good step from the village, as well as from Farmer Horner's house; and the lower end (where the gate was) abutted on the Susscot lane, leading from the ford to Perlycross.

It was now All-Hallows day, accounted generally the farewell of autumn, and arrival of the winter. Birds, and beasts, that know their time without recourse to calendar, had made the best use of that knowledge, and followed suit of wisdom. Some from the hills were seeking downwards, not to abide in earnest yet, but to see for themselves what men had done for their comfort when the pinch should come ; some of more tender kind were gone with a whistle at the storms they left behind ; and others had taken their winter apparel, and meant to hold fast to the homes they understood.

Farmer John, who was getting rather short of breath from the fatness of his bacon, stirred about steadfastly among the rows, exhorting, ordering, now and then up-braiding, when a digger stuck his fork into the finest of the clump. He had put his hunting gaiters on, because the ground would clog as soon as the rime began to melt ; and the fog, which still lingered in the hollows of the slopes, made him pull his triple chin out of his comforter to cough, as often as he opened his big mouth to scold. For he was not (like farmers of the present day) too thankful for anything that can be called a crop, to utter a cross word over it.

Old Mr. Channing, the clerk, came in by the gate from the lane, when the sun was getting high. Not that he meant to do much work—for anything but graves, his digging time was past, and it suited him better to make breeches—but simply that he liked to know how things were going on, and thought it not impossible that if he praised the 'taturs, Churchwarden might say—"Bob, you shall taste them ; we'll drop you a bushel, when the butt comes by your door." So he took up a root or two here and there, and "hefted it," (that is to say, poised it carefully to judge the weight, as one does a letter for the post) and then stroked the sleek skin lovingly, and put it down gingerly for fear of any bruise. Farmer John watched him, with a dry little grin ; for he knew what the old gentleman was up to.

"Never see'd such 'taturs in all my life," Mr. Channing declared with a sigh of admiration. "Talk of varmers ! There be nobody fit to hold a can'le to our Measter John. I reckon them would fry even better than they biled ; and that's where to judge of a 'tatur, I contends."

"Holloa, Mr. Clerk ! How be you then, this fine morning ? " The farmer shouted out, as if no muttering would do for him, while he straddled over a two-foot ridge, with the rime thawing down his gaiters. "Glad to see 'e here, old veller. What difference do 'e reckon now, betwixt a man and a 'tatur?"

Farmer John was famous for his riddles. He made them all himself, in conversation with his wife—for he had not married early—and there was no man in the parish yet with brains enough to solve them. And if any one attempted it, the farmer always snubbed him.

"There now, ye be too deep for me!" Mr. Channing made a hole in the ground with his stick, as if Mr. Horner was at the bottom of it. "It requireth a good deal more than us have got, to get underneath your meaning, sir."

"No, Bob, no! It be very zimple, and zuitable too for your trade. A 'tatur cometh out of ground, when a' be ripe; but a man the zame way goeth underground. And a good thing for him, if he 'bideth there, according to what hath been done in these here parts, or a little way up country. No call for thee to laugh, Bob, at thy time of life, when behooveth thee to think over it. But I'll give thee an order for a pair of corduroys, and thou shalt have a few 'taturs, when the butt comes by. Us, as belongs to the Church, is bound to keep her agoing, when the hogs won't miss it! But there, Lord now, I want a score of nose-rings? Have 'e see'd anything of Joe Crang, this morning? We never heer'd nort of his anvil all the time! Reckon Joe had a drop too much at the *Bush*, last night."

"Why, here a' coom'th!" exclaimed the clerk. "Look, a' be claimbin' of an open gate! Whatever can possess the man? A' couldn't look more mazed and weist, if a hunderd ghostesses was after him?"

Joseph Crang, the blacksmith at Susscot ford, where the Susscot brook passed on its way to the Perle, was by nature of a merry turn, and showed it in his face. But he had no red now, nor even any black about him, and the resolute aspect, with which he shod a horse, or swung a big hammer, was changed into a quivering ghastly stare; his lips were of an ashy blue, like a ring of tobacco smoke; and as for his body, and legs, and clothes, they seemed to have nothing to do with one another.

"What aileth the man?" cried Mr. Channing, standing across, as he had the right to do, after bestraddling so many burials; "Master Joe Crang, I call upon thee to collect thy wits, and out with it."

"Joe, thy biggest customer hath a right to know thy meaning." Farmer John had been expecting to have to run away; but was put in courage by the clerk, and brought up his heels in a line with the old man's.

"Coompany, coompany is all I axes for," the blacksmith gasped weakly, as if talking to himself—"coompany of living volk, as rightly is alive."

"Us be all alive, old chap. But how can us tell as you be?" The clerk was a seasoned man of fourscore years, and knew all the tricks of mortality.

"I wish I wadn't. A'most I wish I wadn't, after all I zee'd last night. But veel of me, veel of me, Measter Channin', if you plaise to veel of me."

"Tull 'e what," the Churchwarden interposed; "gie 'un a drink of zider, Bob. If a' be Joe Crang, a' won't say no to thiccy. There be my own little zup over by the hedge, Joe."

Without any scruple the blacksmith afforded this proof of vitality. The cider was of the finest strain—"three stang three," as they called it—and Joe looked almost like himself, as he put down the little wooden keg, with a deep sigh of comfort.

"Maketh one veel like a man again," he exclaimed, as he flapped himself on the chest. "Master Hornder, I owe 'e a good turn for this. Lord only knoweth where I maight a' been, after a' visited me zo last night. It was a visit of the wicked one, by kitums." Master Crang hitched up his trousers, and seemed ready to be off again. But the Churchwarden gripped him by the collar.

"Nay, man. Shan't have it thy own way. After what us have doed for thy throat, us have a call upon thy breath. Strange ways with strangers; open breast with bellyful."

The honest blacksmith stood in doubt, and some of his terror crept back again. "Bain't for me to zettle. Be a job for Passon Penniloe. Swore upon my knees I did. Here be the mark on my small-clothes. Passon is the only man can set my soul to liberty."

"What odds to us about thy soul? 'Tis thy tongue we want, lad?" the senior Churchwarden cried impatiently.

" Thou shalt never see a groat of mine again, unless thou speakest."

"Passon hath a chill in 's bones, and the doctor hath been called to him," Mr. Channing added, with a look of upper wisdom. " Clerk and Churchwarden, in council assembled, hath all the godliness of a rubric."

The blacksmith was moved, and began to scratch his head. " If a' could only see it so?" he muttered— "howsomever, horder they women vessels out o' zight. A woman hath no need to hear, if her can zee—according as the wise man sayeth. And come where us can see the sun a shinin'; for my words will make 'e shiver, if ye both was tombstones. I feel myself a busting to be rid of them."

Master Crang's tale—with his speech fetched up to the manner of the east of England, and his flinty words broken into our road-metal—may fairly be taken for spoken as follows :—

" No longer agone than last night, I tell you, I went to bed, pretty much as usual, with nothing to dwell upon in my mind ; without it was poor Squire's funeral, because I had been attending of it. I stayed pretty nearly to the last of that, and saw the ground going in again ; and then I just looked in at the *Bush*, because my heart was downsome. All the company was lonesome, and the room was like a barn after a bad cold harvest, with a musty nose to it. There was nobody with spirit to stand glasses round, and nobody with heart to call for them. The Squire was that friendly-minded, that all of us were thinking—' The Lord always taketh the best of us. I may be the one to be called for next.' Then an old man in the corner, who could scarcely hold his pipe, began in a low voice about burials, and doctors, and the way they strip the graves up the country ; and the others fell in about their expe- rience ; and with only two candles and no snuffers but the tongs, any one might take us for a company of sextons.

" The night was cruel cold, when I come out, and everything looking weist and unkid, and the big bear was right across the jags of church-tower ; and with nothing inside to keep me up to the mark, and no neighbour making

company, the sound of my own heels was forced upon my
ears, as you might say, by reason of the gloomy road, and
a spark of flint sometimes coming up like steel-filings, when
I ran to keep heat, for I had not so much as a stick with
me. And when I got home I roused up the forge-fire, so
as to make sure where I was, and comfort my knuckles ;
and then I brushed it down, with coals at present figure,
for the morning.

" As it happened, my wife had been a little put out, about
something or other in the morning ; you know how the
women-folk get into ways, and come out of them again,
without no cause. But when she gets into that frame of
mind, she never saith much, to justify it, as evil-tempered
women do, but keeps herself quiet, and looks away bigly,
and leaves me to do things for myself; until such time as
she comes round again. So I took a drink of water from
the shoot, instead of warming up the teapot, and got into
bed like a lamb, without a word ; leaving her to begin
again, by such time as she should find repentance. And
before I went to sleep, there was no sound to be heard in
the house, or in the shop below ; without it was a rat or
two, and the children snoring in the inner room, and the baby
breathing very peaceful in the cradle to the other side of
the bed, that was strapped on, to come at for nursing of her.

" Well, I can't say how long it may have been, because I
sleep rather heartily, before I was roused up by a thundering noise going through the house, like the roaring of a bull.
Sally had caught up the baby, and was hugging and
talking, as if they would rob her of it ; and when I asked
what all this hubbub was, 'You had better go and see,'
was all she said. Something told me it was no right
thing ; and my heart began beating as loud as a flail, when I
crept through the dark to the window in the thatch ; for
the place was as black almost as the bottom of my dipping-
trough, and I undid the window, and called out, ' Who is
there ?' with as much strength as ever I was master of, just
then.

" ' Come down, or we'll roast you alive,' says a great gruff
voice that I never heard the like of ; and there I saw a red-
hot clinker in my own tongs, a sputtering within an inch
of my own smithy thatch.

"'For God's sake, hold hard!' says I, a thinking of the little ones. 'In less than two minutes I'll be with you.' I couldn't spare time to strike a light, and my hands were too shaky for to do it. I huddled on my working clothes anyhow, going by the feel of them; and then I groped my way downstairs, and felt along the wall to the backway into workshop, and there was a little light throwing a kind of shadow from the fire being bellowsed up; but not enough to see things advisedly. The door had been kicked open, and the bar bulged in; and there in the dark stood a terrible great fellow, bigger than Dascombe, the wrestler, by a foot; so far as I could make out by the stars, and the glimmer from the water. Over his face he had a brown thing fixed, like the front of a fiddle with holes cut through it, and something I could not make out was strapped under one of his arms like a holster.

"'Just you look here, man, and look at nothing else, or it will be worse for you. Bring your hammer and pincers, while I show a light.'

"'Let me light a lantern, sir,' I said, as well as I could speak for shivering; 'if it is a shoeing job, I must see what I am about.'

"'Do what I say, blacksmith; or I'll squash you under your anvil.'

"He could have done it as soon as looked; and I can't tell you how I put my apron on, and rose the step out of shop after him. He had got a little case of light in one hand, such as I never saw before, all black when he chose, but as light as the sun whenever he chose to flash it, and he flashed it suddenly into my eyes, so that I jumped back, like a pig before the knife. But he caught me by the arm, where you see this big blue mark, and handed me across the road like that.

"'Blast the horse! Put his rotten foot right,' he says. And sure enough there was a fine nag before me, quaking and shaking with pain and fright, and dancing his near fore-foot in the air, like a Christian disciple with a bad fit of the gout.

"That made me feel a bit like myself again; for there never was no harm in a horse, and you always know what you are speaking to. I took his poor foot gently, as if I had kid gloves on, and he put his frothy lips into my whiskers, as if he had found a friend at last.

"The big man threw the light upon the poor thing's foot, and it was oozing with blood and black stuff like tar. 'What a d—d fuss he makes about nothing!' says the man, or the brute I should call him, that stood behind me. But I answered him quite spirity, for the poor thing was trying to lick my hand with thankfulness, 'You'd make a d—der, if it was your foot," I said; 'he hath got a bit of iron driven right up through his frog. Have him out of shafts. He isn't fit to go no further.' For I saw that he had a light spring-cart behind him, with a tarpaulin tucked in along the rails.

" 'Do him where he stands, or I'll knock your brains out;' said the fellow pushing in, so as to keep me from the cart. 'Jem, stand by his head. So, steady, steady!'

" As I stooped to feel my pincers, I caught just a glimpse under the nag's ribs of a man on his off-side, with black clothes on, a short square man, so far as I could tell: but he never spoke a word, and seemed ever so much more afraid to show himself than the big fellow was, though he was shy enough. Then I got a good grip on the splinter of the shoe, which felt to me more like steel than iron, and pulled it out steadily and smoothly as I could, and a little flow of blood came after it. Then the naggie put his foot down, very tenderly at first, the same as you put down an over-filled pint.

" 'Gee-wugg's the word now,' says the big man to the other; and sorry I am to my dying bones that I stopped them from doing it. But I felt somehow too curious, through the thicket of my fright, and wise folks say that the Lord hath anger with men that sleep too heartily.

" 'Bide a bit,' I told him, 'till I kill the inflammation, or he won't go a quarter of a mile before he drops;' and before he could stop me, I ran back, and blew up a merry little blaze in the shop, as if to make a search for something, and then out I came again with a bottle in my hand, and the light going flickering across the road. The big man stood across, as if to hide the cart; but the man behind the horse skitted back into a bush, very nimble and clever, but not quite smart enough.

"The pretty nag—for he was a pretty one and kind, and now I could swear to him anywhere—was twitching his bad foot up and down, as if to ask how it was getting on ; and I got it in my hand, and he gave it like a lamb, while I poured in a little of the stuff I always keep ready for their troubles, when they have them so. For the moment I was bold, in the sense of knowing something, and called out to the man I was so mortal frit ot—'Master, just lend a hand for a second, will you ; stand at his head in case it stingeth him a bit.' Horse was tossing of his head a little, and the chap came round me, and took him by the nose, the same as he had squeezed me by the arm.

"'I must have one hind-foot up, or he will bolt,' says I ; though the Lord knows that was nonsense ; and I slipped along the shaft, and put my hand inside the wheel, and twitched up the tarpaulin that was tucked below the rail. At the risk of my life it was ; and I knew that much, although I was out of the big man's sight. And what think you I saw, in the flickering of the light ? A flicker it was, like the lick of a tongue ; but it's bound to abide as long as I do. As sure as I am a living sinner, what I saw was a dead man's shroud. Soft, and delicate, and white it was, like the fine linen that Dives wore, and frilled with rare lace, like a wealthy baby's christening ; no poor man, even in the world to come, could afford himself such a winding-sheet. Tamsin Tamlin's work it was ; the very same that we saw in her window, and you know what that was bought for. What there was inside of it was left for me to guess.

"I had just time to tuck the tarpaulin back, when the big man comes at me with his light turned on. 'What the —— are you doing with that wheel?' says he, and he caught me by the scruff of the neck, and swung me across the road with one hand, and into my shop, like a sack with the corn shot out of it. 'Down on your knees !' he said, with no call to say it, for my legs were gone from under me, and I sprawled against my own dipping-trough, and looked up to be brained with my own big hammer. 'No need for that,' he saith, for he saw me glancing at it ; 'my fist would be enough for a slip such as you. But you be a little too peart, Master Smith. What right have you to call a pair of honest men sheep-stealers?'

F

" I was so astonished that I could not answer, for the thought of that had never come nigh me. But I may have said—*Shish—shish!* to soothe the nag ; and if I did, it saved my life, I reckon.

" ' Now swear, as you hoped to be saved,' says he, ' that never a word shall pass your lips about this here little job to-night.' I swore it by Matthew, Mark, Luke, and John ; but I knew that I never could stick to it. ' You break it,' says he, 'and I'll burn you in your bed, and every soul that belongs to you. Here's your dibs, blacksmith ! I always pay handsome.' He flung me a crown of King George and the Dragon, and before I could get up again, the cart was gone away.

" Now, I give you my word, Farmer Hornder, and the very same to you Clerk Channing, it was no use of me to go to bed again, and there never was a nightcap would stay on my head without double-webbing girths to it. By the mercy of the Lord, I found a thimbleful of gin, and then I roused up light enough to try to make it cheerful ; and down comes Sally, like a faithful wife, to find out whatever I was up to. You may trust me for telling her a cock-and-bull affair ; for 'twas no woman's business, and it might have killed the baby."

CHAPTER IX.

THE NARROW PATH.

" Now, Master Joe Crang," the Churchwarden said firmly, but not quite as sternly as he meant to put it, because he met the blacksmith's eyes coming out of head ; "how are we to know that you have not told us what you call a cock-and-bull affair ? Like enough you had a very fearsome dream, after listening to a lot about those resurrection-men, and running home at night with the liquor in your head."

" Go and see my door ahanging on the hinges, master, and the mark of the big man's feet in the pilm, and the track of wheels under the hedge, and the blood from the poor nag's frog, and the splinter of shoe I pulled out with the pincers.

But mercy upon me, I be mazed almost! I forgot I put the iron in my pocket. Here it is?"

There it was sure enough, with dried blood on the jag of it, and the dint from a stone which had driven it, like a knife through an oyster-shell, into the quick. Such is the nature of human faith, that the men, handling this, were convinced of every word. They looked at each other silently, and shook their heads with one accord, and gave the shivering blacksmith another draught of cider.

"Joe, I beg your pardon for doubting of your word," Farmer John answered, as his own terror grew; "you have been through a most awesome night. But tell us a thing or two you have left out. What way do you reckon the cart came from, and what was the colour, and was there any name on it, and by the sound, which way did it drive off?"

"Ay, ay, he hath hit it," the clerk chimed in; "the finest head-piece in all the county belongeth to the hat of our Master John Horner."

"I'll tell 'e every blessed thing I knows, but one," Joe Crang was growing braver, after handing horrors on; "can't say which way the cart come from, because I was sound in my bed just then. But her hadn't been through the ford, by the look of wheels, and so it seems her must have come from Perlycrass direction. The colour was dark; I should say, a reddish brown, so far as the light supported me. There was no name to see; but I was on her near side, and the name would be t'other side of course, if there wur one. Her drove off the way her was standing, I believe; at least according to the sound of it; and I should have heard the splash, if they had driven through the ford. Any other questions, master?"

"There may be some more, Joe, when I come to think. But I don't see clearly how you could have been on the near side of horse, to the other side of lane, in case they were coming from our village way."

"You'm right enough there, sir, if so be they hadn't turned. I could see by the marks that they went by my shop, and then turned the poor horse, who was glad enough to stop; and then bided under hedge, in a sort of dark corner. Might a' come down the lane a' purpose like,

F 2

seeking of me to do the job. Seemeth as if they had
heard of my shop, but not ezactually where it waz."

" When you come to think of it, might be so." Farmer
John was pretty safe in his conclusions, because they never
hurried him. "And if that was the meaning, we should
all have reason to be very joyful, Joe. You cannot see it
yet; nor even Master Channing. But to my mind it
proveth that the chaps in this queer job—mind, I don't
say but what they may have been respectable, and driving
about because they could afford it—but to my mind it
showeth they were none of our own parish. Nor next
parish either, so far as reason goes. Every child in Perlycross, with legs to go on, knows afore his alphabet, where
Susscot forge be."

"A' knoweth it too well, afore he gets his breeches.
Three quarters of a mile makes no odds to they childer,
when they take it in their heads to come playing with the
sparks. And then their mothers after 'em, and all the
blame on me ! "

"It is the way of human nature, when it is too young.
Master Clerk, a word with you, before we go too far. Sit
down upon this sack, Joe, and try to eat a bit, while the
wiser heads be considering."

The Churchwarden took the ancient clerk aside, and the
blacksmith beginning to be in better heart, renewed his
faith in human nature upon bread and bacon.

Before he was sure that he had finished, the elder twain
came back to him, fortified by each other's sense of right,
and high position in the parish. But Channing was to put
the questions now, because they were unpleasant, and he
was poor.

"According to my opinion, Master Crang, you have
told us everything wonderful clear, as clear as if we had
been there to see it, considering of the time of night. But
still there is one thing you've kept behind, causally
perhaps, and without any harm. But Churchwarden
Horner saith, and everybody knows the value of his
opinion, that the law is such, that every subject of the
King, whatever his own opinion may be, hath to give it
the upper course, and do no more harm than grumble."

" Big or little, old or young, male or female, no distinction, baronet or blacksmith;" said Farmer John, impressively.

"And therefore, Joe, in bounden duty we must put the question, and you must answer. Who was the man according to your judgment, that kept so close behind the horse, and jumped away so suddenlike, when the light of your fire shone into the lane? You said that the big man called him 'Jem,' and you as good as told us that you certified his identity."

"I don't understand 'e, Master Channing. I never was no hand at big words." The blacksmith began to edge away, till the farmer took the old man's staff, and hooked him by the elbow.

"No lies, Crang! You know me pretty well. I am not the man to stand nonsense. Out of this potato-field you don't budge, till you've told us who the short man was."

"A' worn't short, sir; a' worn't short at all—taller than I be, I reckon; but nort to what the other were. Do 'e let go of me, Farmer Hornder. How could I see the man, through the nag?"

"That's your own business, Crang. See him you did. Horse or no horse, you saw the man; and you knew him, and you were astonished. Who was he, if you please, Master Joseph Crang?"

"I can't tell 'e, sir, if I was to drop down dead this minute. And if I said ort to make 'e vancy that I knowed the gentleman, I must a' been mazed as a drummeldrone."

"Oh, a gentleman, was it? A queer place for a gentleman! No wonder you cockle yourself to keep it dark. A five-pound note to be made out of that, Joe; if the officers of justice was agreeable."

"Master Hornder, you'm a rich man, and I be but a poor one. I wouldn't like to say that you behaved below yourself, by means of what I thought; without knowing more than vancy."

"Joe, you are right, and I was wrong;" the farmer was a just man, whenever he caught sight of it; "I was going to terrify of 'e, according to the orders of the evil-thinkers, that can't believe good, because it bain't inside theirselves. But I put it to you now, Joe, as a bit of dooty; and it

must tell up for you, in t'other way as well. For the sake
of all good Christians, and the peace of this here parish,
you be held to bail by your own conscience, the Lord
having placed you in that position, to tell us the full
names of this man, gentleman or ploughboy, gipsy or
home-liver."

The blacksmith was watching Mr. Horner's eyes, and
saw not a shadow of relenting. Then he turned to the old
man, for appeal. But the Clerk, with the wisdom of
fourscore years, said,—" Truth goes the furthest. Who
would go to jail for you, Joe ? "

" Mind that you wouldn't give me no peace ; and that
I says it against my will, under fear of the King and
religion "—Master Crang protested, with a twist, as if a
clod-crusher went over him—" likewise that I look to you
to bear me harmless, as a man who speaketh doubtful of
the sight of his own eyes. But unless they was wrong,
and misguided by the Devil, who were abroad last night
and no mistake, t'other man—in the flesh, or out of it, and
a' might very well a' been out of it upon such occasion, and
with that there thing behind him, and they say that the
Devil doth get into a bush, as my own grandmother zee'd
he once—'twixt a Rosemary tree, which goes far to prove
it, being the very last a' would have chosen——"

" None of that stuff," cried the Churchwarden sternly ;
and the Clerk said, " No beating about the bush, Joe !
As if us didn't know all the tricks of Zatan ! "

" Well then, I tell 'e—it waz Doctor Jemmy Vox."

They both stood, and stared at him, as if to ask whether
his brain was out of order, or their own ears. But he met
their gaze steadily, and grew more positive, on the strength
of being doubted.

" If ever I zee'd a living man, I tell 'e that man, t'other
side of the nag, waz Doctor Jemmy Vox, and no other man."

The men of Devon have earned their place (and to their
own knowledge the foremost one) in the records of this
country, by taking their time about what they do, and
thinking of a thing before they say it. Shallow folk,
having none of this gift, are apt to denounce it as slowness
of brain, and even to become impatient with the sage
deliberators.

Both Horner, and Channing, had excellent reasons for thinking very highly of Dr. Fox. The Churchwarden, because the doctor had saved the life of his pet child Sally, under Providence ; and the Clerk, inasmuch as he had the privilege of making the gentleman's trousers, for working and for rustic use.

"Now I tell 'e what it is," said Farmer John, looking wrathful, because he saw nothing else to do, and Channing shrank back from doing anything ; "either thou art a born liar, Joe ; or the Devil hath gotten hold of thee."

"That's the very thing I been afeared of. But would un let me spake the truth, without contempt of persons ?"

"Will 'e stand to it, Joe, afore a Justice of the Peace ?" The Clerk thought it was high time to put in a word. "Upon occasion, I mean, and if the law requireth."

"There now ! Look at that ! The right thing cometh, soon or late ;" cried the persecuted blacksmith. "Take me afore Squire Walders himself—no, no, can't be, considerin' I were at his funeral yesterday—well take me afore Squire Mockham, if be fitty ; and ax of him to putt, I don't care what it be, stocks, or dead water, or shears atop of me ; and I'll tell un the very zame words I telled to thee. Can't hev no relief from gospel, if the Passon's by the heels ; shall have some relief by law, if the Lord hath left it living. No man can't spake no vairer than that there be."

This adjuration was of great effect. "To Zeiser shalt thou go ?" replied the senior Churchwarden ; "us have no right to take the matter out of Zeiser's hands. I was dwelling in my mind of that all along, and so was you, Clerk."

Mr. Channing nodded, with his conscience coming forward ; and after some directions at the upper end of field—where the men had been taking it easily, and the women putting heads together—the two authorities set off along the lane, with the witness between them, towards Perlycross.

But, as if they had not had enough of excitement to last them for a month of thoughts and words, no sooner did they turn the corner at the four-cross roads (where the rectory stands, with the school across the way), than they came full butt upon a wondrous crowd of people hurrying from the Churchyard.

"Never heard the like of it!" "Can't believe my eyes a'most." "Whatever be us a'coming to?" "The Lord in heaven have mercy on the dead!" "The blessed dead, as can't help theirselves!"

These, and wilder cries, and shrieks, from weeping women along the cottage-fronts; while in the middle of the street came slowly men with hot faces, and stern eyes. Foremost of all was Sergeant Jakes, with his head thrown back, and his gray locks waving, and his visage as hard as when he scaled the ramparts, and leaped into the smoke and swordflash. Behind him was a man upon a foaming horse, and the strength of the village fiercely silent.

"Where be all agoing to? What's up now? Can't any of 'e spake a word of sense?" cried Farmer John, as the crowd stopped short, and formed a ring around him.

"High Jarks, tell un."

"Us was going to your house."

"Hold your tongue, will 'e, and let High Jarks speak."

The Sergeant took discipline, and told his tale in a few strong words, which made the Farmer's hair stand up.

"Let me see the proof," was all he said; for his brain was going round, being still unseasoned to any whirl fiercer than rotation of farm-crops. All the others fell behind him, with that sense of order which still swayed the impulse of an English crowd; for he was now the foremost layman in the parish, and everybody knew that the Parson was laid up. The gloom of some black deed fell upon them; and they passed along the street like a funeral.

"Clap the big gate to, and shoot the iron bar across. No tramping inside more than hath been a'ready."

Master Horner gave this order, and it was obeyed, even by those who excluded themselves. At the west end, round the tower, was a group of "foreign" workmen—as the artisans from Exeter were called—but under orders from Mr. Adney they held back, and left the parish matter to the natives thereof.

"Now come along with me, the men I call for;" commanded the Churchwarden, with his hand upon the bars, as he rose to the authority conferred upon him; "and they be Sergeant Jakes, Clerk Channing, Bob that hath ridden from Walderscourt, and Constable Tapscott, if so be he hath arrived."

"I be here, sure enough, and my staff along o' me—hath the pictur' of His Majesty upon him. Make way, wull 'e, for the Officer of the King?"

Then these men, all in a cold sweat more or less—except Sergeant Jakes, who was in a hot one—backing up one another, took the narrow path which branched to the right from the Churchyard cross, to the corner where brave Colonel Waldron had been laid.

CHAPTER X.

IN CHARGE.

"My young friend, I must get up," Mr. Penniloe exclaimed, if so feeble a sound could be called an exclamation. "It is useless to talk about my pulse, and look so wise. Here have I been perhaps three days. I am not quite certain, but it must be that. And who is there to see to the parish, or even the service of the Church, while I lie like this? It was most kind of you—I have sense enough to feel it—to hurry from your long ride, without a bit to eat—Mrs. Muggridge said as much, and you could not deny it. But up I must get; and more than that, I must get out. It will soon be dark again, by the shadows on the blind, and I am sure that there is something gone amiss, I know not what. But my duty is to know it, and to see what I can do. Now go, and have some dinner, while I just put on my clothes."

"Nothing of that sort, sir, will you do to-day. You are weaker than a cat—as that stupid saying goes. That idiot Jackson has bled you to a skeleton, put a seton in your neck, and starved you. And he has plied you with drastics, by day and by night. Why, the moment I heard of that Perliton booby getting you in his clutches—but thank God I was in time! It is almost enough to make one believe in special Providences."

"Hush, Jemmy, hush? You cannot want to vex me now."

"Neither now, nor ever, sir; as you are well aware. So you must do likewise, and not vex me. I have trouble enough of my own, without rebellion by my patients."

"I forgot that, Jemmy. It was not kind of me. But I am not quite clear in my head just now. I fear I am neglecting some great duty. But just for the moment, I am not sure what it is. In a minute or two, I shall remember what it is."

"No, you won't, my good friend, not for twenty hours yet;" the young doctor whispered to himself. "You have had a narrow shave, and another day of Jackson would have sent you to the world you think too much of. There never was a man who dwelt in shadows—or in glory, as you take it—with his whole great heart, as you do. Well, I wish there were more of them, and that I could just be one."

The peace that had settled on the Parson's face was such as no lineaments of man can win, without the large labours of a pure life past, and the surety of recompense full in view. Fox kept his eye on him, and found his pulse improve, as hovering slumber deepened into tranquil sleep. "Rare stuff that!" he said, referring not to faith, but to a little phial-bottle he had placed upon the drawers; "he shan't go to glory yet, however fit he may be. It is high time,—I take it, for me to have a little peck."

The young man was right. He had ridden thirty miles from his father's house that afternoon, and hearing at the "Old Barn," as he called his present home, of poor Mr. Penniloe's serious illness, had mounted his weary mare again, and spurred her back to the rectory. Of the story with which all the parish was ringing he had not heard a word as yet, being called away by his anxious mother, on the very night after the Squire was buried. But one thing had puzzled him, as he passed and repassed the quiet streets of Perlycross—the people looked at him, as if he were a stranger, and whispered to one another as he trotted by. Could they have known what had happened to his father?

With the brown tops still upon his sturdy legs, and
spurs thickly clotted with Somerset mud (crustier even
than that of Devon) Fox left the bedroom with the door
ajar, and found little Fay in a beehive chair, kneeling with
her palms put together on the back, and striving hard to
pray, but disabled by deep sobs. Her lovely little cheeks
and thick bright curls were dabbled into one another by
the flood of tears ; as a moss-rose, after a thundershower,
has its petals tangled in the broidery of its sheath.

"Will he die, because I am so wicked? Will he die,
because I cannot see the face of God?" She was whispering, with streaming eyes intent upon the sky-light, as if
she were looking for a healthy Father there.

"No, my little darling, he will not die at all. Not for
many years, I mean, when Fay is a great tall woman."

The child turned round with a flash of sudden joy, and
leaped into his arms, and flung her hair upon his shoulders,
and kissed him, vehemently,

> "With a one, two, three !
> If you want any more, you must kiss me."

like a true tiny queen of the nursery. Many little girls
were very fond of Dr. Fox ; although their pretty loves
might end in a sombre potion.

"Now shall I tell you what to do, my dear?" said the
truly starving doctor, with the smell of fine chops coming
up the stairs, sweeter than even riper lips; "you want to
help your dear daddy, don't you?"

Little Fay nodded, for her heart was full again, and the
heel-tap of a sob would have been behind her words.

"Then go in very quietly, and sit upon that chair, and
don't make any noise, even with your hair. Keep the
door as it is, or a little wider; and never take your eyes
from your dear father's face. If he keeps on sleeping, you
stay quiet as a mouse; if he opens his eyes, slip out softly,
and tell me. Now you understand all that, but you must
not say a word."

The child was gazing at him, with her whole soul in her
eyes, and her red lips working up and down across her
teeth ; as if her father's life hung upon her self-control.
Dr. Fox was hard put to it to look the proper gravity.

As if he would have put this little thing in charge, if there had been any real charge in it!

"Grand is the faith of childhood. What a pity it gets rubbed out so soon!" He said to himself, as he went down the stairs, and the child crept into her father's room, as if the whole world hung upon her pretty little head.

Mrs. Muggridge had lighted two new candles, of a size considered gigantic then—for eight of them weighed a pound almost—and not only that, but also of materials scarcely yet accepted as orthodox. For "Composites" was their name, and their nature was neither sound tallow, nor steadfast wax. Grocer Wood had sent them upon trial gratis; but he was a Dissenter, though a godly man; and the housekeeper, being a convert to the Church, was not at all sure that they would not blow up. Therefore she lit them first for Dr. Fox, as a hardy young man, with some knowledge of mixtures.

"He is going on famously, as well as can be, Muggridge;" the doctor replied to her anxious glance. "He will not wake till twelve, or one o'clock, to-morrow; and then I shall be here, if possible. The great point then will be to feed him well. Beef-tea, and arrow-root, every two hours, with a little port wine in the arrow-root. No port wine in the house? Then I will send some, that came from my father's own cellar. Steal all his clothes, and keep a female in the room. The Parson is a modest man, and that will keep him down. But here comes my mutton chop. Well done, Susanna! What a cook! What skill and science, at the early age of ten!"

This was one of Dr. Jemmy's little jokes; for he knew that Susanna was at least seventeen, and had not a vestige of cookery. But a doctor, like a sexton, must be jolly, and leave the gravity to the middleman—the parson.

But instead of cutting in with her usual protest, and claim to the triumph, whatever it might be, Mrs. Muggridge to his surprise held back, and considered his countenance, from the neighbourhood of the door. She had always been ready with her tit-for-tat, or lifting of her hand in soft remonstrance at his youthful levity. But now the good woman, from behind the candles, seemed to want snuffing, as they began to do.

"Anything gone wrong in Perlycross, since I went away, Mrs. Muggridge? I don't mean the great loss the parish has sustained, or this bad attack of Mr. Penniloe's. That will be over, in a few days' time, now his proper adviser is come back again. By the way, if you let Jackson come in at this front door—no, it mustn't lie with you, I will write a little note, polite but firm, as the papers say; it shall go to his house by my boy Jack, to save professional amenities : but if he comes before he gets it, meet him at the door with another, which I will leave with you. But what makes you look so glum at me, my good woman? Out with it, if I have hurt your feelings. You may be sure that I never meant to do so."

"Oh sir, is it possible that you don't know what has happened?" Thyatira came forward, with her apron to her eyes. She was very kind-hearted, and liked this young man; but she knew how young men may be carried away, especially when puffed up with worldly wisdom.

"I have not the least idea what you mean, Mrs. Muggridge." Fox spoke rather sternly, for his nature was strong, and combative enough upon occasion, though his temper was sweet and playful; and he knew that many lies had been spread abroad about him, chiefly by members of his own profession. "My ears are pretty sharp, as suits my name, and I heard you muttering once or twice— 'He can't have done it. I won't believe it of him.' Now if you please, what is it I am charged with doing?"

"Oh sir, you frighten me when you look like that. I could never have believed that you had such eyes."

"Never mind my eyes. Look here, my good woman. Would you like to have wicked lies told about you? I have been away for three days, called suddenly from home, before daylight on Saturday morning. My father was seized with a sudden attack, for the first time in his life. He is getting old; and I suppose a son's duty was to go. Very well, I leave him on Tuesday morning, because I have urgent cases here ; and he has his own excellent doctor. I pass up the village, and everybody looks as if I had cut his throat. I go home, concluding that I must be mazed—as you people call it—from want of food and sleep. But when I get home, my own man, and boy, and old Betty, all rush out, and stare at me. 'Are you mad?' I call out, and instead of answering, they tell me the Parson is dying, and at the mercy of Jervis Jackson. I know what that means, and without quitting saddle come back here and rout the evil one. Then what happens? Why, my very first mouthful is poisoned by the black looks of a thoroughly good woman. Tell me what it is, or by George and the Dragon, I'll ride home, and drag it out of my own people."

"Can you prove you were away, sir? Can you show when you left home?" Thyatira began to draw nearer, and forgot to keep a full-sized chair 'twixt the Doctor and herself.

"To be sure, I can prove that I have been at Foxden, by at least a score of witnesses, if needful."

"Thank the Lord in heaven, that He hath not quite forgotten us! Susanna, have another plate hot, but be sure you don't meddle with the grid-iron. Bad enough for Perlycross it must be anyhow ; a disgrace the old parish can never get over—but ever so much better than if you, our own doctor——"

"Good-bye, Mrs. Muggridge! You'll see me to-morrow."

"Oh no, sir, no. I will tell you now just. How could I begin, when I thought you had done it? At least I never thought that, I am sure. But how was I to contradict it? And the rudest thing ever done outside of London! The poor Squire's grave hath been robbed by somebody, and all Perlycross is mad about it."

"What!" cried Jemmy Fox. "Do you mean Sir Thomas Waldron? It cannot be. No one would dare to do such a thing."

"But some one hath, sir, sure enough. Mr. Jakes it was, sir, as first found it out, and a more truthfuller man never lived in any parish. My master doth not know a word of it yet. Thank the Lord almost for this chill upon his lungs ; for the blow might have killed him, if he had been there, with such a disorderly thing on his back. We must hide it from him, as long as ever we can. To tell the truth, I was frightened to let you go up to him, with every one so positive about the one who did it. But you wouldn't take no denial, and I am very glad you wouldn't. But do have t'other chop, sir ; it's a better one than this was. Oh, I beg your pardon. I forgot to draw the blind down."

The truth was that she had been afraid till now to sever herself from the outer world, and had kept Susanna on the kitchen stairs; but now she felt as certain of the young man's innocence, as she had been of his guilt before.

"Nothing more, thank you," said Fox, sitting back, and clenching his hand upon the long bread-knife; "and so all the parish, and even you, were only too delighted to believe that I, who have worked among you nearly three years now, chiefly for the good of the poor and helpless, and never taken sixpence when it was hard to spare—that I would rob the grave of a man, whom I revered and loved, as if he were my father. This is what you call Christianity, is it? And no one can be saved except such Christians as yourselves! The only Christian in the parish is your parson. Excuse me—I have no right to be angry with— with a woman, for any want of charity. Come tell me this precious tale, and I'll forgive you. No doubt the evidence is very strong against me."

Thyatira was not pleased with this way of taking it. She thought that the charity was on her side, for accepting the doctor's own tale so frankly. So she fell back upon her main buttress.

"If you please, Dr. Fox," she said with some precision; "as women be lacking in charity, therefore the foremost of all godly graces, you might think it fairer to see Sergeant Jakes, a military man and upright. And being the first as he was to discover, I reckon he hath the first right to speak out. Susanna seeth light in the schoolroom still though all the boys be gone, and books into the cupboards. Ah, he is the true branch for discipline. Do 'e good to look in at the window after dusk, and the candles as straight as if the French was coming. 'I am the Vine,' saith the Lord, 'and ye'—but you know what it is, Dr. Jemmy, though seldom to be found, whether Church it be, or Chapel. Only if you make a point of seeing the man that knoweth more than all of us put together, the new pupil, Master Peckover, is a very obliging young gentleman, and one as finds it hard upon him to keep still."

"Oh, he is come, is he? I have heard some tales of him.

It struck me there was more noise than usual in the pupils'
room.   Let me think a moment, if you please.   Yes, I had
better see Sergeant Jakes.   He may be a queer old codger,
but he will stick to what he sees and says.   Tell those
noisy fellows, that they must keep quiet.   They want High
Jarks among them with his biggest vine, as you seem to
call his cane."

CHAPTER XI.

AT THE CHARGE.

STRENUOUS vitality, strong pulse, thick skin, tough bone,
and steadfast brain, all elements of force and fortitude,
were united in this Dr. Fox ; and being thus endowed, and
with ready money too, he felt more of anger than of fear,
when a quarrel was thrust upon him.   While he waited
alone for the schoolmaster, he struck Mr. Penniloe's best
dining-table with a heavy fist that made the dishes ring,
and the new-fashioned candles throw spots of grease upon
the coarse white diaper.   Then he laughed at himself, and
put a calm face on, as he heard the strong steps in the
passage.

"Sit here, Mr. Jakes," he said, pointing to a chair, as
the Sergeant offered him a stiff salute.   "Mrs. Muggridge,
you had better leave the room.   This is not a nice matter
for ladies.   Now Sergeant, what is all this rotten stuff
about me ? "

"Not about you, sir, I hope with all my heart."

Mr. Jakes met the young man's flashing eyes, with a
gaze that replied—"You don't scare me," and drew his
chair close enough to study every feature.   If the young
man was full of wrath, so was the old man—implacable
wrath, at the outrage to his Colonel.

"Well, tell your pack of lies "—Fox was driven beyond
himself, by the other's suspicious scrutiny—"oh, I beg
your pardon, you believe them true, of course.   But out
with your stuff, like a man, sir ! "

"It is your place to prove it a pack of lies ; " said the
old man, with his shaggy eyebrows rigid as a line of

British bayonets; "and if you can't, by the God who made me, I'll run my old sword through your heart."

"Rather hard upon me. Not got it here, I hope. Half an hour for repentance, while you fetch it out of some cheese-toasting rack. A nice man to teach the youth of Perlycross! What a fool you are, Jakes! But that you can't help. Even a fool though may try to be fair. During your long time in the wars, were you ever accused wrong-fully, my friend?"

"Yes, sir, a score of times. And I like your spirit. If you did what they say of you, you would be a cur. Every evil name you call me makes me think the better of you."

"I will call you no more; for I want no favour. All I want is truth about this cursed outrage. Am I to wait all night for it? Now just tell your tale, as if your were sitting at the *Ivy-bush*. You have been in command of men, no doubt—just command yourself."

"That I will," said the veteran with an upward glance—"not like the *Ivy-bush*, but as before the Lord. Sir, I will command myself, as you recommend; and perhaps you would be none the worse, for taking your own medicine."

"Jakes, you are right. It is enough to turn me savage. But you shall not hear me speak again, until you have finished."

"It was just like this, sir," began the Sergeant, looking round for a glass, by force of habit, and then ashamed of himself for such a thought just now; "everybody in this parish knows how much I thought of Colonel Waldron; for a better and a braver man never trod this earth. Even Parson Penniloe will have to stand behind him, when the last muster cometh; because he hath not served his country. But I never was satisfied with any of you doctors. You may be very well in your way, Mr. Fox, for toothing, or measles, or any young complaint; but where is your experience in times of peace? And as for that hang-dog looking chap from London—well, I won't say what I thought of him; for I always keep my own opinions to myself. But I knew it was all over with our poor Colonel, the moment I clapped eyes on that fellow. Why, I went myself at once, and begged the Colonel to have him drummed out of the parish to the rogue's tattoo. But the good Colonel only laughed, and shook my hand—the last time it was, sir, the very last time.

"You were at the funeral, and there never was a truer one. I was proud to my heart, though it felt like lead, to see three old Officers come from miles away, brave men as ever led a storming column, with tears in their eyes, and not a thought of their own ends. There was no firing-party as should have been, being nothing but peace going on nowadays, and only country bumpkins about here. But I see you are impatient; because you know all that.

"As soon as all were gone away, and the ground put tidy, I brought a few of my own white flowers, as they do in Spanish land, and put them in very carefully with a bit of moss below them, and fastened them so as not to blow away, although there was a strong east wind up. Later on at night, I came again by the little wicket from the schoolroom, just to see that all was right; for my mind was uneasy somehow.

"The moon was going low, and it was getting very cold, and not a soul about, that I could see. The flowers showed bright, at the head of the mound; and close by was a little guardian—the Colonel's pet dog, that could never bear to leave him—she was lying there all in the cold by herself, sobbing every now and then, or as it were be-wailing, with her chin along the ground, as if her heart was broken. It struck me so sad, that I could look at her no more.

"In the morning I slept past the usual time, being up so late, and out of spirits. But I saw the white frost on the ground, and I had a few boys to correct before school began, and then lessons to see to till twelve o'clock; and it must have been turned the half hour, when I went to Churchyard again, to see how my flowers had stood the frost. I had brought a bit of victuals in my pocket, for the dog; but little *Jess* was gone; and I could not blame her, considering how easily a man forgets his dog; and yet I was vexed with her, for being so like us; for the poor things have no religion, such as we make smooth with. My flowers were there; but not exactly as I thought I had put them; and the bank appeared to me to be made up sharper.

" Well, Mr. Fox, I am not one of them that notice little things upon the earth so much, (as if there was never any sky above them,) and make more fuss about a blade of grass, than the nature of men and good metal. I thought that old Channing had been at work again, not satisfied with his understrapper's job. Then I drew forth my flowers ; and they looked almost, as if they had been tossed about the yard—crumpled almost anyhow, as well as scorched with frost.

" At this, I was angry, when I thought how kind the poor Colonel had been to that old stick of a clerk, and even let him muck up their liveries ; and so I set off for the old man's cottage, to have a word or two with him, about it. But he was not at home ; and little Polly, his grand-daughter, was sure that he had not been near the church that day, but was gone to help dig Farmer John's potatoes.

" Then back I went again, in a terrible quandary, remembering the wicked doings up the country, and the things that had come across my fancy in the night.

" The first thing I saw, when I came back by south-gate, was a young man, red in the face, and out of breath, jumping, in and out, over graves and tombstones, from the west end, where the contractor's work is. ' What are you doing, Bob ? ' said I, rebuking of him pretty strongly ; for I saw that it was one of my old boys, now become a trusty sort of groom at Walderscourt.

" ' Sergeant, what have you been doing here ? ' says he ' Our little Jess has just come home, with one leg cut in two.'

" All my blood seemed to stand still, and I should have dropped, if I hadn't laid hold of that very tombstone, which the Parson can't endure. The whole of it flashed upon me, in a moment ; and a fool I must have been not to see it all before. But wicked as our men were, and wicked I myself was—as I will not deny it, in the rough-and-tumble times—such a blackguard dastard crime was out of my conception. Considering who the Colonel was ; considering what he was, sir ! "

The Sergeant turned away his face, and desired to snuff

the candles. No snuffers were there, for this new invention
was warranted not to want them. So he fumbled with
his empty sleeve; but it would not come up to order; and
then he turned back, as if brought to bay, and reckless of
public opinion; with his best new handkerchief in his
hand—a piece of cotton goods imprinted with the Union-
Jack in colours.

"My friend, you are a noble fellow," said Fox, with his
own wrongs out of date, in the movement of large feeling.
"Would to God, that I had any one as true to me, as you
are!"

"It is not that," resumed the Sergeant, trying to look
stern again. "It is the cursed cruelty, that makes me
hate mankind, sir. That a man should kill a poor dumb
thing, because it loved its master—there, there, the
Almighty will smite the brute; for all helpless things
belong to Him.

"Well, sir, I hardly know what happened next, or what
I said to Bob Cornish. But he went round the wall, to
fetch his horse; and the news must have spread, like
wildfire. A young man, who had helped to make up the
grave, was going to his dinner through the Churchyard;
and seeing us there, he came and looked, and turned like a
ghost, and followed us. Presently we were in the street,
with half the village after us, going to the chief Churchwarden's house; for we knew how ill the Parson was. At
the cross-roads, we met Farmer John, and old Clerk
Channing along of him, looking doiled as bad as we were,
and between them the blacksmith from Susscot ford; and
a terrible tale we had from them.

"Farmer John, as the head of the parish now, took the
lead; and well he did it. We went back by the big iron
gate, and there we kept the outsiders back; and Mr.
Adney was as good with his, who were working near the
tower. I was ordered to the eastern end, where the stone
stile leads into Perlycombe lane, by which the villains must
have got in; with no house there in view of it, but only
the tumble-down Abbey. Somebody was sent for my old
sword, that I knocked away from the French officer, and
now hangeth over the Commandments; and I swore that
ᵀ would slash off any hand, that was laid on the edge of

the riser; while Adney brought a pile of scaffold-cords, and enclosed all the likelihood of footprints.

"By this time the other Churchwarden was come, and they all put their heads together, and asked what my opinion was; and I said—'Make no bones of it.' But they had done a wiser thing than that, with an eye to the law, and the penalties. They had sent Bob Cornish on the fast young horse, the Colonel thought so much of, to fetch the nearest Justice of the Peace, from his house this side of Perliton. Squire Mockham came, as strong as he could ride, with his mind made up about it; and four digging men were set to work at once. Squire Mockham was as sharp about it, as if he had just had the lid taken off of him, by death of superior officer; and I, who had seen him on the Bench knock under, to half a wink from the Colonel's eye, was vexed with the dignity he took over, by reason of being survivor.

"Clerk Channing will tell you more about the condition of things underground, for I never made them my study; though I have helped to bury a many brave men, in the rough, both French and English. My business it was to keep people away; and while I was putting a stern face on, and looking fit to kill any of the bumpkins, the Lord knows I could never have touched them, for my blood was as cold as snow-water. And when they sang up—'No Colonel here!' just as if it made no difference—I dropped the French sword, and my flesh clave to my bones, the same as it did to King David. And ever since that, I have been fit for Bedlam; and the boys may stand and make mouths at me."

"I can understand that," said Dr. Fox, with his medical instincts moving—generously, as they always do with a man worthy of that high calling—"Jakes, you are in a depressed condition; and this exertion has made it worse. What you want is a course of carminatives. I will send you a bottle this very night. No more excitement for you at present. Lay aside all thought of this sad matter."

"As if I could, sir; as if I could!"

"No, I am a fool for suggesting that. But think of it, as little as you can. Above all things, go in for more physical exertion. Cane half-a-dozen boys, before break-fast."

"There's a dozen and a half, sir, that have been neglected sadly."

"That will be a noble tonic. Making mouths at Sergeant Jakes! You look better already, at the thought of doing duty, and restoring discipline."

"Talk about duty, sir! Where was I? Oh, if I had only gone out again; if I had only gone out again, instead of turning into my bed, like a sluggard! I shall never forgive myself for that."

"You would just have been killed; as poor *Jess* was. Such scoundrels think nothing of adding murder to a crime still worse. But before you go home—which is the best thing you can do, and have a dish of hot kidneys from your brother's shop—one thing I must ask; and you must answer. What lunatic has dared to say, that I had anything to do with this?"

"The whole parish is lunatic; if it comes to that, sir."

"And all the world, sometimes. But who began it? Jakes, you are a just man; or you could not be so loyal. Is it fair, to keep me in the dark, about the black things they are saying of me?"

"Sir, it is not. And I will tell you all I know; whatever enemies I may make. When a thing flares about, you can seldom lay your hand on the man, or the woman, who fired the train. It was Crang, the shoeing smith at Susscot ford, who first brought your name into it."

"Crang is an honest, and a simple-minded man. He would never speak against me, of his own will. He has been most grateful for what I did, when his little girl had scarlet fever. How could he have started this cursed tale?"

"From the evidence of his own eyes, sir; according at least to his use of them."

"Tell me what he saw, or thought he saw. He is not the man to tell a lie. Whatever he said, he believed in."

Fox spoke without any anger now; for this could be no scheme of his enemies.

"You are wonderful fair, sir;" said Sergeant Jakes.

"You deserve to have all above board; and you shall have it."

Tired as he was, and beginning to feel poorly at the threat of medicine, the old soldier told the blacksmith's tale, with as few variations as can contrive to keep themselves out of a repetition. Fox began to see that the case was not by any means so easy, as he first supposed. Here was evidence direct against him, from an impartial witness; a tale coherent, and confirmed by facts independent of it, a motive easily assigned; and the public eager to accept it, after recent horrors. But he was young, and warm of faith in friendship, candour, and good-will; or (if the worst should come to the worst) in absolute pure justice.

"It will not take long to put this to rights," he said, when the Sergeant had finished his account. "No one can really have believed it, except that blockhead of a blacksmith. He was in a blue funk all the time, and no need to be ashamed of it. There are two people I must see to-night—Mr. Mockham, and that Joe Crang himself. I shall borrow a horse from Walter Haddon; my young mare has had enough of it. I shall see how the Parson looks before I go. Now go to bed, Sergeant, as I told you. To-morrow you will find all the wiseacres saying, what fools they have made of one another."

But the veteran shook his head, and said, "If a cat has nine lives, sir; a lie has ninety-nine."

CHAPTER XII.

A FOOL'S ERRAND.

Mr. JOHN MOCKHAM was a short stout man, about five or six and forty years of age, ruddy, kind-hearted, and jocular. He thought very highly of Jemmy Fox, both as a man and a doctor; moreover he had been a guest at Foxden, several times, and had met with the greatest hospitality. But for all that, he doubted not a little, in his heart—though his tongue was not allowed to know it—concerning the young doctor's innocence of this most atrocious outrage. He bore

in mind how the good and gentle mother had bemoaned
(while Jemmy was in turn-down collars) the very sad
perversity of his mind, towards anything bony and splintery.
Nothing could keep him from cutting up, even when his
thumb was done round with oozing rag, anything jointed
or cellular; and the smell of the bones he collected was
dreadful, even in the drawer where his frilled shirts were
laid."

The time was not come yet, and happily shall never—in
spite of all morbid suisection—when a man shall anatomise
his own mind, and trace every film of its histology. Squire
Mockham would have laughed any one to scorn, who had
dared to suggest, that in the process of his brain, there
was any connexion of the frills in Jemmy's drawer with
the blacksmith's description of what he had seen; and yet
without his knowledge, it may even have been so. But
whatever his opinion on the subject was, he did not refuse
to see this young friend; although he was entertaining
guests, and the evening was now far advanced.

Fox was shown into the library, by a very pale footman,
who glanced at the visitor, as if he feared instant dissection,
and evidently longed to lock him in. "Is it come to this
already?" thought poor Fox.

"Excuse me for not asking you to join us in there,"
Mr. Mockham began rather stiffly, as he pointed to the
dining-room; "but I thought you might wish to see me
privately."

"I care not how it is. I have come to you, as a Magistrate, and—and—" "an old friend of the family," was
what he meant to say, but substituted—"as a gentleman,
and a sensible and clear-sighted one, to receive my deposition on oath, concerning the wicked lies spread abroad
about me."

"Of what use will it be? The proper course is for you
to wait, till the other side move in the matter; and then
prove your innocence, if possible; and then proceed against
them."

"That is to say, I am to lie, for six months, perhaps
twelve months, under this horrible imputation, and be
grateful for escaping at last from it! I see that even you
are half inclined to think me guilty."

"All this to a Magistrate is quite improper. It happens that I have resolved not to act, to take no share in any proceedings that may follow; on account of my acquaintance with your family. But that you could not know, until I told you. I am truly sorry for you; but you must even bear it."

"You say that so calmly, because you think I deserve it. Now as you are not going to act in the matter, and have referred to your friendship with my family, I will tell you a little thing in confidence, which will prove to you at once that I am innocent—that I never could by any possibility have done it."

Before Mr. Mockham could draw back, the visitor had whispered a few words in his ear, which entirely changed the whole expression of his face.

"Well, I am surprised! I had no idea 'of it. How could that fool Crang have made such a mistake? But I saw from first how absurd it was, to listen to such fellows. I refused to give a warrant. I said that no connexion could be shown, between the two occurrences. How strange that I should have hit the mark so well! But I seem to have that luck generally. Well, I am pleased, for your dear mother's sake, as well as your own, Master Jemmy. There may be a lot of trouble; but you must keep your heart up, and the winning card is yours. After all, what a thing it is to be a doctor!"

"Not so very fine, unless your nature drives you into it. And everybody thinks you make the worst of him, to exalt your blessed self. So they came for a warrant against me, did they? Is it lawful to ask who they were?"

"To be sure it is, my boy. Everybody has a right to that piece of information. Tapscott was the man that came to swear—strong reason for believing, etc., with two or three witnesses, all from your parish; Crang among the others, hauled in by the neck, and each foremost in his own opinion. But Crang wanted to be last, for he kept on shouting, that if he had to swear against Doctor Jemmy, the Lord would know that he never meant it. This of course made it all the worse for your case; and every one was grieved, yet gratified. You are too young to know the noise, which the newspapers begin to call 'public

opinion,'—worth about as much as a blue-bottle's buzz, and
as eager to pitch upon nastiness. I refused a warrant—as
my duty was. Even if the blacksmith's tale was true—and
there was no doubt that he believed it—what legal connexion could they show betwixt that, and the matter at
the churchyard? In a case of urgency, and risk of disappearance of the suspected person, I might have felt
bound to grant it. But I knew that you would stand it
out; and unless they could show any others implicated,
their application was premature."

"Then, unless you had ventured to stem the ltide, I
suppose that I should have been arrested, when I came
back to-day from my father's sick-bed. A pretty state of
law, in this free country!"

"The law is not to blame. It must act promptly, in
cases of strong suspicion. Probably they will apply to-
morrow, to some younger magistrate. But your father is
ill? How long have you been with him? They made a
great deal out of your disappearance."

"My father has had a paralytic stroke. I trust that he
will get over it; and I have left him in excellent hands.
But to hear of this would kill him. His mind is much
weakened, of course; and he loves me. I had no idea that
he cared much for me. I thought he only cared for my
sister."

"Excuse me for a moment. I must go to my guests;"
Mr. Mockham perceived that the young man was overcome
for the moment, and would rather be alone. "I will make
it all right with them, and be back directly."

Fox was an active, and resolute young fellow, with great
powers of endurance, as behoved a man of medicine.
Honest indignation, and strong sense of injustice, had
stirred up his energy for some hours; but since last Thursday night he had slept very little, and the whole waking
time had been worry and exertion. So that now when he
was left alone, and had no foe to fire at, bodily weariness
began to tell upon him, and he fell back in an easy chair
into a peaceful slumber.

When the guests had all departed, and the Magistrate
came back, he stopped short for a moment, with a broad
smile on his face, and felt proud of his own discretion, in

refusing to launch any criminal process against this trustful visitor. For the culprit of the outcry looked so placid, gentle, good-natured, and forgiving—with the natural expression restored by deep oblivion—that a woman would have longed to kiss his forehead, if she had known of his terrible mishap.

"I have brought you a little drop of cordial, Master Jemmy. I am sure you must want something good, to keep you up." Mr. Mockham put a spirit-stand and glass upon the table, as Fox arose, and shook himself.

"That is very kind of you. But I never take spirits, though I prescribe them sometimes for old folk when much depressed. But a glass of your old port wine, sir, would help me very much—if I am not giving you a lot of trouble."

"You shall have a glass, almost as good as your father has given me. There it is! How sorry I am to hear about his illness! But I will do what he would have wished. I will talk to you as a friend, and one who knows the world better than you can. First, however, you must forgive me, for my vile suspicions. They were founded partly on your good mother's account of your early doings. And I have known certain instances of the zeal of your Profession, how in the name of science and the benefits to humanity—but I won't go on about that just now. The question is, how shall we clear you to the world? The fact that I doubted you, is enough to show what others are likely to conclude. Unluckily the story has had three days' start, and has fallen upon fruitful ground. Your brother doctors about here are doing their best to clench the nail"—Mr. Mockham, like almost everybody else, was apt to mix metaphors in talking—"by making lame excuses for you, instead of attempting to deny it."

"Such fellows as Jervis Jackson, I suppose. Several of them hate me, because I am not a humbug. Perhaps they will get up a testimonial to me, for fear there should be any doubt of my guilt."

"That is the very thing they talk of doing. How well you understand them, my young friend! Now, what have you to show, against this general conclusion? For of course you cannot mention what you confessed to me."

"I can just do this—I can prove an *alibi*. You forget that I can show where I have been, and prove the receipt of the letter, which compelled me to leave home. Surely that will convince everybody, who has a fair mind. And for the rest, what do I care?"

"I don't see exactly what to say to that." Mr. Mockham was beginning to feel tired also, after going through all his best stories to his guests. "But what says Cicero, or some other fellow that old Dr. Richards used to drive into my skin? 'To neglect what everyone thinks of oneself, is the proof not only of an arrogant, but even of a dissolute man.' You are neither of these. You must contend with it, and confound your foes; or else run away. And upon the whole, as you don't belong here, but up the country—as we call it—and your father wants your attention, the wisest thing you can do is, to bolt."

"Would you do that, if it were your own case?" Fox had not much knowledge of Squire Mockham, except as a visitor at his father's house; and whether he should respect, or despise him, depended upon the answer.

"I would see them all d—d first;" the Magistrate replied, looking as if he would be glad to do it; "but that is because I am a Devonshire man. You are over the border; and not to be blamed."

"Well, there are some things one cannot get over," Dr. Jemmy answered, with a pleasant smile; "and the worst of them all is, to be born outside of Devon. If I had been of true Devonshire birth, I believe you would never have held me guilty."

"Others may take that view; but I do not;" said the Magistrate very magnanimously. "It would have been better for you, no doubt. But we are not narrow-minded. And your mother was a Devonshire woman, connected with our oldest families. No, no, the question is now of evidence; and the law does not recognise the difference. The point is—to prove that you were really away."

"Outside the holy county, where this outrage was committed? Foxden is thirty miles from Perlycross, even by the shortest cuts, and nearer thirty-five, to all who are particular about good roads. I was at my father's bed-side, some minutes before ten o'clock, on Saturday morning."

" That is not enough to show. We all know in common sense, that the ride would have taken at least four hours. Probably more, over those bad roads, in the darkness of a November morning. The simplest thing will be for you to tell me the whole of your movements, on the night of this affair."

" That I will, as nearly as I can remember ; though I had no reason then, for keeping any special record. To begin with—I was at the funeral of course, and saw you there, but did not cross over to speak to you. Then I walked home to the Old Barn where I live, which stands as you know at the foot of Hagdon Hill. It was nearly dark then, perhaps half-past five ; and I felt out of spirits, and sadly cut up, for I was very fond of Sir Thomas. I sat thinking of him for an hour or so ; and then I changed my clothes for riding togs, and had a morsel of cold beef and a pipe, and went to look for the boy that brings my letters ; for old Walker, the postman, never comes near the Barn. There was no sign of the boy, so I saddled *Old Rock*—for my man was 'keeping funeral ' still, as they express it—and I rode to North-end, the furthest corner of the parish, to see to a little girl, who has had a dangerous attack of croup. Then I crossed Maiden Down by the gravel-pits, to see an old stager at Old Bait, who abuses me every time, and expects a shilling. Then homewards through Priestwell, and knocked at Gronow's door, having a general permission to come in at night. But he was not at home, or did not want to be disturbed ; so I lost very little time by that. It must have been now at least nine o'clock, with the moon in the south-west, and getting very cold ; but I had managed to leave my watch on the drawers, when I pulled my mourning clothes off.

" From Priestwell, I came back to Perlycross, and was going straight home to see about my letters—for I knew that my father had been slightly out of sorts, when I saw a man waiting at the cross-roads for me, to say that I was wanted at the Whetstone-pits ; for a man had tumbled down a hole, and broken both his legs. Without asking the name, I put spurs to *Old Rock*, and set off at a spanking pace for the Whetstone-pits, expecting to find the foreman there, to show me where it was. It is a long roundabout

way from our village, at least, for any one on horseback,
though not more than three miles perhaps in a straight
line, because you have to go all round the butt of Hagdon
Hill, which no one would think of riding over in the dark.
I should say it must be five miles at least, from our cross-
roads."

"Every yard of that distance," says the Magistrate, who
was following the doctor's tale intently, and making notes
in his pocket-book ; "five miles at least, and road out of
repair. Your parish ought to be indicted."

"Very well. *Old Rock* was getting rather tired. A
better horse never looked through a bridle ; but he can't be
less than sixteen years of age. My father had him eight
years, and I have had him three ; and even for a man with
both legs broken, I could not drive a willing horse to death.
However, we let no grass grow beneath our feet ; and dark
as the lanes were, and wonderfully rough, even for this
favoured county, I got to the pit at the corner of the hill,
as soon as a man could get there, without breaking his
neck."

"In that case he never would get there at all."

"Perhaps not. Or at least, not in working condition.
Well, you know what a queer sort of place it is. I had been
there before, about a year ago. But then it was daylight ;
and that makes all the difference. I am not so very fidgetty
where I go, when I know that a man is in agony ; but how
to get along there in the dark, with the white grit up to
my horse's knees, and black pines barring out the moon-
shine, was—I don't mind confessing it—a thing beyond me.
And the strangest thing of all was, that nobody came near
me. I had the whole place to myself ; so far as I could
see—and I did not want it.

"I sat on *Old Rock ;* and I had to sit close ; for the old
beauty's spirit was up, in spite of all his weariness. His
hunting days came to his memory perhaps ; and you should
have seen how he jumped about. At the risk of his dear
old bones of course ; but a horse is much pluckier than we
are. What got into his old head, who shall say? But I
failed to see the fun of it, as he did. There was all the
white stuff, that comes out of the pits, like a great cascade
of diamonds, glittering in the level moonlight, with broad

bars of black thrown across it by the pines, all trembling, and sparkling, and seeming to move.

"Those things tell upon a man somehow, and he seems to have no right to disturb them. But I felt that I was not brought here for nothing, and began to get vexed at seeing nobody. So I set up a shout, with a hand to my mouth, and then a shrill whistle between my nails. The echo came back, very punctually; but nothing else, except a little gliding of the shale, and shivering of black branches. Then I jumped off my horse, and made him fast to a tree, and scrambled along the rough bottom of the hill.

"There are eight pits on the south side, and seven upon the north, besides the three big ones at the west end of the hill, which are pretty well worked out, according to report. Their mouths are pretty nearly at a level, about a hundred and fifty feet below the chine of hill. But the tumbledown —I forget what the proper name is—the excavated waste, that comes down, like a great beard, to the foot where the pine-trees stop it—"

"*Brekkles* is their name for it;" interrupted Mr. Mockham; "*brekkles*, or *brokkles*—I am not sure which. You know they are a colony of Cornishmen."

"Yes, and a strange outlandish lot, having nothing to do with the people around, whenever they can help it. It is useless for any man to seek work there. They push him down the brekkles—if that is what they call them. However, they did not push me down, although I made my way up to the top, when I had shouted in vain along the bottom. I could not get up the stuff itself; I knew better than to make the trial. But I circumvented them at the further end; and there I found a sort of terrace, where a cart could get along from one pit-mouth to another. And from mouth to mouth, I passed along this rough and stony gallery, under the furzy crest of hill, without discovering a sign of life, while the low moon across the broad western plains seemed to look up, rather than down at me. Into every black pit-mouth, broad or narrow, bratticed with timber or arched with flint, I sent a loud shout, but the only reply was like the dead murmuring of a shell. And yet all the time, I felt somehow, as if I were watched by invisible eyes, as a man upon a cliff is observed from the sea.

"This increased my anger, which was rising at the thought that some one had made a great fool of me ; and forgetting all the ludicrous side of the thing—as a man out of temper is apt to do—I mounted the most conspicuous pile at the end of the hill, and threw up my arms, and shouted to the moon, ' Is this the way to treat a doctor ? '

"The distant echoes answered—' Doctor ! Doctor ! ' as if they were conferring a degree upon me ; and that made me laugh, and grow rational again, and resolved to have one more try, instead of giving in. So I climbed upon a ridge, where I could see along the chine, through patches of white among the blackness of the furze ; and in the distance there seemed to be a low fire smouldering. For a moment I doubted about going on, for I have heard that these people are uncommonly fierce, with any one they take for a spy upon them ; and here I was entirely at their mercy. But whenever I have done a cowardly thing, I have always been miserable afterwards ; and so I went cautiously forward towards the fire, with a sharp look-out, and my hunting-crop ready. Suddenly a man rose in front of me, almost as if he jumped out of the ground, a wild-looking fellow, stretching out both arms. I thought I was in for a nasty sort of fight, and he seemed a very ugly customer. But he only stepped back, and made some enquiry, so far as I could gather from his tone, for his words were beyond my intelligence.

"Then I told him who I was, and what had brought me there ; and he touched his rough hat, and seemed astonished. He had not the least difficulty in making out my meaning ; but I could not return the compliment. ' Naw hoort along o' yussen '—was his nearest approach to English ; which I took to mean—' no accident among us ; ' and I saw by his gestures that he meant this. In spite of some acquaintance with the Mendip miners, and pretty fair mastery of their brogue, this Whetstoner went beyond my linguistic powers, and I was naturally put out with him. Especially when in reply to my conclusion that I had been made a fool of, he answered ' yaw, yaw,' as if the thing was done with the greatest ease, and must be familiar to me. But, in his rough style, he was particularly civil, as if he valued our Profession, and was sorry that any one should play with it.

He seemed to have nothing whatever to conceal; and so far as I could interpret, he was anxious to entertain me as his guest, supposing that time permitted it. But I showed him where my horse was, and he led me to him by a better way, and helped me with him, and declined the good shilling which I offered him. This made me consider him a superior sort of fellow; though to refuse a shilling shows neglected education.

"When I got back to the Ancient Barn—as I call my place, because it is in reality nothing else—it was two o'clock in the morning, and all my authorities were locked in slumber. George was on a truss of hay up in the tallat, making more noise than Perle-weir in a flood, although with less melody in it; and old Betty was under her 'Mark, Luke, and John'—as they called the four-poster, when one is gone. So I let them 'bide, as you would say; gave *Old Rock* a mash myself, because he was coughing; and went in pretty well tired, I can assure you, to get a bit of bread and cheese, and then embrace the downy.

"But there on my table was a letter from my mother; which I ought to have received before I started; but the funeral had even thrown the Post out, it appears. I don't believe that my boy was at all to blame. But you know what Walker the Postman is, when anything of interest is moving. He simply stands still, to see the end of it; sounding his horn every now and again, to show his right to look over other folk's heads. Every one respects him, because he walks so far. Thirty miles a day, by his own account; but it must be eighteen, even when he gets no beer."

"A worthy old soul!" said the Magistrate. "And he had a lot of troubles, last winter. Nobody likes to complain, on that account. He is welcome to get his peck of nuts upon the road, and to sell them next day at Pumpington, to eke out his miserable wages. But this is an age of progress; and a strict line must be drawn some where. The Post is important sometimes, as you know; though we pay so many eightpences, for nothing. Why, my friends were saying, only this very evening, that Walker must submit henceforth to a rule to keep him out of the coppices. When he once gets there, all his sense of time is gone. And people are now so impatient."

"But the nutting-time is over, and he has not that

H

excuse. He must have been four hours late on Friday, and
no doubt he was as happy as ever. But to me it would
have made all the difference; for I should have started that
evening for Foxden. My mother's letter begged me to
come at once; for she feared that my father would never
speak again. There had been some little trifles between us;
as I don't mind telling you, who are acquainted with the
family. No doubt I was to blame; and you may suppose,
how much I was cut up by this sad news. It was folly to
start in that tangle of cross-lanes, with the moon gone down,
and my horse worn out. I threw myself down upon my
bed, and sobbed, as I thought of all the best parts of the
Governor.

"What a fool a man is, when a big blow falls upon him.
For two or three hours, I must have lain like that, as if all
the world were in league against me, and nothing to be
done but feel helpless, and rebel. I knew that there was
no horse near the place, to be hired for the ride to Foxden,
even if the owner could be fetched out of his bed. And all
the time, I was forgetting the young mare that I had
bought about a month ago—a sweet little thing, but not
thoroughly broken, and I did not mean to use her much,
until the Spring. She was loose in a straw-run at the top
of my home-meadow, with a nice bit of aftermath still
pretty fresh, and a feed of corn at night, which I generally
took to her myself. Now she came to the gate, and
whinnied for me, because she had been forgotten; and
hearing the sound I went downstairs, and lit a lantern to
go to the corn-bin. But she had better have gone without
her supper, for I said to myself—why not try her? It was
a long way for a young thing just off grass; but if only she
would take me to the great London road, I might hire on,
if she became distressed.

"Of course I went gently and carefully at first, for I
found her a little raw and bridle-shy; but she carried me
beautifully, when the daylight came, and would have gone
like a bird, if I had let her. She will make a rare trotter,
in my opinion, and I only gave fifteen pounds for her. I
would not look at fifty now, after the style she brought me
back—a mouth like a French kid-glove, and the kindest of
the kind."

"You deserve a good horse, because you treat them well, Jemmy. But what about your good father?"

"Well, sir, thank God, he is in no danger now; but he must be kept very quiet. If he were to hear of this lying tale, it might be fatal to him. And even my mother must not know it. Your Exeter paper never goes that way; but the Bristol ones might copy it. My only sister, Christie, is a wonderful girl, very firm, and quick, and sensible. Some say that she has got more sense than I have; though I don't quite see it. I shall write to her to-morrow, just to put her upon guard, with a line for Dr. Freeborn too—my father's old friend and director, who knows exactly how to treat him. What a rage they will be in, when they hear of this! But they will keep it as close as a limpet. Now what do you advise me to do, about myself?"

"You must look it in the face, like a man, of course; though it is enough to sour you for life almost, after all your good works among the poor."

"No fear of that, sir. It is the way of the world. 'Fair before fierce' is my family motto; and I shall try to act up to it. Though I daresay my temper will give out sometimes, especially with brother pill-box."

"You take it much better than I should, I fear;" Mr. Mockham spoke the truth in this; "you know that I will do my utmost for you; and if you keep your head, you will tide over this, and be the idol of all who have abused you —I mean, who have abused you honestly. You seem to have solid stuff inside you, as is natural to your father's son. But it will take a lot out of your life; and it seems very hard upon a fine young fellow. Especially after what you have told me. Things will be very black there; as you must see."

"Certainly they will. But I am not a boy. I know a noble nature, when I come across it. And if ever there was—but I won't go on with that. If she believes in me, I am content, whatever the low world may say. I have never been romantic."

"I am not at all sure of that, my boy. But I felt that sort of wildness, before I was married. Now let me put one or two questions to you; just to get up your case, as if I was your Counsel. Did any of your people at the

Old Barn see you, after your return from the Whetstone Pits?"

"Not one, to my knowledge. My household is small, in that ramshackle place. Old Betty upstairs, and George over the stables, and the boy who goes home to his mother at night. I have only those three in the domestic line, except upon great occasions. Old Betty was snoring in her bed, George doing the like upon a truss of hay, and the boy of course off the premises. They must have found in the morning that I had been there, but without knowing when, or how long I stayed."

"That is most unlucky. Did you pass near the church? Did you meet any people who would know you, anywhere between midnight and morning?"

"Neither man, woman, nor child did I see, from the time I left the Whetstone Hill, until I passed Perlycombe next morning. It was either too late, or too early, for our very quiet folk to be stirring."

"Bad again. Very bad. You cannot show your whereabouts, during any part of the critical time. I suppose you would know the man on the Whetstone Hill; but that was too early to help you much. The man at the cross-roads—would you know him?"

"Not to be certain. He kept in the shadow, and spoke as if he were short of breath. And the message was so urgent, that I never stopped to examine him."

"Very little comfort anywhere. Is it usual for Dr. Gronow to be from home at night?"

Mr. Mockham put this question abruptly, and pronounced the Doctor's name, as if he did not love him.

"Not very usual. But I have known it happen. He is wild about fishing, though he cannot fish a bit; and he sometimes goes late to his night-lines."

"He would scarcely have night-lines laid in November, however big a poacher he may be. Betwixt you and me, Jemmy, in the very strictest confidence, I believe he is at the bottom of all this."

"I will answer for it, that he is not. In the first place, he is a gentleman, though rough in his manners, and very odd. And again he had no motive—none whatever. He has given up his practice, and cares more for Walton and

Cotton, than for all the Hunterian Museum. And he knew, as well as I do, the nature of the case. No, sir, you must not suspect him for a moment."

"Well, then it must be that man—I forgot his name—who was staying with Mr. Penniloe. A very sarcastic, unpleasant fellow, as several people said who spoke to him. He would take good care to leave no trace. He looked as crafty as Old Nick himself. It will never be found out, if that man did it. No, no, Jemmy, don't attempt to argue. It must be one of you three. It is neither you, nor Gronow; then it must be that Harrison Gowler."

CHAPTER XIII.

THE LAW OF THE LAND.

ONE comfort there was among all this trouble, and terror, and perplexity—little *Jess* was not dead, as reported; nor even inclined to die, just at present. It was true that she had been horribly slashed with a spade, or shovel, or whatever it might have been; and had made her way home on three legs by slow stages, and perhaps with many a fainting fit. But when she had brought her evil tidings, and thrown down her staunch little frame to die, at the spot where she was wont to meet her master, it happened that Mr. Sharland crossed the garden from the stables. This was a Veterinary Surgeon, full of skill, and large of heart, awake to the many pangs he caused in systems finer than the human, and pitiful to the drooping head, and the legs worn out in man's service. In a moment he had gathered up the story of poor *Jess*, and he said, "if any dog deserves to be saved, it is this faithful little dear."

Then he pulled off his coat, and tucked up his sleeves, and pronounced with a little pomposity—for a good man should make his impression—

"Deep cut across the humerus. Compound fracture of the ulna. Will never do much with that limb again. But if the little thing is only half as sagacious as she is faithful, and pyretic action does not supervene, we shall save her life; and it is worth saving."

Jess licked his hand, as if she understood it all, and resigned herself to human wisdom. And now she had a sweet bed in a basket, airy and buoyant, yet proof against cold draughts ; and there she was delighted to receive old friends, with a soft look of gratitude in large black eyes, and a pretty little quiver of the tail too wise to wag, for fear of arousing their anxiety. *Pixie*, the pug, had many qualms of jealousy, as well as some pangs of deep interest —for what dog, however healthy, could feel certain in his heart that he might not be reduced to the same condition? And he was apt to get a human kick, when he pressed his kind enquiries.

But upon the loftier level of anthropic interests, less of harmony prevailed, and more of hot contention. The widowed lady of the house had felt her loss intensely ; and with the deeper pain, because her generous nature told her of many a time when she had played a part a little over the duty of a loyal wife. Her strong will, and rather imperious style, and widely different view-point, had some-times caused slight disagreements between the Spanish lady and the English squire ; and now she could not claim the pleasure of having waived herself to please him. But she had the sorrow of recalling how often she had won the victory, and pushed it to the utmost, and how seldom she had owned herself in the wrong, even when she had perceived it. A kinder and a nobler husband no woman was ever blessed with ; and having lost him, how could she help dis-paraging every other man, as a tribute to his memory?

Even with her daughter Inez, she was frequently pro-voked, when she saw the tears of filial love, or heard the unconsidered sigh. "What is her loss, compared with mine?" "But for this child, he would have loved me more." "Shallow young creature, like a tinkling zither— she will start a new tune, in a week or two." Such were her thoughts ; but she kept them to herself, and was angry with herself for forming them.

So it may be supposed, what her fury was, or rather her boundless and everlasting rage, when she heard of the miscreant villainy, which could not long be concealed from her. Her favourite maid, Tamar Haddon, was the one who first let fall an unwary word ; and that young woman received a shock, which ought to have disciplined her tongue for life. With a gaze, and a gesture, there was no withstanding, her mistress tore out of her everything she knew, and then with a power of self-control which few men could have equalled, she ordered the terrified damsel away, and sat down alone, to think miserably.

How long she stayed thus, was unknown to any; for Tamar made off with all speed to her room, and was seized with a fit of hysterics. But the lady's only movement was to press one hand upon her labouring heart. By and by she rose, and unlocked the door of her little oratory—a place not very often favoured with her presence. There she took down a crucifix of ivory—not the Indian, but the African, which hardens and whitens with the lapse of years, though green at first, as truth is—and she set it upon a velvet shelf, and looked at it without much reverence. In the stormy times, when Spain was writhing under the heel of an infidel, her daughters lost their religious grounding, and gained fierce patriotism. "My Country is my God," was a copy set in schools.

At first she looked with scorn and pity at such meek abandonment. What had her will and heart to do with mild submission, drooping head, and brow of wan benignity? But the sculptor had told more than that. He had filled the sufferer's face with love, and thrilled the gaze of death with sweet celestial compassion. So well had the human hand conveyed the tender heart of heaven.

' The sting of mortal injuries began to grow less venomous. The rancorous glare was compelled to soften, and suffused with quivering tears. She had come to have a curse attested, and a black vow sanctified; but earthly wrong and human wrath were quelled before the ruth of heaven, and conquest of the Tortured One. She fell upon her knees, and laid her hands upon the spike-torn feet; and her face became that of a stricken woman, devoted to sorrow, but not to hate.

How long this higher influence would last is quite another point, especially with a woman. But it proved at least that she was not altogether narrow, and hard, and arrogant. Then she went to her bed, and wept for hours; and perhaps her reason was saved thereby. At any rate

her household, which had been in wretched panic, was
saved from the fearful outburst, and the timid cast-up of
their wages.

On the following morning, she was calm, at least to all
outward semblance, and said not a word to any one of the
shock she had suffered yesterday. But as soon as business-
time allowed, she sent for Mr. Webber, the most active
member of the steady firm, in which her husband had
placed confidence. He was good enough to come at once,
although, as he told his nervous wife, he would have
preferred an interview with the lioness, who had just
escaped from a travelling menagerie.

But like all other terrors, when confronted, this proved
tolerably docile ; and upon his return he described this
foreign lady's majestic beauty, and angelic fortitude, in
warmer terms than his wife thought needful over his own
mahogany. After recounting all he knew, and being heard
with patience, he had taken instructions which he thought
sagacious and to the purpose, for they were chiefly of his
own suggestion.

Now this Mr. Webber was a shrewd, as well as a very
upright man, but of rather hasty temperament, and in many
of his conclusions led astray, without the least suspicion of
it, by prejudices and private feelings. One of his favourite
proverbs was—"A straw will show how the wind blows ;"
and the guiding straw for him was prone to float on the
breath of his own favour. Although he knew little of Dr.
Fox, he was partly prepared to think ill of him, according
to the following inclination.

Waldron Webber, the lawyer's eldest son, and Godson
of the brave Sir Thomas, had shown no capacity for the
law, and little for anything else, except a good thumb for
the gallipots. Good friends said—"What a doctor he will
make ! " and his excellent mother perceived the genius, and
felt how low it would be to lament that such gifts were
seldom lucrative, till half the life is over. So the second
son took to the ruler, and the elder to the pestle, instruments of equal honour, but of different value. And
Waldron, although his kind father had bought him a snug
little practice at Perlycombe, was nibbling at the bottom of
the bag at home, while his brother cast in at the top of it,

Why was this? Simply because young Fox, the heir of a wealthy family, had taken it into his wicked head to drop down from the clouds at Perlycross. It was true that he had bought a practice there; but his predecessor had been a decent fellow, observing the rules of the Profession. If a man could not pay for it, let him not be ill; or at any rate go to the workhouse, and be done for in the lump. But this interloper was addicted to giving tick unlimited, or even remission of all charges, and a cure—when nature would not be denied—without the patient paying for it, if he had no money. One thing was certain —this could not last long. But meanwhile a doctor of common sense was compelled to appeal to his parents.

"All cannot be right," Mr. Webber senior had observed with emphasis, when he heard the same tale from his son's bosom friend, Jervis Jackson of Perliton; "there are certain rules, my dear, essential to the existence of all sound Professions; and one of the most fundamental is, to encourage nobody who cannot pay. This Fox must be a sadly Radical young man, though his family is most respectable. Mischief will come of it, in my firm opinion."

The mischief was come, and in a darker form than the soundest lawyer could anticipate. Mr. Webber lamented it; and his wife (who had seen Jemmy waltzing at a Taunton ball with one of her pretty daughters, and been edified with castles in the air) lifted up her hands, and refused to listen to it; until she thought of her dear son. "If it is the will of God," she said, "we must accept it, Theodore."

But this resignation is not enough for an Attorney with a criminal case in hand. Lady Waldron had urged despatch; and he knew that she was not to be trifled with. He had taken the blacksmith's deposition, which began as if his head were on the anvil, as well as Farmer John's, and Channing's, and that of Mr. Jakes the schoolmaster. And now it was come to Monday night; and nothing had been heard of Fox.

But it was not so easy to know what to do. There was no Police-force as yet to be invoked with certainty of some energy, and the Bow-Street-Runners, as they were called—possibly because they never ran—had been of no service in such cases, even when induced to take them up. Recourse must be had to the ancient gear of Magistrate and constable; for to move any higher authorities would require time and travel. Strong suspicion there might be, but no strong chain of evidence; for no connexion could be established (whatever might be the inference) between the occurrence at Susscot and the sacrilege at Perlycross.

Moreover, our ancient laws are generally rough, and brisk, and able-bodied to stick out bravely for the purse, but leave the person to defend itself. If it cannot do this after death, let it settle the question with its Maker; for it cannot contribute to the Realm, and belongs to the Resurrection. This larger view of the matter will explain to the live content how it came to pass that the legislature (while providing, for the healthy use of anatomy, the thousands of criminal bodies despatched for the good of their choicer brethren) failed to perceive any duty towards those who departed this life in the fear of God, after paying their rates and taxes, for the term prescribed by Heavenly Statute. In a word, when the wicked began to fall short —through clemency human or Divine—no man of the highest respectability could make sure of what he left behind. Only, by the ancient Common Law, to dig him up again, without a Faculty, was indictable as a Misdemeanour.

Mr. Webber was familiar with all these truths, and obliged to be careful of their import. If the theft of a sheep could be brought home to Fox, the proceeding would have been more simple, and the penalties far heavier. But, for his enemies, the social outrage was the thing to look at. As it stood, there was small chance yet of saddling the culprit with legal guilt; nevertheless if the tide of general opinion set against him, even the noblest medical science must fail to make head against it. And the first step was to give some public form to the heinous accusation, without risk of enormous damages. Hence the application to Mr. Mockham, under the name of Tapscott, as before related, and justly refused by that Magistrate.

Mr. Webber of course did not appear, nor allow his name to be quoted, knowing how small the prospect was of the issue of a warrant. But his end was gained, for all who were present—including the Magistrate himself—left the place with dark and strong suspicion against the absent Doctor. The question was certain now to be taken up by County Journals; whereupon the accused might well be trusted to do something foolish, even if nothing more were learned from the stealthy watch kept on him.

There was much to justify this view; for Fox did many foolish things, and even committed blunders, such as none but the sagest of the sage could avoid in his position. He was young, and hot of blood, and raging at the sweet readiness of his friends—as such dastards dared to call themselves—to accept the wicked charge against him, on such worthless evidence. Now was the time for any generous nature to assert itself; for any one with a grain of faith, or even of common charity, to look him in the face, and grasp his hand, and exclaim with honest anger— "Not a word of those cursed lies do I believe. You are an honest fellow, Jemmy, whatever skulks and sneaks may say; and if any one says it in my presence, down he goes like a dabchick."

Did any one do this, of all who had been so much obliged to him, or even of those who without that had praised him in his prosperous days, and been proud of his acquaintance? It made his young heart cold with bitterness, and his kind eyes flash with scorn, when even young fellows of healthy nature, jovial manners, and careless spirit, spied something of deepest interest across the road, as he came by; or favoured him with a distant nod, and a passing—"How doo, Doctor?" perhaps with an emphasis on the title, suggestive of dissection. It was enough to sour any man of even bright intelligence, and fair discrimination; for large indeed is the heart of him, and heavenly his nature, who does not judge of his brethren, by their behaviour to this brother.

Yet there were some few, who did behave to this poor brother, as if they had heard of the name of Christ, or deserved, in a way, to do so. These were the very poor, who feel some gratitude for kindness; because it comes not as a right, but a piece of rare luck to them. "'Tis nort to I, what the lad hath dooed, and I'll never belave a' dooed it. If it worn't for he, our little Johnny would be in Churchyard, instead of 's cot." So spake one or two; and if the reasoning was unsound, why then, so much the worse for reason.

But a fine young farmer, of the name of Gilham (a man who worked hard for his widowed mother, at the North West end of the parish) came forward like a brave Englishman, and left no doubt about his opinion. This young man was no clod-hopper; but had been at a Latin school, founded by a great High-Priest of the Muses in the woollen line, and worthy of the *infula*. Gilham had shown some aptness there, and power in the resurrection of languages, called dead by those who would have no life without them. His farm was known as the "White Post," because it began with a grand old proof of the wisdom of our ancestors. Upon the mighty turnpike road from London even to Devonport, no trumpery stick of foreign fir, but a massive column of British oak had been erected in solid times, for the benefit of wayfarers. If a couple of them had been hanged there, as tradition calmly said of them, it was only because they stopped the others, and owed them this enlightenment.

Frank Gilham knew little of Doctor Fox, and had never swallowed physic; which may have had something to do perhaps with his genial view of the subject.

"A man is a man," he said to his mother, as if she were an expert in the matter; "and Fox rides as straight as any man I ever saw, when his horse has not done too much parish-work. What should I do, if people went against me like this, and wouldn't even stand up to their own lies? That old John Horner is a pompous ass; and Crang loses his head with a young horse, by daylight. Where would his wits be, pulled out of bed at night, with a resurrection-man standing over him? I am thoroughly ashamed of the parish, mother; and though some of our land is under Lady Waldron, I shall go and see Fox, and stick up for him."

So he did; and though he was a younger man than Jemmy, and made no pretence of even offering advice, his love of fair play, and fine healthy courage, were more than a houseful of silver and gold, or a legion of soldiers direct from heaven.

CHAPTER XIV.

REASONING WITHOUT REASON.

ONE of the most unlucky things, that could befall an unlucky man, in the hour of tribulation, had befallen that slandered Fox ; to wit the helpless condition of the leading spirit, and most active head in the troubled parish of Perlycross. Mr. Penniloe was mending slowly ; but his illness had been serious, and the violent chill in a low state of health had threatened to cause inflammation of the lungs. To that it would have led, there can be little doubt, but for the opportune return of Fox, and the speedy expulsion of Jackson. Now the difficulty was to keep the curate quiet ; and his great anxiety to get to work prolonged the disability, even as a broken arm in splinters is not likely to do without them, while the owner works a pump.

The Doctor caught his patient, on the Friday morning, groping his way through the long dark tunnel which underran the rectory, and just emerging, with crafty triumph, into the drive by his own main gate. Thyatira was gone to Jakes the butcher, after locking the front door and carrying off the key. The parson looked miserably thin and wan, but proud of this successful sortie. He was dressed as if for action in his Sunday clothes, though tottering on his black-varnished stick ; while his tortoise-shell eyeglass upon its watered ribbon dangled across his shrunken chest. But suddenly all his scheme collapsed.

"Ah, ah, ah !" he began with his usual exclamation, while his delicate face fell sadly, and his proud simper waned into a nervous smile ; "fine morning, Fox ; I hope you are quite well—pleasant morning for a walk."

"It may be pleasant," returned the Doctor, trying to look most awful ; "but like many other pleasant things it is wrong. Will you do me the honour to take my arm ?"

Fox hooked the baffled parson by the elbow, and gently led him towards his own front door, guilty-looking, sadly smiling, striving vainly to walk as if he were fit to contest a hurdle-race. But the cup of his shame was not full yet.

"Oh sir, oh!" exclaimed Mrs. Muggridge, rushing in from the street with a dish of lamb's fry reposing among its parsley. "I never would have believed it, sir, if an Angel was to speak the words. To think that he have come to this!"

"She refers to my moral condition, I fear;" Mr. Penniloe held his head down, while the key he had thought to elude was used to restore him to safer durance. "Well perhaps I was wrong; but I only meant to go a very short way, I assure you; only as far as the spot where my dear old friend is sleeping."

"What a blessing as we caught you, sir!" cried the impulsive Muggridge; while her master looked up in sharp wonder, and the Doctor frowned at her clumsiness.

"Not to the repairs, sir? Oh come, come, come!" Jemmy cut in rapidly, with this attractive subject.

"No, not even to the repairs, or I might even say—the arrest of ruin. Without the generosity of my dear friend, we never should have achieved so much for the glory of— I will not speak proudly—for the doing up of our old church. Those who should have been foremost—but no doubt they had good reason for buttoning up their pockets. Comparatively, I mean, comparatively; for they really did give something. Possibly, all that they could afford."

"Or all they thought they couldn't help. It was very hard upon them, sir. But you are getting into a rebellious humour. Sit down by the fire, and allow me to examine you."

"I will carry my rebellion further," said the invalid, after sitting down. "I know how kind you have been to me, kinder by far than I ever could deserve. And I believe it was the goodness of the Lord that delivered me from Jackson. He meant well; but he can not be positive whether the lungs should be higher up, or deeper down than the liver. I have been examined, and examiner as well, at Oxford, and in some public schools; but the question has never arisen; and I felt myself unable to throw any light on it. Still it struck me that he ought to know, as a properly qualified medical man."

" No, sir, no. That is quite a trifle. That should never have lessened your confidence in him." Dr. Fox spoke so gravely, that Mr. Penniloe was angry with his own inside.

" Well, after all, the mind and soul are the parts that we should study. I see that I have wronged poor Jackson, and I will apologise. But what I have to say to you is this—even if I am not to take a walk, I must be allowed some communication with people of the parish. I have no idea what is going on. I am isolated as if I had the plague, or the cholera of three years ago. Let me see Channing, or Jakes, or Mr. Horner, or even Robson Adney."

" In a day or two, sir. You are getting stronger fast; and we must not throw you back. You must have a little patience. Not a service has been missed ; and you can do no good."

" That may be true," said the parson with a sigh. " Unhappily they always tell me that ; but it does not absolve me. All my duties are neglected now. Three pupils, and not a lesson have I heard them. How can that new boy get on without me? A very odd youth, from all that I am told. He will require much attention. No, no, it will never do, Fox. I know how kind everybody has been, in doing with only one sermon ; and the Lord has provided an uncommonly good man. But I feel as if there was something wrong. I am sure you are hiding something from me. I am not allowed to see anybody ; and even Fay looks odd sometimes, as if the others were puzzling her. And the pupils too must have heard of something bad ; for poor little Michael has been forbidden to talk to any of them. What is it? It would hurt me less to know, than to keep on wondering, and probably imagine it worse than it is. And good or bad for my bodily health, my first duty is not to myself, but to those entrusted to me."

Mr. Penniloe had spoken with more excitement than he often showed when in his usual health, and the doctor had observed it with some alarm. But he had long foreseen that this must come ; and it might come in a more abrupt and dangerous manner, when he was out of reach. So he made up his mind at once, and spoke without further hesitation.

"Yes, sir, a most disgraceful thing has happened in this parish; and it is better perhaps that you should know it, than be kept in the dark any longer. But you must not be angry with me, though I have given all the orders which puzzled you. It was not for my own sake, you may be sure; for God only knows how much I have longed for your advice in this miserable affair. And yet, before I tell you, you must promise to do nothing whatever about it, for at least three days. By that time you will be yourself again, if we can keep you quiet, and if you take this sad blow with your usual strength of mind—and piety."

The parson began to tremble, and the blue lines on his delicate forehead shone, like little clues of silk. He fingered his open glasses, and began to raise them, until it struck him that he might seem rude, if he thus inspected Fox throughout his narrative. A rude act was impossible to him; so he leaned back in his ancient chair, and simply said—"Be quick, my friend, if you can thus oblige me."

The young man watched him very narrowly, while he told his dreadful tale; and Thyatira in the passage sobbed, and opened her smelling-bottle, for she had been making urgent signs and piteous appeals from the background to the doctor to postpone this trial. But her master only clasped his hands, and closed his quivering eyelids. Without a word he heard the whole; though little starts, and twitching lips, and jerkings of his gaiter'd foot, made manifest that self-control was working at high pressure.

"And who has done this inhuman thing?" asked Mr. Penniloe at last; after hoping that he need not speak, until he felt that he could speak. "Such things have been done about Bristol; but never in our county. And my dear friend, my best friend Tom! We dare not limit the mercy of God; for what are we? Ah, what are we? But speaking as a frail man should, if there is any crime on earth——" He threw his handkerchief over his head; for what can the holiest man pronounce? And there was nothing that moved him more to shame, than even to be called a "holy man."

"The worst of it is," said Dr. Fox, with tears in his eyes, for he loved this man, although so unlike him in his ways of thought ; "the worst of it is—or at least from a wretchedly selfish point of view, the worst—that all the neighbourhood has pitched upon the guilty person."

"Who is supposed to have done this horribly wicked thing? Not Gowler?"

"No sir ; but somebody nearer home. Somebody well-known in the village."

"Tell me who it is, my dear fellow. I am sure there is no one here who would have done it."

"Everybody else is sure there is. And the name of the scoundrel is—James Fox."

"Fox, it is not a time for jokes. If you knew how I feel, you would not joke."

"I am not joking, sir," said Fox, and his trembling voice confirmed his words. "The universal conclusion is, that I am the villain that did it."

"My dear friend, my noble fellow !" The Parson sprang up on his feeble legs, and took both of Jemmy's strong thick hands in his quivering palms, and looked at him ; "I am ashamed of my parish ; and of myself, as a worthless labourer. And with this crushing lie upon you, you have been tending me, day and night, and shown not a sign of your bitter disdain ! "

"I knew that you would acquit me, sir. And what did I care for the rest of them? Except one of course—well you know what I mean ; and I must now give up all hope of that. Now take a little of this strengthening stuff, and rest for a couple of hours."

"I will take the stuff ; but I will not rest, until you have told me, upon what grounds this foul accusation has been brought. That I should be in this helpless state, when I ought to go from house to house—truly the ways of Providence are beyond our poor understanding."

The young man told him in a few hot words, upon what a flimsy tale his foes had built this damning charge, and how lightly those who called themselves his friends had been ready to receive it. He had had a long interview with Crang, and had shaken the simple blacksmith's faith in his own eyes ; and that was all. Owing to the sharp

I

frost of the night, there was no possibility of following the track of the spring-cart up the road, though its course had first been eastward, and in the direction of the Old Barn. For the same reason, all attempts had failed in the immediate scene of the outrage; and the crisp white frost had settled on bruised herbage and heavy footmark.

"There is nothing more to be done in that way;" the Doctor finished with a bitter smile; "their luck was in the right scale, and mine in the wrong one, according to the usual rule. Now what do you advise me to do, dear sir?"

"I am never very quick, as some men are;" Mr. Penniloe replied, without even the reproof which he generally administered to those who spoke of "luck." "I am slow in perceiving the right course, when it is a question of human sagacity. But the Lord will guide this for our good. Allow me to think it over, and to make it a subject of earnest prayer."

Fox was well content with this, though his faith in prayer was limited. But he knew that the clergyman was not of those, who plead so well that the answer tallies with their inclinations. For such devoted labourers, when a nice preferment comes in view, lay it before the "Throne of Grace;" and the heavenly order always is—"Go thou into the fatter Vineyard." Mr. Penniloe had not found it thus, when a College living was offered to him as a former Fellow, at a time when he and his wife could scarce succeed in making both ends meet. The benefice being in a part of Wales where the native tongue alone prevailed, his Ministry could be blest to none but the occupants of the rectory. Therefore he did not pray for guidance, but for grace to himself and wife—especially the latter—to resist this temptation without a murmur. Therein he succeeded, to the huge delight of the gentleman next upon the roll, and equally ignorant of Welsh, whose only prayer upon the occasion was—"Thank the Lord, oh my soul!"

In the afternoon, when Fox returned according to arrangement, he found his much respected patient looking pale and sad, but tranquil. He had prayed as only those who are in practice can accomplish it; and his countenance showed that mind and heart, as well as soul, were fortified. His counsel to Fox was to withstand, and not to be daunted by the most insidious stratagem of the Evil One—whose existence was more personal in those days than it now appears, and therefore met more gallantly—to pay no heed to furtive looks, sly whispers, cold avoidance, or even spiteful insults, but to carry himself as usual, and show an example to the world of a gentleman and a Christian.

Fox smiled in his sleeve, for his fist was sore with knocking down three low cads that day; but he knew that the advice was sound, and agreed with that of Squire Mockham, only it was more pacific, and grounded on larger principles.

"And now, my dear young friend," the Parson continued very earnestly; "there are two things I have yet to speak of, if you will not think me intrusive. You ought to have some one in the Old Barn to comfort and to cheer you. The evenings are very long and dark, and now I suppose you will have to spend the greater part of them at home. Even without such trouble as yours, a lonely man is apt to become depressed and sometimes bitter. I have heard you speak of your sister, I think—your only sister, I believe—and if your father could spare her——"

"My father is much stronger, sir. But I could not think of bringing Christie here. Why, it would be wretched for her. And if anybody insulted her——"

"Who could insult her, in your own house? She would stay at home mostly in that very quiet place, and have her own amusements. She would come across no one, but old Betty and yourself. It would feel lonely at first, no doubt; but a loving sister would not mind that. You would take care not to vex her by speaking of any of the slights you suffered, or even referring to the subject at all, whenever it could be avoided. If it were only for one week, till you get used to this sad state of things, what a difference it would make to you! Especially if she is of a lively nature. What is her character—at all like yours?"

"Not a bit. She has ten times the pluck that I have. I should like to hear any one dare to say a word against me, before Christie. But it is not to be thought of, my dear sir. A pretty coward I should be to bring a girl here to protect me!"

"What is her name? Christine, I suppose. A very

good name indeed ; and I dare say she deserves it." The
curate looked at Fox, to have his inference confirmed ; and
the young man burst into a hearty laugh—his first for a
most unaccustomed length of time.

"Forgive me, sir. I couldn't help it. I was struck
with the contrast between your idea of a Christian, and
Christie's. Though if any one called her anything else, he
would have a specimen of zeal. For she is of the militant
Christian order, girt with the sword of the Spirit. A
great deal of St. Peter, but not an atom of St. John.
Thoroughly religious, according to her lights ; and always
in a flame of generosity. Her contempt for any littleness
is something splendid ; except when it is found in any one
she loves. She is always endeavouring to 'see herself
from the outside,' as she expresses it ; and yet she is inside
all the time. Without any motive that a man can see, she
flares up sometimes like a rocket, and then she lies rolling
in self-abasement. She is as full as she can be of
reasoning ; and yet there is not a bit of reason in her.
Yet somehow or other, everybody is wonderfully fond of
Christie."

"What a valuable addition to this parish ! And the very
one to keep you up, in this mysterious trial. She would
come at once, of course ; if she is as you describe her."

"Come, sir ? She would fly—or at least post with four
horses. What a sensation in Perlycross ! But she is not
the one to live in a cupboard, and keep silence. She would
get up in your pulpit, sir, and flash away at your
Churchwardens. No, I could not think of bringing her
into this turmoil. If I did, it would serve me right
enough, never to get out of it."

"Very well. We shall see," Mr. Penniloe said quietly,
having made up his mind, after Fox's description, to write
for this doughty champion, whatever offence might come of
it. "Now one other matter, and a delicate one. Have
you seen Lady Waldron, since this terrible occurrence ? "

"No ; I have feared to go near the house. It must be
so awful for them. It is horrible enough for me, God
knows. But I am ashamed to think of my own trouble, in
comparison with theirs. I shall never have the courage to
go near them."

"It would be a frightful visit; and yet I think that you should go there. But it is most difficult to say. In all the dark puzzles and trials of this world, few men have been placed, I should say, in such a strange dilemma. If you go, you may shock them beyond expression. If you don't go, you must confirm their worst ideas. But there is one who holds you guiltless."

"I am afraid that you only mean—the Lord," Jemmy Fox said, with his eyes cast down. "It is out of my luck to hope for more. He is very good, of course—but then He never comes and does it. I wish that you meant some one nearer."

"My dear young friend, my dear young friend! Who can be nearer to us?" The Parson thought of his own dark times, and spoke with reproach, but not rebuke. "I ought to have meant the Lord, no doubt. But in plain truth, I didn't. I meant a mere mortal, like yourself. Oh, how we all come down to ground! I should have referred to Providence. What a sad relapse from duty!"

"Relapse more, sir. Relapse more!" cried the young man, insisting on the human vein. "You have gone so far, that you must speak out, as—as a Messenger of good tidings."

"Really, Jemmy, you do mix things up"—the parson's eyes twinkled at this turn upon him—"in a very extraordinary manner. You know what I mean, without any words of mine."

"But how can you tell, sir? Oh, how can you tell? If I could only be sure of that, what should I care for anything?"

"Young man, you are sure," said Mr. Penniloe, placing his hand upon Jemmy's shoulder. "Or if you are not, you are not worthy to have faith in anything. Next to the word of God, I place my confidence in a woman's heart."

Fox said not another word. His heart was as full as the older man's. One with the faithful memory, and the other with the hopeful faith of love. But he kept out of sight, and made a stir, with a box of powders, and some bottles.

When he got home, in a better state of mind than he had been able to afford for a long time, out rushed somebody, and pulled him off his horse, and took the whole command of him with kisses.

"I will never forgive you, never, never!" cried a voice of clear music, out of proper pitch with tears. "To think that you have never told me, Jemmy, of all the wicked things they are doing to you!"

"Why, Christie, what on earth has brought you here? Look out! You are going all to tatters with my spurs! Was there ever such a headlong girl? What's up now?"

"It won't do, Jemmy. Your poor mind is all abroad. I saw the whole thing in the *Exeter Gazette*. You deserve to be called—even worse than they have called you, for behaving so to me."

CHAPTER XV.

FRIENDS AND FOES.

In for a penny, in for a pound. Throw the helve after the hatchet. As well to be hanged for a sheep as a lamb. He that hath the name may as well enjoy the game.— These and other reckless maxims of our worthy grandsires (which they may have exemplified in their own lives, but took care for their own comfort to chastise out of their children) were cited by Miss Christie Fox, with very bright ferocity, for her poor brother's guidance. It was on the morning after her arrival, when she had heard every-thing there was to hear, and had taken the mastery of Old Barn, as if it were her pony-carriage. Fox stood and looked at her in this queer old dwelling-place, which had once been the tithe-barn of the parish, but proving too far from the chief growth of corn had been converted by the Dean and Chapter into a rough and rambling, but com-modious and roomy house; for the tithes of Perlycross were fat, worthy of a good roof and stout walls.

She sat by the window in the full light of the sun,—for she never thought much about her complexion, and no sun could disparage it—a lovely girl, with a sweet expression, though manifest knowledge of her own mind. Her face was not set off by much variety of light and shade, like that of Inez Waldron, dark lashes, or rich damask tint, or contrasts of repose and warmth ; but pure straightforward English beauty (such as lasts a lifetime) left but little to be desired—except the good luck to please it.

"There was not too much of her," as her father said—indeed he never could have enough—and she often felt it a grievance that she could not impress the majesty of her sentiments, through lack of size ; but all that there was of her was good stuff; and there very well may be, as a tall admirer of hers remarked, "a great deal of love in five feet two."

However this specimen of that stature had not discovered that fact yet, as regards any other than her own kin ; and now with the sun from over Hagdon Hill throwing wintry light into her spring-bright eyes, she was making herself quite at home, as an English girl always tries to do, with her own belongings about her, while she was railing at this strange neighbourhood. Not that she meant even half of what she said, but her spirit was up, and being always high it required no great leap to get far above the clouds. And her brother kept saying—"now you don't mean that," in a tone that made her do her very best to mean it.

As for avoiding the subject, and the rest of the cautious policy suggested by the peaceful parson, the young lady met that wise proposal with a puff of breath, and nothing more. In gestures, and what on a plainer place would have been called "grimaces," she was so strong, that those who had not that short-cut of nature to the meaning of the moment, were inclined to scoff and mimic ; which they could not do at all, because it was not in them. Jemmy being some years older, and her only brother, felt himself responsible for the worst part of her character. He was conscious, when he thought about it, that he had spoiled her thoroughly, from the date of her first crawl on the floor, until her path in life was settled. And upon the whole, the result was not so bad as to crush him with much self-reproach.

"All I want is, just to have the names of your chief enemies." This valiant sister, as she spoke, spread forth an ivory *deltis*, as that arrangement then was called, a baby-fan with leaves of no more substance than a wafer.

"Have no fear, Jemmy, I will not kill them, unless my temper rises. You are so abominally forgiving, that I daresay you don't know their names."

"Not I," said the Doctor, beginning to fill his after-breakfast pipe, for now he had no round to make among his patients of the paying class; "Chris, they are all alike; they have no ill-will at all against me, unless it is Jackson, and young Webber, and half a dozen other muffs perhaps, with a grudge because I have saved poor fellows they were killing. I have never interfered in any rich man's case; so they have no right to be so savage."

"They are dummies," answered Christie, just waving her hand, and then stopping it, as if they were not worth the trouble. "I don't mean them. They could never lead opinion. I mean people of intelligence, or at any rate of influence."

"Well really I don't know any of that sort, who have gone against me openly. Such people generally wait to hear both sides, unless their duty drags them into it. Both the Churchwardens are against me, I believe. But that must be chiefly, because they saw with their own wise eyes what had been done. You know, or perhaps you don't, but I do, what an effect is produced on the average mind by the sight of anything. Reason seems to fly, and the judgment is lost. But Horner is a very decent fellow, and I have been of some service to his family. Farrant is a man of great honesty and sense; but carried away perhaps for the moment. I hear that he is coming round to my side."

"Then I won't put down either of them. But come, there must be some one at the head of it."

"Upon my word, I don't think there is. Or if there is, he keeps quite in the background. It seems to be rather a general conclusion, than any conspiracy against me. That makes it so much harder to contend with. One proof of what I say is, that there has been no further application for a warrant, since Mr. Mockham's refusal. If there were any bitter enemy, he would never have been content with that."

"I am not so sure of that," replied sage Christie, longing for a foe more definite; "I am not of course a lawyer, though papa was a Magistrate before I was born, and ever since; and that gives me a great deal of insight. And I have come to the conclusion that there is some one, besides those poor little pill-grinders—you see what comes of taking to the pill-box, Jemmy—some one of a hateful nature, and low cunning, who is working in the dark against you. The mischief has been done, and they know that; and they don't want to give you any chance of putting your own case clearly, and confounding them. You see that reel of silk now, don't you?"

"I see about fifty. What a child you are! Are you going to decorate a doll's house?"

"I never lose my temper with you, dear Jemmy, because you are so stupid. But if you can't see the force of it, I can. That reel of silk is an honest reel, a reel you know how to deal with. The end is tucked into a nick at the side, and you set to at once and thread your needle. But the one next to it is a rogue—same colour, same size, same everything, except that the maker has hidden the end, to hide his own short measure, so that you may hunt for it for half an hour. Even a man can see that, can't he? Very well, apply that to this frightful affair. If your enemies would only come forward, they would give you a chance to clear yourself. You would get hold of the end and unwind it, just as I bite off this knot. There! What can be easier than that, I'd like to know?"

"You are very clever, Christie, but you don't see the real difficulty. Who would believe my denial on oath, any more than they would without it? I can offer no witness except myself. The man at the pits would avail me nothing, even if I could get hold of him. There was plenty of time after I left him, for me to have been in the thick of it. I can prove no *alibi*. I have only my word, to show that I was in this house while the miscreants were at work. It is the blackest piece of luck, that poor George was so tipsy, and old Betty was so buried in slumber. It is no good to deceive ourselves, my dear. I shall never be cleared of this foul charge, till the fellows who did the thing are found out."

This was what Jemmy had felt all along; and no one knew better than himself, how nearly impossible it is to bring such criminals to justice. But his sister was not to be discouraged.

"Oh, as for that, I shall just do this. I have money of my own, or at least I shall have plenty of it, when I come of age next year. I'll find out the cleverest lawyer about here, a man who is able to enter into rogues, and I'll make him advertise a great reward, and promise him the same for himself, if he succeeds. That is the only way to make them look sharp. A thousand pounds will be sure to tempt the poor dirty villains who must have been employed; and a thousand pounds will tempt a good lawyer to sell his own wife and family. Free pardon to every one, except the instigator. I wonder that you never even thought of that."

"I did think of it long ago. It is the first thing that occurs to an Englishman, in any case of wrong-doing. But it would be useless here. I heard much of these cases when I was a student. They are far more frequent than the outer world supposes. But I won't talk about it. It would only make you nervous. It is not a thing for girls to dwell upon."

"I know that very well. I don't want to dwell upon it. Only tell me, why even a large reward would not be of any service."

"Because there is only a very small gang; and a traitor would never live to get his money. Rewards have been tried, but vainly, except in one case, and then the end was dreadful. For the most part, the villains manage so well that no one ever dreams of what has happened. In the present case, though a most daring one, the villainy would scarcely have been discovered, except for the poor little faithful dog. If she had been killed and thrown into the river, perhaps nothing would ever have been heard of it."

"Oh, Jemmy, what a dreadful thing to say! But surely you forget the blacksmith?"

"Not at all. His story would have come to nothing, without this to give it special meaning. Even as it is, no connexion has been proved, though of course there is a strong presumption, between the affair at Susscot, and the crime at Perlycross. There was nothing to show where the cart came from. Those fellows travel miles with them, these long nights. There is an old chapelyard at Monkswell, more than a mile from any house, and I firmly believe—but I will not talk about it."

"Then you know who did this! Oh, Jemmy, Jemmy, is it some horrible secret of your trade?" Christie leaped up, and away from her brother.

"I know nothing, except that it happened. I have not the least idea who the scoundrel is. Now no more of this—or you won't sleep to-night."

"I am not a coward—for a girl at least. But this is a dark and lonely house. I shall have my bed put against the partition of your room, before ever I go into it this night. Then you can hear me knock, if I get frightened."

Miss Fox sat down, and leaned her head upon her hands for a moment, as in deep meditation upon the wrongs of humanity; and then she announced the result of her thoughts.

"One thing is certain. Even you cannot deny it. If the Government of this Country allows such frightful things to be done, it is bound to provide every woman in the land with a husband to protect her, or at any rate to keep her courage up. If I had seen that cart at Susscot, I should have died with terror."

"Not you. But I must make one rule, I see; and you know there are times when I will be obeyed. You have come here, my dear child, with the greatest kindness, and no small courage as well, just to keep up my spirits, and console me in this trouble. I would never have let you come, if I had known it; and now I will not have your health endangered. Back you go, this very day, sad as I shall be without you, unless you promise me two things. One is that you will avoid these subjects, although you may talk of my position. And the other is, that you will not stir from this house, except in my company; and when you are with me, you will be totally unconscious of anything anybody says, or looks,—uncivil, unpleasant, or even uncordial. You understand now, that I am in earnest."

Fox struck his solid legs into a stiff position, and crested up his whiskers with his finger-tips; which action makes a very fine impression on a young man's younger sister.

"Very well, I agree to all of that;" said Christie, a little too airily for one who is impressed with an engagement. "But one thing I must have, before we begin the new code. Here are my tablets. As you won't tell the names of your enemies, Jemmy, I must have the names of your friends to set down. It won't require many lines, I fear, you gentle Jemmy."

"Won't it? Why all the good people about here are on my side, every one of them. First, and best of them all, Philip Penniloe. And then, Mr. Mockham the Magistrate, and then Sergeant Jakes, the schoolmaster. And after him, Thyatira Muggridge, a person of considerable influence, because she takes hot meat, or pudding, in a basin, to half the old women in the village, whenever her master can afford it, and can't get through all of it. That is how they put it, in their grateful way. But it strengthens their tongues against his enemies, and they seem to know them—though he doesn't. Well, then there is Farrant, the junior Churchwarden, coming round fast to my side. And Baker, the cooper, who made me a tub for salting my last pig; and Channing—not the clerk, he is neutral still, but will rally to my side when I pay him twelve shillings, as I shall do to-morrow, for a pair of corduroys—but Channing the baker, a notable man, with a wife who knows everything about it, because she saw a dark man over the wall last summer, and he would not give his name. She has caused a reaction already, and is confident of being right, because she got upon a pair of steps. Oh you must not imagine that I am forlorn. And then there is Frank Gilham, last not least, a fine young fellow, and a thorough Englishman."

"I like that description. I hate foreigners—as a rule I mean of course," said Christie Fox, with a look of large candour, that proved what a woman of the world she was; "there may be good individuals among them, when they have come to know what home-life means; but take them altogether, they are really very queer. But surely we ought to know a little more, as to what it was Mrs. Baker Channing saw; and over the Churchyard wall, you say."

"Waste of time, Christie. Why it was back in August, when Harrison Gowler was staying here. And it was not the Churchyard wall at all, but the wall of the rectory garden,

that she peeped over in the dark. It can have had nothing
to do with it."

"I am not so sure of that. Things come out so oddly. You
remember when my poor *Flo* was poisoned, how I found it out
at last. I never left off. I wouldn't leave off. Prying, listening, tip-toeing, even spying, without any sense of shame. And
I found it out at last—at last ; and didn't I have my revenge ?
Oh, I would have hanged that woman, if the law had been
worth a farthing, and stuck her all over with needles and
pins."

"You spiteful, and meanly vindictive little creature !
But you never found it out by yourself, after all. It came
out quite by accident."

"Well, and so will this. You take my word. I dare
say I am stupid, but I always prove right. Yet we are
bound to use the means of grace, as they tell us in every
blessed sermon. Oh come, I may go and see your pet
parson. I'll be bound, I shall not care for him, an atom of
an atom. I hate those perfect people ; they are such a slur
upon one. I like a good minister, who rides to hounds in
pink, and apologises to the ladies, every time he swears. But,
come, brother Jemmy, are there no more friends ? I have
put down all you mentioned, and the list looks very short.
There must be a few more, for the sake of Christianity."

"To be sure, there is one more, and a frightfully zealous
one—certain to do more harm than good. A mere boy,
though he flies into a fury at the word. Mr. Penniloe's new
pupil—preparing for the church, by tearing all across the
country. He breaks down all the hedges, and he drives the
sheep-dogs mad. He is mad as a March-hare himself, by
all accounts ; but everybody likes him. His name is
Horatio Peckover, but everybody calls him 'Hopper,' by
syncope, as we used to say at school. One of his fellow-
pupils, young Pike, who is a very steady-going young
fellow, and a fine rising fisherman, told me that Hopper is
double-jointed ; and they believe it devoutly. They tied
him on a chair at his own request, the other day, in order
that he might learn his lessons. But that only made him
worse than ever ; for he capered round the room, chair and
all, until Mr. Penniloe sent to ask who was churning
butter."

"What a blessing that boy must be in a sick house! But what has made him take up our case, Jemmy?"

"The demand of his nature for violent motion. Every day of his life, except Sunday, he scours the country for miles around. On foot, mind—not on horseback, which one could understand. Moreover, he is hot in my favour, because he comes from somewhere near Wincaunton, and is a red hot 'Zon ov' Zummerzet,' and contemptuous of Devon. But it is not for me to enquire into motives. I shall want every single friend I can scrape together, if what I heard, this morning is anything like true. You asked me last night, what Lady Waldron thought."

"To be sure, I did. It seemed most important. But now," continued Christie, as she watched her brother's face, "there are reasons why I should scarcely attach so much weight to her opinion."

"The chief reason being that you see it is against me. Well, truly, you are a brave reasoner, my dear. But I fear that it is so. I am told that my name must never again be heard in the house, where once I was so welcome."

"Oh, I am rather glad of that. That will go a long way in our favour. I cannot tell how many times I have heard not from one, but from all who have met her, that she is a most unpleasant haughty person, even for a foreigner. It must lie very heavy on the poor woman's conscience, that everybody says she helped, by her nasty nature to shorten her poor husband's days. Possibly now—well, that throws a new light. What has happened may very well have been done at the order of some of his relatives, who knowing her character suspect foul play. And of course she would like to hear no more about it. You know all those foreigners, how pat they are with poison."

"What a grand thing it is to have a sister!" Fox exclaimed, looking with astonishment at Christie, who was quite excited with her new idea. "Better almost to have a sister than—than—I mean than any one else. I almost feared to tell you my last piece of news, because I thought that it must upset you so. And behold, it has greatly encouraged you! But remember, on no account must you drop a hint, even to our best friends, of your last brilliant idea. What frightful things flow into the sweetest little head!"

"Well, I don't see at all, why I should try to conceal it. I think it is a case for very grave suspicions. And if she spreads shameful reports about you, I'll soon let her know that two can play at that."

"Nonsense, my dear child. There is evidence against me. None, nor even a shadow of suspicion, against her. She loved Sir Thomas devotedly; and I always thought that jealousy was the cause of her coldness to his English friends. But to come to common sense again—what I heard to-day settles my doubts as to what I should do. Penniloe thought that I should call at Walderscourt; though he saw what a difficult thing it was to do, and rather referred it to my own decision. I shrank from it, more than I can describe. In fact, I could not bring myself to go; not for my own sake but for theirs. But this behaviour on her part puts a new aspect upon it. I feel myself bound, as an innocent man, to face her; however unpleasant it may be. It will only be the worse, for putting off. I shall go, this afternoon."

"I love to bring anything to a point. You are quite right;" replied Christie, with her bright colour rising, at the prospect of a brush; "Jemmy dear, let me come with you."

"Not quite, you gallant Chris! No such luck for me. Not that I want you to back me up. But still it would have been a comfort. But you know it is out of the question, for a stranger to call, at such a time.

"Well, I fear it is. Though I shouldn't mind that. But it would look very odd for you. Never mind; I won't be far away. You can leave me outside, and I will wait for you, somewhere in the shrubbery, if there is one. Not that I would dream of keeping out of sight. Only that they might be afraid to see me."

"They might reasonably fear it, if you looked as you do now. Ferocity does not improve the quality of your smile, dear. What will mother say, when you go home? And somebody else perhaps? Now, you need not blush. I have a very high opinion of him."

"Jemmy, I won t have it. Not another word! Get it out of your silly mind for ever. Men never understand such things. There's no romance in me, as Goodness knows. But you'll never catch me marrying a man with none of it in him."

"You are too young to think of such things yet. Though sometimes even younger girls—but come along, let us have a breath of fresh air, after all this melancholy talk. That footpath will take us up to Hagdon in ten minutes. You are eager to try our Old-Barn style of victualling, and it suits the system better than your long late dinners. We dine at two o'clock. Come and get an appetite."

A short sharp climb, and with their lungs expanded, they stood upon the breezy hill, and looked back at the valley. Before them rolled the sweep of upland, black in some places with bights of fired furze; but streaked with long alleys of tender green, where the flames had not fed, or the rains had wept them off. The soft western air, though the winter had held speech with it, kept enough of good will yet, to be a pleasant change for those who found their fellow-creatures easterly. And more than that, the solemn distance, and expanse of trackless grey, hovering with slow wings of sleepy vapour touched with sunshine, if there was no comfort in them, yet spread some enlargement. These things breathed a softer breath, as nature must (though it be unfelt) on young imaginations fluttering, like a wisp of brambled wool, in the bridle-paths, and stray sheep-walks of human trouble.

CHAPTER XVI.

LITTLE BILLY.

WHEN he has refreshed his memory with the map of England, let any man point out upon it, if he can deliberately, any two parishes he knows well, which he can also certify to be exactly like each other, in the character of their inhabitants. Do they ever take alike a startling piece of news, about their most important people? Do they weigh in the same balance the discourses of the parson, the merits of those in authority, or the endeavours of the rich to help them? If a stranger rides along the street, he is pretty sure to be stared at; but not with quite the same expression, as in the last village he came through. Each place has its own style, and tone, vein of sentiment, and lines of attitude, deepened perhaps by the lore and store of many generations.

For instance, Perlycombe, Perlycross, and Perliton, are but as three pearls on one string, all in a line, and contiguous. The string is the stream; which arising at the eastern extremity of Perlycombe parish, passes through the village, then westward through Perlycross, and westward still through the much larger village of Perliton. At Perlycombe it is a noisy little brook, at Perlycross a genial trout-stream—anon of glassy wanderings, anon of flickered hurry—; while Perliton, by the time it gets there, entitles it "the River Perle," and keeps two boats upon it, which are not always more aground than landsmen should desire.

Now any one would fancy, that these three adjoining parishes would, in all their ways and manners, be as like each other as three peas vertebrated in one pod. But the fancy would prove that he was only fit for fiction, not for the clearer heights of history such as this. For these three parishes are quite as distinct, one from another, as all three taken together admit that they are, and deserve to be, from the rest of England.

All three are simple, all old-fashioned, highly respectable, and wonderfully quiet—except when lashed up by some outrage—slightly contemptuous of one another, and decidedly so of the world outside the valley. From it they differ widely, and from one another visibly, in their facial expression, and figure, and walk; perceptibly also, in tone of feeling, habits of thought (when they think at all), voices, pet words, and proclivities of slouch. So that in these liberal times of free disintegration, each of them has nature's right to be a separate nation. And in proof of this, they beat their bounds, and often break each other's heads, upon Saint Clement's day.

"What an extraordinary sound I hear!" said Christie to her brother, as they turned to quit the hill. "Just listen a moment. I can't make it out. It sounds like a frightful lot of people in the distance."

K

"Well, I declare, I had forgotten all about it! How very stupid I am getting now!" cried Jemmy. "Why this is St. Clement's day, and no mistake!"

"Who is he? I never heard of him. And, what right has he got to make such a dreadful noise? He couldn't do it all by himself, Jemmy, even if he was on a gridiron."

"But he has got half of Perlycross to help him. Come here, Chris. Here is a nice dry hollow, away from the damp and the mist; and the noise below follows the curve of it."

Fox led his sister into a little scarp of flint, with brows of grey heather, and russet fern, quivering to the swell of funneled uproar. "Don't be afraid," he said, "it is only our own parish. There ought to be three of them; but this is only ours."

"Well, if your parish can make all that noise, what would all three of them do together? Why ten packs of hounds couldn't equal it!"

"You have hit the very point; you have a knack of doing that;" answered Jemmy, as he landed her upon a grey ledge. "We don't let the other two in, any more. The business had always been triennial. But the fighting grew more and more serious, till the stock of sticking-plaster could not stand it. Then a man of peaceful genius suggested that each parish should keep its own St. Clement's day, at intervals of three years as before; but in succession, instead of all three at once; so that no two could meet upon the frontier in force. A sad falling off in the spirit of the thing, and threatening to be better for the lawyers, than for us. Perlycombe had their time last year; and now Perlycross has to redress it. Our eastern boundary is down in that hollow; and Perlycombe stole forty feet from us last year. We are naturally making a little stir about it."

"If that is a little stir, what would be a big one? But I want to see them; and the fogginess of the trees in that direction stops me. I should say there must be at least five hundred people there. I can't stop up here, like a dummy."

"Very well. If you love a row so much. But there

are no five hundred there, because it is more than thirty miles round this parish, and the beaters start in two companies from Perle-Weir, one lot to the north and the other to the south, and they go round till they meet each other; somewhere at the back of Beaconhill. One church-warden with each party, and the overseers divided, and the constables, and so on. The parson should be in the thickest of the fray; but I strictly forbade Mr. Penniloe, and told him to send Jakes as his deputy. Still I should not be surprised, if he turns up. He is hot upon the rights of his parish. Come round this way; there is no fear of missing them, any more than a pack of hounds in full cry."

Christie was quite up for it. She loved a bit of skirmish, and thought it might fetch her brother's spirits up again. So they turned the steep declivity, and after many scratches, crept along a tangled path, leading down to a wooded gully.

Here they found themselves, rather short of breath, but in a position to command fair view of the crowd, full of action in the dingle and the bramble-land. How it could matter to any sane humanity, whether the parish-bound ran even half a league, on this side or on that of such a desert wild, only those who dwell on human nature can explain.

However so it was; and even Mr. Penniloe had flouted the doctors, and was here, clad in full academicals ac-cording to the ancient rule, flourishing his black-varnished stick, and full of unfeigned wrath at some gross crime.

"Thou shalt not move thy neighbour's land-mark "—he was shouting, instead of swallowing pills; and as many of his flock as heard his text, smote right and left in accord-ance with it.

"What on earth is it all about?" asked Christie, peeping through a holly bush, and flushing with excitement.

"All about that stone down in the hollow, where the water spurts so. Don't be afraid. They can't see us." The girl looked again, and wondered.

Some fifty yards before them was a sparkling little water-course, elbowing its way in hurried zig-zag down the steep; but where it landed in the fern-bed with a toss of tresses,

some ungodly power of men had heaved across its silver
foot a hugeous boulder of the hill, rugged, bulky, beetle-
browed—the "shameless stone" of Homer. And with such
effect, that the rushing water, like a scared horse, leaped
aside, and swerving far at the wrongful impulse, cut a
felonious cantel out of the sacred parish of Perlycross!

Even this was not enough. To add insult to injury,
some heartless wag had chiselled, on the lichened slab of
boulder, a human profile in broad grin, out of whose wicked
mouth came a scroll, inscribed in deep letters—"P. combe
Parish."

The Perlycrucians stood before this incredible sight,
dumb-foundered. Thus far they had footed it in a light
and merry mood, laughing, chaffing, blowing horns, and
rattling bladders, thumping trees and gates and cowsheds,
bumping schoolboys against big posts, and daubing every
corner of contention, from kettles of tar or sheep-wash, with
a big P. +.

But now as this outrage burst upon them, through a tall
sheaf of yellow flags, their indignation knew no bounds,
parochial or human. As soon as they could believe their
eyes, they lifted their hands, and closed their lips; while
the boys, who were present in great force—for Jakes could
not help the holiday—put their fingers in their mouths, and
winked at one another. Five or six otter-hounds, from the
kennels of a sporting yeoman, had joined the procession
with much goodwill; but now they recognised the check,
and sat upon their haunches, and set up a yell with one
accord, in the dismay of human silence.

Not an oath was uttered, nor a ribald laugh; but
presently all eyes were turned upon the pale Mr. Penniloe,
who stood at the side of Mr. Farrant, the junior Churchwarden, who had brought him in his four-wheeled chaise,
as far as wheels might venture. Few were more pained by
this crime than the parson; he nodded under his College
cap, and said—

"My friends, abate this nuisance."

But this was easier said than done, as they very soon
discovered. Some called for crowbars, and some for gun-
powder, and some for a team of horses; but nothing of the
sort was near at hand. Then Sergeant Jakes, as an old

campaigner, came to the rescue, and borrowing a hatchet
(of which there were plenty among them), cut down a
sapling oak, hard and tough and gnarled from want of
nourishment; therewith at the obnoxious rock they rushed,
butting, ramming, tugging, levering, with the big pole
below, and a lot of smaller staves above, and men of every
size and shape trampling, and kicking out, and exhorting
one another. But the boulder had been fanged into its
socket so exactly, probably more by luck than skill, that
there it stuck, like a gigantic molar, and Perlycross
laboured in vain at it.

"What muffs! As if they could do it, like that!
Penniloe ought to know better; why the pressure is
all the wrong way. But of course he is an Oxford man.
Chris, you stay here, till I come back. Cambridge v.
Oxford, any day, when it comes to a question of engineer-
ing."

Speaking too lightly, he leaped in like manner into the
yellow-rib'd breast of the steep; while Christie communed
with herself, like this.

"Oh, what a pity he left St. John's! He must have been
senior-wrangler, if he had stayed on, instead of those
horrible hospitals. And people would have thought so
much more of him. But perhaps he would not have looked
so bright; and he does more good in this line. Though
nobody seems to thank him much. It would be ever so
much better for him, and he would be valued more, if he
did ever so much less good. But I like the look of Mr.
Penniloe."

The man who should have been senior-wrangler—as every
man ever yet sent to Cambridge should have been, if justice
had been done him—went in a style of the purest mathe-
matics along the conic sections of the very noble Hagdon.
The people in the gully shouted to him, for a single slip
would have brought him down upon their hats; but he
kept his breath for the benefit of his legs, and his nerves
were as sound as an oyster's, before its pearly tears begin.
Christie watched him without fear; she had known the
construction of his legs, from the days of balusters and
rocking-horses.

"Give me up a good pole—not too heavy—you see how

I have got to throw my weight; but a bit of good stuff
with an elbow to it."

Thus spake Jemmy, and the others did their best. He
stuck his heel and footside into a soft place he had found,
and let the ledge of harder stuff overlap his boot-vamps,
then he took the springy spar of ash which some one had
handed up to him, for he stood about twelve feet above
them, and getting good purchase against a scrag of flint,
brought the convexity of his pole to bear on the topmost
jag of boulder.

"Slew away as high as you can reach," he cried; "but
don't touch it anywhere near the bottom." As they all
put their weights to it, the rock began to sway, and with a
heavy groan lurched sideways.

"Stand clear!" cried Jemmy, as the whole bunk swang,
with the pillar of water helping it, and then settled
grandly back into the other niche, with the volume of the
fall leaping generously into the parish of Perlycombe.

"Hurrah!" shouted everybody young enough to shout;
while the elder men leant upon their staves, and thanked
the Lord. Not less than forty feet was recovered, and
another forty added from the substance of big rogues.
"'Tis the finest thing done ever since I were a boy," said
the oldest man present, as he wiped his dripping face.
"Measter Vox, come down, and shake hands round. Us
will never believe any harm of thee no more."

This reasoning was rather of the heart than head; but it
held good all round, as it generally does. And now as the
sound of the water went away into its proper course, with
the joy of the just pursuing it, Miss Fox, who had watched
all proceedings from the ridge, could hear how the current
of public opinion was diverted and rushing in her brother's
favour. So she pinned up a torn skirt, and smoothed out
another, and putting back her bright hair, tripped down
the wooded slope, and stood with a charming blush before
them. The labourers touched their hats, and the farmers
lifted theirs, and every one tried to look his best; for
Perlycross being a poetical parish is always very wide
awake to beauty.

"My sister!" explained Dr. Fox with just pride. "My
sister, Mr. Penniloe! My sister, Mr. Farrant! Sergeant

Jakes, my sister! Miss Christie Fox will be glad to know you all."

"And I am sure that everybody will be glad to know Miss Fox," said the Parson, coming forward with his soft sweet smile. "At any time she would be welcome; but now she is come at the time of all times. Behold what your brother has done, Miss Fox! That stream is the parish boundary."

"He maketh the river to run in dry places;" cried Channing the clerk, who had been pulling at his keg, "and lo, he hath taken away the reproach of his people, Israel!"

"Mr. Channing! Fie, Mr. Channing!" began the representative of the upper desk, and then suddenly checked himself, lest he should put the old man to shame, before the children of the parish.

"By the by," said Mr. Farrant, coming in to fill the pause; "Dr. Fox is the likeliest person to tell us what this curious implement is. It looks like a surgical instrument of some sort. We found it, Doctor, in this same watercourse, about a furlong further down, where the Blackmarsh lane goes through it. We were putting our parish-mark on the old tree that overhangs a deep hole, when this young gent who is uncommon spry—I wish you luck of him, I'm sure, Mr. Penniloe—there he spies it, and in he goes, like an otter, and out with it, before he could get wet, almost."

"Not likely I was going to leave it there," young Peckover interrupted; "I thought it was a clot of eels, or a pair of gloves, or something. Though of course a glove would float, when you come to think of it. Perhaps the young lady knows—she looks so clever."

"Hopper, no cheek!" Dr. Fox spoke sharply, for the youth was staring at his sister. "Mr. Farrant, I can't tell you what it is; for I never saw a surgical instrument like it. I should say it was more like a blacksmith's, or perhaps a turner's tool; though not at all a common one, in either business. Is Crang here, or one of his apprentices?"

"No, sir. Joe is at home to-day—got a heavy job," answered some one in the crowd; "and the two prentices be gone with t'other lot of us."

"I'll tell you what I'll do;" volunteered the Hopper, who was fuming at the slowness of parochial demarcation, for he would have been at the back of Beacon Hill by this time; "I'll go straight with it to Susscot, and be back again before these old codgers have done a brace of meadows. It is frightful cold work to stand about like this. I found it, and I'll find out what it is too."

The tool was handed to him, and he set off, like a chamois, in a straight line westward; while two or three farmers, who had suffered already from his steeplechase tracks, would have sent a brief word after him, but for the parson's presence. Fox, who was amused with this specimen of his county, ran part way up the hill to watch his course, and then beckoned to his sister, to return to the Old Barn by the footpath along the foot of Hagdon.

They had scarcely finished dinner, which they had to take in haste, by reason of the shortness of the days, and their intended visit to Walderscourt, when Joe Crang the blacksmith appeared in the yard, pulling his hat off, and putting it on again, and wiping his face with a tongs-swab. Fox saw that the man was in a state of much excitement, and made him come in, while Miss Christie went upstairs, to prepare for their drive to Walderscourt.

"What's the matter, Crang? Take a chair there. You needn't be nervous," said the Doctor kindly; "I have no grudge against you for saying what you believe. It has done me a world of harm, no doubt; but it's no fault of yours. It's only my bad luck, that some fellow very like me, and also a Jemmy, should have been in that black job that night. But I wish you had just shown a little more pluck, as I told you the other day. If you had just gone round the horse and looked; or even sung out—'Is that you, Doctor?' why you might have saved me from—from knowing so much about my friends."

"Oh sir, 'twaz an awesome night! But what I be come for to say, sir, is just this. I absolve 'e, sir; I absolve 'e, Measter Vox. If that be the right word,—and a' cometh from the Baible, I absolve 'e, Measter Vox."

"Absolve me from what, Crang? I have done nothing. You mean, I suppose, that you acquit me?"

"Well now, you would never believe—but that's the very word of discoorse that have been sticking in my throat all the way from the ford. You never done it, sir,—not you. You never done it, sir! You may put me on my oath."

"But you have been very much upon your oath, ever since it happened, that I was the man, and no other man, that did the whole of it, Joseph Crang. And the ale you have had on the strength of it!"

"The ale, sir, is neither here nor there"—the blacksmith looked hurt by this imputation—"it cometh to-day, and it goeth to-morrow, the same as the flowers of the field. But the truth is the thing as abideth, Measter Jemmy. Not but what the ale might come, upon the other view of it. Likewise, likewise—if the Lord in heaven ordereth it, the same as the quails from the sky, sir."

"The miracle would be if it failed to come, wherever you are, Joseph. But what has converted you from glasses against me, to glasses in my favour?"

"Nothing more than this, sir. Seemeth to a loose mind neither here nor there. But to them that knoweth it, beyond when human mind began, perhaps afore the flood waz, there's nought that speaks like Little Billy."

"Why this," exclaimed Fox, as he unrolled the last new leathern apron of the firm of Crang and wife, "this is the thing they found to-day in beating the bounds of the parish. Nobody could make out what it was. What can it have to do with me, or the sad affair at Perlycross?"

"Little Billy, sir," replied the blacksmith, dandling the tool with honest love, as he promptly recovered it from Fox, "have been in our family from father to son, since time runneth not to the contrary. Half her can do is unbeknown to me, not having the brains as used to be. Ah, we was clever people then, afore the times of the New Covenant. It runneth in our race that there was a Joe Crang did the crafty work for the Tabernacle as was set up in the wilderness. And it might a' been him as made Little Billy."

"Very hard indeed to prove. Harder still to disprove. But giving you the benefit of the doubt, Master Crang, how have you used this magic tool yourself?"

"That's where the very pint of the whole thing lies; that's what shows them up so ungrateful, sir. Not a soul in the parish to remember what Little Billy hath been to

them! Mind, I don't say as I understand this tool, though
I does a'most anything with her. But for them not to
know! For them to send to ax the name of 'un, when
there bain't one in ten of 'em as hathn't roared over 'un,
when her was screwed to a big back tooth."

"The ungrateful villains! It is really too bad. So
after all, it proves to be what Mr. Farrant thought it was
—a genuine surgical instrument. But go on, Crang; will
you never tell me how this amounts to any proof, either of
my guilt or innocence?"

"Why according of this here, sir, and no way out of it.
Little Billy were took off my shelf, where her always bideth
from father to son, by the big man as come along of the
lame horse and the cart, that night. When I was a kneeling down, I zeed 'un put his hand to it, though I dussn't
say a word for the life of me. And he slipped 'un into his
pocket, same as he would a penny dolly."

"Come now, that does seem more important," said the
Doctor cogitating. "But what could the fellow have
wanted it for?"

"Can't tell 'e, sir," replied the blacksmith. "For some of
his unchristian work, maybe. Or he might have thought
it would came in handy, if aught should go amiss with the
poor nag again. Many's the shoe I've punched off with
Little Billy."

"A Billy of all trades it seems to be. But how does the
recovery of this tool show that you made a mistake about
me, Crang?"

"By reason of the place where her was cast away. You
can't get from Old Barn to Blackmarsh lane with wheels,
sir, any way, can you? You know how that is, Doctor
Jemmy."

"Certainly I do. But that proves nothing to my mind
at all conclusive."

"To my mind it do prove everything conclusive. And
here be the sign and seal of it. As long as I spoke again'
you, Dr. Vox, I was forced to go without my Little
Billy. Not a day's work hath prospered all that time, and
two bad shillings from chaps as rode away. But now I be
took to the right side again, here comes my Little Billy,
and an order for three harries!"

"But it was the Little Billy that has made you change sides. It came before, and not in consequence of that."

"And glad I be to see 'un, sir, and glad to find you clear of it. Tell 'e what I'll do, Doctor Jemmy. You draw a table up as big as Ten Commandments, and three horse shoes on the top for luck, in the name of the Lord, and King William the Fourth, and we'll have it on Church-door by next Sunday, with my mark on it, and both 'prentices. You put it up, sir, like Nebuchadnezzar; beginning—'I, Joseph Crang, do hereby confess, confirm, and convince all honest folk of this here parish——'"

"No, no; nothing of that, Joe. I am quite satisfied. Let people come round, or not; just as they like. I am having a holiday, and I find it very pleasant."

"Meaning to say, as it have spoiled your trade? Never would I forgive a man as did the like to me. But I see you be going for a trip somewhere, sir, with a pretty lady. Only you mind one thing. Joe Crang will shoe your horses, as long as you bide in Perlycrass, for the wholesale price of the iron, Doctor Jemmy; time, and labour, and nails thrown in, free gratis and for nothing."

CHAPTER XVII.

CAMELIAS.

WHILE at the Old Barn, and Rectory also, matters were thus improving, there was no lifting of the clouds, but even deeper gloom at Walderscourt. The house, that had been so gay and happy, warm and hospitable, brisk with pleasant indoor amusement; or eager to sally forth upon some lively sport, whenever the weather looked tempting; the house that had been the home of many joyful dogs— true optimists, and therefore the best friends of man—and had daily looked out of its windows, and admired (with noddings of pretty heads, and glances of bright eyes) the manner a good horse has of saying—"by your leave, I want to see a little bit of the world. Two days looking at my own breath, and your nasty whitewash! It would grieve me very much to pitch you off. But remember you have seventy years, and I about seventeen, for seeing God's light, and the glories of the earth."

None of these high-mettled things happened now. If a horse had an airing, it was with a cloth on, and heels of no perception sticking under him, like nippers; instead of the kind and intelligent approach of a foot that felt every step, and went with it—though thankful for being above the mud—or better still, that stroking of his goodness with the grain, which every gentlemanly horse throws up his head to answer, when a lady of right feeling floats upon the breeze to please him.

Neither was there any dog about. Volumes of description close with a bang, the moment such a thing is said. Any lawn, where dogs have played, and any gravel-walk, —whereon they have sauntered, with keener observation than even Shakespeare can have felt, or rushed with head-long interest into the life-history of some visitor—lawn, and walk, and even flower-beds (touchy at times about sepulture of bones) wear a desolate aspect, and look as if they are longing to cry, too late—" Oh bark again, as thou wast wont to bark!"

The premises may not have felt it thus; or if they did, were too mute to tell it. But an air of desolation broods over its own breath; and silence is a ghost that grows bigger at each stalk. There were no leaves left, to make a little hush by dropping, as a dead man does from the human tree; for the nip of early frost had sent them down, on the night of their Master's funeral, to a grave more peaceful and secure than his. Neither had men worked over hard, to improve the state of things around them. With true philosophy, they had accepted the sere and yellow leaf; because nobody came to make them sweep it up. The less a man labours, the longer will he last, according to general theory; and these men though plentiful, desired to last long. So that a visitor of thoughtful vein might form a fair table of the course of "earth-currents," during the last three weeks, from the state of the big lawn at Walderscourt; where Sir Thomas used to lean upon his stick, and say—" that man is working almost too hard. He looks as if he ought to have a glass of beer."

But the gentleman, now coming up the drive, was not in

the proper frame of mind for groundling observation. Not that he failed to look about him, as if to expand or improve his mind ; but the only result upon his nervous system was to make it work harder upon his own affairs. He was visited with a depressing sense of something hanging over him—of something that must direct, and shape, the whole course of his future life ; and whether it might be for good or evil, he was hurrying to go through with it.

"I don't care ; I don't care," he kept saying to himself ; but that self was well aware that he did care very much ; as much as for all the rest of the world put together. "I've a great mind to toss up about it," he said, as he felt a lucky sixpence in his pocket ; but his sense of the fitness of things prevailed ; so he put on a fine turn of speed, and rang the bell.

The old house looked so different, and everything around so changed, that our friend Fox had a weak impression, and perhaps a strong hope, that the bell would prove to be out of its duty, and refuse to wag. But alas, far otherwise ; the bell replied with a clang that made him jump, and seek reassurance in the flavour of his black kid glove. He had plenty of time to dwell fully upon that, and even write a report upon the subject, ere ever door showed any loyalty to bell ; and even then, there was stiffness about it. For one of the stiffest of mankind stood there, instead of the genial John, or Bob—Mr. Binstock himself, a tall man of three score, Major of the cellar, and commander of the household. He, in a new suit of black, and bearing a gold chain on his portly front, looked down upon the vainly upstanding Jemmy, as if in need of an introduction.

But Dr. Fox was not the man to cave in thus. The door was a large one, with broad aperture ; and this allowed the visitor to march in, as if he had failed to see the great Binstock. Taking his stand upon a leopard's skin, in the centre of the entrance hall, he gazed around calmly, as if he were the stranger contemplated by the serving-man.

"You will have the goodness to take this card up. No thank you, my man, I will stay where I am."

The butler's face deepened from the tint of a radish to that of the richest beet-root ; but he feared to reply, and took the card without a word. "My turn will come very soon," was in his eyes.

Acquainted as he was with the domestic signs and seasons, Fox had not a shadow of a doubt about his fate, so far as the lady of the house could pronounce it. But for all that he saw no reason to submit to rudeness; and all his tremors vanished now at this man's servile arrogance. How many a time had that fat palm borne the impress of a five-shilling piece, slipped into it by the sympathetic Jemmy! And now, to think that this humbug did not know him, and looked at him as a young man aiming at the maids, but come to the wrong door! If anything is wormwood to an Englishman,—that a low, supercilious, ungrateful lacquey—well, here he comes again! Now for it.

Binstock descended the old oak staircase, in a very majestic manner, with the light from a long quarled window playing soft hop-scotch, upon his large countenance. The young doctor, as in absent mood, felt interest in the history, value, and propable future, of the beings on the panels,— stags, otters, foxes, martens, polecats, white hares, badgers, and other noble members of West county suffrage; some entire, and too fat to live, some represented by a very little bit.

Binstock descended, in deep silence still. He felt that the crown had passed away. No other five-shilling piece would ever flutter—as a tip on the sly should have the wings to do —from the gentleman of phials, to the man of bottles.

The salver in his hand was three times as large as the one upon which he had received the card; but the little card was on it, very truly in the centre, squaring the circle of a coat of many arms.

The butler came down, and brought his heels together; then made a low bow, and without a word, conveyed to the owner of that piece of pasteboard, how frankly and cordially it lay at his disposal. Fox had been expecting at least some message, some shade, however cold it might be, of courtesy and acknowledgment. But this was a queer sort of reception. And Binstock did not even grin. The turn of his lips suggested only, that others might do so— not he, at such a trifle.

Fox should have taken all, with equal silence. The Foxes were quite as old a race as any Waldrons; Foxden was a bigger place than Walderscourt; and stouter men than Binstock wore in service there. But the young man was in love; and he forgot those spiteful things.

"No message, Binstock?" He asked with timid glance, while he fumbled very clumsily with his nails (now bitten short, during many sad hours of dark brooding) to get his poor card out of graven heraldry—"not a word of any sort, from—from anybody?"

"Had there been a message, sir, I should have delivered it."

"I beg your pardon, Binstock. To be sure—of course, you would. Very well. Good afternoon. There is nothing more to say. I will put this in my pocket, for—for a last remembrance."

He put the rejected card in his waistcoat-pocket, and glanced round, as if to say "Good bye," to the old haunt of many a pleasant hour.

Then Binstock, that grave and majestic butler, surprised him by giving a most unmajestic wink. Whether he was touched with reminiscence of his youth—for he had been a faithful man, in love, as well as wine—or whether sweeter memory of crown-pieces moved him; from sympathy, or gratitude, or both combined, beyond any question, Binstock winked. Fox felt very thankful, and received a lasting lesson, that he had not given utterance to the small contempt within him.

"There was a little pipe, sir," said the butler, glancing round, and speaking in a low voice rather fast, "That our poor Sir Thomas gived to you, from the Spanish, now called the provincial war. John Hutchings made the observation, that he had heard you pronounce opinion that it was very valuable; and never would you part with it, high or low. And John says that to his certain knowledge now, it is lying in our Camelia house."

"Oh never mind about it now. It is kind of you to think of it. Perhaps you will put it by for me."

"Moreover John was a-saying, sir," continued Mr. Binstock, with a still more solemn wink, "that you ought almost to have a look at our poor little dog, that all the parish is so full of, including our Miss Nicie, sir. Vets may be all very well in their way; but a human doctor more immortal. And that makes the young lady so particular no doubt, to keep her in the Camelia house, because of being cool and warm, sir."

"Oh to be sure! That poor dear little *Jess!* What a fine heart you have, Binstock! I suppose I may go out that way?"

"The same to you, sir;" said Binstock, as he proved the truth of the proverb—"a fine heart is a vein of gold." "The shortest way out, sir, John always says, when her ladyship's nerves have locked her up. And the quietest way, with no one about, unless it should happen to be Miss Nicie, certainly is through the west quarry door."

The butler closed the front door with a bang, as if he had thrust the intruder forth; while Jemmy, with his heart in his mouth, hurried down the west corridor to the Green-house.

Colonel Waldron, while in Portugal, five and twenty years ago, had been greatly impressed with the glorious sight of noble Camelia-trees in full bloom, a sight perhaps unequalled in the world of flowers. He had vowed that if ever he returned alive, and could afford the outlay, Camelias he would have in England; not so magnificent of course, but worthy to remind him of Parque da Pena. He had studied the likings of the race, and built a house on purpose for them; and here they were in this dark month, beginning to offer bright suggestion of the Spring. Fine trees of twenty years' sturdy growth, flourishing in the prime flush of health, with the dark leaves glancing like bulls'-eyed glass, and the younger ones gleaming like gauffered satin. And these but a cushion, and a contrast, for the stately luxuriance of blossom; some in the perfect rosette already, of clean-cut, snow-white ivory; some just presenting the pure deep chalice; others in the green bud, tipped with snow, or soft maiden blush, or lips of coral.

For the trees were planted in a border of good soil, cut from healthy pasture; instead of being crammed and jammed in pots, with the roots like a ganglion, or burr-knot wen. Hence the fibres spread, and sucked up strength, and poured the lush juices into elastic cells, ready to flow into grace of form and colour, and offer fair delight, and pride, to the eyes and heart of watchful men.

But Fox was not a watchful man at all of any of the charming feats of vegetation now. Flowers were all very well in their way; but they were not in his way just at present, or—worse again—some of them were, and stopped him from clear view of something worth all the flowers, all the fruit, and all the fortunes of the wide wide world.

For lo, not far away, betwixt a pink tree and a white one, sat Miss Inez Waldron, in a square-backed garden chair. At her feet was a cushioned basket, with an invalid dog asleep in it; while a sound dog, of pug race, was nudging in between, fain to push it out of sight, if his body had been big enough. Jealousy lurked in every wrinkle of his face, and governed every quiver of his half-cocked tail.

The girl looked very pale and sad, and could not even raise a smile, at all the sharp manœuvres and small-minded whines of *Pixie*. Heartily as she loved the dogs, their sorrows, views, and interests now were not the first she had to dwell on. With the colour gone from her cheeks, and her large deep-gray eyes dulled with weeping, her face was not so lovely as in gayer times, but even yet more lovable and tender.

Following *Pixie's* rush, without much expectation in her gaze—for she thought it was her mother coming—her eyes met those of the young man, parted by such a dark cloud from her. For an instant her pale cheeks flushed, and then the colour vanished from them, and she trembled so that she could not rise. Her head fell back on the rail of the chair; while trees, and flowers, and lines of glass began to quiver, and lose their shape, and fade away from her languid eyes.

"You are faint—she has fainted!" cried Fox in dismay, as he caught up the handkerchief she had dropped, and plunged it into a watering pot, then wrung and laid it gently on her smooth white forehead. Then he took both her hands in his, and chafed them, kneeling at her side in a state of agitation, unlikely to add to his medical repute. And from time to time, he whispered words, of more than

L

sympathy or comfort, words that had never passed between them yet.

For a while she knew not what he said, until as she slowly revived, one word attracted her vague attention. "Happy!" she said, only conscious yet of speaking to some kind person; "no, I must never think of such a thing again." The sadness of her own voice told upon her, reacting on the sad heart from which it came. She looked, as if for somebody to comfort her; perhaps the dear father who had always loved to do it. He was not to be found—oh, piteous grief! If he could come, would he ever leave her thus?

Then the whole of her misery broke upon her. She knew too well where she was, and what. Turn away the face there is none to kiss, and toss back the curls there is nobody to stroke. From a woman, she fell back into a petted child, spoiled by sweet love, and now despoiled by bitter fate. She could look at nothing more. Why did consciousness come back? The only thing for her was to sob, and weep—tears that rolled more big and heavy, because they must ever roll in vain.

Fox had never been in such a state of mind before. Hundreds of times he had been driven to the end of his wits, and the bottom of his heart, to know what to do with wailing women, stricken down at last by inexorable death, from the hope that laughs at doctors. But the difference was this—he was the doctor then; and now he was the lover. The lover, without acknowledged right to love; but the shadow of death, and worse than that, betwixt him and the right to love.

While he was feebly holding on, knowing that he could not leave her thus—for there was a large tank near her—yet feeling that no man—save husband, or father—should be admitted to this deep distress, he heard the light steps of a woman in the corridor, and he muttered—"Thank God! There is some kind person coming."

But his joy was premature. The branches of a fine Camelia-tree were swept aside like cobwebs, and there stood Lady Waldron, drawing the heavy black folds around her, and bearing him down with her cold dark eyes. Her gaze of contemptuous loathing passed from him—as if he were not worth it—to the helpless embodiment of anguish in the chair; and even then there was no pity.

Inez turned and faced her, and the meeting of their eyes was not of the gentle sweetness due betwixt a mother and her daughter. Without another glance at Fox, Lady Waldron swept by, as if he were not present; and standing before her daughter, spoke a few Spanish words very slowly, pronouncing every syllable. Then with a smile far worse to see than any frown, she turned away, and her stately figure disappeared in the shadows of the corridor.

The maiden watched her without a word, and the sense of wrong renewed her strength. Her eyes met the light, as if they had never known a tear, and she threw up her head, and swept her long hair back. For her proud spirit rose through the storm of her trouble, as a young palm stands forth from the cloud it has defied. She cast a glance at Fox, and to her great relief saw nothing in his face but anxiety about herself. But she must have his ignorance confirmed.

"What trouble I have given you!" she said, with her usual clear soft tones, and gentle look. "I am quite ashamed of myself, for having so very little strength of mind. I cannot thank you as I ought to do. My mother would have done it, I—I suppose at least, if she had been at all like herself. But she has not been well, not at all as she used to be, ever since—I need not tell you what. We are doing our best to bear things; but we find it very, very hard. As the Spanish proverb is—but I beg your pardon, you don't know Spanish?"

"I am nothing of a linguist. I am no exception to the general rule of Englishmen, that their own tongue is enough for them."

"Please to tell me plainly. My memory seems confused. But I think you have shown some knowledge of it. And I think, I have heard my father say that you could read Don Quixote very fairly from his copy."

"No; but just a little, very badly, and with the help of a dictionary, and my own recollection of Latin."

"Then you know what my mother said just now? I hope not. Oh I should grieve so!"

"Well, Miss Waldron, if you insist upon the truth, I cannot deny that I understood her."

Nicie's eyes flashed as he spoke : then she rose, and went to him hastily ; for he was going, and had taken up his hat to leave her, inasmuch as she now could take care of herself.

"Put down your hat," she said in her own pretty style of issuing orders, in the days of yore ; "now give me both your hands, as you held mine just now, and look at me honestly, and without reserve."

"All that I am doing," answered Jemmy Fox, happy to have her so, and throwing the dawn of a smile into the depth of her dear eyes. " Miss Waldron, I am doing it."

"Then go on like this—'Miss Waldron,' or you may even for once say, 'Nicie—I have never been base enough, for a moment, to imagine that you had any doubt of me.' Say all that from the bottom of your heart."

" Nicie, I say from the bottom of my heart, that I knew you were too noble to have any doubt of me, in that way."

"I should hope so ; " she said, as she dropped her eyes, for fear of showing all that was in them. "You have done me justice, and it will be done to you. I was only afraid, though I knew better, that you might—for men are not like us——"

"No, they are not. And more shame for them. Oh Nicie, what do I care now, if the whole world goes against me ? "

She gave him one steadfast look, as if that recklessness had no shock for her, and in fact had been duly expected. Then knowing by the eyes what had been nursing in her heart for months, she smiled the smile that is deeper almost in the human kind than tears, and happily more lasting. The young man proved himself worthy of her, by cherishing it, without a word.

" I may never see you again," said Nicie, coming back to proper form, though they both knew that was humbug ; " never again, or not for years. It will be impossible for you now to come—to come, as you used to do. But remember, if it is any comfort to you, and I think it will be a little, that no one is more miserable about this wicked, wicked charge, than the one who has more right than any

—yes much more than she has"—and she waved her hand after her mother's steps.

"Yes. Or at any rate quite as much. Darling, darling Nicie dear. Don't get excited again, for my sake."

"I am not excited. And I don't mean to be. But you are welcome to tell everybody, everybody, Jemmy, exactly what I think of you. And my dear father thought the same."

"You are an angel, and nothing less. Something considerably more, I think," said Jemmy, confining himself to moderation.

"Hush!" she replied, though not in anger; for ladies like that comparison. And then, as he could not better it, he whispered, "God bless you, dear, as you have blessed me!" Before she could answer, he was gone.

CHAPTER XVIII.

CONCUSSION.

ALL the time these things were going on, the patient Christie had been waiting, or rather driving to and fro, on the outskirts of the private grounds. These were large, and well adorned with trees of ancient growth, and clumps of shrubs, and ferny dingles. Southward stretched the rich Perle valley, green with meadows beloved by cows, who expressed their fine emotions in the noblest cream; on the north-east side was the Beacon Hill, sheltering from the bitter winds, and forming a goodly landmark; while to the north and west extended heathery downs with sweet short grass, knolls of Scotch fir here and there, and gorse for ever blooming. Across these downs, and well above the valley-margin ran one of the two great western roads, broad and smooth as a ball-room floor, and ringing some forty times a day, with the neigh, and the tramp, and the harness-rattle of four steeds tossing their heads up, and the musical blast of long brass horn, or merry notes of key-bugle.

Christie Fox in her own opinion was an exceedingly fine whip. Tandem-driving was then much in vogue; and truly to be a good tandem-whip was one of the loftiest aspirations

of the rational being who could afford it. Christie was
scarcely up to that mark yet, although she had been known
to "tool a team," when her father had the gout, and there
was some one at her side. So it may be supposed, with
what sweet contempt her sparkling eyes regarded Churchwarden Farrant's rattle-trap, and his old cob *Punch* ante-
ceding it.

"Now don't you go capering about, Miss Chris;" her
brother had said when he left her. "I should have
brought George, or at any rate the boy. These lanes are
so narrow, and the ditches such a depth."

"Well, Jemmy, it shows how little you have been at
home! Why I can drive Sparkler, and Wild-oats, and
Hurricane. To think of my coming to grief with this old
screw!"

"You are a wonder, no doubt. But at any rate, be
careful. He is a quiet old buffer, but he has got a temper
of his own. Why he upset the Reverend, last summer."

"He won't spill me, I can tell him that. The Reverend
is a muff—he should have let him say his prayers."

For a long time the young lady proved that she was
right. *Punch* went up and down, and even on the common,
as grave as a Judge, and as steady as a Church. "Poor
old chap!" said Christie to him; "Why you haven't got
the pluck to call your soul your own." *Punch* only replied
with a whisk of his tail, as if to say—"well, I can call this
my own," and pursued his reflections, with a pensive head.

But suddenly the scene changed. A five-barred gate was
flung mightily open, half across the lane, with a fierce creak
of iron, and a shivering of wood; and out poured a motley
crowd of all sorts and sizes, rattling tea-kettles, and beating
frying-pans, blowing old cow's horns, and flourishing a
blown dozen of Bob Jake's bladders, with nuts inside them.
Punch was coming past, in a moody state of mind, down
upon his luck in some degree, and wondering what the
world was made for, if a piece of iron in a horse's mouth
was allowed to deny him the Almighty's gift of grass.
However he resigned himself about all that.

But when this tremendous uproar broke upon him—for
it happened to be the Northern party of the parish, beating
bounds towards the back of Beacon Hill, and eager to win

a bet about where they met the other lot—and when a gate was flung almost into his shaky knees, which had begun for some time to " come over," up rose the spirit of his hunting days, for he had loved the hounds, when he was young. There was no room to rise the gate ; or perhaps he would have tried it, for the mettle of springier times sprang up, and he had never heard a louder noise, in the most exciting burst. Surely his duty was at least to jump a hedge.

He forgot altogether that he stood between two shafts, and that a young lady was entrusted to his care. Swerving to the off-side, he saw a comely gap, prepared no doubt by Providence, for the benefit of a horse not quite so young as he used to be. And without hesitation he went at it, meaning no harm, and taking even less heed of the big ditch on this side of it. Both shafts snapped, though of fine lance-wood, the four-wheeler became two vehicles, each with a pair of wheels to it, and over the back flew Christie, like a sail blown out of the bolt-ropes.

Luckily she wore large bell-sleeves, as every girl with self-respect was then compelled to do ; and these, like parachutes expanding, broke the full speed of her headlong flight. Even so it must have fared very badly with her—for her hat being stringless had flown far away—had she been allowed to strike the earth ; but quicker than thought a very active figure sprang round the head of the gate, and received the impact of her head upon a broad staunch breast. The blow was severe, and would have knocked the owner down, had he not been an English yeoman.

Upon a double-breasted waistcoat, made of otter skin, soft and elastic, he received the full brunt of the young lady's head, as the goal-keeper stops a football. Throwing forward his arms, he was just in time to catch more of her, as it descended ; and thus was this lovely maiden saved from permanent disfigurement, if not from death. But for the time, she knew nothing of this.

Frank Gilham held her very firmly in his arms, and wondered, as well he might do, at her good fortune and his own. Others came crowding round the gate, but none had the least idea who she was, and Gilham would not permit one of them to touch her, though many would gladly have shared his load. Throughout all history, it has been the nature of the British yeoman to bear his own burden, be it good or be it evil.

"Her be crule doiled," "A' vear her neck be bracken," "Look e' zee what purty hair her hath !" "Vetch a drap watter," "Carr' un up to big 'ouze," "Her be scrunched like a trummot"—in this way they went on, all gaping and staring, eager to help, but not sure of the way.

"Lift the gate from its hinges, and lay it down here ; " said Gilham, for she still remained senseless ; " run to yon rick—they've been hay-binding there; bring a couple of trusses, and spread them on the gate."

In two minutes Christie was lying on the gate—for Devonshire men can be quick when they like—bedded and pillowed among sweet hay, with Frank Gilham's coat spread across her pretty dress, and his hand supporting her fair head, and easing the jerks as they bore her up the road. But before they had gone more than ten or twenty yards towards Walderscourt, whom should they come upon but Dr. Jemmy Fox, looking very joyful, until he met them?

"My sister ! My own dear Chris ! " he exclaimed ; and they fell away, while he examined her.

"Concussion. Only slight, I hope. Thank God ! " he said, with his eyes full of tears ; "keep her head like that, I will take this end ; now, who the other ? But not to the Court—anywhere but that. Never mind why. I can't stop to explain. What is the nearest house, this other way ? "

"Mother's is not more than half a mile away, and good level road," answered Gilham. "She'd be well-treated there. You may trust us for that."

"You are a brick. Take the other end, Frank. Some fellow with good legs run in front, and tell Mrs. Gilham what her son has said. No crowding round there ; we want all the air. One or two of you run and catch Mr. Farrant's horse before he tumbles through that harrow. The rest of you go on with your beating work." For *Punch* was careering across a ploughed field, like a wrecker with his plunder at his heels.

By the time they arrived at White Post Farm, Mrs. Gilham was ready to receive them, a kind old lady as ever lived, sensible, quiet, and ready-witted. A bed on the ground-floor was ready, and poor Christie, who still lay as if in a heavy sleep, was carried in very gently; and placed as well as might be upon it. Sometimes she was breathing with long gasps, and at other times showing no life at all, and her eyes were closed as in a soft deep sleep. "The pretty dear! The poor young thing!" cried Mrs. Gilham, and a real cry it was.

"I shall not leave her till she comes to herself—that is if you will let me stop," said her brother, who was much more anxious than he cared to let them see. "But if you could send a note to my Old Barn, George would come over, with a little chest I want."

"In twenty minutes, I will be there," answered Gilham, "and back in another fifteen with it, if it will come on horseback."

He had saddled a horse, and was off in two minutes, while Fox called after him down the lane, to see on his road through Priestwell whether Dr. Gronow was at home, and beg him to come up if possible.

Gronow came at once, when called; for if anything is remarkable among the professors of the healing art (beyond their inability to heal) it is the good-will with which they always try their best, and the largeness of their ministrations to each other's families. Parsons appeal to one another for a leg-up very freely; but both reading-desk and pulpit feel that the strange foot is not up to much, unless it has its footing paid.

But Dr. Gronow (besides the kindness of his kind profession, always at the service of its members) had an especial regard for Fox, as a young man much of his own type, one who dared to think for himself, and being thoroughly well-grounded, often felt impatient at the vast uncertainty above. Whatever faith a young man may feel in his own powers of perception, it is a happy moment, when a veteran confirms him.

"She will be all right," said the man of long practice, after careful examination; "only she must have her time, which you know as well as I do. Never mind if she lies like this, for twelve or even for twenty-four hours; though I do not think that it will last so long. She ought to have a face she knows and loves, to meet her own, when her

consciousness returns. Then you know how to treat her.
Verbum sat. But I want to have a long talk with you,
when this anxiety is over. Why have you kept so long out
of my way? Come down to my house, when your sister
can spare you."

Fox would have found it hard to say, or at any rate to
tell Gronow, what were his reasons for avoiding Priestwell,
while the present black cloud hung over him. In fact to
himself his own motives had not been very clear or well
considered; but pride was perhaps the foremost. If Gronow
intended to take his part, the first thing to do was to call
at Old Barn, and let everybody know it. And the young
man failed to recollect, that the elder might have good
reasons of his own, for keeping his distance just at first.
Nothing but kind consideration had prevented Gronow
from calling upon Fox straightway, for he knew what
significance people would attach to such a visit. Suspicion
had fallen upon him as well; and many of the baser sort
declared, that old and young doctor had arranged that
piece of work between them.

Liberal as he was, and kind, whenever a case of real
want or trouble was brought before him, the retired
physician was not beloved yet by his neighbours, and he
knew it, and was well content to have it so.

"A queer old chap"—was the usual summary of his
character in the parish; and the charitable added, "no
call to blame him; a little bit touched in the upper storey."

To the vast relief of her brother, and the delight of her
kind hostess, Christie Fox that very night contrived to
come to herself, almost as suddenly as she had left it.

"What is all this about?" she asked, opening her clear
eyes strongly. "Why, Jemmy, you have got no hat on!
And where is mine? Oh dear! oh dear! Thirty shillings,
without the trimming."

"There it is, dear, as large as life, and not a speck upon
it. Now drink this cup of tea; and then I'll finish what I
was saying."

"No, you always talk so fast, and you never let me say
a word. I might just as well have no tongue at all."

The young lady spoke in such fine ignorance of the self
she had come back to, that there could be no doubt of her

being all there. And presently the "cup of tea" had such a tranquillising power that she fell into a sweet deep sleep, and did not awake until the sun was as high as he meant to go at that time of the year. At first she had a slow dull headache, and felt still all over. But Mrs. Gilham appearing with a napkin'd tray, thin toast and butter, a couple of pullet's eggs just laid, and one or two other brisk challenges at the hands of her youngest daughter, nature arose with an open mouth to have the last word about it, and Christie made a famous breakfast.

Very soon Dr. Gronow looked in again, and smiled in his dry way at her, for he was not a man of many words. She gave her round wrist to be felt, and the slim pink tongue to be glanced at, and the bright little head to be certified cool and sound under the curls; and passing this examination with high honours, she thought him a "very nice old man;" though his face was not at first sight perhaps of the sweet and benevolent order.

Then the old doctor took the young doctor aside—for Jemmy had not been out of hail all night—and said, "She will do. I congratulate you. No serious lesion, no feverish symptons—just a bump on her head from a mother-of-pearl button. But she has been severely shaken. I would not move her for a day or two."

"May she get up?" asked Jemmy in that spirit of pure submission, with which a doctor resigns his own family to the care of another, who knows perhaps less than he himself does. But the plan is wise for the most part, inasmuch as love is apt to cloud the clearest eyes.

"To be sure she may. It will do her good. But not to walk about yet. These people are the kindest of the kind. You may safely leave all that to the ladies. Meanwhile you are better out of the way. Come down for an hour or two, and share my early dinner. You want looking to yourself. You have not had a bit for some twenty-four hours."

It was little more than ten minutes' walk to Gronow's house at Priestwell, and Fox accepted the invitation gladly. Neither in the course of their walk, nor during their meal, did his entertainer refer to the mysterious subject, which was always in the mind of one, and often in that of the

other. But Gronow enlarged upon his favourite topic—
the keen sagacity, and almost too accurate judgment
possessed by trout, and the very great difficulty he experienced in catching them, unless the stream was muddy.

"But you can't fish at this time of year," observed Fox ;
"at least so people say. I know nothing about it.
Hunting and shooting are more to my taste."

"You can fish every day in the year," replied Gronow ;
"at any rate in this river. There is nothing against it,
but prejudice. The little ones are as bright as a new
shilling now, and the old ones as a guinea."

"But surely they should be allowed time to breed."

"That is their business, and none of mine. If they
choose to neglect what they should be doing, and come to
my hook, why I pull them out—that is to say, if they
don't slip off."

"But your hook has no right to be there just then."

"Is it for a fish to dictate to me, how I should employ
my time? I bought this property for the fishing. The
interest of my money runs all the year round, and so must
what I spent it on."

Fox saw that he would only irritate this concise logician,
by further contention on behalf of the fish ; and he was
quite disarmed, when the candid doctor added—

"I don't mean to say, that such a fellow as young Pike,
Penniloe's senior pupil, should be allowed to fish all the
year round ; for he never goes out without catching
something. But my case is different ; the winter owes me
all the blank days I had in the summer ; and as they were
nine out of every ten, I shall not have caught up the
record, by the time the May-fly comes back again."

"Then you can't do much harm now," thought Fox ;
"and the trout will soon have their revenge, my friend—
a fine attack of rheumatism, well in season."

"And now," said Dr. Gronow, when dinner was over,
and "red and white wine," as they were always called
then, had been placed upon the table, not upon a cloth,
but on the dark red sheen ; "now you can smoke if you
like. I don't, just at present. Let us talk of all this
botheration. What an idiot world it is! You are young,
and will have to wag your tail to it. I go along, with my

tail straight; like a dog who does not care to fight, but is ready, if it comes to that."

"I know pretty well how you look at things. And it is the best way, for those who can afford it. Of course, I am bound to pretend not to care; and I keep up pretty well, perhaps. But for all that, it is not very jolly. If my sister had not turned up, I am not sure how I should have got on at all. Though Penniloe ¦was very good, and so were several others, especially Mockham. I must have a pipe, if you don't mind. It makes me feel so grateful."

"That is something in its favour, and shows how young you still remain. I would cultivate the pipe more than I do; if so it would bring back my youth; not for the youth—blind puppyhood—but for thinking better of my race, and of myself as one of them."

"It is not for me to reason with you," Fox answered humbly, as he blew a gentle cloud; "you are far above me, in every way. I am stupid enough; but I always know, when I come across a stronger mind."

"Not a stronger, but a harder one. We will not go into that question now. Reams have been written about it, and they leave us none the wiser. The present point is—how are you to get out of this very nasty scrape?"

"I don't care to get out. I will face it out. When a man knows his own innocence——"

"That is all very fine; but it won't work. Your prospects do not depend, I know, at all upon your profession. But for the sake of all your friends, your sweet high-spirited sister, your good mother, and all your family, you must not rest upon that manly view. Your innocence may be a coat of mail to yourself. But it will not shelter them."

"I have thought of all that. I am not so selfish. But who can prove a negative?"

"The man who can prove the positive. You will never be quit, until you show who was the real perpetrator. A big word to use; for, after all, the horror at such things is rather childish. The law regards it so, and in its strong perception of mortal rights, has made it a felony to steal the shroud, to steal the body an indictable offence, to be punished with fine, or (if a poor man did it) with imprisonment."

"Is that the law? I could scarcely have believed it. And they talk of the absurdities of our profession!"

"Yes, that is the law. And perhaps you see now, why your enemies have not gone further. They see that it damns you ten times more, to lie under the imputation, than it would to be brought to trial, and be acquitted, as you must be. You have not to thank them for any mercy, only for knowing their own game."

"It is enough to make one a misanthrope for life," said Fox, looking really fierce once more. "I hoped that they had found their mistake about me, and were sorry for accusing an innocent man."

"Alas for the credulity of youth! No Jemmy, the Philistines are upon thee. You have to reckon with a wily lot, and an implacable woman behind them. They will take every advantage of the rank cowardice of the clodhopper, and the terror of all those pitch-plaster tales. You know how these things have increased, ever since that idiotic Act of two or three years back. That a murderer should be prevented even from affording some posthumous expiation! And yet people call it a religious age—to rob a poor wretch of his last hope of heaven!"

"Your idea is a grim one;" answered Fox with a smile; "I never saw it in that light before. But now tell me one thing—and it is a main point. You know that you can trust me with your opinion. I confess that I am at my wits' ends. The thing must have been done, to solve some doubt. There is no one about here who would dare the risk, even if there were any one zealous enough; and so far as I know, short of Exeter, there are none but hum-drums, and jog-trots."

"You have expressed your opinion already a little too freely to that effect, Master Jemmy."

"Perhaps I have. But I never meant it to go round. It was young and silly of me. But what I want to ask you is this—do you think it possible that, you know who——"

"Harrison Gowler?" said Dr. Gronow calmly. "It is possible, but most improbable. Gowler knew what it was, even better than you did, or I from your account of it. Introsusception is not so very rare, even without a strain, or the tendency to it from an ancient wound. Putting aside all the risk and expense—and I know that friend Gowler sticks close to his money—and dropping all the feelings of a gentleman—what sufficient motive could Gowler have? An enthusiastic tiro might have longed to verify, etc., but not a man of his experience. He knew it all, as well as if he had seen it. No, you may at once dismiss that idea, if you ever formed it."

" I never did form it. It was suggested ; and all that you have said occurred to me. Well, I know not what to think. The mystery is hopeless. All we can be certain of is, that the thing was done."

" Even of that I am not quite so certain. I am never sure of anything, unless I see it. I have come across such instances of things established beyond doubt—and yet they never occurred at all. And you know what a set of fools these fat-chopped yokels are, when scared. Why they actually believe in Spring-heeled Jack, Lord Somebody, and the ten thousand guinea bet ! And they quake in their beds, if the windows rattle. Look at that idiot of a blacksmith, swearing that he saw you with the horse ! A horse? A night-mare, or a mare's nest, I should say. Why it would not surprise me a bit, if it proved that the worthy baronet is reposing in his grave, as calmly as his brave and warlike spirit could desire. If not, it is no fault of our profession, but the result of some dark history, to which as yet we have no clue."

Dr. Gronow had a manner of saying things, in itself so distinct and impressive, and seconded so ably by a lowering of his eyebrows, and wrinkling of his large steep forehead, that when he finished up with his mouth set close, and keen eyes fixed intently, it was hard to believe that he could be wrong—supposing at least that he meant to be right.

" Well, sir," said the young man, strongly feeling this effect; " you have often surprised me by the things you have said. And strange as they seemed, they have generally proved correct in the end. But as to your first suggestion, it is impossible, I fear, to think of it ; after what at least a dozen people saw, without hurry, and in broad daylight. The other matter may be as you say. If so, it only makes it worse for me. What hope can I have of ever getting at the bottom of it?"

"Time, my dear fellow, time will show. And the suspicion against you will be weakening every day, if you meet it with calm disdain. You already have the blacksmith's recantation—a blow in the teeth for your enemies. I am not exactly like your good parson, who exhorts you devoutly to trust in the Lord. 'The Lord helps those who help themselves,' is my view of that question. Though I begin to think highly of Penniloe. He was inclined to be rude about the flies I use, once or twice last summer. But I shall look over that, as he has been so ill. I shall call and enquire for him to-morrow."

"But what am I to do, to help myself? It is so easy to say, 'take it easily.' What is the first step for me to take? I could offer rewards, and all that sort of thing. I could send for experienced men from London. I have written to a friend of mine there already, but have had no answer. I could put myself in a clever lawyer's hands. I could do a lot of things, no doubt, and spread the matter far and wide. But the first result would be to kill my dear father. I told you in what a condition he lies."

"Yes. You are terribly 'handicapped' as the racing people call it. Penniloe's illness was much against you. So was your own absence. So were several other things. But the worst of all is your father's sad state. And the better he gets, the worse the danger. But for all that, I can give you one comfort. I have never yet known things combine against a man, persistently and relentlessly, if he went straight ahead at them. They jangle among themselves, by and by, even as his enemies are sure to do; and instead of being hunted down, he slips out between them. One thing I can undertake perhaps. But I won't talk of it until I know more, and have consulted Penniloe. What, have you never had a glass of wine? Well, that is too bad of me! These are the times, when even a young man wants it, and an old one should sympathise with him thus. Oh, you want to get back to the fair Miss Christie? Very well, take her half a dozen of my pears. These people about here don't know what a pear is, according to my interpretation of the word."

CHAPTER XIX.

PERCUSSION.

THIS was not the right time of year for spring of hope, and bounding growth ; the first bloom-bud of the young heart growing milky, and yet defiant; and the leaf-bud pricking up, hard and reckless, because it can never have a family. Not the right time yet for whispered openings, and shy blush of petals, still uncertain of the air, and creeping back into each other's clasp lest they should be tempted to come out too soon. Neither was there in the air itself that coy, delusive, tricksome way, which it cannot help itself for having, somewhere about the month of April, when the sun is apt to challenge and then shirks the brunt.

In a word (though no man can prove a negative, as Jemmy Fox had well remarked) it was the very time when no young man, acquainted with the calendar of his Church, should dream of falling into love, even though he had a waistcoat of otterskin, and fourteen pearl-buttons upon it.

In spite of all that, it was the positive which prevailed in this case. Frank Gilham had received such a blow upon his heart, that the season and the weather were nothing to it. The fall of the leaf, and retirement of the sap—though the Saps now tell us that it never does retire —had less than no effect upon his circulation. He went in vainly for a good day's ploughing, for he could hold as well as drive ; but there was his waistcoat, and his heart inside it ; and even when he hung the one upon an oak-tree, the other kept going on, upon its private business ; and "Whoa ! Stand still, hossy !" had no effect upon it.

He sneaked into the house, as if he had no right there— though his mother had only a life-interest—and he made a serious matter of the shortness of his nails, and felt a conscientious longing, when he saw his whiskers, to kick the barber at Pumpington, who had shorn them with a

M

pair of tailor's scissors, so abominably on the last market-day. But last market-day, this young man's heart had been inditing of pigs and peas, whereof he had made a tidy penny, because he was a sharp fellow then.

"How is she now?" he asked his young sister Rose, when he came down at last, discontented with himself, though appearing unusually smart to her.

"Well, thank you, Frank, mother is not quite the thing to-night. She did not get quite her proper rest, you know, on account of the strange young lady. And she never took her hore-hound lozenges. She thinks too much of others, and too little of herself——"

"As if I did not know all that! Will you never tell me anything I want to know? But I suppose the young lady won't keep her up to-night?"

"She? Oh she is all right enough. You should just see her eat. My goodness! Talk of farmhouse appetites!"

"Rose, who are you to understand such things? You have seen so very little of the world; and you judge it entirely by yourself. I suppose the door is not open?"

"Oh yes. Anybody can look in, if that's what you want to do. She has been sitting up ever so long, with mother's dressing-gown and Sunday shawl on. Such a guy you never see in all your life!"

"A pity you can't be a guy then. Why Rose, if you only had a hundredth part——"

"Yes, I dare say. But I don't want, don't you see? I am quite contented as I am; and better judges than you will ever be—why that coloured hair is quite out of fashion now. Everybody goes in for this sort of tint, and a leaden comb to make it darker. Corkscrews are all the rage, and they can't be too black. Why Minnie Farrant told me, last Sunday, that she read on the best authority——"

"Her Bible, or her Prayer-book?"

"Don't be so absurd. The very best authority, that Queen Adelaide herself told His Majesty as much, and he said he was a Tar, and the best pitch wasn't black. That was to please her, you know. Wasn't it clever of him? Oh Frank, why don't you fall in love with Minnie Farrant —your own Godfather's favourite child, and they say she'll have four thousand pounds?"

" Minnie Far rant! Why, I'd rather have a broomstick. Though she is a.1 very well in her way, of course."

" She is the prettiest girl in this parish, by long chalks, except of course Nicie Waldron. And I suppose you wouldn't quite stick up to her."

" Stick up indeed! Is that the way you learn to express yourself at a finishing school ? But do look sharp with the frying-pan, if your corkscrews are not too precious. I don't want Minnie Farrant, nor even Miss Waldron—I want my little bit of supper, and you know it well enough. I am sorry for the ninny that ever falls in love with you."

" So am I. Because I won't have him. But what fun it will be! I shall starve him out. All you men think about is eating ; and I shall say——"

" Rose again, as usual ! Her long tongue running away with her." Mrs. Gilham looked very serious, for every day she found stronger proof that girls were not as they used to be. " You have had your tea, child, and you want nothing more. I am sure you should be the very last to talk as if eating were a sin. Go and help Mary with your dear brother's supper. He has been hard at work all day."

> " Sticks to his work, wants no diverting—
> A model young man in the farming line !
> Never goes hunting, dancing, flirting,
> Doesn't know the flavour of a glass of wine."

Away danced Rosie to the tune of her own song, with her light figure frisking from side to side of the long stone passage.

" Ah me ! I fear we shall have trouble yet with that very thoughtless girl. She can only see the light side of everything. It is high time for her now ; why before I was seventeen— But Frank, you don't look like yourself to-night ! " The old lady went up to him, and pushed aside his hair, as crisp and curly as a double hyacinth. " I am almost sure, there is something on your mind. Your dear father had exactly that expression upon his face, at periods of his married life. But then it was always the times when he had rheumatics in his left shoulder blade ;

and I used to iron them out with brown paper, the darkest
brown that you can get, and a sprinkle of vinegar underneath, as hot as ever you can bear it; in fact, until it
begins to singe, and then——"

"Well, nobody will ever do that to me, thank God!"
Frank spoke in a very reckless tone, and strictly avoided
his mother's eyes.

"I will, my son, if I live long enough. Old Mrs.
Horner used to say—not the present Mrs. John, you
know, but her husband's mother——"

"Excuse me, dear mother, but I thought I heard a call.
Shall I go, and knock at the young lady's door?"

"Frank, how can you ask such a question? Not that
she is not in very pretty order, and fit for any one to look
at her; with my dressing-gown on, as good as new, and the
big picture-Bible on one side of her, and 'The Fashionable
Lady's Vade Mecum' on the other."

"How queer she must look in your dressing-gown,
mother! Quite an old frump, I suppose?"

"I am very much obliged to you, my son. But as it
happens, Miss Christie Fox does not look at all like an old
frump; though your poor mother would of course, and
must expect it—though not perhaps quite to be told of it.
On the contrary, Miss Fox looks very bright and blooming,
with her eyes like the sky itself, and her lovely hair
flowing all down her shoulders."

"I had better go and see whether she has knocked for
something. I need not go in of course. In fact I should
not think of it, only just to pop my head inside the door,
and then——"

"No, you won't pop it, sir, in any place of the kind.
Remember that it is a bedroom; and you are a gentleman
—or ought to be."

"Oh, come, mother! That's a little too hard on me.
I never meant anything, except to save you trouble, by
just asking— Well, I didn't think you would speak to
me in that way."

"Well my boy, perhaps I spoke too hastily. Words
turn so different, outside the lips! But I should not like
a visitor of ours to think she had fallen among savages.
But here comes your supper at last; and small thanks to

Rosie. Why at her time of life, I should have been too proud to serve my only brother, hand and foot. But I must just run back, and get my young lady tucked up. High time for her to be in bed again. Her brother has sent her box full of things, and so we shall be able to get her out a bit to-morrow, if the weather permits, and Dr. Gronow."

Dr. Gronow permitted, and so did the weather. Can any man remember when he was stopped from making a fool of himself by the weather, or encouraged in any wisdom by it? How many a youth under vast umbrella, warranted to shelter two, if their shoulders came nice and close together, with the storm beating on them, and suggesting—but such umbrellas are not made now, fine canopies of whalebone—who would buy them? Who thinks of more than his own top-hat?

Unless he sees a chance of a gold-band round it. And that, to tell the truth, has been very charming always. But here was Frank Gilham, without any thought of that. He knew that Jemmy Fox was a fine young fellow, perhaps a little bit above him in the social scale, and likely to be a wealthy man, some day. But of sweet Christie he knew nothing, except that he wanted to know a great deal.

Therefore he found that the young mare was puffing, and wanted wet bandages, and a day in stable—excess of synovial oil is a serious study. While on the other hand old *Tommy*, as hard and as dry as a brick-bat, was not altogether free from signs of rheumatism, and had scraped up his litter, in a manner that meant something. He put it to his mother, whether they should plough to-day. It might be all right, and the horses were hers. If she thought wise to venture it——

"It is no use trying to persuade me, Frank," Mrs. Gilham answered; "I won't risk it. Your dear father lost a good horse once, although I advised him to the contrary. Under Providence, our first duty is to the faithful and long-suffering creatures, provided by Him for the benefit of mankind. You may try to persuade me, as much as you like. But you don't seem to have got your ploughing trousers on!"

"That is not a question of ten minutes. When I looked out of window, the first thing this morning——"

"Yes to be sure. You were considering the weather. Your dear father did the same; though always wrong about it. But it is useless to argue with me, Frank. I must have my own way, sometimes."

"Very well. Very well, then I won't go. I have got a lot of little things to see to here. Why the rack in the kitchen would soon be rack and ruin."

"Frank, you do say the very cleverest things. And I feel in myself that it never comes from me. Thank God that I have such a dutiful son, though his mind is so superior."

The young man exerted his superior mind upon a very solid breakfast, topped up with honey, gushing limpid from the comb, sweeter than the softest beeswing of the meed of love. Then he sauntered in the mow-yard with his ginger terrier Jack; whom no wedded love could equal, in aptitude to smell a rat. But hay was sweet, and clover sweeter, and the rich deep ricks of wheat—golden piles on silver straddles—showed the glossy stalk, and savoured of the glowing grain within. A man might thrust his arm into the yellow thicket here and there, and fetch the chined and plump ear out, and taste the concrete milkiness.

"Rose told me that I should just see her eat," Frank Gilham meditated; "what a greedy thing to say! Was it because eggs are now so scarce, and Rose wanted all of them for herself? But if she likes good things, I could have this rick of brown wheat threshed to-morrow. The bread is ten times as sweet and toothsome—oh by the by, what teeth she has, like wind-flower buds among roses. Two or three times, her lips just showed them, while she was lying upon that hay. But what are her teeth to compare with her lips? And did anybody ever see such cheeks, even with the pink flown out of them? There's nothing that you could find a flaw in; forehead, hair, and eyes, and nose—though I can't pretend quite that I have seen her eyes yet—merely a sort of a flash in the air, while she was flying over the backrail of the trap. Only there is no denying that they must be like heaven itself, full of Angels. Mother says the sky, but that sounds so common.

So far as that goes, everybody is allowed to look at the sky; but who would care ever to see it again, after a glimpse—Jack, what are you about there? Got into a gin? Well, serves you right for mooning."

"Frank! Frank! Frank!" A loud call rang among the ricks. "Got away smoking again, I'll be bound. I never can understand how it is, he doesn't set every blessed rick on fire."

"Not smoking at all, as it happens. But how frightfully shrill your voice is, Rosie!"

"What a swell we are, to be sure, to-day! And getting quite nervous. Wants cotton wool in his ears, poor dear! But the precious young lady is just coming out. And mother says you should be somewhere handy, in case of her being taken faint. About as likely to faint as I am, I should say. Now mind your P's and Q's, in spite of all your Greek and Latin. You may make your bow, about ten miles off; but not to speak, until spoken to. That's right, flourish your hair up. But you needn't run twenty miles an hour."

On the gravel walk bordered by hollyhocks—now a row of gaunt sceptres without any crowns—the kind Mrs. Gilham was leading her guest, who did not require to be led at all, but was too well-bred to reject the friendly hand. Christie was looking a little delicate, and not quite up to the mark of her usual high spirits; but the man must have been very hard to please, who could find much fault on that score.

"Oh what a beautiful view you have!" she exclaimed, as the sun broke through the mist, spreading Perle valley with a veil of purest pearl. "I had no idea it was such a lovely place. And the house, and the garden, and the glen that slopes away. Why that must be Perlycross tower in the distance, and that tall white house the rectory. Why, there's the bridge with seven lofty arches, and the light shining through them! More light than water, I should say. What on earth induced them to put such a mighty bridge across such a petty river? I dare say they knew best—but just look at the meadows, almost as green as they would be in May! No wonder you get such lovely butter. And the trees down the valley, just in the right places to make the most of themselves, and their neighbour-hood. Why half of them have got their leaves on still, here nearly at the end of November—and such leaves too, gold, red, and amber, straw-colour, cinnamon, and russet!"

"And if you come up to that bench, my dear," replied Mrs. Gilham, as proud as Punch, at the praises of her native vale, "that bench at the top of our little orchard—my poor dear husband had such taste, he could find the proper place for everything—gravel-walk all the way, and nothing but a little spring to cross; why, there you can hear the key-bugle of the *Defiance!* Punctual every day at half-past ten. We always set our kitchen clock by it. The Guard, as soon as he sees our middle chimney, strikes up as loud as ever he can blow, 'Oh the roast-beef of Old England,' or 'To glory we steer,' for the horses to be ready. So some people say; but I happen to know, that it is done entirely to please us. Because we sent cider out every day, when that hot week was, last summer."

"What a grateful man! Oh I must go and hear him. I do think there's nothing like gratitude. By the by, I am not acting up to that. I have never even seen your son, to thank him."

"Oh Miss Fox, it is not fair to him, for any young lady to try to do that. He has no opinion of anything he does; and the last time he saved a young lady's life, he ran away, because—because it wouldn't do to stay. You see, she had been at the very point of drowning, and the people on the bank declared that she came up three times. My son Frank never pulled his coat off—he would have despised himself, if he had stopped to do it—he jumped in, they said it was forty feet high, but there is no bank on the river (except the cliff the church stands on) much over five and twenty. However, in he went, and saved her; and everybody said that she was worth £10,000, but carried away by the current. And from that day to this, we heard nothing more about it; and my son, who has a very beautiful complexion, blushes—oh he blushes so, if he only hears of it!"

"Oh, he is too good, Mrs. Gilham! It is a very great mistake, with the world becoming all so selfish. But I am not the young lady that went with the current. I go against the current, whenever I find any. And your son has had the courage to do the same, in the question of my dear brother. I say what I mean, you must understand, Mrs. Gilham. I am not at all fond of shilly-shally."

"Neither is my son, Miss Fox. Only he thinks so very little of himself. Why there he is! Hard at work as usual. Don't say a syllable of thanks, my dear; if he comes up to pull his hat off. He can stand a cannon-ball; but not to be made much of."

"Won't I though say 'thank you' to him? I am bound to consider myself, and not only his peculiar tendencies. Mr. Frank Gilham, do please to come here, if—I mean supposing you can spare just half-a-minute."

Frank had a fair supply of hard, as well as soft, in his composition. He was five and twenty years old, or close upon it, and able to get a dog out of a trap, in the deepest of his own conditia He quitted his spade—which he had found, by the by, left out all night, though the same is high treason—as if he could scarcely get away from it, and could see nothing so fine as a fat spit of sod. And he kept his eyes full upon Christie's, as if he had seen her before, but was wondering where.

This was the proper thing to do. Though he knew himself to be in no small fright, throughout all this bravery. But there is no monopoly of humbug; though we all do our utmost to establish one.

"Miss Fox, I believe you have seen my son before." The old lady took to the spirit of the moment, with the quickness, in which ladies always take the front. "And my son Frank has had the honour of seeing you."

"And feeling me too—pretty sharp against his chest"— Christie thought within herself, but she only said—"Yes; and it was a happy thing for me."

"Not at all, Miss Fox—a mere casual accident, as the people about here express it. I explained to you, that Frank cannot help himself. Be kind enough not to speak of it."

"That won't do," replied Christie, looking stedfast. "It may do for him, but not for me. Allow me one moment, Mrs. Gilham."

Without more ado, she ran up to Frank Gilham, who

was turning away again towards his work, and gave him both hands, and looked full at him, with the glitter of tears in her deep blue eyes.

"My senses have not quite forsaken me," she said: "and I know whom I have to thank for that: and in all probability for my life as well. It is useless to talk about thanking you, because it is impossible to do it. And even before that I was deeply in your debt, for the very noble way in which you took my brother's part, when everybody else was against him. It was so brave and generous of you."

It was more than she could do, with all her spirit, to prevent two large and liberal tears from obeying the laws of nature; in fact they were not far from obtaining the downright encouragement of a sob, when she thought of her poor brother.

"Well, you are a sweet simple dear!" exclaimed the fine old lady, following suit in the feminine line, and feeling for her pocket-handkerchief. "Frankie should be proud to his dying day, of doing any trifle for such a precious dear. Why don't you say so, Frankie, my son?"

"Simply because my mother has said it so much better for me." He turned away his eyes, in fear of looking thus at Christie, lest they should tell her there was no one else in the world henceforth for them to see.

"Here comes the *Defiance!* Hurrah, hurrah!" shouted Rose, rushing in, for once just at the right moment. "I can hear the horses' hoofs springing up the rise. If you want to know anything about roast beef, you must put on a spurt up the periwinkle walk. Here goes number one. Slow coaches come behind."

"I am not a slow coach. At least I never used to be," cried Christie, setting off in chase.

"Miss Fox, Miss Fox, don't attempt to cross the brook, without my son's hand," Mrs. Gilham called after them; for she could not live the pace. "Oh Rose is wrong as usual—it's 'To glory we steer,' this time."

The obliging guard gave it three times over, as if he had this team also in full view; then he gave the "Roast beef," as the substance of the glory; and really it was finer than a locomotive screech.

Presently Rose heard the cackle of a pullet which had laid, and off she ran to make sure of the result, because there was an old cock sadly addicted to the part that is least golden in the policy of Saturn. So the three who remained sat upon the bench and talked, with the cider apples piled in pink and yellow cones before them, and the mossy branches sparkling (like a weeping smile) above, and the sun glancing shyly, under eaves and along hedgerows, like the man denied the privilege of looking at the horse. By this light however Frank Gilham contrived to get many a peep round his mother's bonnet—which being of the latest fashion was bigger than a well-kept hedgerow —at a very lovely object on the other side thereof, which had no fear as yet of being stolen.

Miss Fox had fully made up her mind, that (happen what might) she would not say a single word, to sadden her good hostess with the trouble her brother had fallen into, or the difficulties now surrounding him. But ladies are allowed to unmake their minds, especially if it enlarges them ; and finding in the recesses of that long bonnet a most sympathetic pair of ears, all the softer for being " rather hard of hearing," and enriched with wise echoes of threescore years, she also discovered how wrong and unkind it would be, to withhold any heart-matter from them.

"And one of the most dreadful things of all," Christie concluded with a long-drawn sigh, "is that my dear father, who has only this son Jemmy, is now in such a very sad state of health, that if he heard of this it would most likely take him from us. Or if he got over it, one thing is certain, he would never even look at my brother again. Not that he would believe such a wicked thing of him ; but because he would declare that he brought it on himself, by going (against his father's wishes) into this medical business. My father detests it ; I scarcely know why, but have heard that he has good reason. We must keep this from him, whatever it costs us ; even if it keeps poor Jemmy under this cloud for months to come. Luckily father cannot read now very well, and his doctor has ordered him not to read at all ; and mother never looks at a newspaper : and the place being five and thirty miles away, and in another county, there is no great risk, unless some spiteful friend should rush in, to condole with him. That is what I dread to hear of sometimes; though good Dr. Freeborn, who attends him, will prevent any chance of it, if possible. But you see, Mrs. Gilham, how it cripples us. We cannot move boldly and freely, as we ought, and make the thing the topic of the county; as we should by an action of libel for instance, or any strong mode of vindication. I assure you, sometimes I am ready to go wild, and fly out, and do anything. And then I recollect poor father."

"It is a cruel cruel thing, my dear. I never heard of anything resembling it before. That's the very thing that Frank says. From the very first he saw what a shameful thing it was to speak so of Dr. Fox. I believe he has knocked down a big man or two; though I am sure I should be the last to encourage him in that."

"Come, mother, come! Miss Fox, you must not listen to a quarter of what mother says about me. I dare say, you have found that out, long ago."

"If so, it is only natural, and you deserve it;" this Hibernian verdict was delivered with a smile too bright to be eclipsed by a score of hedgerow bonnets; "but there is one thing I should like to ask Mr. Frank Gilham, with his mother's leave; and it is this—how was it that you Mr. Frank, almost alone of all the parish of Perlycross, and without knowing much of my brother at the time, were so certain of his innocence?"

"Because I had looked in his face;" replied Frank, looking likewise into the sister's face, with a gaze of equal certainty.

"That is very noble; Christie said, with a little toss meaning something. "But most people want more to go upon than that."

CHAPTER XX.

DISCUSSION.

Now Mrs. Fox, Doctor Jemmy's mother, was an enthusiastic woman. She was twenty years younger than her husband, and felt herself fifty years his senior (when genuine wisdom was needed) and yet in enterprise fifty years junior. The

velocity of her brain had been too much for the roots of
her hair, as she herself maintained, and her best friends
could not deny it. Except that the top of her head was
snow-white, and she utterly scorned to disguise it, she
looked little older than her daughter Christie, in some
ways; though happily tougher. She was not too fat, and
she was not too thin; which is more than most people can
tell themselves, at the age of eight and forty. Into this
ancient County race, which had strengthened its roots by
banking, she had brought a fine vein of Devonian blood,
very clearing for their complexions. She had shown some
disdain for mercantile views; until she began to know
better, when her father, and others of her landed lineage
slipped down the hilltop into bankruptcy, without any
Free-trade, or even tenants' superior rights, to excuse them.
Then she perceived that mercantile views are the only ones
left to ensure a quiet man a fair prospect from his own
front windows. She encouraged her husband to cherish
the Bank, which at one time she had derided; and she
quite agreed with him, that no advances could save her
own relations in their march downhill.

The elder James Fox, who like his father had refused a
title—for although they were not Quakers now, they held
to their old simplicity—Mr. James Fox of Foxden was a
fine sample of the unmixed Englishman. He had never
owed a penny of his large fortune to any unworthy trick of
trade, or even to lucky gambling in stocks, or bitter mort-
gages. Many people called him stubborn, and they were
welcome to take that view of it. In business that opinion
served him well, and saved a lot of useless trouble. But
he himself knew well, and his wife knew even better, that
though he would never budge an inch, for claim, or threat,
or lawsuit, there was no man who gave a longer ell, when
drawn out by mercy, or even gentle equity.

But in the full vigour of his faculties, mental if not
bodily—and the latter had not yet failed him much—that
mysterious blow descended, which no human science can
avert, relieve, or even to its own content explain. One
moment he was robust and active, quick with the pulse of
busy life, strong with the powers of insight, foresight,
discrimination, promptitude—another moment, and all was

gone. Only a numb lump remained, livid, pallid, deaf and
dumb, sightless, breathless (beyond a wheezy snore) incapable even of a dream or moan. And knowing all these
things, men are proud !

His strong heart, and firm brain, bore him through; or
rather they gradually shored him up; a fabric still upon
the sands of time, but waiting only for the next tidal
wave.

Now the greatest physician, or metaphysician, that ever
came into the world, can tell us no more than an embryo
could, what the relics of the mind will be in such a case,
or how far in keeping with its former self. Thoroughly
pious men have turned blasphemers; very hard swearers
have taken to sweet hymns; tempers have been changed
from diabolical to angelic; but the change more often has
been the other way. Happily for himself, and all about
him, this fine old man was weakened only, and not
perverted from his former healthful self. His memory
was deranged, in veins and fibres, like an ostrich-plume
draggled in a gale of wind and rain; but he knew his old
friends, and the favoured of his heart, and before and
above all, his faithful wife. He had fallen from his pride,
with the lapse of other powers; and to those who had
known him in his stronger days, his present gentleness
was touching, and his gratitude for trifles affecting; but
notwithstanding that, he was sometimes more obstinate
than ever.

"I wonder why Chris stays away so long;" he said as
he sat one fine day upon the terrace, for he was ordered to
stay out of doors as much as possible, and his wife as usual
sat beside him. "She is gone to nurse Jemmy through a
very heavy cold, as I understood you to say, my dear.
But my memory is not always quite clear now. But it
must be some days since I heard that; and I miss little
Chrissy with her cheerful face. You are enough of course,
my dear Mary, and I very seldom think much of anybody
else. Still I long sometimes to see my little Chrissy."

"To be sure; and so do I. The house seems very sad
without her;" replied Mrs. Fox, as if it could be merry
now. "We won't give her more than another day or two.
But we must remember, dear, how differently poor Jemmy

is placed from what we are in this comfortable house. Only one old rough Devonshire servant; and everybody knows what they are—a woman who would warm his bed, as likely as not, with a frying-pan, and make his tea out of the rain water boiler."

" He has no one to thank for it but himself."

After this delivery, the father of the family shut his mouth, which he still could do as well as ever, though one of his arms hung helpless.

" And I did hear that there was some disturbance there, something I think about the clergyman, who is a great friend of Jemmy's ;" Mrs. Fox spoke this in all good faith, for Dr. Freeborn had put this turn upon a story, which had found its way into the house; "and you know what our Chris is, when she thinks any one attacks the Church— you may trust her for flying to the rescue. At any rate so far as money goes."

" And money goes a long way, in matters eccles—you know what I mean—I can't pronounce those long words now. Christie is too generous with her good aunt's money. The trustees let her have it much too freely. I should not be much surprised if they get a hundred pounds out of Chris, at—let me see, what is the place called—something like a brooch or trinket. Ah there, it's gone again ! "

" You must not talk so much, my dear ; and above all you must not try your memory. It is wonderfully good, I am sure, thank God ! I only wish mine was half as good."

Now Mrs. Fox was quite aware that she had an exceedingly fine memory.

" Well, never mind ; " resumed the invalid, after roving among all the jewels he could think of. " But I should be very glad before I die, to see Chrissy married to Sir Henry Haggerstone, a man of the highest character, as well as a very fine estate. Has he said anything to you about it lately ? "

" No, father ; " Mrs. Fox always called him " father," when a family council was toward ; "how could he while you—I mean why should he be in such a hurry ? Christie is a girl who would only turn against him, if he were to worry her. She is a very odd child ; she is not like her mother. A little spice of somebody else, I think, who has always contrived to have his own way. And she hates the idea of being a stepmother; though there are only two little girls after all, and Chrissy's son would be the heir of course. She says it is so frightfully unromantic, to marry a wealthy widower. But talk of the—I am sure I beg his pardon—but here comes Sir Henry himself, with Dr. Freeborn. You had better see the Doctor first, my dear, while I take a turn with Sir Henry."

This gentleman was, as Mr. Fox had pronounced, of the very highest character, wealthy moreover, and of pleasant aspect, and temper mild and equable. Neither was his age yet gone fatally amiss; though a few years off would have improved it, as concerning Christie; for he was not more than thirty-three, or thirty-four, and scarcely looked that, for he led a healthful life. But his great fault was, that he had no great fault; nothing extreme in any way about him, not even contempt for "extreme people." He had been at Oxford, and had learned, by reading for a first class in classics (which he got) that virtue is a "habit of fore-choice, being in the mean that concerns ourselves, defined by reason, and according as the man of perception would define it."

Sir Henry was a man of very clear perception, and his nature was well-fitted to come into definitions. He never did much thinking of his own; for deeper minds had saved him all that trouble, and he was quite content to accept the results. There was nobody who could lead him much, and no one who could not lead him a little, when he saw a clear path to go along. This was not altogether the man to enchant romantic maidenhood.

Christie cared for him about as much as she would for a habit, that was in a mean. Not that he was in any way a prig, or laid down the law to any one. He had not kept up his Classics, for he had no real love for them; and in those days, a man might get a first at Oxford, who could scarcely scan a Latin hexameter, if he were exceptionally strong in "Science"—then meaning Philosophy, before the age of "Stinks." To none of these subjects did Christie pay heed—she did not care for the man; and that was all about it.

"You are quite right, Mrs. Fox. I think exactly as you do;" this gentleman was replying to the lady of the house, as they walked upon the gentle slope towards the flower-garden; "there are no real Whigs, in the present headlong days. Men, like your husband, and myself, who have fancied ourselves in the happy mean, are either swept aside, or carried down the deluge. For the moment there seems to be a slight reaction; but it will not last. The rush will only be more headlong. And in private life it is just the same. Individual rights are to be no more respected. Everything belongs to everybody. I will tell you a little thing that happened to myself, just as a specimen of the spirit of the age. A year or two ago, I bought some old manorial rights, in a thinly peopled part of Devonshire; in fact at the Western end of the great Blackdown Range, a barren, furzy, flinty sort of place. By the by, not many miles away from the place where your son has gone to live—Perlycross. I only bought the manor to oblige a friend, who wanted a little ready money, and to go there now and then perhaps for a little rough shooting, for the country is beautiful, and the air very fine. Well, the manorial rights included some quarries, or pits, or excavations of some sort, where those rough scythe-stones are dug, such as you see lying on that lawn. The land itself was actually part of the manor, from a time beyond memory or record; but it seems as if strangers had been allowed to settle on the hillside, and work these ancient quarries, and sell the produce on their own account, only paying a small royalty to the manor, every Martinmas, or about that time; not so much for the value of the money, (though it would perhaps be considerable under a proper computation) but as an acknowledgment of the ownership of the manor. But I fear I am tiring you."

"Not at all, Sir Henry; I like any story of that sort. Our laws are so very very queer."

"Sometimes they are. Well, my friend had not deceived me. He said that this Whetstone money was very hard to get, and was so trifling that he had let it go sometimes, when the people objected to paying it, as they did after any bad season. Last Martinmas, the matter slipped my

memory, through domestic trouble. But this year, as the
day approached, I sent orders to a man, (a rough sort of
Game-keeper, who lives near there, and looks after the
shooting and gravel and peat,) to give notice at the pits
that I meant to have my money. A very close corporation they seem to have established, and have made their
encroachments uncommonly secure, being quite distinct in
race, and character, dialect, and even dress, I believe, from
the settled people round them. Now what message do you
think they sent me ? "

"Something very insolent, I have no doubt." Mrs. Fox
did not call herself even a Whig, but a downright determined Tory.

"This was it—my man got the schoolmaster to put it
into writing, and I happen to have it in my pocket. 'Not
a penny will we pay this year. But if you like to come
yourself, and take a turn at the flemmer'—something they
use for getting out the stone—'we won't charge you
anything for your footing.' "

"Your footing on your own land ! Well, that is very
fine. What do you mean to do, Sir Henry ? "

"Grin, and bear it, I suppose, Mrs. Fox. You know
what the tendency of the time is, even in the Law-courts.
And of course, all the Press would be down upon me, as a
monster of oppression, if I ventured to assert my rights.
And though I am out of the House ever since the 'Broom
of Reform' (as the papers call it) swept my two little seats
away, I might like to stand again some day ; and what a
Whetstone this would be for my adversaries ! And I hear
that these people are not a bad lot, rough, and uncivilized,
and wonderfully jealous over the 'rights' they have robbed
me of ; but among themselves faithful, and honest, and
quiet, and sober, which is the strangest thing of all in
England. As for their message, why they speak out
plainly, and look upon their offer as a great concession to
me. And we in this more enlightened part must allow for
the manners of that neighbourhood. In fact this is such a
perfect trifle, after what they have been doing at Perlycross.
If I were a magistrate about there——"

"At Perlycross ! . What do you mean? Some little
matter about the clergyman? I want to know all about

that, Sir Henry. It seems so strange, that Christie never mentioned it."

Sir Henry perceived that he had "put his foot in it." Dr. Freeborn had warned him that the "Sacrilege in Devon"—as the Somerset papers had begun to call it—must be kept most carefully from the knowledge of his patient, and from that of the lady also; for there was no saying how she might take it. And now Mrs. Fox could not fail to find out everything. He was ready to bite off his tongue, as ladies put it.

"Oh, ah—I was thinking of something—which had better not be referred to perhaps. Not quite fit to be discussed, when one has the honour of being with ladies. But about those very extraordinary people. I have heard some things that are highly interesting, things that I am certain you would like to hear——"

"Not half so much as I want to hear the story about the parish, where my son lives, and my daughter is staying, and will not come back— for some reason which we cannot make out. I must insist, Sir Henry, upon hearing all that you know. I am not a young woman, and know the world pretty well by this time. You will not offend me, by anything you say; but you will, by anything you hide."

Sir Henry Haggerstone looked about, and saw that he was in for it. The elderly lady—as some might call her—looked at him, with that pretty doubt, which ladies so thoroughly understand how to show, and intend to be understood without expression. The gentleman glanced at her; he had no moustache to stroke—for only cavalry officers, and cads of the most pretentious upturn, as yet wore ginger hackles—a relief still to come in a downier age.

'My dear Mrs. Fox, there is nothing improper, from a lady's point of view, I mean, in the very sad occurrence at Perlycross. It is a question for the local authorities. And not one for me to meddle with."

"Then why did you speak of it? Either tell me all; or say that you won't, and leave me to find out." The lady had the gentleman, the Tory had the temporizer, on the nail.

"We are nothing in your hands;" he murmured, and

N 2

with perfect truth; for when the question comes to the pulling out of truth, what chance has a man against a clever woman, ten times as quick as he is, and piercing every glance?

"I am truly sorry that it has come to this;" Mrs. Fox did not sympathise with his regret, but nodded, as if to say—"no cure now for that; for my part, I am rather glad." "It was simply through terror of distressing you, that all your best friends have combined, as I may say, at least have thought it wiser——"

"Then they made a great mistake. And I am not at all thankful to any of them. Let me sit down here. And now for all this frightful wonder! Is Jemmy dead? Let me have the worst at once."

This was a sudden relief to Sir Henry, enabling him to offer immediate comfort, and to whisper—"how could you imagine such a thing?"

"No my dear madam," he continued, having now the upper hand, and hers beneath it, "I have the pleasure of assuring you that your noble son is in the very best of health, and improving by his admirable knowledge of medicine the health of all around him. It is acknowledged that he has advanced the highest interests of the Profession."

"That he was sure to do, Sir Henry. And he has a copy of my dear grandmother's recipe for the pounded cherry-stone elixir."

"With all the resources of modern science added, and his own trained insight in their application. But the worst of it is, that these leading intellects, as you must have experienced long ago, can never escape a sad amount of narrow professional jealousy. Your son must have fallen among those heavy-witted Devonshire doctors, like a thunderbolt—or worse, a phenomenon come to heal their patients *gratis*."

"That would drive them to do anything—to poison him, if they had the courage. For every one knows how they run up their bills."

Having brought the lady thus to the practical vein, Sir Henry (as gently as possible, and as it were by the quarter drachm) administered the sombre draught he was now bound to exhibit. Jemmy's dear mother took it with a closeness of attention, and critical appreciation, seldom found in the physical recipients in such cases. But to the administrator's great surprise, her indignation was by no means vivid, in the direction anticipated.

"I am heartily glad that I know this at last. I ought to have been told of it long ago;" said Mrs. Fox, looking resolutely at Sir Henry Haggerstone. "A very great mistake, and want of judgment on the part of Dr. Freeborn. What a frightful risk to run—supposing my husband had been told suddenly of this!"

"All has been done for the best, my dear madam. The great anxiety was to keep it from him."

"And who was the proper one, to see to that? I should have thought, his wife and constant nurse. Was it thought impossible that I should show discretion? Clever men always make one great mistake. They believe that no woman can command her tongue. If they had their own only half as well controlled, there would not be a tenth part of the mischief in the world."

"You are quite right there. That is a very great truth, and exceedingly well expressed;" replied Sir Henry, not that he was impressed with it so deeply, but that he wanted to appease the lady. "However, as regards Dr. Freeborn's ideas, I really know very little; no doubt he thought it was for your own good too, not to be burdened at such a time with another great anxiety."

"He has taken too much upon himself. It would have been no great anxiety to me. My son is quite capable of fighting his own battles. And the same orders issued to my son and daughter! At last I can understand poor Christie's letters—why she has been so brief, for fear of losing all self-control, like her mother. Stupid, stupid, clever men! Why there is infinitely less chance now of Mr. Fox ever knowing it. You may tell our sapient doctor that. Perhaps I shall astonish him a little. I'll prove to him that I can control my tongue, by never mentioning the subject to him."

"Excuse me, Mrs. Fox, if I make one or two remarks. May I speak without reserve, as an old friend of the family, and one who has had a great deal to do with criminal—at least I mean to say with public proceedings in this county?"

"To be sure, Sir Henry. I shall be much obliged by any suggestions you may make."

"In the first place then, it is quite impossible to leave your son under this imputation. I can quite understand how he has been impeded in taking any steps for his own vindication, by his sense of duty towards his father and yourself. In that respect, his behaviour has been most admirable. He has absolutely done nothing; not even protested publicly, and challenged any evidence against him, but been quite content to lie at the mercy of any wicked slanderers. And for this there can be no reason but one—that public proceedings would increase the stir, and make it certain that the whole must come to his father's knowledge."

"To be sure, Sir Henry. There can be no other reason." The old friend of the family was surprised at the tone in which Mrs. Fox uttered this opinion.

"Of course not. And so it is all the more incumbent upon his family to clear him. Let me tell you what I should do, if I were his father, in sound health, and able to attend to business. Of course I am too young to speak so" —he had suddenly remembered Christie—"but that you understand; and you also admit that I am not likely to offer advice, unless asked for."

"I beg you particularly to give it. You are a Magistrate of large, if not long, experience. And I know that you are our true friend."

"That you may rely upon, Mrs. Fox. And you know how much I admire your son; for enthusiasm is a rare gift now, and becoming rarer every year, in these days of liberal sentiment. If the case were my own, I should just do this. I should make application at once to the Court of King's Bench, to have the matter sifted. It is no use shilly-shallying with any County Authorities. A Special Commission has been granted in cases less important. But without pressing for that, it is possible to get the whole question investigated by skilled officers from head-quarters. Those who bring the charge should have done it, and probably would have done it, if they had faith in their own case. But they are playing a deeper game ; according at least to my view of the matter. They have laid themselves open to no action. Your son lies helpless, and must 'live it down ;' as people say glibly, who have never had to do it. Is this a thing you mean to allow ?"

"You need scarcely ask me that, Sir Henry. But remember that I know nothing of the particulars, which have been kept so—so amiably from my knowledge."

"Yes. But I know them all—at least so far as they can be gathered from the Devonshire Journals, and these are very careful what they say. In spite of all the enemies who want to keep it going, the whole thing may be brought to a point at once, by applying for a warrant in the Court of King's Bench, with the proper information sworn. They would grant it at once. Your son would appear, and be released of course on bail ; for the case is only one of misdemeanour. Then the proper officers would be sent down, and the real criminals detected."

"A warrant against my Jemmy ! Oh, Sir Henry, you can never mean that."

"Simply as a matter of form, Mrs. Fox. Ask your solicitors. They are the proper people. And they should have been consulted long ago, and would have been, but for this terrible disadvantage. I only suggest the quickest way to bring the matter to an issue. Otherwise the doubt will hang over your son, with his friends and his conscience to support him. And what are these among so many ?"

This was not altogether a counsel of perfection, or even of a very lofty view ; but unhappily we have to contend with a world neither perfect nor very lofty. There was no other hole to be found in the plan, or even to be picked by the ingenuity of a lady. But who that is worthy of that name cannot slip round the corner gracefully, whatever is presented ?

"I thank you so deeply, Sir Henry, for your very kind interest in this strange matter," said Mrs. Fox, looking all gratitude, with a smile that shone through tears ; "and for your perfectly invaluable advice. You see everything so distinctly, and your experience is so precious. To think of my poor boy in such a position ! Oh dear, oh

dear! I really have not the courage to discuss it any
more. But a kind heart like yours will make every
allowance for the feelings of a mother."

Thus was Sir Henry neatly driven from the hall of
council to the carpeted chamber of comfort. But he knew
as well as if the lady had put it into so many words, that
she meant to accept none of his advice. Her reason,
however, for so resolving was far beyond his perception,
simple as it was and natural.

Mrs. Fox had known little of the young doctor's doings,
since he had settled at Perlycross, having never even paid
him a visit there, for her husband was sore upon that
subject. So that she was not acquainted with the depth
of Jemmy's regard for Sir Thomas, and had never dreamed
of his love for Inez; whereas she was strongly and bitterly
impressed with his lifelong ardour for medical research.
The mother felt no indignant yearning for prompt and
skilled inquiry; because she suspected, in the bottom of
her heart, that it would prove her son the criminal.

CHAPTER XXI.

BLACKMARSH.

A long way back among the Blackdown Hills, and in
nobody knows what parish, the land breaks off into a
barren stretch, uncouth, dark, and desolate. Being
neither hill nor valley, slope nor plain, morass nor wood-
land, it has no lesson for the wanderer, except that the
sooner he gets out of it the better. For there is nothing
to gratify him if he be an artist, nothing to interest him if
his tastes are antiquarian, nothing to arouse his ardour,
even though he were that happy and most ardent creature,
a naturalist free from rheumatism. And as for any honest
fellow mainly concerned with bread and butter, his head
will at once go round with fear and with looking over his
shoulders. For it is a lonesome and gruesome place, where
the weather makes no difference; where Nature has not
put her hand, on this part or on that, to leave a mark or

show a preference, but slurred the whole with one black frown of desolate monotony.

That being so, the few and simple dwellers on the moorland around, or in the lowland homesteads, might well be trusted to keep their distance from this dreary solitude. There were tales enough of hapless travellers last seen going in this direction, and never in any other; as well as of spectral forms, low groans, and nightly processions through the air.

Not more than a hundred years ago, there had been a wicked baronet, profane, rapacious, arrogant, blackhearted, foul, and impious. A blessed curate prayed him not to hunt on Holy Friday. He gave the blessed curate taste of whip-thong from his saddle; then blew seven blasts of his horn, to proclaim that he would hunt seven days in every week, put spurs to his black horse, and away. The fox, disturbed on Holy Friday, made for this "Forbidden land;" which no fox had ever done before. For his life he plunged into it, feeling for the moment that nothing could be worse than to be torn in pieces. The hounds stopped, as if they were turned to stone in the fury of their onslaught. The huntsman had been left far behind, having wife and family. But the wicked baronet cracked his whip, blew three blasts on his horn, leaned forward on his horse and gave him the rowel. The hounds in a frenzy threw up their sterns, and all plunged headlong into it. And ever since that, they may be seen (an hour after sun-down, on every Sunday of the season, and any Holy Friday) in full cry scouring through the air, with the wicked baronet after them, lashing his black horse, and blowing his horn, but with no fox in front to excuse them.

These facts have made the Forbidden land, or the Blackmarsh, as some call it, even less desirable than its own complexion shows it. And it is so far from Perly-cross, that any man on foot is tired by the time he gets there, and feels that he has travelled far enough, and in common sense must go home again.

But there was one Perlycrucian now—by domicile, not nativity—of tireless feet, and reckless spirit, too young for family ties, and too impetuous for legends. By this time he was admitted to the freedom of every hedge and ditch in the parish, because he was too quick to be caught, and too young to be prosecuted. "Horatio Peckover" was his name, by usage cut short into "Hopper"; a lad in advance of his period, and the precursor of all "paper-chases."

Like many of those who are great in this line, he was not equally strong in the sedentary uses of that article. Mr. Penniloe found him so far behind, when pen and ink had to be dealt with, that he put him under the fine Roman hand of Sergeant Jakes, the schoolmaster. Jakes was not too richly endowed by a grateful country, for years of heroism; neither was his stipend very gorgeous, for swinging cane in lieu of gun. Sixpence an hour was his figure, for pen-drill of private pupils, and he gladly added Hopper to the meagre awkward-squad.

Soon an alliance of the closest kind was formed; the veteran taking warm interest in the spirited sallies of youth, and the youth with eager thirst imbibing the fine old Peninsular vintage of the brightest ruby, poured forth in the radiance of a yellow tallow candle. For the long school-room was cleared at night of coats, and hats, and green-baize bags, cracked slates, bead-slides, and spelling-books, and all the other accoutrements, and even toys of the youthful Muse; and at seven o'clock Horatio stepped across the road from the rectory, sat down at the master's high black desk, and shouldered arms for the copy-drill. The Sergeant was famed for his flourishes, chiefly of his own invention, and had promised to impart that higher finish, when the fancy capitals were mastered.

"What a whack of time it does take, Sergeant!" cried Hopper, as he dipped his pen, one Friday night. "Not half so bad as Latin though, and there is something to look at afterwards. Capitals almost captured now. Ah, you have taken the capitals of many a country, Sergeant. Halloa! 'Xerxes was conqueror at Marathon,' to-night! Sergeant, are you quite sure of that? I thought it was another fellow, with a longer name—Milly, Tilly, something."

"No, Master Hopper; if it had been, we must have passed him long ago, among the big M's."

"To be sure. What a muff I was, not to think of that!

I beg your pardon, Sergeant. There's scarcely anything you don't know."

" I had that on the highest authority—right elbow more in to your side, sir, if you please—that Xerxes copy was always set by commanding officer at Turry Vardoes—could not tell what to do with the men at night—so many ordered to play at nine-pins, and so many told off to learn roundhand. If it had not been for that, sir, I should never have been equal to my present situation."

" Then it must have been Xerxes, Sergeant. And after all, how can it matter, when it happened so long ago? A blot again? D—n it."

" Master Hopper, I am very sorry, but it is my duty to reprimand you, for the use of profane language. Never permitted, sir, in school-hours. Would you do it, before Mr. Penniloe?"

" I should rather hope not. Wouldn't old Pen stare? And then he'd be down upon me, like the very—capital D. Sergeant, pray excuse me; I only thought of him, without any name. I suppose we may call him 'Old Nick' though, without having to go to him, for doing it. I never could see what the difference was. But, my eye, Sergeant, I expected to see the old chap yesterday, cloven hoof, tail, eyes of fire, and everything!"

" What do you mean, sir? Where was he? Not in Perlycross, I hope." Sergeant Jakes glanced down the long dark room, and then at the pegs where his French sword was hanging.

" No, not here. He daren't come so near the church. But in the place where he lives all day, according to the best authorities. You have heard of Blackmarsh, haven't you? No marsh at all—that's the joke of it—but the queerest place I ever saw in all my life. Criky jimminy, but it is a rum un!"

" You don't mean to say you were there, sir!" The Sergeant took his hand from Hopper's shoulder, and went round to see whether he was joking.

" To be sure I was, as large as life, and twice as natural! Had a holiday, as you know, and got leave off from dinner. Mother Muggridge gave me grub enough to go to Halifax. I had been meaning to go there ever so long, because every-

body seems to funk it so. Why there's nothing there to
be afraid of : though it makes you look about a bit. And
you aren't sorry to come out of it."

"Did you tell Mr. Penniloe, you had been there, Master
Hopper?"

"Sergeant, do you see any green in my eye?" Horatio
dropped his pen, and enlarged the aperture of one eye, in a
style very fashionable just then, but never very elegant.

"No sir, I can't answer fairly that I do. And I don't
believe there ever was much, even when you was a babby."

"Mum's the word, you see then—even to old Muggridge,
or she might be fool enough to let out. But I say, Sergeant,
I've got a little job for you to do. Easy enough. I know
you won't refuse me."

"No sir, that I won't. Anything whatever that lays in
my power, Master Hopper."

"Well, it's only this—just to come with me to-morrow—
half-holiday, you know, and I can get off, plum-duffs—
always plum-duffs on a Saturday, and you should just see
Pike pitching into them—and we'll give the afternoon to
it, and examine Blackmarsh pretty thoroughly."

"Blackmarsh, Master Hopper! The Forbidden land—
where Sir Robert upon his black horse, and forty hounds
in full cry before him, may be seen and heard, sweeping
through the air, like fiends!"

"Oh, that's all my eye, and Betty Martin! Nobody
believes that, I should hope. Why Sergeant, a man who
knows all about Xerxes, and has taken half the capitals in
Europe—oh, I say, Sergeant, come, you are not afraid now,
and a fellow of sixteen, like me, to go there all by myself,
and stop—well, nearly half-an-hour!"

"Afraid! Not I. No certainly not, after mountains,
and forests, and caverns, and deserts. But the distance,
Master Hopper, for a man of my age, and troubled with
rheumatism in the knee-joint."

"Oh, that's all right! I have planned out all that. Of
course I don't expect you to go ten miles an hour. But
Baker Channing's light cart goes, every other Saturday, to
Crooked-post quarry, at the further end of Hagdon, to
fetch back furze enough to keep his oven going, from a
stack he bought there last summer. To-morrow is his day;

and you have no school, you know, after half-past ten or eleven. You ride with old Tucker to the Crooked-post, and come back with him, when he is loaded up. It shan't cost you a farthing. I have got a shilling left, and he shall have it. It is only two miles, or so, from Crooked-post to this end of Blackmarsh; and there you will find me waiting. Come, you can't get out of that."

"But what do you want me there for, sir? Of course, I'd go anywhere you would venture, if I could see any good in it."

"Sergeant, I'll tell you what. You thought a great deal of Sir Thomas Waldron, didn't you?"

"More than of any man that ever lived, or ever will see the light of this wicked world."

"And you didn't like what was done to him, did you?"

"Master Hopper, I tell you what. I'd give ten years off my poor life, if I could find out who did it."

"Then I fancy I have found out something about it. Not much, mind; but still something, and may come to more if we follow it up. And if you come to-morrow, I'll show you what it is. You know that my eyes are pretty sharp, and that I wasn't born yesterday. You know who it was that found 'Little Billy.' And you know who wants to get Fox out of this scrape, because he is a Somerset man, and all that, and doesn't deserve this trouble. And still more, because——"

"Well, Master Hopper, still more, because of what?"

"I don't mind telling you something, Sergeant—you have seen a lot of the world, you know. Because Jemmy Fox has got a deuced pretty sister."

"Oh come, Master Hopper, at your time of life! And not even got into the flourishes!"

"It doesn't matter, Jakes. I may seem rather young to people who don't understand the question. But that is my own business, I should hope. Well, I shall look out for you to-morrow. Two o'clock at the latest."

"But why shouldn't we tell Dr. Fox himself, and get him to come with us? That seems the simplest thing."

"No. There are very good reasons against that. I have found this out; and I mean to stick to it. No one would have dreamed of it, except for me. And I won't

have it spoiled, by every nincompoop poking his nose into
it. Only if we find anything more, and you agree with me
about it, we will tell old Pen, and go by his opinion."

" Very well, sir. It all belongs to you ; as it did to
me, when I was first after Soult's arrival to discover the
advance of the French outposts. You shall have the credit,
though I didn't. Anything more, sir ? The candle is
almost out."

" Sergeant, no more. Unless you could manage—I
mean, unless you should think it wise to bring your fine
old sword with you. You say there is no such piece of
steel——"

" Master Hopper, there is no such piece, unless it was
Lord Wellington's. They say he had one that he could
lean on—not a dress-sword, not flummery, but a real workman—and although he was never a heavy man, a stone and
a half less than I was then, it would make any figure of the
multiplication-table that he chose to call for, under him,
But I mustn't carry arms in these days, Master Hopper. I
shall bring a bit of Spanish oak, and trust in the Lord."

On the following day, the sun was shining pretty well
for the decrepitude of the year. There had been no frost
to speak of, since that first sharp touch about three weeks
back. The air was mild, and a westerly breeze played
with the half ripe pods of gorse, and the brown welting of
the heather. Hopper had brought a long wand of withy,
from the bank of the last brook he had leaped, and he
peeled it with his pocket-knife, and sat (which he seldom
did when he could help it) on a tuft of rush, waiting for
the Sergeant. He stretched his long wiry legs, and counted
the brass buttons on his yellow leathern gaiters, which
came nearly to his fork, and were made fast by narrow
straps to his brace-buttons.

This young man—as he delighted to be called—had not
many grievances, because he ran them off so fast ; but the
two he chiefly dwelt upon, in his few still moments, were
the insufficiency of cash and calf. For the former he was
chiefly indebted to himself, having never cultivated powers
of retention ; for the deficiency of calves, however, nature
was to blame, although she might plead not unfairly that
they were allowed no time to grow. He regarded them

now with unmerited contempt, and slapped them in some indignation, with the supple willow wand. It might well be confessed that they were not very large, as is often the case with long-distance runners ; but for all that they were as hard as nails, and endowed with knobs of muscle, tough and tense as coiled mainspring. In fact there was not a bit of flabby stuff about him ; and his high clear colour, bright eyes, and ready aspect made him very pleasant to behold, though his nose was rather snubby, and his cheek-bones high, and his mouth of too liberal aperture.

"Come along, Sergeant, what a precious time you have taken!" Hopper shouted, as the angular outline of the veteran appeared at last in a gap between two ridges. "Why, we shall scarcely have two hours of good daylight left. And how do you know that Tucker won't go home without you?"

"He knows a bit better than that," replied Jakes, smiling with dark significance. "Master Hopper, I've got three of Tucker's boys in Horseshoe. Tucker is bound to be uncommon civil."

Now the "Horseshoe" was a form in the school at Perlycross especially adapted for corporal applications, snug as a cockpit, and affording no possibility of escape. And what was still better, the boys of that class were in the very prime of age for attracting, as well as appreciating, healthy and vigorous chastisement ; all of them big enough to stand it, none of them big enough to kick, and for the most part newly trouser'd into tempting chubbiness. Truly it might be said, that the parents of playful boys in the "Horseshoe" had given hostages to education.

"But bless my heart—what—what?" continued the ancient soldier, as he followed the rapid steps of Hopper, "why, I don't like the look of this place at all. It looks so weist—as we say about here, so unwholesome, and strange, and ungodly, and—and so timoursome."

"It is ever so much worse further on ; and you can't tell where you are at all. But to make sure of our coming back, if—if there should be nothing to prevent us, I have got this white stick ready, and I am going to fix it on the top of that clump. There now, we shall be able to see that for miles."

"But we are not going miles I hope, Master Hopper. I'm a little too stiff for such a walk as that. You don't know what it is to have a pain in your knee."

"Oh don't I? I come down on it often enough. But I don't know exactly how far we are going. There is nothing to measure distance by. Come along, Sergeant! We'll be just like two flies going into one of your big ink-pots."

"Don't let me lose sight of you, Master Hopper. I mean, don't you lose sight of me. You might want somebody to stand by you. It is the darkest bit of God's earth I ever did see. And yet nothing overhead to darken it. Seems almost to make its own shadow. Good Lord! what was that came by me?"

"Oh, a bat, or an owl, or a big dor-beetle; or it might be a thunder-bolt—just the sort of place for them. But—what a bad place it is for finding things!"

There could scarcely have been a worse one, at least upon dry and unforested land. There was no marsh whatever, so far as they had come, but a dry uneven shingly surface, black as if fire had passed over it. There was no trace however of fire, neither any substance sufficient to hold it, beyond the mere passage of a shallow flame. The blackness that covered the face of the earth, and seemed to stain the air itself, and heavily dim the daylight, was of something unknown upon the breezy hills, or in the clear draught of a valley. It reflected no light, and received no shadow, but lay like the strewing of some approach to quarters undesirable. Probably from this (while unexamined by such men as we have now), the evil repute of the place had arisen, going down generations of mankind, while the stuff at the bottom renewed itself.

This stuff appeared to be the growth of some lanky trailing weed, perhaps some kind of *Persicaria*, but unusually dense and formless, resembling what may be seen sometimes, at the bottom of a dark watercourse, where the river slides without a wrinkle, and trees of thick foliage overhang it. And the same spread of life, that is more like death, may be seen where leagues of laver strew the foreshore of an Atlantic coast, when the spring-tides are out, and the winds gone low.

"By George, here we are at last. Thought I should

never have made it out, in the thick of this blessed cobobbery," shouted Hopper, stopping short and beckoning; "now, Sergeant, what do you say to that? Queer thing, just here, isn't it?"

The veteran's eyes, confused and weary with the long monotony, were dazzled by sudden contrast. Hitherto the dreary surface, uniform and trackless, had offered only heavy plodding, jarred by the jerk of a hidden stone sometimes, but never elastic. All the boundary-beaters of the parish, or even a regiment of cavalry, might have passed throughout, and left no trace upon the padded cumber. But here a glaring stripe of silver sand broke through the blackness, intensely white by contrast, though not to be seen a few yards off, because sunk below the level. Like a crack of the ground from earthquake, it ran across from right to left, and beyond it all was black again.

The ancient soldier glanced around, to be sure that no surprise was meant; and then with his big stick tried the substance of the white material. With one long stride he could have reached the other side, but the caution of perilous days awoke.

"Oh there's nothing in that, and it is firm enough. But look here;" said his young companion, "this is what floors me altogether."

He pointed to a place where two deep tracks, as of narrow wheels, crossed the white opening; and between them were three little pits about the size and depth of a gallon saucepan. The wheel-tracks swerved to the left, as if with a jerk to get out of the sandy hollow, and one of the three footprints was deeper and larger than the other two.

"Truly this is the doing of the arch-enemy of mankind himself." Sergeant Jakes spoke solemnly, and yet not very slowly; for he longed to make off with promptitude.

"The doing, more likely, of those big thieves who couldn't let your Colonel rest in his grave. Do you mean to turn tail upon them, Sergeant Jakes?"

"May the Lord turn His back upon me, if I do!" The veteran's colour returned to his face, and all thoughts of flight departed. "I would go to the ends of the world, Master Hopper, after any living man; but not after Satan."

"The Devil was in them. No doubt about that. But he made them do it for Him. Does Old Nick carry whipcord? You see how that was, don't you?"

The youth leaped across, and brought back the lash of a whip which he had concealed there. "Plain as a pikestaff, Sergeant. When the wheels plunged into this soft stuff, the driver must have lashed like fury, to make him spring the cart out again. Off came the old lash, and here it is. But wait a minute. I've got something more to show you, that spots the villains pretty plain."

"Well, sir," said Jakes, regarding Hopper with no small admiration, "you deserve your stripes for this. Such a bright young gent shouldn't be thrown away in the Church. I was just going to say—'how can we tell they did it?' Though none but thundering rogues would come here. Nothing can be clearer than that, I take it."

"Then you, and I, are thundering rogues. Got you there, Sergeant; by gum, I did! Now come on a few steps further."

They stepped out boldly, having far less fear of human than of superhuman agency; though better had they met Apollyon perhaps, than the wild men they were tracing. Within less than a furlong, they reached an opening where the smother of the black weeds fell away, and an open track was left once more. Here the cart-wheels could be traced distinctly, and at one spot something far more convincing. In the middle of the track a patch of firm blue clay arose above the surface, for a distance of perhaps some fifty yards; and on it were frequent impressions of the hoofs of a large horse, moving slowly. And of these impressions one (repeated four or five times, very clearly) was that of the near fore-foot, distinctly showing a broken shoe, and the very slope and jag of the fracture.

"What do you think of that now, Sergeant?" asked Hopper, as he danced in triumph, but took good care not to dance upon the clay. "They call me a hedger and ditcher, don't they? Well, I think I am a tracker too."

"Master Hopper, to my mind, you are an uncommonly remarkable young gent. The multiplication-table may not be strongly in your line, sir. But you can put two and two together, and no fear to jump on top of them."

"Oh, but the bad luck of it, Sergeant! The good luck for them, and the shocking luck for me. I never came to old Pen's shop, you see, till a day or two after that wicked job was over. And then it took me a fortnight, or more, to get up the lay of the country, and all that. And I was out of condition for three days, with a blessed example in the Eton Grammar. *Percontatorem fugito*, that frightened me no end, and threw me off the hooks. But I fancy, I am on the right hook now."

"That you are, sir, and no mistake. And a braver young man never came into a regiment, even in Sir Arthur's time. Sir, you must pitch away copy-books. Education is all very fine for those who can't do no better. But it spoils a young man, with higher gifts."

"Don't say a good word of me, till you know all," replied the candid Hopper. "I thought that I was a pretty plucky fellow, because I was all by myself, you understand, and I knew that no fellow could catch me, in a run across the open. But I'll show you where I was stodged off; and it has been on my conscience ever since. Just come to that place, where the ground breaks off."

He led the way along a gentle slope, while the light began to fail behind them, until they stood upon the brink of a steep descent, with a sharp rise upon the other side. It was like the back-way to the bottom of a lime-kiln, but there was no lime for many leagues around. The track of cart-wheels was very manifest, and the bottom was dark with the approach of night.

"My turn, Master Hopper, to go first now. No wife, or family, and nought to leave behind." With these words spoken in a whisper, the Sergeant (who had felt much self-reproach, at the superior courage of a peaceful generation) began to go stiffly down the dark incline, waving his hand for the other to wait there.

"In for a penny, in for a pound. I can kick like winkin', though I can't fight much." With these words, the gallant Hopper followed, slowing his quick steps to the heavier march in front.

When they came to the bottom, they found a level space, with room enough to turn a horse and cart. It was getting very dusky where they stood, with the grim sides gathering

round them, and not a tree or bush to give any sign of life,
but the fringe of the dominant black weed, like heavy
brows, shagging the outlook. But on the left hand, where
the steep fell back, was the mouth as of a cave scooped
roughly. Within it, all was black with gloom, and the low
narrow entrance showed little hospitality.

"I don't care a d—n," said Sergeant Jakes, forgetful of
school discipline; "if there's any scoundrel there, I'll drag
him out. If it's old Colonel's bones—well I'm not afraid
of them." There remained just light enough to show that
the cart had been backed up to the entrance.

"Where you go, I go;" replied the dauntless Hopper;
and into it they plunged, with their hearts beating high,
but their spirit on fire for anything.

The sound of their steps, as they passed into the darkness,
echoed the emptiness of the place. There was nothing to
be felt, except rugged flinty sides, and the damp chill which
gathered in their hair; and in the middle, a slab of broken
stone, over which they stumbled into one another's arms.
They had no means of striking a light; but as their eyes
grew accustomed to the gloom, they assured themselves that
there was nothing more to learn, unless it might be from
some small object on the floor. There seemed to be no
shelves, no sort of fixture, no recesses; only the bare and
unoccupied cave.

"I tell you what," said Sergeant Jakes, as they stood in
the open air again; "this has been a smuggler's store in
the war-time; a natural cave, improved no doubt. What
we thought to find is gone further on, I fear. Too late,
Master Hopper, to do any more to-day, and perhaps too
late to do any more at all. But we must come again with
a light, if possible on Monday."

"Well, one thing we have proved—that the villains, whoever they were, must have come from up the country; perhaps
as far off as the Mendip Hills. But keep it to yourself, till
we have settled what to do. Not a word to Tucker, or the
news will be all over Perlycross to-night. Come back to the
hoof-marks, and I'll take a copy. If we could only find the
impressions of the men's feet too! You see after all, that
Joe Crang spoke the truth. And it was the discovery of his
'Little Billy' that led me on in this direction."

There was light enough still, when they came back to the clay-patch, to make a rough tracing of the broken shoe, on the paper in which the youth had brought his bread and bacon; and even that great steeple-chaser was glad to go home in company, and upon a truss of furze, with a flour-sack to shield him from the stubs and prickles.

CHAPTER XXII.

FIRESHIP AND GALLEON.

MEANWHILE, the fair Christie was recovering nerve so fast, and established in such bouncing health again, by the red-wheat bread of White Post Farm, that nothing less would satisfy her than to beard—if the metaphor applies to ladies—the lion in the den, the arch-accuser, in the very court of judgment. In a word, she would not rest until she stood face to face with Lady Waldron. She had thought of it often, and became quite eager in that determination, when her brother related to her what had passed, in his interview with Miss Waldron.

Truly it was an enterprise of great pith, for a fair young English girl, to confront the dark majestic foreign lady, stately, arrogant, imperious, and above all, embittered with a cruel wrong, fierce, malignant, rancorous. But for all that, Christie was resolved to do it; though perfectly aware that the Spanish lady would never be "at home" to her, if she could help it.

For this reason, and this alone, as she positively assured herself, did Miss Fox make so long a stay with Mrs. Gilham, the while she was quite well enough to go back to Old Barn, and the path of duty led her to her brother's side. But let her once return to that side, and all hope would be lost of arranging an encounter with the slanderer; inasmuch as Dr. Jemmy would most sternly interdict it. Her good hostess, all the while, was only too glad to keep her; and so was another important member of the quiet household; and even the flippant Rosie was delighted to have such patterns. For Miss Fox had sent for a large supply of dresses, all the way to Foxden, by the key-bugleman of the

Defiance; because it would save such a vast amount in carriage, while one was so near the Great Western road. " I can't understand it," protested Doctor Jemmy. "As if men ever could ! " replied the young lady.

However, the sweetest slice of sugar-cane must have empty pores too soon, and the last drop of honey drains out of the comb, and the silver voice of the flute expires, and the petals of the fairest rose must flag. All these ideas (which have been repeated, or repeated themselves, for some thousands of years) were present for the first time in all existence—according to his conviction—in the mind of an exalted, yet depressed, young farmer, one fine Monday morning. Miss Fox had received her very last despatch, to the tune of "Roast beef," that morning, and sad to say she had not cut the string, though her pretty fingers flirted with it.

"My dear," said Mrs. Gilham, longing much to see within, inasmuch as she still had a tender heart for dainty tint, and true elegance of tone, "if you wish to save the string—fine whipcord every inch of it—Frank has a picker in the six-bladed knife his Godfather Farrant gave him, that will undo any knot that was ever tied by Samson." Upon him, she meant perhaps; however the result is quite the same.

"No, thank you," answered Christie, with a melancholy glance ; "it had better be put in my trunk, as it is. What induced them to send it, when I'm just going away ? "

"Going away ! Next week, my dear, you may begin to think about it."

"To-morrow, I must go. I am as well as ever. Better a great deal, I ought to say. What did Dr. Gronow say on Saturday ? And I came down here ; not to enjoy myself, but to keep up the spirits of my poor dear brother."

"Why his spirits are fine, Miss Fox. I only wish my poor dear Frank had a quarter of them. Last night I am sure—and a Sunday too, when you and my son were gone to church——"

"To the little church close by, you mean, with Mrs. Coombes and Mary; because the sermon in the morning had felt so—so edifying."

"Yes to be sure. But when your brother came in, and

was surprised not to find you with us, you know; his conversation—oh dear, oh dear, rather worldly-minded I must confess, bearing in mind what day it was—but he and Rose they kept it up together, for the tip of her tongue is fit for anybody's ear-ring, as the ancient saying goes,—laughing, Miss Fox, and carrying on, till, although I was rather put out about it, and would have stopped any one but a visitor, I was absolutely compelled, I assure you, to pull out my pocket-handkerchief. Oh, I don't think, there need be much fear about Doctor Jemmy's spirits!"

"But don't you think, Mrs. Gilham, it is chiefly his pride that supports him? We do the same sort of thing sometimes. We go into the opposite extreme, and talk and laugh, as if we were in the highest spirits,—when we—when we don't want to let somebody know that we care what he thinks."

"Oh, you have learned that, have you, my dear?" The old lady looked at her, with some surprise. "Well, well! Happy will be the man that you do it for."

Christie felt that she was blushing, and yet could not help giving one sharp glance at her simple hostess. And it would have gone hard with Frank Gilham's chances, if the maiden had spied any special meaning in the eyes of his dear mother. But the elderly lady gazed benignant, reflecting softly upon the time when she had been put to those disguises of the early maidenhood; which are but the face, with its first bloom upon it. For the plain truth was, that she did not wish her son to fall in love, for some ten years yet, at the age that had suited his father. And as for Miss Fox, half a glimpse at her parcels would show her entire unfitness.

"I shall never do it for any man," said Christie, in scorn of her own suggestion; "if I am anything, I am straightforward. And if ever I care for any man, I shall give him my hand, and tell him so. Not, of course, till I know that he is gone upon me. But now I want to do a crafty thing. And money can do almost anything—except in love, Mrs. Gilham. I would not do it without your knowledge; for that would be a very mean return for all your kindness to me. I have made up my mind to see Lady Waldron, and tell her just what I think of her."

"My dear, Lady Waldron is nothing to me. The
Gilhams have held their own land, from the time of cross-
bows and battle-axes. Besides our own, we rent about fifty
acres of the outside of the Waldron property. But if they
can get more for it, let them do so. Everybody loved poor
Sir Thomas; and it was a pleasure to have to deal with
him. But there is no such feeling about her ladyship;
noble enough to look at, but best to deal with at a
distance."

"Well, I mean to see her at close quarters. She has
behaved shamefully to my brother. And who is she to
frighten me? She is at the bottom of all these wicked,
wretched falsehoods, that go about. And she would not
even see him, to let him speak up for truth and justice. I
call that mean, and low, and nasty. Of course the subject
is horrible to her; and perhaps,—well, perhaps I should
have done the same. But for all that, I mean to see her;
for I love fair play; and this is foul play."

"What a spirit you have, my dear! I should never
have thought it was in your gentle face. But you are in
the right. And if I can help you—that is, if you are equal
to it——"

"I am more than equal to it, my dear friend. What is
there to fear, with the truth against black falsehoods?"

Mrs. Gilham turned her wedding-ring upon her "marriage-
finger"—a thing she never failed to do, when her heart was
busy with the bygone days. Then she looked earnestly at
her guest, and saw that the point to be considered was—
not shall we attempt it, but how shall it be done?

"Your mind is entirely set upon it. And therefore we
will do our best;" she promised. "But it cannot be
managed in a moment. Will you allow me to consult my
son? It seems like attacking a house almost. But I
suppose it is fair, in a case like this."

"Perfectly fair. Indoors it must be, as there is no other
chance. A thief must be caught inside a house, when he
will not come out of it. And a person is no better than a
thief, who locks her doors against justice."

When Frank was consulted, he was much against the
scheme; but his opposition was met more briefly than his
mother's had been.

"Done it shall be ; and if you will not help, it shall be done without you "—was the attitude taken, not quite in words ; but so that there was no mistaking it. Then he changed sides suddenly, confuted his own reasoning, and entered into the plan quite warmly ; especially when it was conceded that he might be near the house, if he thought proper, in case of anything too violent, or carried beyond what English ladies could be expected to endure. For as all agreed, there was hardly any saying what an arrogant foreigner might not attempt.

"I am quite aware that it will cost a large amount of bribery," said Christie, with a smile which proved her faith in her own powers in that line ; "will ten pounds do it, Mr. Frank, should you suppose ? "

Though far gone in that brilliant and gloomy, nadir and zenith, tropical and arctic, condition of the human mind, called love, Frank Gilham was of English nature ; which, though torn up by the roots, ceases not to stick fast to the main chance. And so much the nobler on his part was this, because the money was not his, nor ever likely so to be.

"I think that three pounds ought to do it, or even fifty shillings," he replied, with an estimate perhaps too low of the worth of the British domestic. "If we could choose a day when old Binstock is off duty, it would save the biggest tip of all. And it would not matter what he thought afterwards, though doubtless he would be in a fury."

"Oh, I won't do it. I don't think I can do it. It does seem so nasty, and underhanded."

Coming now to the practical part, Miss Fox was suddenly struck with the objections.

"My dear, I am very glad that you have come to see it in such a proper light ;" cried Mrs. Gilham a little prematurely, while her son nodded very sagely, ready to say "Amen" to either side, according to the final jump of the vacillating reasoner.

"No, but I won't then. I won't see it so. When people behave most improperly to you, are you bound to stand upon propriety with them ? Just answer me that, if you can, Mrs. Gilham. My mind is quite settled by that consideration. I'll go in for it wholesale, Binstock and all, if he means a five-pound note for every stripe in his waist-coat."

"Mr. Binstock is much too grand to wear a striped waistcoat;" said Frank with the gravity of one who understands his subject. But he goes to see his parents every Wednesday. And he will not be wronged in reality, for it will be worth all that to him, for the rise he will get by his absence."

"Binstock's parents! Why he must be over sixty!" exclaimed Frank's mother in amazement. She had greatly undervalued her son's knowledge.

"They are both in the poorhouse at Pumpington, the father eighty-five and the mother eighty-two. They married too early in life," said Frank, "and each of their fifteen children leaves the duty of supporting them to the other fourteen. Our Binstock is the most filial of the whole, for he takes his parents two ounces of tobacco every Wednesday."

"The inhuman old miser!" cried Miss Fox. "He shall never have two pence out of me. That settles it. Mr. Frank, try for Wednesday."

"Well, Frank, you puzzle me altogether," said Mrs. Gilham with some annoyance. "To think of your knowing all those things, and never telling your own mother!"

"I never talk of my neighbour's affairs, until they become my own business." Frank pulled up his collars, and Christie said to herself that his mind was very large. "But don't run away with the idea, mother, that I ever pry into such small matters. I know them by the merest accident. You know that the gamekeeper offers me a day or two when the woodcocks come in; and Batts detests old Binstock. But he is on the very best terms with Charles, and Bob, and Tamar Haddon. Through them I can manage it perhaps for Wednesday, if Miss Fox thinks fit to entrust me with the matter."

It happened that Lady Waldron held an important council with Mr. Webber, on the following Wednesday. She had long begun to feel the helplessness, and sad disadvantages of her position, as a foreigner who had never even tried to understand the Country in which she lived, or to make friends of any of the people round her. And this left her so much the more at the mercy of that dawdling old solicitor.

"Oh that I could only find my dear brother!" was the constant cry of her sorrow, and her wrath. "I wonder that he does not rush to help me. He would have done so long ago, if he had only known of this."

"No reply, no reply yet?" she asked, after listening, with patience that surprised herself, to the lawyer's long details of nothing, and excellent reasons for doing still less. "Are you certain that you have had my demand, my challenge, my supplication to my only brother entered in all the Spanish journals, the titles of which I supplied to you? And entered in places conspicuous?"

"In every one of them, madam, with instructions that all replies should be sent to the office of the paper, and then direct to you. Therefore you would receive them, and not our firm. Shall we try in any other country?"

"Yes, oh yes! That is very good indeed. I was thinking of that only yesterday. My brother has much love for Paris sometimes, whenever he is in good—in affluence, as your expression is. For I have not concealed from you, Mr. Webber, that although of the very first families of Spain, the Count is not always—through caprice of fortune, his resources are disposed to rise and fall. You should there-fore try Paris, and Lyons, and Marseilles. It is not in my power to present the names of the principal journals. But they can be discovered, even in this country."

Mr. Webber was often hard put to it, by the lady's calm assumption that barbarism is the leading characteristic of an Englishman. For Theodore Webber was no time-server; only bound by his duty to the firm, and his sense of loyal service to a client of lofty memory. And he knew that he could take the lead of any English lady, because of her knowledge of his character, and the way in which he pro-nounced it. But with this Spanish lady, all his really solid manner, and true English style were thrown away.

"Even in this country, madam, we know the names of the less enlightened Journals of the Continent. They are hard to read because of the miserable paper they are printed on; but my younger son has the gift of languages, and nothing is too outlandish for him. That also shall be

attended to. And now about this question that arises
between yourself and Mr. Penniloe?"

"I will not yield. I will sign nothing. Everything
shall be as my husband did intend. And who can declare
what that was, a stranger, or his own wife, with the most
convincing?"

"Yes, madam, that is true enough. But according to
English law, we are bound by the words of the will; and
unless those are doubtful, no evidence of intention is admis-
sible, and even then——"

"I will not be bound by a—by an adaptation of words
that was never intended. What has a heretic minister to
do with my family, and with Walderscourt?"

"But, madam, excuse me. Sir Thomas Waldron asked
you, and you consented, to the appointment of the Rev.
Philip Penniloe, as your co-executor, and co-trustee for
your daughter, Miss Inez."

"If I did, it was only to please my husband, because he
was in pain so severe. It should have been my brother, or
else my son. I have said to you before, that after all
that has been done, I refuse to adhere to that interpretation."

The solicitor fixed his eyes on her, not in anger, but in
pure astonishment. He had deep grey eyes in a rugged
setting, with large wrinkles under, and dark gabled brows
above; and he had never met a lady yet—except his own
wife—who was not overpowered by their solemn wisdom.
Lady Waldron was not overpowered by them. In her
ignorance of English usage, she regarded this gentleman
of influence and trust, as no more than a higher form of
Binstock.

"I shall have to throw it up," said Mr. Webber to
himself; "but oh, what gorgeous picking, for that very
low-principled Bubb and Cockshalt!" The eminent firm
he thought of thus were always prepared to take anything
he missed.

"Your ladyship is well aware," he said, being moved by
that last reflection, "that we cannot have anything perfect
in this world, but must take things as we find them.
Mr. Penniloe is a most reasonable man, and acknowledges
the value of my experience. He will not act in any way

against your wishes, so far as may be in conformity with sound legal practice. That is the great point for us to consider, laying aside all early impressions—which are generally loose when examined—of—of Continental codes, and so on. We need not anticipate any trouble from your co-executor, who as a clergyman is to us a layman, if proper confidence is reposed in us. Already we are taking the regular steps to obtain Probate of a very simple will, prepared very carefully in our Office, and by exceedingly skilful hands. We act for Mr. Penniloe, as well as for your ladyship. All is proceeding very smoothly, and exactly as your dear husband would have wished."

"Then he would have wished to have his last rest dishonoured, and his daughter estranged from her own mother."

"The young lady will probably come round, madam, as soon as you encourage her. Your mind is the stronger of the two, in every way. With regard to that sad and shameful outrage, we are doing everything that can be done. We have very little doubt that if matters are left to our judgment, and discreet activity——"

"Activity, sir! And what have you done? How long is it—a month? I cannot reckon time, because day and night are the same thing to me. Will you never detect that abominable crime? Will you never destroy those black miscreants? Will you never restore—oh, I cannot speak of it—and all the time you know who did it all! There is no word strong enough in your poor tongue, for such an outcast monster. Yet he goes about, he attends to his business, they shake him by the hand, they smile at him; instead of spit, they smile at him! And this is called a Christian land! My God, what made You make it?"

"I implore your ladyship not to be excited. Hitherto you have shown such self-command. Day and night, we are on the watch, and something must speedily come of it. We have three modes of action, each one of them sure to be successful, with patience. But the point is this—to have no mistake about it, to catch him with evidence sufficient to convict him, and then to punish and disgrace him for ever."

"But how much longer before you will begin? I am so tired, so weary, so worn out—can you not see how it is destroying me?"

Mr. Webber looked at her, and could not deny that this was a very different Lady Waldron from the one who had scarcely deigned to bow to him, only a few months ago. The rich warm colour had left her cheeks, the large dark eyes were wan and sunken, weariness and dejection spread, where pride and strength of will had reigned. The lawyer replied in a bolder tone than he would have employed, last summer.

"Lady Waldron, we can do no more. If we attempted any stronger measures, the only result would be to destroy our chance. If you think that any other firm, or any kind of agency, would conduct matters more to your satisfaction, and more effectually than we have done, we would only ask you to place it in their hands. I assure you, madam, that the business is not to our liking, or even to our benefit. For none but an old and most valued client, would we have undertaken it. If you think proper, we will withdraw, and hand over all information very gladly to our successors."

"To whom can I go? Who will come to my rescue in this wicked, impious, accursed land? If my brother were here, is it possible to doubt what he would do—how he would proceed? He would tear that young man, arm from arm, and leg from leg, and lay him in the market-place, and shoot any one who came to bury him. Listen, Mr. Webber, I live only for one thing—to find my noble brother, and to see him do that."

The lady stood up, with her eyebrows knitted, her dark eyes glowing, and her white hands thrown apart and quivering, evidently tearing an imaginary Jemmy.

"Let us hope for the best, madam, hope for the best, and pray for the blessing of the Almighty, upon our weak endeavours."

This was anything but a kind view to take of the dispersion of poor Jemmy; but the lawyer was terrified for the moment by the lady's vehemence. That she who had hitherto always shown such self-command and dignity—he began to fear that there was too much truth in her account of the effect upon her.

Suddenly, as if all her passion had been feigned—though none who had seen, or even heard her, could believe that possible—she returned to her tranquil, self-possessed, and even cold and distant style. The fire in her eyes, and the fury of her gestures sank and were gone, as if by magic ; and the voice became soft and musical, as the sound of a bell across a summer sea.

"You will pardon me," she said, as she fell back into the chair, from which in her passion she had risen ; "but sometimes my trouble is more great than I can bear. Ladies of this country are so delicate and gentle, they cannot have much hatred, because they have no love. And yet they can have insolence, very strong, and very wonderful. Yesterday, or two days ago, I obtained good proof of that. The sister of that man is here—the man who has overwhelmed me thus—and she has written a letter to me, very quiet, very simple, very polite, requesting me to appoint an interview for her in my own house ;"— this had been done on Monday, at the suggestion of Frank Gilham, that fair means should be exhausted first—"but after writing thus, she has the insulting to put in under— something like this, I remember very well—' if you refuse to see me, I shall be compelled to come, without permission.' Reflect upon that, Mr. Webber."

"Madam, it was not the proper thing to say. But ladies are, even when very young, a little—perhaps a little inclined to do, what they are inclined to."

"I sent her letter back, without a word, by the insolent person who brought it. Just in the same manner as her wicked brother's card. It is quite certain that she will never dare to enter into my presence."

"You have made a mistake there, Lady Waldron. Here I am, to thank you for your good manners ; and to speak a few truths, which you cannot answer."

Christie Fox walked up the room, with her eyes fixed steadfastly upon the other's, made a very graceful curtsey, and stood, without even a ribbon trembling. She was beautifully dressed, in dove-coloured silk, and looked like a dove, that has never been fluttered. All this Lady Waldron perceived at a glance ; and knew that she had met her equal, in a brave young Englishwoman.

Mr. Webber, who longed to be far away, jumped about with some agility, and manœuvred not to turn his back upon either of the ladies, while he fetched a chair for the visitor. But his trouble was lost, for the younger lady declined with a wave of her hand; while the elder said— "Sir, I will thank you to ring the bell."

"That also is vain," said Miss Fox, calmly. "I will not leave this room, Lady Waldron, until I have told you my opinion of your conduct. The only question is—do you wish to hear it, in the presence of this gentleman; or do you wish me to wait until he is gone?"

To all appearances, the lawyer was by far the most nervous of the three; and he made off for the door, but received a sign to stop.

"It is just as well, perhaps, that you should not be alone," Christie began in a clear firm voice, with her bright eyes flashing, so that the dark Spanish orbs were but as dead coals in comparison, "and that you should not be ashamed; because it proves at least that you are honest in your lunatic conclusions. I am not speaking rudely. The greatest kindness that any one can do you, is to believe that you are mad."

So great was the force of her quiet conviction that Lady Waldron raised one hand, and laid it upon her throbbing temples. For weeks she had been sleepless, and low, and feverish, dwelling on her wrongs in solitude, and estranged from her own daughter.

"Hush, hush, my good young lady!" pleaded the old Solicitor; but his client gazed heavily at her accuser, as if she could scarcely apprehend; and Christie thought that she did not care.

"You have done a most wicked thing;" Miss Fox continued in a lower tone, "as bad, in its way as the great wrong done to you. You have condemned an innocent man, ruined his life to the utmost of your power, and refused to let him even speak for himself. Is that what you call justice?"

"He was not innocent. He was the base miscreant. We have the proof of the man who saw him."

Lady Waldron spoke slowly, in a strange dull tone, while her lips scarcely moved, and her hands fell on her lap.

" There is no such proof. The man owns his mistake.
My brother can prove that he was miles away. He was
called to his father's sick bed, that very night. And
before daylight he was far upon the road. He never
returned till days afterwards. Then he finds this black
falsehood ; and you for its author ! "

" Is there any truth in this ? "

Lady Waldron turned slightly towards Mr. Webber, as
if she were glad to remove her eyes from her visitor's
contemptuous and overpowering gaze.

" There may be some, madam. I believe it is true that
the blacksmith has changed his opinion, and that Dr. Fox
was called suddenly away."

The old Solicitor was beginning to feel uneasy about his
own share in the matter. He had watched Miss Fox
intently through his glasses ; and long experience in law-
courts told him, that she thoroughly believed every word
she uttered. He was glad that he had been so slow and
careful ; and resolved to be more so, if possible, henceforth.

" And now if you are not convinced of the great wrong
you have done," said Christie coming nearer, and speaking
with a soft thrill in her voice, for tears were not far
distant ; " what have you to say to this ? My brother,
long before your husband's death, even before the last
illness, had given his heart to your daughter Inez. Her
father more than suspected that, and was glad to think it
likely. Inez also knew it well. All this also I can prove,
even to your satisfaction. Is it possible, even if he were a
villain, and my brother is a gentleman of as good a family
as your own, Lady Waldron—ask yourself, would he offer
this dastard outrage to the father of the girl he loved ? If
you can believe it, you are not a woman. And that would
be better for all other women. Oh, it is too cruel, too
atrocious, too inhuman ! And you are the one who has
done it all. Lay this to heart—and that you may think
of it, I will leave you to yourself."

Brave as she was, she could not quite accomplish this.
It is a provision of Nature, that her highest production
should be above the rules of inferior reason ? When this
fair young woman ceased to speak, and having discharged
her mission should have walked away in silence—strange

P

to say, she could do nothing of the kind. As if words had been her spring and motive power, no sooner were they exhausted than she herself broke down entirely. She fell away upon the rejected chair, covered her face with both hands, reckless of new kid gloves just come from Paris, and burst into a storm of tears and sobs.

"You have done it now," cried Mr. Webber; "I thought you would; but you wouldn't be stopped." He began to rush about helplessly, not on account of the poor girl's plight—for he had wife and daughter of his own, and knew that tears are never fatal, but often highly beneficial; "you have done it now; I thought you would." His prophetic powers seemed to console him.

Christie looked up through her dabbled gloves, and saw a sight that frightened her. Lady Waldron had been sitting at a large oak table covered with books and papers,—for the room was chiefly used for business, and not a lady's bower—and there she sat still; but with this change, that she had been living, and now was dead. Dead to all perception of the life and stir around her, dead to all sense of right or wrong, of daylight or of darkness; but living still to the slow sad work that goes on in the body, when the mind is gone. Her head lay back on the stout oak rail; her comely face showed no more life than granite has, or marble; and her widow's hood dropped off, and shed the coils of her long black hair around.

"I can't make it out;" cried Mr. Webber, hurrying to the bell-rope, which he pulled to such purpose that the staple of the crank fell from the ceiling, and knocked him on the head. But Christie, recovering at a glance, ran round the end of the table, and with all her strength supported the tottering figure.

What she did afterwards, she never knew, except from the accounts of others; for she was too young to have presence of mind, when every one else was distracted. But from all that they said—and they were all against her—she must have shown readiness, and strength, and judgment, and taken Mr. Webber under her command.

One thing she remembered, because it was so bitter, and so frightfully unjust; and if there was anything she valued —next to love and truth and honour, most of which are parts of it—Christie valued simple justice, and impartiality. To wit—as Mr. Webber might have put it—when she ran out to find Mr. Gilham, who had been left there, only because he did not choose to go away, and she only went to find him that he might run for Dr. Gronow—there was her brother standing with him, and words less friendly than usual were, as it seemed to her, passing between them.

"No time for this sort of thing now," she said, as well as her flurried condition would permit; and then she pulled her brother in, and sent Frank, who was wonderfully calm and reasonable, to fetch that other doctor too. Her brother was not in a nice frame of mind, according to her recollection; and there was no time to reason with him, if he chose to be so stupid. Therefore she sent him where he was wanted; and of course no doctor could refuse to go, under such frightful circumstances. But as for herself, she felt as if it mattered very little what she did; and so she went and sat somewhere in the dark, without even a dog for company, and finished with many pathetic addenda the good cry that had been broken off.

CHAPTER XXIII.

A MAGIC LETTER.

"Oh here you are at last then, are you?" said somebody entering the room with a light, by the time the young lady had wept herself dry, and was beginning to feel hungry; "what made you come here? I thought you were gone. To me it is a surprising thing, that you have the assurance to stay in this house."

"Oh, Jemmy, how can you be so cruel, when every bit of it was for you?"

"For me indeed! I am very much obliged. For your own temper, I should say. Old Webber says that if she dies, there may be a verdict of manslaughter."

"I don't care two pins, if there is; when all the world is so unjust to me. But how is she, Jenmy? What has happened to her? What on earth is it all about?"

"Well, I think you ought to know that best. Webber

says he never heard any one like you, in all his experience of Criminal Courts."

"Much I care what he says—the old dodderer! You should have seen him hopping about the room, like a frog with the rheumatism. You should have seen him stare, when the bell-rope fell. When I said the poor thing's hands were cold, he ran and poked the fire with his spectacles. But can't you tell me how she is? Surely I have a right to know, if I am to be manslaughtered."

"Well," replied Dr. Fox, with that heavy professional nod which he ridiculed in others; "she is in a very peculiar state. No one can tell what may come of it."

"Not a fit, Jemmy? Not like dear father's; not a mild form of—no, it seemed quite different."

"It is a different thing altogether, though proceeding probably from the brain. An attack of what we call catalepsy. Not at all a common thing, and quite out of my own experience, though I know of it from the books a little. Gronow knew it, of course, at a glance. Fortunately I had sense enough not to try any strong measures till he came. Any other young fellow in this part of the world would have tried venesection instantly, and it might have killed her. My treatment happened to be quite right, from my acquaintance with principles. It is nothing less than a case of entirely suspended animation. How long it may last, none can foretell."

"But you don't think it will kill her, Jemmy? Why my animation was suspended ever so long, the other day——"

"That was quite a different thing—this proceeds from internal action, overpowering emotion in a very anæmic condition; yours was simply external concussion, operating on a rather highly charged——"

"You are very polite. My own fault in fact. Who gave me the horse to drive about? But surely if a dis-ordered brain like mine contrives to get right again——"

"Christie, I wish to do you good. You have brought me into a frightful mess, because you are so headlong. But you meant it for the best, I know; and I must not be too hard upon you."

"What else have you been for the last five minutes?

Oh, Jemmy, Jemmy, I am so sorry! Give me a kiss, and I will forgive you."

"You are a very quick, warmhearted girl; and such have never too much reason."

The Doctor kissed his sister, in a most magnanimous manner; and she believed implicitly (until the next time of argument) that she had done the injury, and her brother sweetly borne it.

"Now come, while it is hot," said he; "get your courage up, and come. Never let a wound grow cold. Between you two there must be no ill-will; and she is so noble."

"Oh, indeed! Who is it then? It is so good, and so elevating to be brought into contact with those wonderfully lofty people."

"It is exactly what you want. If you can only obtain her friendship, it will be the making of your character."

"For goodness' sake, don't lose a moment. I feel myself already growing better, nobler, loftier."

"There is nothing in you grave, and stable, none of the stronger elements;" said the Doctor, as he led the way along an empty passage.

"Don't you be too sure of that;" his sister answered, in a tone which he remembered afterwards.

Lady Waldron lay on a broad and solid sofa, well-prepared for her; and there was no sign left of life or movement in her helpless figure. She was not at all like " recumbent marble"—which is the ghost of death itself—neither was she stiff or straight; but simply still, and in such a condition, that however any part of her frame might be placed, so it would remain; submissive only to the laws of gravitation, and to no exercise of will, if will were yet surviving. The face was as pale as death, the eyes half open but without expression; the breathing scarcely perceptible, and the pulse like the flutter of eider down, or gossamer in a sheltered spot.

There was nothing ghastly, repulsive, or even greatly distressing at first sight; for the fine, and almost perfect, face had recovered in placid abandonment the beauty impaired by grief and passion. And yet the dim uncertainty, the hovering between life and death, the touching frailty of human power over-tried and vanquished, might move the bitterest foe to tears, and waken the compassion planted in all human hearts by heaven.

Christie was no bitter foe, but a kind impulsive generous maiden, rushing at all hazards to defend the right, ready to bite the dust when in the wrong, if properly convinced of it. Jemmy stepped back, and spread forth his hand more dramatically than was needed, as much as to say—"See what you have done! Never forget this, while you live. I leave you to self-abasement."

The sensitive and impetuous girl required no such admonishment. She fell on her knees, and took one cold hand, while her face turned as pale as the one she watched. The pity of the sight became more vivid, deep, and overpowering; and she whispered her little bedside prayer, for that was the only one she recalled. Then she followed it up with confession.

"I know what ought to be done to me. I ought to be taken by the neck—no, that's not right—I ought to be taken to the place of execution, and there hanged by the neck, till I am dead, dead, dead."

All this she may have deserved, but what she got was very different.

Around her bended neck was flung no hangman's noose, but a gentle arm, the softest and loveliest ever felt, while dark eyes glistened into her own, and seeming to be encouraged there, came closer through a clustering bower; and in less time than it takes to tell, two fair young faces touched each other, and two quick but heavy hearts were throbbing very close together.

"It is more my fault than yours," said Nicie, leading the way to another room, when a few soft words of comfort and good-will had passed; "I am the one who has done all this; and Dr. Gronow says so—or at least he would, if he said what he thinks. It was the low condition caused by long and lonely thinking, and the want of sufficient food and air, and the sense of having no one, not even me."

"But that was her fault. She discouraged you; she showed no affection for you; she was even very angry with you; because you dared to think differently, because you had noble faith and trust."

"For that I deserve no credit, because I could not help

it. But I might have been kinder to her, Christie; I might have shown less pride and temper. I might have said to myself more often—'she is sadly shattered; and she is my mother.' It will teach me how to behave another time. For if she does not get well, and forgive me, I shall never forgive myself. I must have forgotten how much easier it is, to be too hard, than to be too soft."

"Probably you never thought about it;" said Christie, who knew a great deal about what were then called "the mental processes"—now gone into much bigger names, but the same nut in a harder shell. "You acted according to your sense of right; and that meant what you felt was right; and that came round to mean—Jemmy."

Nicie, who never examined her mind—perhaps the best thing to be done with it—was not quite satisfied with this abruptly concrete view of the issue. "Perhaps, I did," she said and sighed; because everything felt so cloudy.

"Whatever you did—you are a darling;" said the more experienced one. "There is a lot of trouble before us both. Never mind, if we only stick together. Poor Jemmy believes that he is a wonder. Between us, we will fetch him down."

Nicie could perceive no call for that, being as yet of less practical turn. She was of that admirable, and too rare, and yearly diminishing, type of women, who see and feel that Heaven meant them, not to contend with and outdo, but to comfort, purify, and ennoble that stronger, coarser, and harder half, called men.

"I think that he wants fetching up," she said, with very graceful timidity; "but his sister must know best, of course. Is it right to talk of such things now?"

"Decidedly not;" Miss Fox replied. "In fact it is downright wicked. But somehow or other, I always go astray. Whenever I am out of sorts with myself, I take a turn at other people. But how many turns must I have at others before I get my balance now! Did you ever see anything so sad? But how very beautiful she is! I never noticed it this afternoon, because I was in such a rage, I suppose. How long is she likely to remain like this?"

"Dr. Gronow cannot say. He has known one case which lasted for a month. But then there was no consciousness at all. He thinks that there is a little now. But we can perceive no sign of it."

"Well, I think I did. I am almost sure I did ;" Christie answered eagerly ; "when I said 'dead, dead, dead,' in that judicial manner, there came a little gleam of light into her eyes, as if she approved of the sentence. And again when you called me your sister, there seemed to be a sparkle of astonishment, as if she thought you were in too much of a hurry ; and perhaps you were, my darling. Oh, what a good judge Jemmy is ! No wonder he is getting so conceited."

" If there is any consciousness at all," said Nicie, avoiding that other subject, " this trance (if that is the English word for it) will not last long—at least Dr. Gronow says so ; and Doctor Jemmy—what a name for a gentleman of science !—thoroughly confirms it. But Dr. Fox is so diffident and modest, that he seems to wait for his friend's opinion ; though he must know more, being younger."

" Certainly he ought," Miss Fox replied, with a twinkle of dubious import ; " I hear a great deal of such things. No medical man is ever at his prime, unless it is at thirty-nine years and a half. Under forty, he can have no experience, according to the general public ; and over forty he is on the shelf, according to his own Profession. For that one year, they ought to treble all their fees."

"'That would only be fair ; for they always charge too little."

" You are an innocent duck ;" said Christie. " There is a spot on your cheek that I must kiss ; because it always comes, when you hear the name of Jemmy. Abstract affection for unknown science. Oh do have a try at Dr. Gronow. He knows fifty times as much as poor Jemmy."

" But he doesn't know how to please me," replied Nicie ; " and I suppose that ought to count for something ; after all. I must go and tell him what you thought you saw. That is his step in the passage now ; and he ordered us to watch for any symptoms of that sort. Oh what will he think of me, for leaving Nurse alone ? Good night, dear Christie ; I shall come away no more. But Binstock, our great man, is come back. He will attend to you, and see that you don't go home starving, or by yourself."

"Positive statements suit young men," Dr. Gronow declared, as he buttoned up his coat, about an hour afterwards; "and so does sitting up all night. Fox, you had better act up to that. But I shall just see your sister safe, as far as the hospitable White Post, and then I shall go home to my supper. There is not the slightest danger now, but constant attention is needful, in case of sudden revival. That I do not at all expect; but you know what to do, if it happens. The third day will be the most likely time; and then any pleasing excitement, or attraction—but I shall be here, and see to that."

"Oh Dr. Gronow," exclaimed Miss Fox, as she fastened her cloak to go with him; "how I wish I had been born a little sooner, to see you more positive than you are now!"

"Miss Fox, it is a happy thing for me, that I anticipated all such views. Young ladies, I meant of course—and not young men. Yet alas, the young ladies are too negative."

On the third day from Lady Waldron's seizure, the postman of the name of Walker finding not even a mushroom left to retard the mail-delivery, and having a cold north wind at his back, brought to the house, soon after noon, a very large letter, marked "Ship Despatch. Two shillings and tenpence to pay," and addressed to Lady Waldron.

"It must be from dear Tom," pronounced Nicie; "we have not heard from him since he sailed for India. There is no other person in the world, capable of such a frightful scrawl."

"Why, this is the very thing we want," said Gronow, who was present according to promise; "large, conspicuous, self-assertive. Let somebody fetch me a green flower-stick."

Slitting one end of the stick, he inserted the lower edge of the letter, and fixed it upright in the scroll-work at the bottom of the couch. Then he drew the curtain back, and a slant of cheerful sunshine broke upon the thick bold writing. But the figure on the couch lay still, without a sign of interest, cold, rigid, and insensible.

"I'll keep out of sight," the Doctor whispered, "and let no one say a word. But presently when I hold my hand up, let Miss Nicie strike a few notes, not too rapidly, on her guitar—some well-known Spanish melody."

Gliding round the back of the couch, with a very gentle touch he raised the unconscious lady's head, and propped it with a large firm pillow; so that the dim half-open eyes were level with and set point-blank upon the shining letter. Securing it so, he withdrew a little, and held up his hand to Nicie.

She, upon a low chair further off, touched the strings of her mother's own and in younger days much loved guitar; gently at first, like a distant ripple; then with a strong bold swell arising into a grand melodious strain—the March of Andalusia. All present held their breath to watch, and saw a strange and moving sight.

The Spanish lady's eyes began to fill with soft and quivering light, like a lake when the moon is rising; the fringe of their dark lashes rose; a little smile played on her lips, and touched them with a living tint; then all the brilliance of her gaze flashed forth, and fastened on that letter. She lifted both her trembling hands, and the letter was put into them. Her face was lit with vivid joy, and her lips pronounced—" My son, my son !" Then wanting nothing more, she drew the precious token to her breast, concealed it there, and sank into profound, and tranquil, and sweet sleep.

"She will be all right, when she awakes, and then she will want a lot of food ;" said Dr. Gronow with a quiet grin, while Nicie and Chris wept tears of joy, and Dr. Fox and the Nurse looked queer. "Mind she can't live on her son's letter. Beef-tea, arrowroot, and port-wine, leg of mutton gravy, and neat's foot jelly—finer than the sweetest sweetheart's letters, let alone a boy who writes with the stump of a cigar. Ladies and gentlemen, my job is over ; what a blessing Penniloe is gone to London! We should have had a prayer meeting every day. Miss Fox, I think I shall call you ' Christie,' because you are so unchristian."

"You may call me anything you like—that is so long as it is something you do like. I shall almost begin to have faith in doctors now, in spite of poor Jemmy being one."

"Jemmy, you had better throw up the trade. Your sister understands it best. The hardest work, and the hardest paid—however I go a trout-fishing, ere ever the river freezes."

The wind was very cold, and everybody there shivered at the shudders he would have to undergo, as they saw him set forth with an eager step. He waved his hand back from a turn of the walk which reminded him of the river, and his shoulders went up, as if he had a trout on hook.

" He is happy. Let him be," said the percipient Christie ; " he won't catch anything in fact ; but the miraculous draught in fancy."

" He ought to be pitched in," replied her brother, who was put out about something, possibly the fingering of the second fiddle ; " the least that can be done to him is to pitch him in, for trying to catch trout in December. Pike had vowed to do it ; but those fellows are gone home, Hopper and all, just when the world was most in want of them. Christie, you will just come back with me, to the Old Barn."

" Why does Dr. Gronow address nearly all his very excellent remarks to me ? And why does he always look at me, when he speaks ? "

" Because you are so pretty, dear. And because you catch his meaning first. They like that sort of thing ; " said Nicie.

" For looks I am nowhere, with Nicie present. But he sees advanced intelligence in me. And he comes from where they appreciate it. I shall go back to Old Barn, just when I think right."

" We are coming to something ! " cried Doctor Jemmy, who looked pleasantly, but loftily, at all the female race— save Nicie, who was saved perhaps, till two months after marriage—" stay, if you like, where you are appreciated, so highly, so very highly."

Christie's face became red as a rose, for really this was too bad on his part, and after all she had done for him, as witnessed those present.

" They like me," she said in an off-handed manner ; " and I like them—which is more than one can do to everybody. But it makes very little difference, I am afraid, for I shall never see them any more, unless they come to Foxden. I had made up my mind to go home, the moment Lady Waldron was out of danger. I did not come here to please myself ; and this is all I get for it. Good-bye to fair

Perlycross to-morow! One must not neglect one's dear father and mother, even for—even for such a dear as Nicie."

"Well, I never knew what it was to be out of temper." There was some truth in this assertion, though it seems a large one ; for Jemmy Fox had a remarkably sweet temper ; and a man who takes stock of himself, when short of that article, has already almost replaced it. "But how will you go, my dear little Cayenne pepper? Will you pack up all your grandeur, and have a coach and four?"

"Yes that I will," answered Christie quick as light, "though it won't cost me quite as much as the one I hired, when I came post-haste to your rescue. The name of my coach is the *Defiance ;* and the Guard shall play ' Roast-beef ' all the way, in honour of the coming Christmas-time. Won't we have a fine time at Foxden, if father is in good health again?"

Jemmy wisely left her to her own devices—for she generally "took the change out of him"—and consoled himself with soft contemplation of a lovelier, nicer, and (so far as he knew yet) ten thousand times sweeter-tempered girl, whose name was Nicie Waldron.

Now that sweet creature had a worry of her own, though she did not afflict the public with it. She was dying with anxiety, all the time, to know the contents of her brother Tom's letter, which had so enlivened her dear mother.

It is said that the only thing the all-wise Solomon could not explain to the Queen of Sheba, was the process of her own mind, or rather perhaps the leaps of it, which landed her in conclusions quite correct, yet unsupported even by the shadow of an enthymem. Miss Waldron was not so clever as the Queen of Sheba, or even as Miss Christie Fox ; yet she had arrived at a firm conviction that the one, who was destined to solve the sad and torturing question about her dear father, was no other than her brother, Tom Rodrigo. She had observed that his letter bore no token of the family bereavement, neither was that to be expected yet, although six weeks had now elapsed since the date of their sore distress.

Envelopes was not as yet in common use, and a letter was a cumbrous and clumsy-looking thing, one of the many reasons being that a writer was bound by economy, and very often by courtesy as well, to fill three great pages, before he began to double in. This naturally led to a vast sprawl of words, for the most part containing very little ; and "what shall I say next?" was the constant enquiry of even the most loving correspondent. Nicie knew well, that her brother was not gifted with the pen of a ready writer, and that all his heart indited of was—" what shall I put, to get done with it ?" This increased the value of his letters (by means of their rarity) and also their interest, according to the canon that plenty of range should be allowed for the reader's imagination.

But now even too much range was left, for that of the affectionate and poetic maiden, inasmuch as her mother lay asleep for hours with this fine communication to support her heart. There was nothing for Nicie to do, except to go to sleep patiently on her own account, and that she did in her own white bed, and saw a fair vision through tears of joy.

Behold, she was standing at the door, the sacred portal of Walderscourt, gazing at trees that were full of singing birds, with her milk-white pony cropping clover honey-sweet, and *Pixie* teetotuming after his own tail. All the air was blossoming with dance of butterflies, and all the earth was laughing at the flatteries of the sun. And behold a very tall form arose, from beyond the weeping willow, leading a form yet taller, and looking back for fear of losing it. Then a loud voice shouted, and it was brother Tom's— " Here he is at last ! No mistake about it. I have found the Governor—hurrah, hurrah !" The maiden sprang up with a bounding heart, to embrace her darling father. But alas, there was nothing, except the cold moon, and a pure virgin bosom that glistened with tears.

When Tom's letter came to the reading at last, there was plenty of blots in it, and brown sand, but not a blessed bit of poetry. The youth had been at Eton, and exhausted there all the tendency of his mind towards metre. Even now people, who ought to know better, ask why poetry will not go down with the tall, and imaginative, and romantic public. It must be from the absence of the spark divine among them. Nay rather because ere they could spell,

their flint was fixed for life, with the "fire" used up by
Classic hammer.

Of these things the present Sir Thomas Rodrigo Waldron
had neither thought nor heed. For him it was enough to
be released ; and the less he saw of book and pen, for the
rest of his natural life, the better for the book, the pen,
and him. So that on the whole he deserved much credit,
and obtained even more (from his mother) as the author of
the following fine piece of correspondence. Though all the
best bits were adapted from a book, entitled " The young
man's polite letter-writer, to his parents, sisters, sweethearts,
friends, and the Minister of his native parish, etc., etc.—also
when applying for increase of wages."

"Valetta, in the Island of Malta, Mediterranean Sea, etc. November
the 5th, also Guy Fawkes' Day, A.D. 1835.

" MY BELOVED AND RESPECTED MOTHER,—I take up
my pen with mingled feelings of affection and regret. The
bangs "—oh, he ought to say "pangs," thought Nicie, as
her mother read it on most gravely—" which I have suffered,
and am suffering still, arise from various sources. Affection, because of your unceasing and unmerited parental
goodness ; regret because absence in a foreign land enhances
by a hundred fold the value of all those lost endearments. I
hope that you will think of me, whenever you sit on the old
bench by the door, and behold the sun setting in the east."

" It is very beautiful," said Lady Waldron, animated by a
cup of strong beef-tea ; " but Rodrigo was so hard to kiss.
Very often, I have knocked my head—but he is competent
to feel it in his own head now."

" Mother, there is no bench by the door. And how can
the sun set in the east ?   Oh I see it was ' west,' and he has
scratched it out, because of his being in the east himself."

" That means the same thing ; " replied Lady Waldron ;
" Inez, if you intend to find fault with your dear brother's
letter about such trifles, you deserve to hear no more of it."

" Mother, as if it made any difference where the sun
sets ; so long as he can see it ! "

" He always had large thoughts," reflected his mother ;
" he is not of this cold geography.   Hearken how beautifully
he proceeds to write—

"' But it is vain to indulge these contemplations. Thanks to your careful tuition, and the lofty example set before me, I trust that I shall never be found wanting in my duty to the Country that gave me birth. Unfortunately in these foreign parts, the price of every article is excessive ; and although I am guided, as you are well aware, by the strictest principles of economy, my remembrance of what is due to you, and the position of a highly respected family, have in some degree necessitated an anticipation of resources. Feeling assured of your sympathy, and that it will assume a practical form by return of post, I venture to state for your guidance that the house of Plumper, Wiggins, and Golightly in this City have been advised, and have consented to receive on my behalf a remittance of £120, which will, I trust, appear a very reasonable sum.' "

" Mother, dear mother, let me go on," cried Nicie, as the letter dropped from her mother's hand ; " the pleasure and excitement have been too much for you, although the style is so excellent."

" It is not the style ; but my breath has been surprised, by —by the expressions of that last sentence. The sum that I myself placed to his credit, out of my bonds of the City of Corduba, was in addition, and without his father's knowledge—but no doubt he will give explanation more further down ; though the writing appears now to become of a different kind, shorter and less polished. But why is he in Malta, when the ship sailed for Bombay? Oh I am terrified there will be some war. The English can never stay without fighting very long. And behold his letter seems to go into three pieces ! See now, it is quite crooked, Inez, and of less correction. Nevertheless I approve more of it so. Listen again, child.

"' I was almost forgeting to say that we were mett before we had got very far on our way by a Despatch Vessle bringing urgent orders for all of the Draught to be sent to this place, which is not half so hot as the other place would be, and much more convenient, and healthy but too white. But it does make the money fly, and they are a jolley sett. I have long been wanting to write home, but waited untill there was some news to tell, and we could tell where we are going next. But we shall have to stay here for some time, because most of our things were sent to West Indies, and the other part went on to East India. It will all be for the best because so strong a change of climate will be almost certain to destroy the moths. I have bought three dogs. There is a new sort here, very clever, and can almost speak. I hope all the dogs at home are well. I miss the shooting very much, and there are no horses in the Mediterranean big enough to cary me. Now I must conclude with best love and duty to the Governor and you, and Nicie, and old nurse Sweetland, and anybody else who inquires for

"'remaining your affectionate and dutiful Son,

"'TOM R. WALDRON.

"'P.S.—Your kind letter of Aug. 30th just come. They must be very clever to have found us here. I am dredfully cutt up to hear dear Governor not at all well when you wrote. Shall hope for better news every day. There is a Greek gentleman here with a pill waranted to cure everything yet discovered. They are as large as yellow sluggs, and just the same shape. He will let me have 10 for my amathist studds which are no good to me. Shall try to send them by the next ship that goes home. Do write at once, because I never heard before of anything wrong with dear Governor.

"'T. R. W.'"

"Poor darling!" said his mother with tears in her eyes, while Nicie was sobbing quietly; "by this time he may be aware of it perhaps, though not of the dreadful thing that happened since. It will not be for his happiness that he should ever know. Remember that, Inez. He is of so much vigour and high blood of the best Andalusian, that he would become insane, and perhaps do himself deep injury. He would cast away his office—what you call the Commission,—and come back to this country, and be put in prison for not accepting quietly the sacrilegious laws."

"Mother, you have promised never to speak of that subject. If it is too much for poor Tom, what is it likely to be for us? All we can do is to leave it to God."

"There is not the same God in this Country as we have. If there was, He would never endure it."

CHAPTER XXIV.

A WAGER.

IT was true enough that Mr. Penuiloe was gone to London, as Gronow said. But it was not true that otherwise he would have held a prayer-meeting every day in Lady Waldron's room, for the benefit of her case. He would have been a great support and strength to Inez in her anxiety, and doubtless would have joined his prayers with hers; that would have been enough for him. Dr. Gronow was a man who meant well upon the whole, but not in every crick and cranny, as a really fine individual does. But the Parson was even less likely than the Doctor, to lift a latch plugged by a lady against him.

"Thyatira, do you think that you could manage to see to the children, and the butcher's bill, during the course of next week," he enquired, when the pupils were off for their holiday, with accordions, and pan-pipes and pea-shooters; " I have particular business in London. Only Betty Cork, and old Job Tapscott, have come to my readings of Solomon's Song, and both of them are as deaf as milestones. Master Harry will be home again in three days' time, and when he is in the house you have no fear; though your confidence should be placed much higher. Master Michael is stronger of late, and if we can keep shocking stories from him, his poor little head may be right again. There really has been no proof at all of the existence of any Spring-heeled Jack; and he would never come here to earn his money. He may have been mentioned in Prophecy, as the Wesleyan Minister declared, but I have failed to come across the passage. Our Church does not deal in those exciting views, and does not recognise dark lanterns."

"No sir, we are much soberer like; but still there remains the Seven Vials."

The Parson was up to snuff—if the matter may be put upon so low a footing. Mrs. Muggridge had placed her arms akimbo, in challenge Theological. He knew that her views were still the lowest of the low, and could not be

Q

hoisted by any petard to the High Church level. And the worst of it is that such people are pat with awkward points of Holy Writ, as hard to parry as the stroke of Jarnac. In truth he must himself confess that partly thus had Thyatira, at an early and impressible age, been induced to join the Church, when there chanced to be a vacancy for a housemaid at the Parsonage. It was in his father's parish, where her father, Stephen Muggridge, occupied a farm belonging to the Rev. Isaac Penniloe. Philip, as a zealous Churchman, urged that the Parson's chief tenant should come to church, but the Rev. Isaac took a larger view, preferring his tangible cornland to his spiritual Vineyard.

"You had better let Stephen alone," he said, "you would very soon get the worst of it, with all your new Oxford theology. Farmer Steve is a wonderfully stout Antipædobaptist; and he searches the Scriptures every day, which leaves no chance for a Churchman, who can only find time on a Saturday."

This dissuasion only whetted the controversial appetite, and off set Philip with his Polyglot Bible under his arm. When Farmer Stephen saw him coming, he smiled a grim and gallant smile, being equally hot for the combat. Says he, after a few preliminary passes,

"Now, young sir, look here! I'll show 'e a text as you can't explain away, with all Oxford College at the back of thee. Just you turn to Gospel of John, third chapter and fifth verse, and you read it, after me. 'Except a man be born of water and of the spirit, he cannot enter into the Kingdom of God.' The same in your copy, bain't it now? Then according to my larning, m. a. n. spells man, and b. a. b. e. spells babe. Now till you can put b. a. b. e. in the place of m. a. n. in that there text, what becomes of your Church baptism?"

The farmer grinned gently at the Parson, in the pride of triumph, and looked round for his family to share it.

"Farmer Stephen, that sounds well;" replied the undaunted Philip, "but perhaps you will oblige me, by turning over a few leaves, as far as the sixteenth chapter of the same Gospel, and verse twenty-one. You see how it begins with reference to the pains of a mother, and then occur these words—'she remembereth no more the anguish, for joy that a *man* is born into the world.' Now was that man born full-grown, Farmer Stephen?"

The farmer knitted his brows, and stared; there was no smile left upon his face; but in lieu of it came a merry laugh from beside his big oaken chair; and the head of her class in the village school was studying his countenance.

"Her can go to Parsonage," quoth the Antipædo-baptist, "her won't take no harm in a household where they know their Bible so."

Farmer Stephen was living still; and like a gentleman had foregone all attempts to re-capture his daughter. With equal forbearance, Penniloe never pressed his own opinions concerning smaller matters upon his pious house-keeper, and therefore was fain to decline, as above, her often proffered challenges.

"There are many things still very dark before us," he answered with his sweet sad smile; "let us therefore be instant in prayer, while not neglecting our worldly duties. It is a worldly duty now, which takes me from my parish, much against my own desires. I shall not stay an hour more than can be helped, and shall take occasion to forward, if I can, the interests of our restoration fund."

Mrs. Muggridge, when she heard of that, was ready at once to do her best. Not that she cared much about the church repairs, but that her faithful heart was troubled by her master's heavy anxieties. As happens (without any one established exception) in such cases, the outlay had proved to be vastly vaster than the most exhaustive estimate. Mr. Penniloe felt himself liable for the repay-ment of every farthing; and though the contractors at Exeter were most lenient and considerate (being happily a firm of substance), his mind was much tormented- at the lower tides of faith—about it. At least twelve hundred pounds was certain to fall due at Christmas, that season of peace and good-will for all Christians, who can pay for it. Even at that date there were several good and useful Corporations, Societies, Associations, ready to help the Church of England, even among white men, when the case was put well before them. The Parson had applied by letter vainly; now he hoped to see the people, and get a trifle out of them.

The long and expensive journey, and the further expense
of the sojourn, were quite beyond his resources—drained so
low by the House of the Lord—but now the solicitors to
the estate of Sir Thomas Waldron Bart. deceased required
his presence in London for essential formalities, and gladly
provided the *viaticum*. Therefore he donned his warmest
clothes, for the weather was becoming wintry, put the
oilskin over his Sunday hat—a genuine beaver, which had
been his father's, and started in life at two guineas, and
even now in its Curate stage might stand out for twenty-
one shillings—and committing his household solemnly to the
care of the Almighty, met the first up-coach before daylight
on Monday, when it changed horses at the *Blue Ball* Inn,
at the north-east corner of his parish.

All western coaches had been quickened lately by
tidings of steam in the North, which would take a man
nearly a score of miles in one hour ; and though nobody
really believed in this, the mere talk of it made the horses
go.   There was one coach already, known by the rather
profane name of *Quicksilver*, which was said to travel at the
almost impious pace of twelve miles an hour.   But few had
much faith in this break-neck tale, and the *Quicksilver* flew
upon the southern road, which never comes nigh the Perle
valley.   Even so, there were coaches on this upper road
which averaged nine miles an hour all the way, foregoing
for the sake of empty speed, breakfast, and dinner, and
even supper on the road.   By one of these called the
Tallyho, Mr. Penniloe booked his place for London, and
arrived there in good health but very tired, early on
Tuesday morning.

The curate of Perlycross was not at all of the rustic
parson type, such as may still be found in many an out-of-
the-way parish of Devon.   He was not likely to lose himself in the streets of " Mighty Babylon," as London was
generally called in those days—and he showed some
perception of the right thing to do, by putting up at the
" Old Hummums."   His charges for the week were borne
by the lawyers, upon whose business he was come ; and
therefore the whole of his time was placed at the disposal
of their agents, Messrs. Spindrift, Honeysweet, and
Hoblin, of Theobald's Road, Gray's Inn.   That highly

respected firm led him about from office to office, and pillar
to post, sometimes sitting upon the pillar, sometimes leaning
against the post, according to the usage immemorial of
their learned Profession. But one of the things he was
resolved to do between Doe and Roe, and Nokes and
Styles, was to see his old friend Harrison Gowler, concerning the outrage at Perlycross.

There happened to be a great run now upon that eminent
Physician, because he had told a lady of exalted rank, who
had a loose tendon somewhere, that she had stepped on a
piece of orange-peel five and twenty years ago. Historical
research proved this to be too true, although it had entirely
escaped the august patient's memory. Dr. Gowler became
of course a Baronet at once, his practice was doubled,
though it had been very large, and so were all his fees,
though they had not been small. In a word, he was the
rage, and was making golden hay in the full blaze of a
Royal sun.

No wonder then that the simple friend for a long time
sought the great man vainly. He could not very well
write, to ask for an interview on the following day, because
he never knew at what hour he might hope to be delivered
from the lawyers; and it never occurred to him to prepay
the postage of his card from door to table, through either of
the haughty footmen. Slow as he was to take offence, he
began to fear that it must be meant, for the name of his
hotel was on his cards; until as he was turning away once
more, debating with himself whether self-respect would
allow him to lift that brass knocker again, the great man
himself came point-blank upon him. The stately footman
had made a rush for his pint of half-and-half round the
corner, and Sir Harrison had to open his own door to show
a noble patient forth.

" What, you in London, Penniloe !" And a kind grasp
of the hand made it clear, that the physician was not
himself to blame. In a few quick words it was arranged
that the Parson should call again at six o'clock, and share
his old friend's simple meal. " We shall have two good
hours for a talk," said Gowler, " for all the great people
are at dinner then. At eight, I have a consultation on."

" I never have what can be called a dinner ;" Sir

Harrison said, when they met again; "only a bit of—I forgot what the Greek expression is. There is an American turn for it."

"You must indeed be overdone, if you are forgetting your Greek," replied his friend; "you were far in front of me there always; though I think I was not so far behind, in Latin."

"I think you were better in both. But what matter? We have little time now for such delights. How often I wish I were back again at Oxford; ten times poorer, but a thousand times happier. What is the good of my hundred pounds a day? I often get that; and am ashamed of it."

The Parson refrained from quoting any of the plentiful advice upon that matter, from the very highest authorities. He tried to look cheerfully at his old friend, and did not even shake his head. But a very deep sadness was in his own heart; and yet a confirmation of his own higher faith.

Then knowing that the time was very short and feeling his duty to his own parish, he told the tale he was come to tell; and Sir Harrison listened intently to it.

"I scarcely know what to think," he said; "even if I were on the spot, and knew every one whom it was possible to suspect, it would be a terrible puzzle to me. One thing may be said, with confidence, amounting almost to certainty, that it is not a medical matter at all. That much I can settle, beyond all doubt, by means which I need not specify. Even with you I cannot enter upon questions so professional. We know that irregular things are done, and the folly of the law compels them. But this is quite out of the course they pursue. However I can make quite certain about all that within a week. Meanwhile you should look for a more likely clue. You have lost invaluable time by concluding, as of course the stupid public would, especially after all the Burke and Hare affairs, that 'the doctors must be at the bottom of it.' Most unlucky that you were so unwell, or you might have set the enquiry on the right track from the first. Surely it must have occurred to you that medical men, as a general rule, are the sharpest fellows of the neighbourhood, except of course—of course excepting the parsons?"

"They are sharper than we are," said the Parson with a

smile ; " but perhaps that is the very thing that tells against
our faith in them."

" Very likely. But still it keeps them from utterly mad
atrocities. Sir Thomas Waldron, a famous man, a grand
old soldier, and above all a wealthy man ! Why they
could have done no more to a poor old wretch from the
workhouse ! "

" The crime in that case would have been as great ;
perhaps greater, because more cowardly."

" You always were a highflyer, my friend. But never
mind the criminality. What we want to know is the
probability. And to find out that, we have to study not
the laws of morality, but the rules of human conduct.
What was the name of the man I met about the case, at
your house ? Oh, I remember—Gronow ; a very shrewd
clear-headed fellow. Well, what does he say about it ? "

" As nearly as possible what you have said. Some slight
suspicion has fallen upon him. But as I told you, Jemmy
Fox has come in for the lion's share of it."

" Poor young fellow ! It must be very hard to bear. It
will make him hate a Profession in which he would have
been sure to distinguish himself, because he really loves it.
What a thick-headed monster the English public is ! They
always exult in a wild-goose chase. Are you sure that the
body was ever carried off at all ? "

" The very question Doctor Gronow asked ! Unhappily,
there can be no doubt whatever upon that point. As I
ought to have told you, though I was not there to see it,
the search was made in the middle of the day, and with a
dozen people round the grave. They went to the bottom,
found the brickwork broken down, and no sign of any
coffin."

" Well, that ought to lead us to something clear. That
alone is almost certain proof of what I said just now.
' Resurrection-men,' as the stupid public calls them—would
have taken the body alone. Not only because they escape
all charge of felony by doing so, but that it is so much
easier ; and for many other reasons which you may imagine.
I begin to see my way more clearly. Depend upon it, this
is some family matter. Some private feud, or some motive
of money, or perhaps even some religious scruple lies at the

bottom of this strange affair. I begin to think that you
will have to go to Spain, before you understand it all. How
has Lady Waldron behaved about it ? "

" She has been most bitter against poor Jemmy." Mr.
Penniloe had not heard of what was happening this very
week at Walderscourt. " She will not see him, will not
hear his name, and is bitter against any one who takes his
part. She cannot even bring herself to speak to me,
because in common fairness I have done my best for him,
against the general opinion, and her own firm conclusion.
That is one reason why I am in London now. She will not
even act with me in taking probate of the will. In fact it
has driven her, as I fear, almost to the verge of insanity ;
for she behaves most unkindly even to her daughter. But
she is more to be pitied than blamed, poor thing."

" I agree with you ; in case of all this being genuine.
But is it so ? Or is it a bit of acting over-acted ? I have
known women, who could act so as to impose upon their
own brains."

" It has never once entered my head," replied the simple-
minded Parson, " to doubt that all she says, and does, is
genuine. Even you could not doubt, if you beheld her."

" I am not so sure of that," observed Sir Harrison very
drily ; " the beauty of your character is the grand simplicity. You have not the least idea of any wickedness."

" My dear fellow," cried the Parson deeply shocked ; " it
is, alas, my sad duty to find out and strive with the darkest
cases of the depravity of our fallen race ! "

" Of course. But you think none the worse of them for
that. It is water on a duck's back, to such a man as you.
Well, have it so ; if you like. I see the worst of their
bodies, and you the worst of their souls, as you suppose.
But I think you put some of your own into them—infusion
of sounder blood, as it were."

" Gowler, you may think as ill, as fallen nature can make
you think, of all your fellow-creatures ; " Mr. Penniloe spoke
with a sharpness very seldom found in words of his. " But
in fair truth, it is beyond the blackest of all black bitterness to doubt poor Lady Waldron's simple and perfect
sincerity."

" Because of her very magnificent eyes," Sir Harrison

answered, as if to himself, and to meet his own too
charitable interjections. "But what has she done, to carry
out her wild revenge at an outrage, which she would feel
more keenly perhaps than the most sensitive of English
women? Has she moved high and low, ransacked the earth,
set all the neighbourhood on fire, and appealed with tears,
and threats, and money, (which is the strongest of all
appeals) to the Cæsar enthroned in London? If she had
done any of these things, I fancy I should have heard of
them."

For the moment Mr. Penniloe disliked his friend; as a
man may feel annoyance at his own wife even, when her
mind for some trivial cause is moving on a lower level than
his own.

"As yet she has not taken any strong steps," he confessed
with some reluctance; "because she has been obliged to act
under her lawyer's guidance. Remember that she is a
foreigner, and knows nothing of our legal machinery."

"Very likely not. But Webber does—Webber her
solicitor. I suppose Webber has been very energetic."

"He has not done so much as one might have expected.
In fact he has seemed to me rather remiss. He has had his
own private hands at work, which as he says is the surest
plan; but he has brought no officers from London down.
He tells me that in all such cases they have failed; and
more than that, they have entirely spoiled the success of all
private enquiry."

"It looks to me very much as if private enquiry had no
great desire to succeed. My conclusion grows more and
more irresistible. Shall I tell you what it is?"

"My dear fellow, by all means do. I shall attach very
great importance to it."

"It is simply this," Sir Harrison spoke less rapidly than
usual; "all your mystery is solved in this—*Lady Waldron
knows all about it.* How you all have missed that plain
truth, puzzles me. She has excellent reasons for restricting
the enquiry, and casting suspicion upon poor Fox. Did I
not hear of a brother of hers, a Spanish nobleman I think
he was?"

"Yes, her twin-brother, the Count de Varcas. She has
always been warmly attached to him; but Sir Thomas did

not like him much. I think he has been extravagant.
Lady Waldron has been doing her utmost to discover
him."

"I dare say. To be sure she has! Advertised largely
of course. Oh dear, oh dear! What poor simple creatures
we men are, in comparison with women!"

Mr. Penniloe was silent. He had made a good dinner,
and taken a glass of old port-wine; and both those proceedings were very rare with him. Like all extremely
abstemious men, when getting on in years, he found his
brain not strengthened, but confused, by the unusual supply.
The air of London had upon him that effect which it often
has at first upon visitors from the country—quick increase
of appetite, and hearty joy in feeding.

"Another thing you told me, which confirms my view,"
resumed the relentless Doctor—"the last thing discovered
before you came away—but not discovered, mark you, by
her ladyship's agents—was that the cart supposed to have
been employed had been traced to a smuggler's hiding-place,
in a desolate and unfrequented spot, probably in the
direction of the coast. Am I right in supposing that?"

"Partly so. It would be towards the sea; though
certainly not the shortest way."

"But the best way probably of getting at the coast, if
you wished to avoid towns and villages? That you admit?
Then all is plain. Poor Sir Thomas was to be exported.
Probably to Spain. That I will not pretend to determine;
but I think it most likely. Perhaps to be buried in
Catholic soil, and with Catholic ceremonial; which they
could not do openly here, because of his own directions.
How simple the very deepest mystery becomes, when once
you have the key to it! But how strange that it never
occurred to you! I should have thought Gronow at any rate
would have guessed it."

"He has more penetration than I have; I am well aware
of that," replied the humble Parson; "and you of course
have more than either of us. But for all that, Gowler, and
although I admit that your theory is very plausible, and
explains many points that seemed inexplicable, I cannot,
and I will not accept it for a moment."

"Where is your difficulty? Is it not simple—consistent

with all that we know of such people, priest-ridden of course,
and double-faced, and crafty? Does it not solve every difficulty? What can you urge against it?"

"My firm belief in the honesty, affection, and good faith
of women."

" Whew ! " The great physician forgot his dignity, in
the enjoyment of so fine a joke. He gave a long whistle,
and then put his thumb to his nose, and extended his fingers,
as schoolboys of that period did. " Honesty of women,
Penniloe ! At your age, you surely know better than that.
A very frail argument indeed."

" Because of my age it is perhaps that I do know better.
I would rather not discuss the subject. You have your
views ; and I have mine."

" I am pleased with this sort of thing, because it reminds
one so much of boyhood ; " Sir Harrison stood by the fire,
and began to consult his short gray locks. " Let me
see, how many years is it, since I cherished such illusions ?
Well, they are pleasant enough while they last. I suppose
you never make a bet, Penniloe ? "

" Of course not, Gowler. You seem to be as ignorant of
clergymen, as you are of women."

" Don't be touchy, my dear fellow. Many of the cloth
accept the odds, and have privilege of clergy when they
lose. Well, I'll tell you what I will do. You see that
little cupboard in the panelling? It has only one key, and
the lock is peculiar. Here 1 deposit— behold my act and
deed—these two fifty-pound notes. You take the key. Now
you shall come, or send either churchwarden, and carry them
off for the good of your church-restoration fund, the moment
you can prove that my theory is wrong."

" I am not sure," said the clergyman, with a little agitation, as the courage of that single glass of port declined,
" that this is not too much in the nature of a wager."

" No, there is no wager. That requires two parties. It
is simply a question of forfeiture. No peril to a good cause
—as you would call it—in case of failure. And a solid
gain to it, if I prove wrong. Take the key, my friend. My
time is up."

Mr. Penniloe, the most conscientious of mankind, and
therefore the most gentle, had still some qualms about the

innocence of this. But his friend's presumptuous manner hushed them. He dropped the key into his deep watch-pocket, specially secured against the many rogues of London ; and there it was when he mounted on the *Magnet* coach, at two o'clock on the Friday afternoon, prepared for a long and dreary journey to his home.

The *Magnet* was one of those calm and considerate coaches which thought a great deal more of the comfort and safety of their passengers and horses, than of the fidgety hands of any clock—be it even a cathedral clock—on the whole road from London to Exeter. What are the most important hours of the day ? Manifestly those of feeding. Each of them is worth any other three. Therefore, you lose three times the time you save, by omitting your dinner. This coach breakfasted, dined, and supped, and slept on the road, or rather out of it, and started again as fresh as paint, quite early enough in the morning.

With his usual faith in human nature, Mr. Penniloe had not enquired into these points, but concluded that this coach would rush along in the breathless manner of the *Tallyho*. This leisurely course began to make him very nervous, and when on the Saturday at two o'clock, another deliberate halt was made at a little wayside inn, some fifty miles still from Perlycross, and every one descended with a sprightly air, the clergyman marched up to the coachman to remonstrate.

" Unless we get on a little faster," he said, with a kind but anxious smile ; " I shall not be at home for Sunday."

" Can't help that, sir. The coach must dine ;" replied the fat driver, as he pulled his muffler down, to give his capacious mouth fair play.

" But—but consider, Mr. Coachman ; I must get home. I have my church to serve."

" Must serve the dinner first, sir, if you please," said the landlord coming forward with a napkin, which he waved as if it were worth a score of sermons: " all the gents are waiting, sir, for you to say the grace—hot soup, knuckle of veal, boiled round, and baked potatoes. Gents has to pay, if they dine, or if they don't. Knowing this, all gents does dine. Preach all the better, sir, to-morrow for it."

If this preparation were needful, the curate's sermon

would not have been excellent, for anxiety had spoiled his
appetite. When at length they lumbered on again, he
strove to divert his thoughts by observing his fellow-
passengers. And now for the first time he descried, over
the luggage piled on the roof, a man with a broad slouched
hat and fur cloak, who sat with his back towards him, for
Mr. Penniloe had taken his place on the hinder part of the
coach. That man had not joined the dinner party, yet no
one remained on the coach or in it during the dinner hour ;
for the weather was cold and windy, with a few flakes of
snow flying idly all day, and just making little ribs of white
upon the road. Mr. Penniloe was not a very observant
man, least of all on a Saturday, when his mind was dwelling
chiefly upon Scriptural subjects ; but he could not help
wondering how this man came there; for the coach had
not stopped since they left the little inn.

This perhaps drew his attention to the man, who appeared
to be " thoroughly a foreigner," as John Bull in those days
expressed it. For he wore no whiskers, but a long black
beard streaked with silver, as even those behind could see,
for the whirl of the north wind tossed it now and then
upon his left shoulder. He kept his head low behind the
coachman's broad figure, and appeared to speak to nobody,
but smoked cigars incessantly, lighting each from the stump
of its predecessor, and scattering much ash about, to the
discomfort of his neighbours' eyes. Although Mr. Penniloe
never smoked, he enjoyed the fragrance of a good cigar,
perhaps more than the puffer himself does (especially if he
puff too vehemently), and he was able to pronounce this
man's tobacco very fine.

At length they arrived at Pumpington, about six miles
from Perlycross, and here Mr. Penniloe fully expected
another halt for supper, and had made up his mind in that
case to leave the coach and trudge home afoot. But to his
relief, they merely changed horses, and did that with some
show of alacrity ; for they were bound to be at Exeter that
night, and the snow was beginning to thicken. At the
turnpike-gate two men got up ; one of them a sailor, going
probably to Plymouth, who mounted the tarpaulin that
covered the luggage, and threw himself flat upon it with a
jovial air, and made himself quite at home, smoking a short

pipe, and waving a black bottle, when he could spare time from sucking it. The other man came and sat beside the Parson, who did not recognise him at first; for the coach carried only two lamps, both in front, and their light was thrown over their shoulders now and then, in rough streams, like the beard of the foreigner. All the best coaches still carried a guard, and the Royal Mail was bound to do so; but the *Magnet* towards the end of its career had none.

Mr. Penniloe meekly allowed the new-comer to edge his feet gradually out of the straw nest, and work his own into the heart of it; for now it was truly a shivering and a shuddering night. The steam of the horses and their breath came back in turbid clouds, and the snow, or soft hail (now known as *graupel*), cut white streaks through them into travellers' eyes, and danced on the roof like lozenges. Nobody opened mouth, except the sailor; and his was stopped, as well as opened, by the admirable fit of the neck of his rum-bottle. But this being over-strained became too soon a hollow consolation; and the rim of the glass rattled drily against his chattering teeth, till he cast it away.

"Never say die, mates. I'll sing you a song. Don Darkimbo, give us a cigar to chaw. Never could smoke them things, gentlemen and ladies. Can't 'e speak, or won't 'e then? Never mind, here goes!"

To his own encouragement this jolly fellow, with his neck and chest thrown open, and his summer duds on, began to pour forth a rough nautical ballad, not only beyond the pale of the most generous orthodoxy, but entirely out of harmony with the tone of all good society. In plainer words, as stupid a bit of ribaldry and blasphemy as the most advanced period could produce.

Then up rose Mr. Penniloe, and in a firm voice clear above the piping of the wind, and the roar of wheels, and rattle of loose harness, administered to that mariner a rebuke so grave, and solemn, and yet so full of large kindness and of allowance for his want of teaching, that the poor fellow hung his head, and felt a rising in his throat, and being not advanced beyond the tender stage of intoxication, passed into a liquid state of terror and repentance.

With this the clergyman was content, being of longer experience than to indulge in further homily. But the moment he sat down, up rose the gentleman who had cribbed his straw, and addressed the applauding passengers.

" My friends, the Reverend Penniloe has spoken well and eloquently. But I think you will agree with me, that it would be more consistent of him, and more for the service of the Lord, if he kept his powers of reproof for the use of his own parishioners. He is the clergyman of Perlycross, a place notorious throughout the country for the most infamous of crimes—a place where even the dead are not allowed to sleep in peace."

After this settler, the man sat down, and turned his back on the Parson, who had now recognised him, with deep sorrow at his low malevolence. For this was no other than Solomon Pack, watchmaker and jeweller at Pumpington, well known among his intimates as " Pack of lies," from his affection for malignant gossip. Mr. Penniloe had offended him by employing the rival trades-man, Pack's own brother-in-law, with whom he was at bitter enmity.

" Mr. Pack, you have done much harm, I fear; and this is very unjust of you "—was all that the Parson deigned to say. But he had observed with some surprise, that while Pack was speaking, the foreigner turned round and gazed intently, without showing much of his swarthy face, at himself—Philip Penniloe.

Before silence was broken again, the *Magnet* drew up at the *Blue Ball* Inn, where the lane turns off towards Perlycross, and the clergyman leaving his valise with the landlord, started upon his three-mile trudge. But before he had walked more than a hundred yards he was surprised to see, across the angle of the common, that the coach had stopped again at the top of a slight rise, where a footpath led from the turnpike road towards the northern entrance to Walderscourt. The clouds were now dispersing, and the full moon shining brightly, and the ground being covered with newly fallen snow, the light was as good as it is upon many a winter afternoon. Mr. Penniloe was wearing a pair of long-sight glasses, specially adapted to his use by a skilful optician in London, and he was as proud of them as a child is of his first whistle. Without them the coach might have been a haystack, or a whale, so far as he could tell; with them he could see the horses, and the passengers, and the luggage.

Having seen too much of that coach already, he was watching it merely as a test for his new glasses; and the trial proved most satisfactory. "How proud Fay will be," he was thinking to himself, "when I tell her that I can see the big pear-tree from the window, and even the thrushes on the lawn!" But suddenly his interest in the sight increased. The man, who was standing in the road with his figure shown clearly against a snowy bank, was no other than that dark foreigner, who had stared at him so intently. There was the slouched hat, and there was the fur cloak, and even the peculiar bend of the neck. A parcel was thrown to him from the roof, and away he went across the common, quite as if he knew the way, through furze and heather, to the back entrance of Walderscourt grounds. He could not see the Parson in the darker lane below, and doubtless believed himself unseen.

The circumstance aroused some strange ideas in the candid mind of Penniloe. That man knowing who he was from Pack's tirade, must have been desirous to avoid him, otherwise he would have quitted the coach at the *Blue Ball*, and taken this better way to Walderscourt; for the lane Mr. Penniloe was following led more directly thither by another entrance. What if there were something, after all, in Gowler's too plausible theory? That man looked like a Spaniard, probably a messenger from Lady Waldron's scapegrace brother; for that was his character if plain truth were spoken, without any family gloss upon it. And if he were a messenger, why should he come thus, unless there were something they wanted to conceal?

The Curate had not traversed all this maze of meditations, which made him feel very miserable—for of all things he hated suspiciousness, and that £100, though needed so sadly, would be obtained at too high a cost, if the cost were his faith in womankind—when, lo, his own church-tower rose grandly before him, its buttresses and stringing courses capped with sparkling snow, and the yew-tree by the battlements feathered with the same, and away to the east the ivy mantle of the Abbey, laced and bespangled with the like caprice of beauty, showered from the glittering stores of heaven.

He put on a spurt through the twinkling air, and the frozen snow crushed beneath his rapid feet ; and presently he had shaken hands with Muggridge, and Fay in her nightgown made a reckless leap from the height of ten stairs into his gladsome arms.

CHAPTER XXV.

A SERMON IN STONE.

Now Sergeant Jakes was not allowed to chastise any boys on Sunday. This made the day hang very heavy on his hands ; and as misfortunes never come single, the sacred day robbed him of another fine resource. For Mr. Penniloe would not permit even Muggridge, the pious, the sage, and the prim, to receive any visitors—superciliously called by the front-door people " followers "—upon that blessed day of rest, when surely the sweeter side of human nature is fostered and inspirited, from reading-desk and lectern, from gallery and from pulpit.

However even clergymen are inconsistent, as their own wives acknowledge confidentially ; and Mr. Penniloe's lectures upon Solomon's Song—a treatise then greatly admired, as a noble allegory, by High Churchmen—were not enforced at home by any warmth of practice. Thus stood the law ; and of all offences upon the Sergeant's Hecatologue, mutiny was the most heinous ; therefore he could not mutiny.

But surely if Mr. Penniloe could have received, or conceived, a germ of the faintest suspicion concerning this faithful soldier's alternatives on the afternoon of the Sabbath—as Churchmen still entitled it—he would have thrown open every door of kitchen, back-kitchen, scullery, and even pantry to him, that his foot might be kept from so offending. Ay, and more than his foot, his breast, and arm—the only arm he had, and therefore leaving no other blameless.

It is most depressing to record the lapse of such a lofty character, so gallant, faithful, self-denying, true, austere,

R

and simple—though some of these merits may be refused
him, when the truth comes out—as, alas, it must. All that
can be pleaded in his favour, is that ancient, threadbare,
paltry, and (as must even be acknowledged) dastardly
palliation—the woman tempted him, and he fell! Fell
from his brisk and jaunty mien, his noble indifference to
the fair, and severity to their little ones, his power of
example to the rising age, and his pure-minded loyalty to
Thyatira, watered by rivers of tea, and fed by acres of
bread and butter. And the worst of it was, that he had
sternly resolved, with haughty sense of right and hearty
scorn of a previous slip towards backsliding, that none of
this weakness should ever, even in a vision, come anigh him
any more. Yet see, how easily this rigid man was wound
round the finger of a female "teener"—as the Americans
beautifully express it!

He was sitting very sadly at his big black desk, one
mild and melancholy Sabbath eve, with the light of the
dull day fading out, and failing to make facets from the
diamonds of the windows, and the heavy school-clock ticking
feebly, as if it wished time was over: while shadows, that
would have frightened any other unmarried man in the
parish, came in from the silent population of the old churchyard, as if it were the haze of another world. A little
cloud of smoke, to serve them up with their own sauce,
would have consoled the school-master; but he never
allowed any smoking in this temple of the Muses, and as
the light waned he lit his tallow candle, to finish the work
that he had in hand.

This was a work of the highest criticism, to revise,
correct, and arrange in order of literary merit all the
summaries of the morning sermon prepared by the head-
class in the school. Some of these compositions were of
extreme obscurity, and some conveyed very strange
doctrinal views. He was inclined to award the palm to the
following fine epitome, practical, terse, and unimpeachably
orthodox—" The Sermon was, sir, that all men ort to be
good, and never to do no wikked things whennever they can
help it." But while he yet paused, with long quill in hand,
the heavy oak door from the inner yard was opened very
gently, and a slender form attired in black appeared at the
end of the long and gloomy room.

Firm of nerve as he was, the master quailed a little at
this unexpected sight; and therefore it became a very
sweet relief, when the vision brightened into a living and
a friendly damsel, and more than that a very charming one.
All firm resolutions like shadows vanished; instead of a
stern and distant air and a very rigid attitude, a smile of
delight and a bow of admiration betrayed the condition of
his bosom.

That fair and artless Tamar knew exactly how to place
herself to the very best advantage. She stood on the
further side of the candle, so that its low uncertain light
hovered on the soft curve of her cheeks, and came back in a
flow of steady lustre from her large brown eyes. She blushed
an unbidden tear away, and timidly allowed those eyes to
rest upon the man of learning. No longer was she the gay
coquette, coying with frolic challenge, but the gentle, pensive, submissive maiden, appealing to a loftier mind. The
Sergeant's tender heart was touched, up sprang his inborn
chivalry; and he swept away with his strong right hand
the efforts of juvenile piety, and the lessons of Holy Writ.

"Sergeant Schoolmaster, no chair for me;" Tamar
began in a humble voice, as he offered his own official
seat. " I have but a moment to spare, and I fear you will
be so angry with me, for intruding upon you like this.
But I am so—oh so unhappy!"

" What is it, my dear? Who has dared to vex you?
Tell me his name, and although it is Sunday—ah just let
me come across him!"

" Nobody, nobody, Sergeant Schoolmaster;" here she
pulled out a handkerchief, which a woman would have
pronounced, at a glance, the property of her mistress.
"Oh how shall I dare to tell you who it is?"

" I insist upon knowing," said the Sergeant boldly, taking
the upper hand, because the maiden looked so humble; " I
insist upon knowing who it is, this very moment."

" Then if I must tell, if you won't let me off," she
answered with a sweet glance, and a sweeter smile; " it is
nobody else but Sergeant Jakes himself."

" Me !" exclaimed the veteran; " whatever have I done?
You know that I would be the last in the world to vex
you."

"Oh it is because you are so fierce. And that of course is, because you are so brave."

"But my dear, my pretty dear, how could I ever be fierce to you ?"

"Yes, you are going to cane my brother Billy, in the morning."

This was true beyond all cavil—deeply and beautifully true. The Sergeant stared, and frowned a little. Justice must allow no dalliance.

"And oh, he has got such chilblains, sir ! Two of them broke only yesterday, and will be at their worst in the morning. And he didn't mean it, sir, oh he never meant it, when he called you an 'Old beast' !"

"The discipline of the school must be maintained." Mr. Jakes stroked his beard, which was one of the only pair then grown in the parish, (the other being Dr.Gronow's) for the growth of a beard in those days argued a radical and cantankerous spirit, unless it were that of a military man. Without his beard Mr. Jakes would not have inspired half the needful awe ; and he stroked it now with dignity, though the heart beneath it was inditing of an *infra dig.* idea. "Unhappily he did it, Miss, in the presence of the other boys. It cannot be looked over."

"Oh what can I do, Sergeant? What can I do? I'll do anything you tell me, if you'll only let him off."

The Schoolmaster gave a glance at all the windows. They were well above the level of the ground outside. No one could peep in, without standing on a barrel, or getting another boy to give him a leg up.

"Tamar, do you mean what you say ?" he enquired, with a glance of mingled tenderness and ferocity—the tenderness for her, the ferocity for her brother.

"If you have any doubt, you have only got to try me. There can't be any harm in that much, can there ?" She looked at him, with a sly twinkle in her eyes, as much as to say—"Well now, come, don't be so bashful."

Upon that temptation, this long-tried veteran fell from his loyalty and high position. He approached to the too fascinating damsel, took her pretty hand, and whispered something through her lovely curls. Alas, the final word of his conditions of abject surrender was one which rhymed with "this," or "Miss," or—that which it should have been

requited with—a hiss. Oh Muggridge, Muggridge, where
were you? Just stirring a cup of unbefriended tea, and
meditating on this man's integrity!

"Oh you are too bad, too bad, Sergeant!" exclaimed the
young girl starting back, with both hands lifted, and a
most becoming blush. "I never did—I never could have
thought that you had any mind for such trifles. Why,
what would all the people say, if I were only to mention it?"

"Nobody would believe you;" replied Mr. Jakes, to
quench that idea, while he trembled at it; adding thereby
to his iniquities.

"Well perhaps they wouldn't. No I don't believe they
would. But everybody likes a bit of fun sometimes. But
we won't say another word about it."

"Won't we though? I have got a new cane, Tamar—
the finest I ever yet handled for spring. The rarest thing
to go round chilblains. Bargain, or no bargain, now?"

"Bargain!" she cried; "but I couldn't do it now. It
must be in a more quieter place. Besides you might cheat
me, and cane him after all. Oh it is too bad, too bad to
think of. Perhaps I might try, next Sunday."

"But where shall I see you next Sunday, my dear?
'Never put off; it gives time for to scoff.' Give me one
now, and I'll stick to it."

"No, Sergeant Jakes. I don't like to tell you, and my
father would be so angry. But I don't see what right he
has to put me in there. And oh, it is so lonely! And I
am looking out for ghosts, and never have a happy mouthful.
That old woman will have something to answer for. But
it's no good to ask me, Sergeant; because—because ever
so many would be after me, if they only got a hint of it."

This of course was meant to stop him; but somehow it
had quite the opposite effect; and at last he got out of the
innocent girl the whole tale of her Sunday seclusion. The
very best handmaid—as everybody knows—will go through
the longest and bitterest bout of soaking, shivering, freezing,
starving, dragging under wheels, and being blown up to the
sky, rather than forego her "Sunday out." Miss Tamar
Haddon was entitled always to this Sabbath travail; and
such was her courage that have it she would, though it
blew great guns, and rained cats and dogs.

Now, her father, as may have been said before, was

Walter Haddon of the *Ivy-bush*, as respectable a man as ever lived, and very fond of his children. This made him anxious for their welfare; and welfare meaning even then —though not so much as now it does—fair wealth, and farewell poverty, Mr. Haddon did his best to please his wealthy aunt, a childless widow who lived at Perlycombe. For this old lady had promised to leave her money among his children, if they should fail to offend her. In that matter it was a hundredfold easier to succeed, than it was to fail; for her temper was diabolical. Poor Tamar, being of flippant tongue, had already succeeded fatally; and the first question Mrs. Pods always asked, before she got out of her pony-carriage, was worded thus—"Is that minx Tamar in the house?"

Whatever the weather might be, this lady always drove up with her lame pony to the door of the *Ivy-bush*, at half-past one of a Sunday, expecting to find a good hot dinner, and hot rum and water afterwards. For all this refreshment she never paid a penny, but presented the children with promises of the fine things they might look forward to. And thus, like too many other rich people, she kept all her capital to herself, and contrived to get posthumous interest upon it, on the faith of contingent remainders.

Now Tamar's mother was dead; and her father knowing well that all the young sparks of the village were but as the spoils of her bows and bonnets, had contrived a very clever plan for keeping her clear of that bitter Mrs. Pods, without casting her into the way of yokel youths, and spry young bachelors of low degree. At the back of his hostelry stood the old Abbey, covered with great festoons of ivy, from which the Inn probably took its name; and the only entrance to the ruins was by the arched gateway at the end of his yard, other approaches having been walled up; and the key of the tall iron gate was kept at this Inn for the benefit of visitors.

The walls of the ancient building could scarcely be seen anywhere for the ivy; and the cloisters and roofless rooms inside were overgrown with grass and briars. But one large chamber, at the end of a passage, still retained its vaulted ceiling, and stone pavement scarred with age. Perhaps it had been the refectory, for at one side was a deep fireplace, where many a hearty log had roared; at present its chief business was to refresh Miss Tamar Haddon. A few sticks kindled in the old fireplace, and a bench from the kitchen of the Inn, made it a tolerable keeping-room, at least in the hours of daylight; though at night the bold Sergeant himself might have lacked the courage for sound slumber there.

To this place was the fair Tamar banished, for the sake of the moneybags of Mrs. Pods, from half-past one till three o'clock, on her Sunday visits to the *Ivy-bush*. Hither the fair maid brought her dinner, steaming in a basin hot, and her father's account-book of rough jottings, which it was her business to verify and interpret; for, as is the duty of each newer generation, she had attained to higher standard of ennobling scholarship.

In a few words now she gave the loving Sergeant a sketch of this time-serving policy, and her exile from the paternal dinner-table, which aroused his gallant wrath; and then she told him how she had discovered entrance unknown to her father, at a spot where a thicket of sycamores, at the back of the ruins, concealed a loop-hole not very difficult to scale. She could make her escape by that way, if she chose, after her father had locked her in, if it were not for spoiling her Sunday frock. And if her father went on so, for the sake of pleasing that ugly old frump, she was blest if she would not try that plan, and sit on the river bank far below, as soon as the Spring dried up the rubbish. But if the Sergeant thought it worth his while, to come and afford her a little good advice, perhaps he might discover her Sunday hat waving among the ivy.

This enamoured veteran accepted tryst, with a stout heart, but frail conscience. The latter would haply have prevailed, if only the wind had the gift of carrying words which the human being does not utter, but thinks and forms internally. For the sly maid to herself said this, while she hastened to call her big brother Watty, to see her safe back to Walderscourt.

"What a poor old noodle! As if I cared twopence, how much he whacks Billy! Does he think I would ever let him come anigh me, if it wasn't to turn him inside out? Now if it were Low Jarks, his young brother, that would be quite another pair of shoes."

On the following Sunday it was remarked, by even the less observant boys, that their venerated Master was not wearing his usual pair of black Sunday breeches, with purple

worsted stockings showing a wiry and muscular pair of legs.
Strange to say, instead of those, he had his second best small-
clothes on, with dark brown gaiters to the knee, and a pair
of thick laced shoes, instead of Sunday pumps with silk
rosettes.   So wholly unversed in craft, as yet, was this good
hero of a hundred fights.   Thyatira also marked this change,
with some alarm and wonder ; but little dreamed she in her
simple faith of any rival Delilah.

Mr. Penniloe's sermon, that Sunday morning, was of a
deeply moving kind.   He felt that much was expected of
him, after his visit to London ; where he must have seen the
King and Queen, and they might even have set eyes on him.
He put his long-sight glasses on, so that he could see anybody that required preaching at ; and although he was never
a cushion-thumper, he smote home to many a too comfortable bosom.   Then he gave them the soft end of the rod to
suck, as a conscientious preacher always does, after smiting
hip and thigh, with a weapon too indigenous.   In a word,
it was an admirable sermon, and one even more to be loved
than admired, inasmuch as it tended to spread good-will
among men, as a river that has its source in heaven.

Sergeant Jakes, with his stiff stock on, might be preached
at for ever, without fetching a blink.   He sat bolt upright,
and every now and then flapped the stump of his left arm
against his sound heart, not with any eagerness to drive the
lesson home, but in proof of cordial approbation of hits, that
must tell upon his dear friends round about.   One cut
especially was meant for Farmer John ; and he was angry
with that thick-skinned man, for staring at another man,
as if it were for him.   And then there was a passage, that
was certain to come home to his own brother Robert, who
began to slaughter largely, and was taking quite money
enough to be of interest to the pulpit.   But everybody present
seemed to Jakes to be applying everything to everybody
else—a disinterested process of the noblest turn of thought.

However those who have much faith—and who can fail
to have some ?—in the exhortations of good men who practise
their own preaching, would have been confirmed in their
belief by this man's later conduct.   Although the body of
the church had been reopened for some weeks now, with
the tower-arch finished and the south wall rebuilt, yet there
were many parts still incomplete, especially the chancel

where the fine stone screen was being erected as a reredos; and this still remained in the builder's hands, with a canvas partition hiding it.

When the congregation had dispersed, Mr. Jakes slipped in behind that partition, and stood by a piece of sculpture which he always had admired. In a recess of the northern wall, was a kneeling figure in pure white marble of a beautiful maiden claimed by death on the very eve of her wedding-day. She slept in the Waldron vaults below; while here the calm sweet face, portrayed in substance more durable than ours, spoke through everlasting silence of tenderness, purity, and the more exalted love.

The Sergeant stood with his hard eyes fixed upon that tranquil countenance. It had struck him more than once that Tamar's face was something like it; and he had come to see whether that were so. He found that he had been partly right, but in more important matters wrong. In profile, general outline, and the rounding of the cheeks, there was a manifest resemblance. But in the expression and quality of the faces, what a difference! Here all was pure, refined and noble, gentle, placid, spiritual. There all was tempting, flashing, tricksome, shallow, earthly, sensuous.

He did not think those evil things, for he was not a physiognomist; but still he felt the good ones; and his mind being in the better tone—through commune with the preacher's face, which does more than the words sometimes, when all the heart is in it—the wonted look of firmness, and of defiance of the Devil, returned to his own shrewd countenance. The gables of his eyebrows, which had expanded and grown shaky, came back to their proper span and set; he nodded sternly, as if in pursuit of himself with a weapon of chastisement; and his mouth closed as hard as a wrench-hammer does, with the last turn of the screw upon it. Then he sneered at himself, and sighed as he passed the empty grave of his Colonel—what would that grand old warrior have thought of this desertion to the enemy?

But ashamed as he was of his weak surrender and treachery to his colours, his pride and plighted word compelled him to complete his enterprise. The Abbey stood near the church-yard wall, but on that side there was no entrance; and to get at the opposite face of the buildings, a roundabout way must be taken; and Jakes resolved now that he would not skulk by the lower path from the corner, but walk boldly across the meadow from the lane that led to Perlycombe. This was a back way with no house upon it, and according to every one's belief here must have lurked that horse and cart, on the night of that awful outrage.

Even to a one-handed man there was no great difficulty in entering one of the desolate courts, by the loophole from the thicket; and there he met the fair recluse in a manner rather disappointing to her. Not that she cared at all to pursue her light flirtation with him, but that her vanity was shocked, when he failed to demand his sweet reward. And he called her "Miss Haddon," and treated her with a respect she did not appreciate. But she led him to her lonely bower, and roused up the fire for him, for the weather was becoming more severe, and she rallied him on his clemency, which had almost amounted to weakness, ever since he allowed her brother Billy to escape.

"Fair is fair, Miss;" the Master answered pensively. "As soon as you begin to let one off, you are bound to miss the rest of them."

"Who have they got to thank for that? I am afraid they will never know," she said with one of her most bewitching smiles, as she came and sat beside him. "Poor little chaps! How can I thank you for giving them such a nice time, Sergeant?"

The veteran wavered for a moment, as that comely face came nigh, and the glossy hair she had contrived to loosen fell almost on his shoulders. She had dressed herself in a killing manner, while a lover's knot of mauve-coloured ribbon relieved the dulness of her frock, and enhanced the whiteness of her slender neck. But for all that, the Sergeant was not to be killed, and his mind was prepared for the crisis. He glanced around first, not for fear of anybody, but as if he desired witnesses; and then he arose from the bench, and looked at this seductive maiden, with eyes that had a steady sparkle, hard to be discomfited by any storm of flashes.

"Tamar," he said, "let us come to the point. I have been a fool; and you know it. You are very young; but somehow you know it. Now have you meant, from first to last, that you would ever think of marrying me?"

It never should have been put like that. Why you must

never say a word, nor use your eyes except for reading, nor even look in your looking-glass, if things are taken in that way.

" Oh Sergeant, how you frighten me ! I suppose I am never to smile again. Who ever dreamed of marrying ? "

" Well, I did ; " he answered with a twinkle of his eyes, and squaring of his shoulders. " I am not too old for everybody ; but I am much too old for you. Do you think I would have come here else ? But it is high time to stop this fun."

" I don't call it fun at all ; " said Tamar, fetching a little sob of fright. " What makes you look so cross at me ? "

" I did not mean to look cross, my dear." The Sergeant's tender heart was touched. " I should be a brute, if I looked cross. It is the way the Lord has made my eyes. Perhaps they would never do for married life."

" That's the way all of them look," said Tamar ; " unless they get everything they want. But you didn't look like that, last Sunday."

" No. But I ought. Now settle this. Would you ever think of marrying me ? "

" No. Not on no account. You may be sure of that. Not even if you was dipped in diamonds." The spirit of the girl was up, and her true vulgarity came out.

" According to my opinion of you, that would make all the difference ; " said the Sergeant, also firing up. " And now, Miss Haddon, let us say ' Good-bye.' "

" Let me come to myself, dear Sergeant Jakes. I never meant to be rude to you. But they do court me so different. Sit down for a minute. It is so lonely, and I have heard such frightful things. Father won't be coming for half an hour yet. And after the way you went on, I am so nervous. How my heart goes pit a pat ! You brave men cannot understand such things."

At this moving appeal, Mr. Jakes returned, and endeavoured to allay her terrors.

" It is all about those dreadful men," she said ; " I cannot sleep at night for thinking of them. You know all about them. If you could only tell me what you are doing to catch them. They say that you have found out where they went, and are going to put them in jail next week. Is it true ? People do tell such stories. But you found it all out by yourself, and you know all the rights of it."

With a little more coaxing, and trembling, and gasping, she contrived to get out of him all that he knew, concerning the matter to the present time. Crang had identified the impressions as the footmarks of the disabled horse; and a search of the cave by torchlight showed that it must have been occupied lately. A large button with a raised rim, such as are used on sailors' overalls, had been found near the entrance, and inside were prints of an enormous boot, too big for any man in Perlycross. Also the search had been carried further, and the tracks of a horse and a narrow-wheeled cart could be made out here and there, until a rough flinty lane was come to, leading over the moors to the Honiton road. All these things were known to Dr. Fox, and most of them to Mr. Penniloe, who had just returned from London, and the matter was now in skilful hands. But everything must be kept very quiet, or the chance of pursuing the clue might be lost.

Tamar vowed solemnly that she would never tell a word; and away went the Sergeant, well pleased with himself, as the bells began to ring for the afternoon service.

CHAPTER XXVI.

THE OLD MILL.

COMBING up on the South like a great tidal wave, Hagdon Hill for miles looks down on the beautiful valley of the Perle, and then at the western end breaks down into steep declivities and wooded slopes. Here the Susscot brook has its sources on the southern side of the long gaunt range, outside the parish of Perlycross; and gathering strength at every stretch from flinty trough, and mossy runnel, is big enough to trundle an old mill-wheel, a long while before it gets to Joe Crang's forge.

This mill is situated very sweetly for those who love to be outside the world. It stands at the head of a winding hollow fringed along the crest with golden gorse, wild roses by the thousand, and the silvery gleam of birch. Up this pretty "goyal"—as they call it—there is a fine view of the ancient mill, lonely, decrepit, and melancholy, with the flints dropping out of its scarred wall-face, the tattered thatch rasping against the wind, and the big wheel dribbling idly;

for the wooden carrier, that used to keep it splashing and spinning merrily, sprawls away on its trestles, itself a wreck, broken-backed and bulging.

And yet in its time this mill has done well, and pounded the corn of a hundred farms; for, strange as it may be, the Perle itself is exceedingly shy of mill-work, being broken upon no wheel save those of the staring and white-washed factory which disfigures the village of Perlycross. Therefore from many miles around came cart, and butt, and van, and wain, to this out-of-the-way and hard to find, but flourishing and useful Tremlett mill. That its glory has departed and its threshold is deserted, came to pass through no fault of wheel, or water, or even wanton trade seduced by younger rivals. Man alone was to blame, and he could not—seldom incapable as he is of that—even put the fault on woman.

The Tremletts were of very ancient race, said to be of Norman origin, and this mill had been theirs for generations. Thrifty, respectable, and hard-working, they had worn out many millstones—one of which had been set up in the churchyard, an honour to itself and owner—and patched up a lot of ages of mill-wheels (the only useful revolution) until there came into the small human sluice a thread of vile weed, that clogged everything up. A vein of bad blood that tainted all, varicose, sluggish, intractable.

What man can explain such things, even to his own satisfaction? Yet everybody knows that it is so, and too often with the people who have been in front of him. Down went the Tremletts for a hundred years—quite a trifle to such an old family—and the wheel ceased to turn, and the hearth had nought to burn, and the brook took to running in a low perverted course.

But even sad things may be beautiful—like the grandest of all human tragedies,—and here before Mr. Penniloe's new long-sighted glasses, which already had a fine effect upon his mind, was a prospect, worth all the three sovereigns he had paid, in addition to the three he had lived under. No monarch of the world—let alone this little isle—could have gilded and silvered and pearled and jewelled his most sumptuous palace, and his chambers of delight, with a tithe of the beauty here set forth by nature, whose adornments come and go, at every breath.

For there had just been another heavy fall of snow, and the frost having firm hold of the air, the sun had no more power than a great white star, glistening rather than shining, and doubtful of his own domain in the multitude of sparkles. Everything that stood across the light was clad with dazzling raiment; branch, and twig, and reed, and ozier, pillowed with lace of snow above, and fringed with chenille of rime below. Under and through this arcade of radiance, stood the old mill-wheel—for now it could stand—black, and massive, and leaning on pellucid pillars of glistering ice.

Mr. Penniloe lifted up his heart to God, as he always did at any of His glorious works; and then he proceeded to his own less brilliant, but equally chilling duty. Several times he knocked vainly at the ricketty door of the remaining room, until at last a harsh voice cried—" Come in, can't 'e? Nort for 'e to steal here."

Then he pulled the leather thong, an old boot-lace, and the grimy wooden latch clicked up, and the big door staggered inwards. Everything looked cold and weist and haggard in the long low room he entered, and hunger-stricked, though of solid fabric once, and even now tolerably free from dirt. At the further end, and in a gloomy recess, was a large low bedstead of ancient oak, carved very boldly and with finely flowing lines. Upon it lay a very aged woman, of large frame and determined face, wearing a high yellow cap, and propped by three coarse pillows, upon which fell the folds of a French shawl of rich material.

She had thick eyebrows, still as black as a coal, and fierce gray eyes with some fire in them still, and a hooked nose that almost overhung a pointed chin; and her long bony arms lay quivering upon a quilt of well-worn patchwork. She looked at Mr. Penniloe, discerning him clearly without the aid of spectacles, and saluted him with a slight disdainful nod.

" Oh, Passon is it? Well, what have 'e got to say to me? " Her voice was hard and pitched rather high, and her gaunt jaws worked with a roll of wrinkles, intended for a playful grin.

" Mrs. Tremlett, I was told that you wished to see me, and that it is a solemn moment with you—that soon you will stand in the presence of a merciful but righteous Judge."

Mr. Penniloe approached her with a kind and gentle

look, and offered to take one of her clenched and withered hands, but she turned the knuckles to him with a sudden twist, and so sharp were they that they almost cut his palm. He drew back a little, and a flash of spiteful triumph told him that she had meant this rasper for him.

"Bain't a gwäin' to die yet," she said; "I be only ninety-one, and my own moother wor ninety-five afore her lost a tooth. I reckon I shall see 'e out yet, Master Passon; for 'e don't look very brave—no that 'e don't. Wants a little drap out o' my bottle, I conzider."

The clergyman feared that there was little to be done; but he never let the Devil get the best of him, and he betook himself to one of his most trustworthy resources.

"Mrs. Tremlett, I will with your permission offer a few simple words of prayer, not only for you but for myself, my friend. You can repeat the words after me, if you feel disposed."

"Stop!" she cried, "stop!" and threw out both hands with great vigour, as he prepared to kneel. "Why, you han't gi'en me the zhillin' yet. You always gives Betty Cork a zhillin', afore 'e begins to pray to her. Bain't my soul worth every varden of what Betty Cork's be?"

The Parson was distressed at this inverted view of the value of his ministrations. Nevertheless he pulled out the shilling, which she clapped with great promptitude under her pillow, and then turned her back upon him.

"Goo on now, Passon, as long as ever 'e wull; but not too much noise like, case I might drop off to sleep."

Her attitude was not too favourable; but the Curate had met with many cases quite as bad, and he never allowed himself to be discouraged. And something perhaps in his simple words, or the powers of his patient humility, gave a better and a softer turn to the old woman's moody mind.

"Passon, be you a *honest* man?" she enquired, when he had risen, affording that adjective a special roughness, according to the manner of Devon. "B'lieve 'e be a good man. But be 'e *h*onest?"

"My goodness, as you call it, would be very small indeed, unless I were honest, Mrs. Tremlett. Without honesty, all is hypocrisy."

"And you bain't no hypocrite; though 'e may be a vule. Most fine scholards is big vules, and half-scholards always maketh start for rogues. But I'll trust 'e, Passon; and the Lord will strike 'e dead, being in his white sleeves, every Zunday, if 'e goo again the truth. What do 'e say to that, Passon Penniloe? What do 'e think now of that there? And thee praying for me, as if I hadn't got ne'er a coffin's worth!"

The old lady pulled out a canvas bag, and jingled it against Mr. Penniloe's gray locks. Strong vitality was in her face. How could she die, with all that to live for?

"Vifty-two guineas of Jarge the Zecond. T'other come to the throne afore I did it; but his head wasn't out much, and they might goo back of his 'en. So I took 'un of the man as come afore, and there they has been ever since— three score years, and ten, and two. The Lord knoweth, if He reckon'th up the sparrows, what a fine young woman I were then. There bain't such a one in all the County now. Six foot high, twenty inch across the shoulders, and as straight as a hazel wand sucker'd from the root. Have mercy on you, Passon! Your wife, as used to come to see me, was a very purty woman. But in the time of my delight, I could 'a taken her with one hand, and done— well, chucked her over Horse-shoe."

"What do you mean?" Mr. Penniloe asked, and his quiet eyes bore down the boastful gaze, and altered the tone of the old virago.

"Nort, sir, nort. It bain't no use to worrit me. Her tumbled off the clift, and her bruk her purty nack. Her was spying too much after coney's holes, I reckon. But her always waz that tender-hearted. You bain't fit to hold a can'le to her, with all your precious prayers and litanies. But I'll trust 'e, Passon, for her zake. Vetch thiccy old book out o' cubbert."

In the cupboard near the fireplace he found an ancient Bible, bound in black leather, and fortified with silver clasps and corners.

"Hold that there book in your right hand, and this here bag in t'other;" the old lady still clave to the bag, as if far more precious than the Bible—"and then you say slowly after me, same as I was to do the prayers, 'I, Passon Penniloe, of Perlycross, Christian Minister, do hereby make oath and swear that I will do with this bag of money as Zipporah Tremlett telleth me, so help me God Almighty.'"

"Stop, if you please. I will make no such promise, until I know all about it;" objected Mr. Penniloe, while she glared at him with rising anger, and then nodded as something occurred to her.

"Well, then, I'll tell 'e fust; and no call for prabbles. This money bain't none o' they Tremletts; every varden of theirs is gone long ago, although they had ten times so much as this, even while I can mind of 'un. All this, except for a bit of a sto'un in the lower cornder, and that hath been hunderds of years with the Tremletts, but all the rest cometh from my own father, and none on 'em knoweth a word of it. Wouldn't believe if they did, I reckon. Zippy, that's my grand-darter as minds me, her hath orders to hurn for her life and vetch you—night or day, mind,—fust moment the breath be gone out of my body. And every varden of it is for she. You be to take it from this here little nestie, wi'out a word to no one, and keep it zealed up under lock and key, till Zippy be eighteen year of age, and then, accordin' to your oath, you putt it into her two hands. If 'e do that, Passon, I'll die a Christian, and you be welcome of me to your churchyard. But if 'e wun't do it, then I'll die a hatben, and never go to no churchyard, same as scores and scores of the Tremletts is. Now, do 'e care for the soul of an old 'ooman? Or would 'e soonder her went to the Devil?"

By this alternative the Curate felt much pressure put upon his conscience. If there were no other way to save her, he must even dispense with legal form, and accept a trust, which might for all he knew defraud the Revenue of legacy duty, and even some honest solicitor of a contribution to his livelihood. But first he must be certain that the scheme was just and rational.

"No fear of robbing nobody. They Tremletts be a shocking lot," she said, with amiable candour. "Just slip the wedge on top of latch, for fear one on 'em should come to see if I be dead; though I reckon, this weather, it would be too much for either son or darter. Wouldn't 'em hurn, if 'em knowed of this? But here I may lie and be worm-eaten. And chillers of my own—my own buys and girls. Dree quarters of a score I've had, and not one on 'em come anigh me! Never was a harrier-bird could fly so

s

fast as every one on 'em would, to this old bed, if 'em knowed what be in it. No, I be a liar—every one on 'em can't, because the biggest half be gone. Twelve buys there was, and dree wenches of no count. Dree buys was hanged, back in time of Jarge the Third, to Exeter jail, for ship-staling, and one to Gibbet-moor, for what a' did upon the road. Vour on 'em was sent over seas, for running a few bits of goods from France. Two on 'em be working to Whetstone pits, 'cording to their own account, though I reckon they does another sort of job, now and again. And as for t'other two, the Lord, or the Devil, knoweth what be come to they. Not one on 'em comes nigh poor old moother, who might a' died years ago 'cep for little Zippy. Though little Zip's father have a' been here now and then. The biggest and the wildest of the dozen I call him, though a' kapeth wonderful out of jail. 'Tis his cheel he comes to see, not his poor old moother. Look 'e ere, Passon, all the ins and outs of 'un be set down rarely in that there book ; same as the game with lines and crosses we used to play with a oyster-shell, fourscore years agone and more."

On three or four leaves of the ancient Bible, bound in for that purpose, was a pedigree of these Tremletts of the Mill, descending from the fourteenth century. Mr. Penniloe looked at it with no small interest. What a pity to find them come to this! The mill itself had been a fall no doubt ; but the Whetstone pits were a great descent from that.

"Tremletts has always had one or two fine scholards"— the old woman had a strange theory about this. "'Twor all along o' that they come down so. Whenever any man taketh much to books, a' stoppeth up his ears to good advice, and a' heedeth of his headpiece, and robbeth of 's own belly. But there, no matter. I can do a bit myself. Have 'e made up your mind about my poor soul?"

From the toss of her nose, Mr. Penniloe was afraid that she was not much in earnest about that little matter. And in common sense, he was loth to get entangled with the nettles and briars of such a queer lot.

"I think, Mrs. Tremlett," he said, with a smile containing some light of wavering, "that your wisest plan by far would be to have a short will drawn up, and leave the money——"

"Gi'e me my bag, and go thy ways," she screamed in a fury, though the bag was in her claws. "No churchyard for me, and my soul at thy door, thou white-livered, black-smocked Passon!"

Her passion struck into her lungs or throat, and she tore at her scraggy chest, to ease the pain and gripe of a violent coughing-fit. Mr. Penniloe supported her massive head, for if it fell back, it might never rise again.

"A drap out o' bottle!" she gasped at last, pointing to the cupboard where the Bible had been. He propped up her head with a pillow on end, and took from the cupboard a long-necked bottle of the best French brandy, and a metal pannikin.

"No watter! No watter!" the old woman shrieked, as he went towards a pitcher that stood by the chimney. "Watter spileth all. No vear. Vill up!"

He gave her the pannikin full, and she tipped it off, like a mouthful of milk, and then sat up and looked at him steadily.

"I be no drunkard," she said, "though a man as knoweth nort might vancy it. Never touches that stuff, excep' for physic. I've a' seed too much what comes of that. Have a drap, wull 'e? Clane glass over yanner."

She seemed annoyed again at his refusal, but presently subsided into a milder vein, as if she were soothed by the mighty draught, instead of becoming excited.

"Naden't have troubled 'e, Passon," she said, "but for zending of little Zip away. I'll tell 'e why, now just. Better cheel never lived than little Zip. Her tendeth old grannie night and day, though her getteth a tap on the head now and then. But her mustn't know of this here money, or her father 'd have it out of her in two zeconds. Now 'e see why I won't make no will. Now, will 'e do what I axed of 'e?"

After some hesitation the Parson gave his promise. He had heard from his wife about poor little Zip, and how faithful she was to her old grandmother; and he felt that it would be unfair to the child to deprive her of the chance in life this money might procure; while he knew that if he

s 2

declined the trust, not a penny would she ever see of it. He insisted however upon one precaution—that the owner should sign a memorandum of the gift, and place it with the guineas in the bag, and then hand the whole to him as trustee, completing by delivery the *donatio mortis causâ*. In spite of her sufferings from the ruinous effects of the higher education, Zipporah could sign her name very fairly, and a leaf of her grandchild's copybook served very well for the memorial prepared by Mr. Penniloe.

"Now rouse up the fire there, 'e must be frore a'most," Mrs. Tremlett said when that was finished, and she had shown him where she concealed the treasure. "'One good toorn desarves another,' as I've heerd say, though never had much chance of proving it; and I could tell 'e a thing or two, 'e might be glad to know, Passon Penniloe, wi'out doing harm to nobody. Fust place then, you mind hearing of the man as gi'ed that doiled zany of a blacksmith such a turn—how long agone was it? I can't say justly; but the night after Squire Waldron's vuneral."

"To be sure. The big man with the lame horse, at Susscot Ford."

"Well, that man was my son Harvey, little Zip's father. You see the name in big Bible. French name it waz then, spelled different, and with a stroke to the tail, as maight be. Tremletts had a hankering after foreign languages. See 'un all down the page you can."

"What, Mrs. Tremlett!" exclaimed the Parson. "Are you aware what you are doing? Informing against your own son—and one of the very few remaining!"

"Zober now, zober! Don't 'e be a vule, Passon. I knows well enough what I be adoing of. Just I wants 'un out of way, till arter I be buried like. I zent his little darter to the pits to-day, to tell 'un as how you knowed of it. That'll mak 'un cut sticks, till I be underground, I reckon."

As the old woman grinned and nodded at her own sagacity, a horrible idea crossed the mind of Mr. Penniloe. Could she be afraid that her own son would dig up her body, and dispose of it?

Before he had condemned himself for such a vile suspicion, Mrs. Tremlett seemed to have read his thoughts; for she smiled with bitter glory, as if she had caught a pious man yielding to impiety.

"No, Harvey bain't no body-snatcher—leastways not as I ever heer'd on; though most volk would say a' was bad enough for anything. All that I wants 'un out of way for, is that he mayn't have the chance to rob his darter. He loveth of the little maid, so much as Old Nick 'loweth him. But he could never kape his hands out of this here bag, if a' zeed 'un. And as for your folk doin' any hurt to 'un, 'twould be more use for 'e to drive nails into a shadow, than to lay hold of Harvey when he knoweth you be arter 'un. And even if 'e wor to vind 'un, man alive, it would be a bad job for you, or for zix such men as you be, to come nigh the hands of Harvey Tremlett. Volk about these parts don't know nort of un', else they'd have had un' for the 'rastling long ago. He hath been about a good deal among the Gipsies, and sailor-folk, and so on; and the Lord knows He musn't look for too very much of good in 'un."

"We must make allowances, Mrs. Tremlett. We never do justice to our fellow-men, in that way." Mr. Penniloe was saying to himself, while he spoke—"and a great deal must be allowed for such bringing-up as yours, ma'am." "But have you anything more to tell me, about that shocking thing, that is such a sad disgrace to Perlycross?" The Parson buttoned up his Spencer, as if he still felt that dirty Pack's hits below the belt.

"I could tell 'e a saight of things, if I waz so minded, about what they vules to Perlycross, and you among t'others be mazed about. I can't make 'un out myself; but I be free to swear you'm a passel of idiots. Tremletts was bad enough; no vamley could be worse a'most; and much older they was than any Waldrons. But none on 'em never was dug up for generations. Won'erful things has come to them—things as would fill books bigger than this Bible; because 'em always wor above the lids of the ten Commandments. But 'em always had peace, so soon as they was dead, till such time as the Devil could come for 'un, and he don't care for no corpses. They Waldrons is tame—no French blood in 'em. Vitted for big pews in church, and big vunerals. Vellers not laikely to be dug up, when that waz never done to Tremletts. Passon, I could tell 'e such a saight of things, as would make the hair creep round the head of thee. Can't talk no more, or my cough will come on. Will tell 'e all about your little boy, Mike ; if 'e come again when this vrost is over. And then I'll show 'e Zip. But I can't talk vair, while the houze be so cold. I've a dooed too much to-day, for a 'ooman in her ninety-zecond year. You come again about this day wake. I trust 'e now, Passon. You be a good man, because you'm got no good blood in you. A old 'ooman's blessing won't do 'e no harm."

Vast is the power of a good kind face, and of silence at the proper moment. The Curate of Perlycross possessed that large and tender nature, at which the weak are apt to scoff, because they are not afraid of it. Over them no influence can last, for there is nothing to lay hold of. But a strong-willed person, like that old woman, has substance that can be dealt with, if handled kindly and without pretence. Thus Mr. Penniloe indulged some hope of soothing and softening that fierce and flinty nature, and guiding it towards that peace on earth, which is the surest token of the amnesty above.

But while he was at breakfast on the following day, he was told that a little maid was at the front door, crying very bitterly, and refusing to come in. He went out alone, but not a syllable would she utter, until he had closed the door behind him. There she stood, shivering in the snow, and sobbing, very poorly dressed, and with nothing on her head, but mopping her eyes and nose, as she turned away, with a handkerchief of the finest lace.

"Zip," was all the answer Mr. Penniloe could get to his gentle enquiry as to who she was ; and then she looked at him with large and lustrous eyes, beautifully fringed below as well as above, and announcing very clearly that she was discussing him within. Although he guessed what her errand was, the clergyman could not help smiling at her earnest and undisguised probation of his character; and that smile settled the issue in his favour.

"You be to coom to wance ;" her vowel-sounds were of the purest Devonshire air, winged by many a quill, but never summed in pen by any ; "Wi'out no stapping to think, you be to coom !"

" What an imperious little Zenobia ! " said Mr. Penniloe, in self-commune.

" Dunno, whatt thiccy be. Grandmoother zayeth, 'e must coom to wance. But her be dead, zince the can'le gooed out." Her eyes burst into another flood, and she gave up the job of sopping it.

" My dear. I will come with you, in half a minute. Come and stand in the warmth, till I am ready."

" Noo. Noo. I bain't to stop. Putt on hat, and coom raight awai. Vire gooed out, and can'le gooed out, and Grannie gooed out, along wi' 'un."

Mr. Penniloe huddled his Spencer on, while the staring child danced with impatience in the snow ; and quiet little Fay came and glanced at her, and wondered how such things could be. But Fay would not stare, because she was a little lady.

The clergyman was very quick of foot ; but the child with her long Tremlett legs kept easily in front of him all the way, with the cloud of her black hair blowing out, on the frosty air, to hurry him.

" I bain't aveared of her. Be you ? " said the little maid, as she rose on tip-toe, to pull the thong of the heavy latch. " If her coom back, her would zay—' Good cheel, Zippy ! ' "

CHAPTER XXVII.

PANIC.

CHRISTMAS DAY fell on a Friday that year, and the funeral of that ancient woman took place on the previous afternoon. The Curate had never read the burial-service, before so small an audience. For the weather was bitterly cold, and poor Mrs. Tremlett had outlived all her friends, if she ever had any ; no one expected a farthing from her, and no one cared to come and shudder at her grave. Of all her many descendants none, except the child Zip, was present ; and she would have stood alone upon the frozen bank, unless Mrs. Muggridge had very kindly offered to come and hold the shivering and streaming little hand.

What was to be done with Zip ? Nobody came forward. There were hundreds of kind people in the parish, and

dozens to whom the poor waif would have been a scarcely
perceptible burden. Yet nobody cared to have a Tremlett
at his hearth, and everybody saw the duty marked out for
his neighbour.

"Then I will take her;" said Mr. Penniloe with his
true benevolence, "but the difficulty is where to place her.
She cannot well be among my children yet, until I know
more about her. And, although the old family is so
reduced, the kitchen is scarcely the place for her." However, that question soon answered itself; and though little
Zip was at first a sad puzzle (especially to the staid Muggridge), her grateful and loving nature soon began to win
a warm hold and a tranquil home for her.

That winter, although it began rather early, was not of
prolonged severity, for the frost broke up on Christmas
night, at least in the west of England, with a heavy fall of
snow which turned to rain. But Christmas Day itself was
very bright and pleasant, with bracing air, hard frozen
snow, and firm sunshine throwing long shadows on it, and
sparkling on the icicles from thatch and spout and window-
frame. As the boys of the Sunday school filed out, at the
call of the bells in the tower chiming (after long silence
while the arch was being cut) and as they formed into
grand procession, under the military eye of Jakes, joyfully
they watched their cloudy breath ascending, or blew it in
a column on some other fellow's cap. Visions were before
them,—a pageantry of joy, a fortnight of holidays, a fortnight of sliding, snow balling, bone-runners, Cooper Baker's
double-hoops, why not even skates?

But alas, even now the wind was backing, as the four
vanes with rare unanimity proclaimed, a white fog that
even a boy could stand out of was stealing up the valley,
while the violet tone of the too transparent sky, and the
whiteness of the sun (which used to be a dummy fireball),
and even the short sharp clack of the bells, were enough to
tell any boy with weather eyes and ears, that the nails on
his heels would do no cobbler's click again, till the holiday
time was over.

But blessed are they who have no prophetic gift, be it of
the weather, or of things yet more unstable. All went to
church in a happy frame of mind; and the Parson in a like

mood looked upon them. Every head was there that he
had any right to count, covered or uncovered. Of the
latter perhaps more than a Sunday would produce; of the
former not so many, but to a Christian mind enough; for
how shall a great church-festival be kept without a cook?
But the ladies who were there were in very choice attire,
happy in having nothing but themselves to dress; all in
good smiling condition, and reserving for home use their
candid reviews of one another.

There was the genial and lively Mrs. Farrant, whose
good word and good sayings everybody valued; close at
her side was her daughter Minnie, provided by nature with
seasonable gifts—lips more bright than the holly-berry,
teeth more pearly than mistletoe, cheeks that proved the
hardiness of the rose in Devon, and eyes that anticipated
Easter-tide with the soft glance of the Forget-me-not.
Then there was Mrs. John Horner, *interdum aspera cornu*,
but *fœnum habens* for the roast-beef time; and kind Mrs.
Anning (quite quit of this tale, though the Perle runs
through her orchard), and tall Mrs. Webber with two pretty
girls—all purely distinct from the lawyer—and Mrs. James
Hollyer, and Mrs. John Hollyer, both great in hospitality;
and others of equally worthy order, for whom the kind
hearts of Bright and Cobden would have ached, had they
not been blind seers.

To return to our own sheep, themselves astray, there
was no denying Mrs. Gilham, looking still a Christian, up
a fathom of sea-green bonnet; and her daughter Rose, now
so demure if ever she caught a wandering eye, that it had
to come again to beg pardon; and by her side a young
man stood, with no eyes at all for the prettiest girl inside
the sacred building!

But strange as it may seem, he had eyes enough and to
spare, for a young man opposite; whose face he perused
with perpetual enquiry, which the other understood, but
did not want to apprehend. For instance, "How is your
very darling sister? Have you heard from her by the
latest post? Did she say anything about me? When is
she coming to Perlycross again? Do you think she is
reading the same Psalm that we are? Have they got any
Christmas parties on? I hope there is no mistletoe up

that way, or at any rate no hateful fellow near her with
it?"

These, and fifty other points of private worship, not to
be discovered in the Book of Common Prayer—even by the
cleverest anagram of Ritualist—did Frank Gilham vainly
strive to moot with Jemmy Fox across the aisle, instead of
being absorbed and rapt in the joyful tidings of the day.

Neither was Jemmy Fox a ha'porth more devout. With
the innate selfishness of all young men, he had quite
another dish of fish to fry for his own plate. As for
Frank Gilham's, he would upset it joyfully, in spite of all
sympathy or gratitude. And, if so low a metaphor can
ever be forgiven, Jemmy's fish, though not in sight but in
a brambly corner, was fairly hooked and might be felt;
whereas Frank Gilham's, if she had ever seen his fly, had
(so far as he could be sure) never even opened mouth to
take it; but had sailed away upstream, leaving a long
furrow, as if—like the celebrated trout in Crocker's Hole
—she scorned any tackle a poor farmer could afford.

Fox, on the other hand, had reasonable hopes, that
patience and discretion and the flowing stream of time,
would bring his lovely prize to bank at last. For the chief
thing still against him was that black and wicked charge :
and even now he looked at all the women in the church,
with very little interest in their features, but keen enquiry
as to their expression. His eyes put the question to them,
one after another,—" My good madam, are you still afraid
of me?" And sad to say, the answer from too many of them
was—" Well, I had rather not shake hands with you, till
you have cleared your reputation." So certain is it that if
once a woman has believed a thing—be it good, or be it
evil—nothing but the evidence of her own eyes will uproot
that belief ; and sometimes not even that.

Especially now with Lady Waldron, Fox felt certain
that his case stood thus ; that in spite of all the arguments
of Christie and of Inez, he was not yet acquitted, though
less stubbornly condemned ; and as long as that state of
things lasted, he could not (with proper self-respect) press
his suit upon the daughter. For it should be observed
that he had no doubt yet of the genuine strength of her
ladyship's suspicions. Mr. Penniloe had not thought it

right or decent, placed as he was towards the family, to impart to young Jemmy Sir Harrison Gowler's hateful (because misogynic) conclusions.

That excellent preacher, and noble exemplar, the Reverend Philip Penniloe, gave out his text in a fine sonorous voice, echoing through the great pillars of his heart, three words —as many as can ever rouse an echo—and all of them short,—"On earth, peace."

He was gazing on his flock with large good will, and that desire to see the best side of them which is creditable to both parties ; for take them altogether they were a peaceful flock—when a crack, as of thunder and lightning all in one, rang in every ear, and made a stop in every heart. Before any body could start up to ask about it, a cavernous rumble rolled into a quick rattle ; and then deep silence followed.

Nervous folk started up, slower persons stared about, even the coolest and most self-possessed doubted their arrangements for the Day of Judgment. The sunlight was shining through the south aisle windows, and none could put the blame on any storm outside.

Then panic arose, as at a trumpet-call. People huddled anyhow, to rush out of their pews, without even sense enough to turn the button-latch. Bald heads were plunging into long-ribboned bonnets, fathers forgot their children, young men their sweethearts, but mothers pushed their little ones before them. "Fly for dear life"—was the impulse of the men ; "save the life dearer than my own" —was of the women. That is the moment to be sure what love is.

"Sit still boys, or I'll skin you"—Sergeant Jakes' voice was heard above the uproar ; many believed that the roof was falling in ; every kind of shriek and scream abounded.

"My friends," said Mr. Penniloe, in a loud clear voice, and lifting up his Bible calmly, "remember in Whose house, and in Whose hands we are. It is but a fall of something in the chancel. It cannot hurt you. Perhaps some brave man will go behind the screen, and just tell us what has happened. I would go myself, if I could leave the pulpit."

People were ashamed, when they saw little Fay run from her seat to the newly-finished steps, and begin groping at the canvas, while she smiled up at her father. In a moment three men drew her back and passed in. They were Jemmy Fox, Frank Gilham, and the gallant Jakes; and a cloud of dust floated out as they vanished. Courage returned and the rush and crush was stayed, while Horner and Farrant, the two churchwardens, came with long strides to join the explorers.

Deep silence reigned when Doctor Fox returned, and at the request of Farmer John, addressed the Parson so that all could hear. "There is no danger, sir, of any further fall. There has been a sort of settlement of the south-east corner. The stone screen is cracked, and one end of it has dropped, and the small lancet window has tumbled in. All is now quite firm again. There is not the smallest cause for fear."

"Thank God!" said Mr. Penniloe, "and thank you my friends, for telling us. And now, as soon as order is quite restored, I shall beg to return to the discussion of my text, which with your permission I will read again."

As soon as he had finished a very brief discourse, worthy of more attention than it could well secure, his flock hurried gladly away, with much praise of his courage and presence of mind, but no thought of the heavy loss and sad blow cast upon him. Fox alone remained behind, to offer aid and sympathy, when the Parson laid his gown aside and came to learn the worst of it. They found that the south-east corner of the chancel-wall, with the external quoin and two buttresses, had parted from the rest, and sunk bodily to the depth of a yard or more, bearing away a small southern window, a portion of the roof and several panels of that equally beautiful and unlucky screen.

At a rough guess, at least another hundred pounds would be required to make good the damage. It was not only this, but the sense of mishaps so frequent and unaccountable — few of which have been even mentioned here—that now began to cast heavy weight and shadow, upon the cheerful heart of Penniloe. For it seemed as if all things combined against him, both as regarded the work itself, and the means by which alone it could be carried on. And this last disaster was the more depressing, because no cause whatever could be found for it. That wall had not been

meddled with in any way externally, because it seemed
quite substantial. And even inside there had been but
little done to it, simply a shallow excavation made, for the
plinth, or footings, of the newly erected screen.

"Never mind, sir," said Fox; "it can soon be put to
rights; and your beautiful screen will look ever so much
better without that lancet window, which has always
appeared to me quite out of place."

"Perhaps," replied the Parson, in a sad low voice, and
with a shake of his head which meant—"all very fine; but
how on earth am I to get the money?"

Even now the disaster was not complete. Subscriptions
had grown slack, and some had even been withdrawn, on
the niggardly plea that no church was worth preserving,
which could not protect even its own dead. And now the
news of this occurrence made that matter worse again, for
the blame of course fell upon Penniloe. "What use to
help a man, who cannot help himself?" "A fellow
shouldn't meddle with bricks and mortar, unless he was
brought up to them." "I like him too well, to give him
another penny. If I did he'd pull the tower down upon his
own head." Thus and thus spoke they who should have
flown to the rescue; some even friendly enough to deal the
coward's blow at the unfortunate.

Moreover, that very night the frost broke up, with a fall
of ten inches of watery snow, on the wet back of which
came more than half an inch of rain, the total fall being
two inches and three quarters. The ground was too hard
to suck any of it in; water by the acre lay on streaky
fields of ground-ice; every gateway poured its runnel, and
every flinty lane its torrent. The Perle became a roaring
flood, half a mile wide in the marshes; and the Susscot
brook dashed away the old mill-wheel, and whirled some of
it down as far as Joe Crang's anvil, fulfilling thereby an old
prophecy. Nobody could get—without swimming horse or
self—from Perlycombe to Perlycross, or from Perlycross to
Perliton; and old mother Pods was drowned in her own
cottage. The view of the valley, from either Beacon Hill
or Hagdon, was really grand for any one tall enough to
wade so far up the weltering ways. Old Channing vowed
that he had never seen such a flood, and feared that the big

bridge would be washed away ; but now was seen the value of the many wide arches, which had puzzled Christie Fox in the distance. Alas for the Hopper, that he was so far away at this noble time for a cross-country run ! But he told Pike afterwards, and Mrs. Muggridge too, that he had a good time of it, even in the Mendips.

In this state of things, the condition of the chancel, with the shattered roof yawning to the reek of the snow-slides, and a Southern gale hurling floods in at the wall-gaps, may better be imagined than described, as a swimming rat perhaps reported to his sodden family. And people had a fine view of it at the Sunday service, for the canvas curtain had failed to resist the swag and the bellying of the blast, and had fallen in a squashy pile, and formed a rough break-water for the mortary lake behind it.

There was nothing to be done for the present except to provide against further mischief. The masons from Exeter had left work, by reason of the frost, some time ago ; but under the directions of Mr. Richard Horner the quoin was shored up, and the roof and window made waterproof with tarpaulins. So it must remain till Easter now ; when the time of year, and possibly a better tide of money, might enable beaten Christians to put shoulder to the hod again. Meanwhile was there any chance of finding any right for the wrong, which put every man who looked forward to his grave out of all conceit with Perlycross ?

" Vaither, do 'e care to plaze your luving darter, as 'e used to doo ? Or be 'e channged, and not the zame to her ? "

" The vurry za-am. The vurry za-am," Mr. Penniloe answered, with his eyes glad to rest on her, yet compelled by his conscience to correct her vowel sounds. It had long been understood between them, that Fay might forsake upon occasion what we now call ' higher culture,' and try her lissome tongue at the soft Ionic sounds, which those who know nothing of the West call *Doric*.

" Then vaither," cried the child, rising to the situation ; " whatt vor do 'e putt both han's avore the eyes of 'e ? The Lard in heaven can zee 'e, arl the zaam."

The little girl was kneeling with both elbows on a chair, and her chin set up stedfastly between her dimpled hands, while her clear eyes, gleaming with the tears she was repressing, dwelt upon her father's downcast face.

"My darling, my own darling, you are the image of your mother," Mr. Penniloe exclaimed, as he rose, and caught her up. "What is the mammon of this world to heaven's angels?"

After that his proper course would have been to smoke a pipe, if that form of thank-offering had been duly recommended by the rising school of Churchmen. His omission however was soon repaired; for, before he could even relapse towards "the blues," the voice of a genuine smoker was heard, and the step of a man of substance, the time being now the afternoon of Monday.

"Halloa, Penniloe!" this gentleman exclaimed; "How are you, this frightful weather? Very glad to see you. Made a virtue of necessity; can't have the hounds out, and so look up my flock. Never saw the waters out so much in all my life. *Nancy* had to swim at Susscot ford. Thought we should have been washed down, but Crang threw us a rope. Says nobody could cross yesterday. *Nancy* must have a hot wash, please Mrs. Muggridge. I'll come and see to it, if you'll have the water hot. Harry's looking after her till I come back. Like to see a boy that takes kindly to a horse. What a job I had to get your back-gate open! Never use your stable-yard, it seems. Beats me, how any man can live without a horse! Well, my dear fellow, I hope the world only deals with you, according to your merits. Bless my heart, why, that can never be Fay! What a little beauty! Got a kiss to spare, my dear? Don't be afraid of me. Children always love me. Got one little girl just your height. Won't I make her jealous, when I get home? Got something in my vady, that will make your pretty eyes flash. Come, come, Penniloe, this won't do. You don't look at all the thing. Want a thirty mile ride, and a drop of brown mahogany—put a little colour into your learned face. Just you should have a look at my son, Jack. Mean him for this little puss, if ever he grows good enough. Not a bad fellow though. And how's your little Mike? Why there he is, peeping round the corner! I'll have it out with him, when I've had some dinner. Done yours, I daresay? Anything will do for me.

A rasher of bacon, and a couple of poached eggs is a dinner for a lord, I say. You don't eat enough, that's quite certain. Saw an awful thing in the papers last week. Parsons are going to introduce fasting! Protestant parsons, mind you! Can't believe it. Shall have to join the Church of Rome, if they do. All jolly fellows there—never saw a lean one. I suppose I am about the last man you expected to turn up. Glad to see you though, upon my soul! You don't like that expression—ha, how well I know your face! Strictly clerical I call it though; or at any rate, professional. But bless my heart alive—if you like that better—what has all our parish been about? Why a dead man belongs to the parson, not the doctor. The doctors have done for him, and they ought to have done with him. But we parsons never back one another up. Not enough colour in the cloth, I always say. Getting too much of black, and all black."

The Rev. John Chevithorne, Rector of the parish, was doing his best at the present moment to relieve "the cloth" of that imputation. For his coat was dark green, and his waistcoat of red shawl-stuff, and his breeches of buff corduroy, while his boots—heavy jack-boots coming half-way up the thigh—might have been of any colour under the sun, without the sun knowing what the colour was, so spattered, and plastered, and cobbed with mud were they. And throughout all his talk, he renewed the hand-shakes, in true pump-handle fashion, at short intervals, for he was strongly attached to his Curate. They had been at the same College, and on the same staircase; and although of different standing and very different characters, had taken to one another with a liking which had increased as years went on. Mr. Penniloe had an Englishman's love of field-sports; and though he had repressed it from devotion to his calling, he was too good a Christian to condemn those who did otherwise.

"Chevithorne, I have wanted you most sadly," he said, as soon as his guest was reclad from his vady, and had done ample justice to rashers and eggs; "I am really ashamed of it, but fear greatly that I shall have to be down upon you again. Children, you may go, and get a good run before dark. Things have been going on—in fact the Lord has not seemed to prosper this work at all."

"If you are going to pour forth a cloud of sorrows, you won't mind my blowing one of comfort."

The Rector was a pleasant man to look at, and a pleasant one to deal with, if he liked his customer. But a much sharper man of the world than his Curate; prompt, resolute, and penetrating, short in his manner, and when at all excited, apt to indulge himself in the language of the laity.

"Well," he said, after listening to the whole Church history, "I am not a rich man, as you know, my friend. People suppose that a man with three livings must be rolling in money, and all that. They never think twice of the outgoings. And Jack goes to Oxford in January. That means something, as you and I know well. Though he has promised me not to hunt there; and he is a boy who never goes back from his word. But Chancel of course is my special business. Will you let me off for fifty, at any rate for the present? And don't worry yourself about the debt. We'll make it all right among us. Our hunt will come down with another fifty, if I put it before them to the proper tune, when they come back to work, after this infernal muck. Only you mustn't look like this. The world gets worse and worse, every day, and can't spare the best man it contains. You should have seen the rick of hay I bought last week, just because I didn't push my knuckles into it. Thought I could trust my brother Tom's churchwarden. And Tom laughs at me; which digs it in too hard. Had a rise out of him last summer though, and know how to do him again for Easter-offerings. Tom is too sharp for a man who has got no family. Won't come down with twopence for Jack's time at Oxford. And he has got all the Chevithorne estates, you know. Nothing but the copyhold came to me. Always the way of the acres, with a man who could put a child to stand on every one of them. However, you never hear me complain. But surely you ought to get more out of those Waldrons. An offering to the Lord *in memoriam*—a proper view of chastisement; have you tried to work it up?"

"I have not been able to take that view of it," Mr. Penniloe answered, smiling for a moment, though doubtful of the right to do so. "How can I ask them for another

T

farthing, after what has happened? And leaving that aside, I am now in a position in which it would be unbecoming. You may have heard that I am Trustee for a part of the Waldron estates, to secure a certain sum for the daughter, Nicie."

"Then that puts it out of the question," said the Rector; "I know what those trust-plagues are. I call them a tax upon good repute. 'The friendly balm that breaks the head.' I never understood that passage, till in a fool's moment I accepted a Trusteeship. However, go on with that Waldron affair. They are beginning to chaff me about it shamefully, now that their anger and fright are gone by. Poor as I am, I would give a hundred pounds, for the sake of the parish, to have it all cleared up. But the longer it goes on, the darker it gets. You used to be famous for concise abstracts. Do you remember our Thucydides? Wasn't it old Short that used to put a year of the war on an oyster-shell, and you beat him by putting it on a thumbnail? Give us in ten lines all the theories of the great Perlycrucian mystery. Ready in a moment. I'll jot them down. What's the Greek for Perlycross? Puzzle even you, I think, that would. Number them, one, two, and so on. There must be a dozen by this time."

Mr. Penniloe felt some annoyance at this too jocular view of the subject; but he bore in mind that his Rector was not so sadly bound up with it, as his own life was. So he set down, as offering the shortest form, the names of those who had been charged with the crime, either by the public voice, or by private whisper.

1. Fox.
2. Gronow.
3. Gowler.
4. Some other medical man of those parts—conjecture founded very often upon the last half-year's account.
5. Lady Waldron herself.
6. Some relative of hers, with or without her knowledge.

"Now I think that exhausts them," the Curate continued, "and I will discuss them in that order. No. 1 is the general opinion still. I mean that of the great majority, outside the parish, and throughout the county. None who knew Jemmy could conceive it, and those who know nothing of him will dismiss it, I suppose, when they hear of his long attachment to Miss Waldron.

"Nos. 2, 3, and 4, may also be dismissed, being founded in each case on personal dislikes, without a *scintilla* of evidence to back it. As regards probability, No. 4 would take the lead; for Gronow, and Gowler, are out of the question. The former has given up practice, and hates it, except for the benefit of his friends. And as for Gowler, he could have no earthly motive. He understood the case as well as if he had seen it; and his whole time is occupied with his vast London practice. But No. 4 also is reduced to the very verge of impossibility. There is no one at Exeter, who would dream of such things. No country practitioner would dare it, even if the spirit of research could move him. And as for Bath, and Bristol, I have received a letter from Gowler disposing of all possibility there."

"Who suggested No. 5? That seems a strange idea. What on earth should Lady Waldron do it for?"

"Gowler suggested it. I tell you in the strictest confidence, Chevithorne. Of course you will feel that. I have told no one else, and I should not have told you, except that I want your advice about it. You have travelled in Spain. You know much of Spanish people. I reject the theory altogether; though Gowler is most positive, and laughs at my objections. You remember him, of course?"

"I should think so," said the Rector, "a wonderfully clever fellow, but never much liked. Nobody could ever get on with him, but you; and two more totally different men—however, an opinion of his is worth something. What motive could he discover for it?"

"Religious feelings. Narrow, if you like—for we are as Catholic as they are—but very strong, as one could well conceive, if only they suited the character. The idea would be, that the wife, unable to set aside the husband's wishes openly, or unwilling to incur the odium of it, was secretly resolved upon his burial elsewhere, and with the rites which she considered needful."

"It is a most probable explanation. I wonder that it never occurred to you. Gowler has hit the mark. What a clever fellow! And see how it exculpates the parish! I

T 2

shall go back, with a great weight off my mind. Upon my
soul, Penniloe, I am astonished that you had to go to
London, to find out this *a, b, c.* If I had been over here
a little more often, I should have hit upon it, long ago."

"Chevithorne, I think that very likely," the Curate
replied, with the mildness of those who let others be rushed
off their legs by themselves. "The theory is plausible,—
accounts for everything,—fits in with the very last
discoveries, proves this parish, and even the English nation,
guiltless. Nevertheless, it is utterly wrong; according at
least to my view of human nature."

"Your view of human nature was always too benevolent.
That was why everybody liked you so. But, my dear
fellow, you have lived long enough now, to know that it
only does for Christmas-day sermons."

"I have not lived long enough, and hope to do so never,"
Mr. Penniloe answered very quietly; but with a manner,
which the other understood, of the larger sight looking over
hat-crowns. "Will you tell me, Chevithorne, upon what
points you rely? And then, I will tell you what I think
of them."

"Why, if it comes to argument, what chance have I
against you? You can put things, and I can't. But I
can sell a horse, and you can buy it—fine self-sacrifice on
your side. I go strictly upon common sense. I have heard
a lot of that Lady Waldron. I have had some experience
of Spanish ladies. Good and bad, no doubt, just as English
ladies are. It is perfectly obvious to my mind, that Lady
Waldron has done all this."

"To my mind," replied Mr. Penniloe, looking stedfastly
at the Rector, "it is equally obvious that she has not."

"Upon what do you go?" asked the Rector, rather
warmly, for he prided himself on his knowledge of mankind,
though admitting very handsomely his ignorance of books.

"I go upon my faith in womankind." The Curate spoke
softly, as if such a thing were new, and truly it was not
at all in fashion then. "This woman loved her husband.
Her grief was deep and genuine. His wishes were sacred
to her. She is quite incapable of double-dealing. And
indeed, I would say, that if ever there was a straightforward simple-hearted woman——"

"If ever, if ever," replied Mr. Chevithorne, with a fine indulgent smile. "But upon the whole, I think well of them. Let us have a game of draughts, my dear fellow, where the Queens jump over all the poor men."

"Kings, we call them here," answered Mr. Penniloe.

CHAPTER XXVIII.

VAGABONDS.

ALTHOUGH Mr. Penniloe's anxiety about the growth of Church-debt was thus relieved a little, another of his troubles was by no means lightened through the visit of the Rector. That nasty suspicion, suggested by Gowler, and heartily confirmed by Chevithorne, was a very great discomfort, and even a torment, inasmuch as he had no one to argue it with. He reasoned with himself that even if the lady were a schemer, so heartless as to ruin a young man (who had done her no harm) that she might screen herself, as well as an actress so heaven-gifted as to impose on every one—both of which qualifications he warmly denied—yet there was no motive, so far as he could see, strong enough to lead her into such a crooked course. To the best of his belief, she was far too indifferent upon religious questions; he had never seen, or heard, of a priest at Walderscourt; and although she never came to church with the others of the family, she had allowed her only daughter to be brought up as a Protestant. She certainly did not value our great nation, quite as much as it values itself, and in fact was rather an ardent Spaniard, though herself of mixed race. But it seemed most unlikely, that either religion or patriotism, or both combined, were strong enough to drive her into action contrary to her dead husband's wishes and to her own character, so far as an unprejudiced man could judge it.

There remained the last theory, No. 6, as given above. To the Curate it seemed the more probable one, although surrounded with difficulties. There might be some Spanish relative, or even one of other country, resolute to save the soul of Sir Thomas Waldron, without equal respect for his body ; and in that case it was just possible, that the whole thing might have been arranged, and done, without Lady Waldron's knowledge. But if that were so, what meant the visit of the foreigner, who had tried to escape his notice, when he left the coach ?

Before Mr. Penniloe could think it out—Jemmy Fox (who might have helped him, by way of Nicie, upon that last point) was called away suddenly from Perlycross. His mother was obliged, in the course of nature, to look upon him now as everybody's prop and comfort ; because her husband could not be regarded in that light any longer. And two or three things were coming to pass, of family import and issue, which could not go aright, except through Jemmy's fingers. And of these things the most important was concerning his sister Christina.

"I assure you, Jemmy, that her state of mind is most unsatisfactory," the lady said to her son, upon their very first consultation. "She does not care for any of her usual occupations. She takes no interest in parish matters. She let that wicked old Margery Daw get no less than three pairs of blankets, and Polly Church go without any at all—at least she might, so far as Christie cared. Then you know that admirable Huggins' Charity—a loaf and three halfpence for every cottage containing more than nine little ones ;—well, she let them pass the children from one house to another ; and neither loaves nor halfpence held out at all! 'I'll make it good,' she said, 'what's the odds?' or something almost as vulgar. How thankful I was, that Sir Henry did not hear her ! 'Oh I wish he had, rayther,' she exclaimed with a toss of her head. You know that extremely low slangish way of saying *rayther* to everything. It does irritate me so, and she knows it. One would think that instead of desiring to please as excellent a man as ever lived, her one object was to annoy and disgust him. And she does not even confine herself to— to the language of good society. She has come back from Perlycross, with a sad quantity of Devonshirisms ; and she always brings them out before Sir Henry, who is, as you know, a fastidious man, without any love of jocularity. And it is such a very desirable thing. I did hope it would have been all settled, before your dear father's birthday."

"Well, mother, and so it may easily be. The only point is this—after all her bad behaviour, will Sir Henry come to the scratch?"

"My dear son! My dear Jemmy, what an expression! And with reference to wedded life! But if I understand your meaning, he is only waiting my permission to propose; and I am only waiting for a favourable time. The sweetest tempered girl I ever saw; better even than yours, Jemmy, and yours has always been very fine. But now—and she has found out, or made up, some wretched low song, and she sings it down the stairs, or even comes singing it into the room, pretending that she does not see me. All about the miseries of stepmothers. Oh, she is most worrying and aggravating! And to me, who have laboured so hard for her good! Sometimes I fancy that she must have seen somebody. Surely, it never could have been at Perly-cross?"

"I'll put a stop to all that pretty smartly"—the doctor exclaimed, with fine confidence. "But—but perhaps it would be better, mother, for me not to seem to take Sir Henry's part too strongly. At any rate until things come to a climax. He is coming this afternoon, you said; let him pop the question at once; and if she dares to refuse him, then let me have a turn at her. She has got a rare tongue; but I think I know something—at any rate, you know that I don't stand much nonsense."

They had scarcely settled their arrangements for her, when down the stairs came Christie, looking wonderfully pretty; but her song was not of equal beauty.

"There was an old dog, and his name was 'Shep;'
Says he to his daughter—don't you ever be a Step."

She nodded to her mother very dutifully, and to her brother with a smile that made him laugh; and then she went out of the front-door, almost as if she felt contempt for it.

"Won't do. Won't do at all;" said Jemmy. "She'll say 'no,' this afternoon. Girls never know what they are about. But better let him bring it to the point. And then leave it to me, mother. I understand her. And she knows I am not to be trifled with."

Sir Henry Haggerstone came in time for luncheon, showed no signs of nervousness, and got on very well with everybody. He knew something of everything that is likely to be talked of anywhere ; and yet he had the knack of letting down his knowledge, as a carpet for his friends to walk upon. Everybody thought—" Well, I have taught him something. He could not be expected to understand that subject. But now, from his own words, I feel that he will. What a fool Smith is, to be bothering a man like Sir Henry with the stuff that is *a. b. c.* to him ! I wonder that he could put up with it."

But however great Sir Henry was in powers of conversation, or even of auscultation, his eloquence—if there was any—fell flat, and his audience was brief, and the answer unmistakable.

" It can't be. It mustn't be. It shan't be, at any price." That last expression was a bit of slang, but it happened to fit the circumstances.

" But why can it not be ? Surely, Miss Fox, I may ask you to give me some reason for that."

The gentleman thought—" What a strange girl you are ! " While the lady was thinking—" What a difference there is between an artificial man and a natural one ! "

" What o'clock is it, by that time-piece, if you please, Sir Henry Haggerstone ? "

" Half-past two, within about two minutes."

" Thank you ; can you tell me why it isn't half-past ten ? Just because it isn't. And so now you understand."

" I am sorry to say, that I do not very clearly. Probably it is very stupid of me. But can you not give me a little hope, Miss Fox ? "

" Yes, a great deal ; and with my best wishes. There are thousands of nice girls, a thousand times nicer than I ever was, who would say ' yes,' in a minute."

" But the only one, whose ' yes ' I want, says ' no,' in less than half a minute ! "

" To be sure, she does—and means it all over ; but begs to offer no end of thanks."

" Perhaps it is all for the best," he thought as he rode homeward slowly ; " she is a very sweet girl ; but of late she seems to have grown so fond of slang expressions—all very well for a man, but not at all what I like in a woman. I should have been compelled to break her of that trick ; and even the sweetest tempered woman hates to be corrected."

This gentleman would have been surprised to hear that the phrases he disliked were used, because he so thoroughly disliked them. Which, to say the least, was unamiable.

"All settled? Hurrah! My dear Chris, let me congratulate you," cried Jemmy rushing in with a jaunty air, though he well knew what the truth was.

"Amen! It is a happy thing. That golden parallelogram, all tapered and well-rounded, will come to harass me no more."

"What a mixture of quotations! A girl alone could achieve it. A tapered parallelogram! But you have never been fool enough to refuse him?"

"I have been wise enough to do so."

"And soon you will be wise enough to think better of it. I shall take good care to let him know, that no notice is to be taken of your pretty little vagaries."

"Don't lose your temper, my dear Jemmy. As for taking notice of it, Sir Henry may be nothing very wonderful. But at any rate he is a gentleman."

"I am heartily glad that you have found that out. I thought nobody could be a gentleman, unless he lived in a farm-house, and could do a day's ploughing, and shear his own sheep."

"Yes, oh yes! If he can roll his own pills, and mix his own black draughts, and stick a knife into any one."

"Now, it is no use trying to insult me, my dear girl. My profession is above all that."

"What, above its own business? Oh Jemmy, Jemmy! And yet you know, you were afraid sometimes of leaving it all to that little boy George. However George did the best part of it."

"Christie, I shall be off, because you don't know what you are talking of. I am sorry for any man, who gets you."

"Ha! That depends upon whether I like him. If I do, wouldn't I polish his boots? If I don't, wouldn't I have the hair off his head?"

"Good-bye, my dear child. You will be better, by and by."

"Stop," exclaimed Christie, who perceived that dear Jemmy preferred to have it out with her, when she might be less ready ; "don't be in such a hurry. There is no child with the measles, which is about the worst human complaint that you can cure. Just answer me one question. Have I ever interfered, between you and Nicie Waldron ?"

"The Lord look down upon me ! What an idea ! As if you could ever be so absurd ! "

"The Lord looks down upon me, also, Jemmy ;" said Christie, passing into a different mood. "And He gives me the right to see to my own happiness, without consulting you ; any more than you do me."

The Doctor made off, without another word ; for he was not a quarrelsome fellow ; especially when he felt that he would get the worst of it.

"Let her alone a bit ;" he told his mother. "She has been so much used to have her own way, that she expects to have it always. It will require a little judgment, and careful handling, to bring her out of her absurdities. You must not expect her to have the sense a man has. And she has got an idea that she is so clever ; which makes her confoundedly obstinate. If you had heard how insolent she was to me, you would have been angry with her. But she cannot vex me with her childish little talk. I shall go for a thirty mile ride, dear mother, to get a little fresh air after all that. Don't expect me back to dinner. Be distant with her, and let her see that you are grieved ; but give her no chance of arguing—if indeed she calls such stuff argument."

In a few minutes he was on the back of *Perle*—as he called the kindly and free-going little mare, who had brought him again from Perlycross—and trotting briskly towards the long curve of highlands, which form the western bulwark of the Mendip Hills. The weather had been very mild and rather stormy, ever since the Christmas frost broke up, and now in the first week of the year, the air was quite gentle and pleasant. But the roads were heavy and very soft, as they always are in a thaw ; and a great deal of water was out in the meadows, and even in the ditches alongside of the lanes.

In a puzzle of country roads and commons, further from

home than his usual track, and very poorly furnished with
guide-posts, Fox rode on without asking whither; caring
only for the exercise and air, and absorbed in thought
about the present state of things, both at Perlycross and
Foxden. To his quick perception and medical knowledge
it was clear that his father's strength was failing, gradually,
but without recall. And one of the very few things that
can be done by medical knowledge is that it can tell us
(when it likes) that it is helpless.

Now Jemmy was fond of his father, although there had
been many breezes between them; and as nature will have
it, he loved him a hundredfold, now that he was sure to
lose him. Moreover the change in his own position, which
must ensue upon his father's death, was entirely against
his liking. What he liked was simplicity, plain living and
plain speaking, with enough of this world's goods to help a
friend in trouble, or a poor man in distress; but not enough
to put one in a fright about the responsibility, that turns
the gold to lead. But now, if he should be compelled to
take his father's place at Foxden, as a landowner and a
wealthy man, he must give up the practice of his beloved
art, he must give up the active and changeful life, the free
and easy manners, and the game with Bill and Dick; and
assume the slow dignity and stiff importance, the consciousness of being an example and a law, and all the other
briars and blackthorns in the paradise of wealth and station.
Yet even while he sighed at the coming transformation, it
never occurred to him that his sister was endowed with
tastes no less simple than his own, and was not compelled
by duty to forego them.

Occupied thus, and riding loose-reined without knowing
or caring whither, he turned the corner of a high-banked
lane, and came upon a sight which astonished him. The
deep lane ended with a hunting-gate, leading to an open
track across a level pasture, upon which the low sun cast
long shadows of the rider's hat, and shoulders, and elbow
lifted to unhasp the gate. Turning in the saddle he beheld
a grand and fiery sunset, such as in mild weather often
closes a winter but not wintry day.

A long cloud-bank, straight and level at the base, but
arched and pulpy in its upper part, embosomed and turned

into a deep red glow the yellow flush of the departing sun.
Below this great volume of vapoury fire, were long thin
streaks of carmine, pencilled very delicately on a background of limpid hyaline. It was not the beauty of the
sky however, nor the splendour, nor the subtlety, that
made the young man stop and gaze. Fine sunsets he had
seen by the hundred, and looked at them, if there was time
to spare; but what he had never seen before was the
grandeur of the earth's reply.

On the opposite side of the level land, a furlong or so in
front of him, arose the great breastwork to leagues of plain;
first a steep pitch of shale and shingle, channelled with
storm-lines, and studded with gorse; and then, from its crest,
a tall crag towering, straight and smooth as a castle-wall.
The rugged pediment was dark and dim, and streaked with
sombre shadows; but the bastion cliff above it mantled
with a deep red glow, as if colour had its echo, in answer
to the rich suffusion of that sunset cloud. Even the ivy,
and other creepers, on its kindled face shone forth, like
chaplets thrown upon a shield of ruddy gold. And all the
environed air was thrilling with the pulses of red light.

Fox was smitten with rare delight—for he was an
observant fellow—and even *Perle's* bright eyes expanded,
as if they had never seen such a noble vision. "I'll be up
there before it is gone," cried Jemmy, like a boy in full
chase of a rainbow; "the view from that crag must be
glorious."

At the foot of the hill stood a queer little hostel, called
the *Smoking Limekiln;* and there he led his mare into the
stable, ordered some bread and cheese for half an hour
later, and made off at speed for the steep ascent. Active
as he was, and sound of foot, he found it a slippery and
awkward climb, on account of the sliding shingle; but after
a sharp bout of leaping and scrambling he stood at the
base of the vertical rock, and looked back over the
lowlands.

The beauty of colour was vanishing now, and the glory
of the clouds grown sombre, for the sun had sunk into a
pale gray bed; but the view was vast and striking. The
fairest and richest of English land, the broad expanse of
the western plains for leagues and leagues rolled before him,

deepening beneath the approach of night, and shining with veins of silver, where three flooded rivers wound their way. Afar towards the north, a faint gleam showed the hovering of light, above the Severn sea ; whence slender clues of fog began to steal, like snakes, up the watercourses, and the marshy inlets. Before there was time to watch them far, the veil of dusk fell over them, and things unwatched stood forth, and took a prominence unaccountable, according to the laws of twilight, arbitrary and mysterious.

Fox felt that the view had repaid his toil, and set his face to go down again, with a tendency towards bread and cheese ; but his very first step caused such a slide of shingle and loose ballast, that he would have been lucky to escape with a broken bone, had he followed it. Thereupon instead of descending there, he thought it wiser to keep along the ledge at the foot of the precipice, and search for a safer track down the hill. None however presented itself, until he had turned the corner of the limestone crag, and reached its southern side, where the descent became less abrupt and stony.

Here he was stepping sideways down, for the pitch was still sharp and dangerous, and the daylight failing in the blinks of hills, when he heard a loud shout—"Jemmy ! Jemmy !"—which seemed to spring out of the earth at his feet. In the start of surprise he had shaped his lips for the answering halloa, when good luck more than discretion saved him ; for both his feet slipped, and his breath was caught. By a quick turn he recovered balance ; but the check had given him time to think, and spying a stubby cornel-bush, he came to a halt behind it, and looked through the branches cautiously.

Some twenty yards further down the hill, he saw a big man come striding forth from the bowels of the earth—as it seemed at first—and then standing with his back turned, and the haze beyond enlarging him. And then again, that mighty shout rang up the steep and down the valley— "Jemmy, Jemmy, come back, I tell thee, or I'l let thee know what's what !"

Fox kept close, and crouched in his bush, for he never had seen such a man till now, unless it were in a caravan ; and a shudder ran through him, as it came home that his friend down there could with one hand rob, throttle, and throw him down a mining shaft. This made him keep a very sharp look-out, and have one foot ready for the lightest of leg-bail.

Presently a man of moderate stature, who could have walked under the other's arm, came panting and grumbling back again from a bushy track leading downwards. He flung something on the ground and asked—

"What be up now ; to vetch me back up-hill for ? Harvey, there bain't no sense in 'e. Maight every bit as well a' had it out, over a half pint of beer."

"Sit you there, Jem," replied the other, pressing him down on a ledge of stone with the weight of one thumb on his shoulder. Then he sat himself down on a higher ridge, and pulled out a pipe, with a sigh as loud as the bellows of a forge could compass ; and then slowly spread upon the dome of his knee a patch of German punk, and struck sparks into it.

There was just light enough for Fox to see that the place where they sat was at the mouth of a mining shaft, or sloping adit ; over the rough stone crown of which, standing as he did upon a higher level, he could descry their heads and shoulders, and the big man's fingers as he moved them round his pipe. Presently a whiff of coarse brown smoke came floating uphill to the Doctor's nostrils ; and his blood ran cold, as he began to fear that this great Harvey must be the Harvey Tremlett, of whom he had heard from Mr. Penniloe.

"Made up my maind I have. Can't stand this no longer ;" said the big man, with the heavy drawl, which nature has inflicted upon very heavy men. "Can't get no more for a long day's work, than a hop o' my thumb like you does."

"And good raison why, mate. Do 'e ever do a hard day's work ?" Fox could have sworn that the smaller throat gave utterance to the larger share of truth. "What be the vally of big arms and legs, when a chap dothn't care to make use of 'un ?"

But the big man was not controversial. Giants are generally above that weakness. He gave a long puff, and confined himself to facts.

"Got my money : and d—d little it is. And now I means to hook it. You can hang on, if you be vule enough."

"What an old Turk it is!" Jem replied reproachfully. "Did ever you know me throw you over, Harvey? Who is it brings you all the luck? Tell 'e what—let's go back to Clampits. What a bit o' luck that loudering wor!"

"Hor, hor, hor!" the big man roared. "A purty lot they be to Perlycrass! To take Jemmy Kettel for a gentleman! And a doctor too! Oh Lord! Oh Lord! Doctor Jemmy Vox Kettel! Licensed to deal in zalts and zenna, powders, pills, and bolusses. Oh Jemmy, Jemmy, my eye, my eye!"

"Could do it, I'll be bound, as well as he doth. A vaine doctor, to dig up the Squire of the parish, and do it wrong way too, they zay of 'un! Vaine doctor, wasn't 'un? Oh Lord! Oh Lord!"

As these two rovers combined in a hearty roar of mirth at his expense, Dr. Jemmy Fox, instead of being grateful for a purely impartial opinion, gave way to ill feeling, and stamped one foot in passionate remonstrance. Too late he perceived that this movement of his had started a pebble below the cornel-bush, and sent it rolling down the steep. Away went the pebble with increasing skips, and striking the crown of the pit-mouth flew just over the heads of the uncouth jokers.

"Halloa, Jemmy! Anybody up there? Just you goo, and look, my boy."

Fox shrunk into himself, as he heard those words in a quicker roar coming up to him. If they should discover him, his only chance would be to bound down the hill, reckless of neck, and desperate of accident. But the light of the sky at the top of the hill was blocked by the rampart of rock, and so there was nothing for him to be marked upon.

"Nort but a badger, or a coney there, I reckon," Jem Kettel said, after peering up the steep; and just then a rabbit of fast style of life whisked by; "Goo on, Harvey. You han't offered me no 'bacco!"

"You tak' and vinish 'un;" said the lofty-minded giant, poking his pipe between the other fellow's teeth. "And now you give opinion; if the Lord hath gived thee any."

" Well, I be up for bunkum, every bit so much as you be. But where shall us be off to? That's the p'int of zettlement. Clampits, I say. Roaring fun there, and the gim'-keepers aveared of 'e."

" Darsn't goo there yet, I tell 'e. Last thing old moother did was to send me word, Passon to Perlycrass had got the tip on me. Don't want no bother with them blessed Beaks again."

" Wonder you didn't goo and twist the Passon's neck." The faithful mate looked up at him, as if the captain had failed of his duty, unaccountably.

" Wouldn't touch a hair of that man's head, if it wor here atwixt my two knees." Harvey Tremlett brought his fist down on his thigh, with a smack that made the stones ring round him. "Tell 'e why, Jem Kettel. He have took my little Zip along of his own chiller, and a' maneth to make a lady on her. And a lady the little wench hath a right to be—just you say the contrairy—if hanncient vam'ley, and all that, have right to count. Us Tremletts was here, long afore they Waldrons."

The smaller man appeared afraid to speak. He knew the weak point of the big man perhaps, and that silence oils all such bearings.

" Tull 'e what, Jemmy," said the other coming round, after stripping his friend's mouth of his proper pipe; " us 'll go up country—shoulder packs and be off, soon as ever the moon be up. Like to see any man stop me, I would."

He stood up, with the power of his mighty size upon him ; a man who seemed fit to stop an avalanche, and able to give as much trouble about stopping him.

" All right, I be your man ; " replied the other, speaking as if he were quite as big, and upon the whole more important. " Bristol fust ; and then Lunnon, if so plaise 'e. Always a bit of louderin' there. But that remindeth me of Perlycrass. Us be bound to be back by fair-time, you know. Can't afford to miss old Timberlegs."

" Time enow for that ; " Harvey Tremlett answered. " Zix or zeven weeks yet to Perlycrass fair. What time wor it as old Timberlegs app'inted ? "

" Ten o'clock at naight, by Churchyard wall. Reckon the old man hath another job of louderin' handy. What a spree that wor, and none a rap the wiser ! Come along, Harvey, let's have a pint at the *Kiln*, to drink good luck to this here new start."

The big man took his hat off, while the other jumped nimbly on a stump and flung over his head the straps of both their bundles ; and then with a few more leisurely and peaceful oaths they quitted their stony platform, and began to descend the winding path, from which Jem Kettel had been recalled.

Fox was content for a minute or two with peeping warily after them, while his whole frame tingled with excitement, wrath, and horror, succeeded by a burning joy at the knowledge thus vouchsafed to him, by a higher power than fortune. As soon as he felt certain that they could not see him, even if they looked back again, he slipped from his lurking-place, and at some risk of limb set off in a straighter course than theirs for the Public house in the valley, where a feeble light was twinkling. From time to time he could hear the two rovers laughing at their leisure, probably with fine enjoyment of very bad jokes at his expense. But he set his teeth, and made more speed, and keeping his distance from them, easily arrived first at the Inn, where he found his bread and cheese set forth, in a little private parlour having fair view of the Bar.

This suited him well, for his object was to obtain so clear a sight of them, that no change of dress or disguise should cast any doubt upon their identity ; and he felt sure that they were wending hither to drink good speed to their enterprise. There was not much fear of their recognising him, even if his face were known to them, which he did not think at all likely. But he provided against any such mishap, by paying his bill beforehand, and placing his candle so that his face was in the dark. Then he fell to and enjoyed his bread and cheese ; for the ride and the peril had produced fine relish, and a genuine Cheddar—now sighed for so vainly—did justice to its nativity. He also enjoyed, being now in safety, the sweet sense of turning the tables upon his wanton and hateful deriders.

For sure enough, while his mouth was full, and the froth on his ale was winking at him, in came those two scoffing fellows, followed by a dozen other miners. It appeared to

U

be pay-night, and generous men were shedding sixpences on
one another; but Fox saw enough to convince him that
the rest fought shy of his two acquaintances.

When he saw this, a wild idea occurred to him for a
moment—was it not possible to arrest that pair, with the
aid of their brother miners? But a little consideration
showed the folly of such a project. He had no warrant,
no witness, no ally, and he was wholly unknown in that
neighbourhood. And even if the miners should believe his
tale, would they combine, to lay hands on brother workmen, and hand them over to the mercies of the law?
Even if they would, it was doubtful that they could, sturdy
fellows though they were.

But the young man was so loth to let these two
vagabonds get away, that his next idea was to bribe
somebody to follow them, and keep them in view until he
should come in chase, armed with the needful warrant, and
supported by stout *p sse comitatus*. He studied the faces
of his friends at the Bar, to judge whether any were fitted
for the job. Alas, among all those rough and honest
features, there was not a spark of craft, nor a flash of swift
intelligence. If one of them were put to watch another,
the first thing he would do would be to go and tell him
of it.

And what Justice of the Peace would issue warrant
upon a stranger's deposition of hearsays? Much against
his will, Jemmy Fox perceived that there was nothing for
it, but to give these two rogues a wide berth for the
present, keep his own counsel most jealously, and be ready
to meet them at Perlycross fair. And even so, on his long
homeward ride, he thought that the prospect was brighten-
ing in the west; and that he with his name cleared might
come forward, and assert his love for the gentle Nicie.

CHAPTER XXIX.

TWO PUZZLES.

"THEN if I understand aright, Lady Waldron, you wish me to drop all further efforts for the detection of those miscreants? And that too at the very moment, when we had some reason to hope that we should at last succeed. And all the outlay, which is no trifle, will have been simply thrown away! This course is so extraordinary, that you will not think me inquisitive, if I beg you to explain it."

Mr. Webber, the lawyer, was knitting his forehead, and speaking in a tone of some annoyance, and much doubt, as to the correctness of his own reluctant inference. Meanwhile the Spanish lady was glancing at him with some dismay, and then at Mr. Penniloe, who was also present, for the morning's discussion had been of business matters.

"No, I doubt very much if you quite comprehend," she answered, with Mr. Penniloe's calm eyes fixed upon her. "I did not propose to speak entirely like that. What I was desirous of describing to you is, that to me it is less of eagerness to be going on with so much haste, until the return of my dear son. He for instance will direct things, and with his great—great command of the mind, will make the proceedings to succeed, if it should prove possible for the human mind to do it. And there is no one in this region, that can refuse him anything."

Mr. Penniloe saw that she spoke with some misgivings, and shifted her gaze from himself to the lawyer and back again, with more of enquiry, and less of dictation, than her usual tone conveyed.

"The matter is entirely one for your ladyship's own decision," replied Mr. Webber, beginning to fold up the papers he had submitted. "Mr. Penniloe has left that to us, as was correct, inasmuch as it does not concern the trust. I will stop all enquiries at once, upon receiving your instructions to that effect."

"But—but I think you do not well comprehend. Perhaps I could more clearly place it with the use of my own tongue. It is nothing more than this. I wish that my dear son should not give up his appointment as Officer, and come back to this country, for altogether nothing. I wish that he should have the delight of thinking that—that it shall be of his own procuration, to unfold this mysterious case. Yes, that is it—that is all that I wish—to let things wait a little, until my son comes."

If either of her listeners had been very keen, or endowed with the terrier nose of suspicion, he would have observed perhaps that the lady had found some relief from an afterthought, and was now repeating it as a happy hit. But Mr. Penniloe was too large, and Mr. Webber too rough of mind—in spite of legal training—to pry into a lady's little turns of thought.

"Very well, madam," said the lawyer, rising, "that finishes our business for to-day, I think. But I beg to congratulate you on your son's return. I cannot call to mind that I have heard of it before. Every one will be delighted to see him. Even in his father's time, everybody was full of him. When may we hope to see him, Lady Waldron?"

"Before very long, I have reason for good hope," the lady replied, with a smile restoring much of the beauty of her careworn face. "I have not heard the day yet; but I know that he will come. He has to obtain permission from all the proper authorities, of course. And that is like your very long and very costful processes of the Great British law, Mr. Webber. But now I will entreat of you to excuse me any more. I have given very long attention. Mr. Webber, will you then oblige me by being the host to Mr. Penniloe? The refreshment is in the approximate room."

"Devilish fine woman," Mr. Webber whispered, as her ladyship sailed away. "Wonderfully clever too! How she does her w's—I don't know much about them, but I always understood, that there never was any one born out of England, who could make head or tail of his w's. Why, she speaks English quite like a native! But I see you are looking at me. Shocking manners, I confess, to swear in the presence of a parson, sir; though plenty of them do it—ha, ha, ha!—in their own absence, I suppose."

"It is not my presence, Mr. Webber. That makes it

neither better nor worse. But the presence of God is everywhere."

"To be sure! So it is. Come into the next room. Her ladyship said we should find something there. I suppose we shan't see Missy though," said the lawyer, as he led the Parson to the luncheon-table. "She fights very shy of your humble servant now. Girls never forgive that sort of thing. I don't often make such a mistake though, do I? And it was my son Waldron's fault altogether. Waldron is a sharp fellow, but not like me. Can't see very far into a milestone. Pity to stop the case, before we cleared Fox. I don't understand this new turn though. A straw shows the way the wind blows. Something behind the scenes, Mr. Penniloe. More there than meets the eye. Is it true that old Fox is dropping off the hooks?"

"If you mean to ask me, Mr. Webber, what I have heard about his state of health, I fear that there is little hope of his recovery. Dr. Fox returns to-morrow, as you may have heard through—through your especial agents. You know what my opinion is of that proceeding on your part."

"Yes, you spoke out pretty plainly. And, by George, you were right, sir! As fine a property as any in the county. I had no idea it was half as much. Why, bless my heart sir, Jemmy Fox will be worth his £8000 a year, they tell me!"

"I am glad that his worth," Mr. Penniloe said quietly, "is sufficient *per annum* to relieve him from your very dark suspicion."

"Got me there!" replied Webber, with a laugh. "Ah, you parsons always beat the lawyers. Bury us, don't you? If you find no other way. But we get the last fee after all. Probate, sir, Probate is an expensive thing. Well, I must be off. I see my gig is ready. If you can make my peace with Jemmy Fox, say a word for me. After all it looked uncommonly black, you know. And young men should be forgiving."

Scarcely had his loud steps ceased to ring, when a very light pit-a-pat succeeded, and Mr. Penniloe found himself in far more interesting company. Nicie came softly, and put back her hair, and offered her lovely white forehead to be kissed, and sat down with a smile that begged pardon for a sigh.

" Oh, Uncle Penniloe, I am so glad! I thought I should never have a talk with you again. My fortune has been so frightful lately. Everything against me, the same as it has been with this dear little soul here."

She pointed to *Jess*, the wounded one, who trotted in cheerfully upon three legs, with the other strapped up in a white silk pouch. The little doggie wagged her tail, and looked up at the Clergyman, with her large eyes full of soft gratitude and love; as by that reflex action, which a dog's eyes have without moving, they took in—and told their intense delight in—that vigilant nurse, and sweet comrade, Nicie.

" Oh, she is so proud ;" Miss Waldron said, looking twice as proud herself; "this is the first time that she has had the privilege of going upon three legs, without anybody's hand; and she does think so much of herself! *Jess*, go and show Uncle Penniloe what she can do, now her health is coming back. *Jess*, go and cut a little caper—very steadily, you know, for fear of going twisty; and keep her tail up, all the time! Now *Jess* come, and have a pretty kiss; because she has earned it splendidly.

" She takes my breath away, because she is so good ;" continued Nicie, leaning over her. " I have studied her character for six weeks now, and there is not a flaw to be found in it, unless it is a noble sort of jealousy. *Pixie*"—here *Jess* uttered a sharp small growl, and showed a few teeth as good as ever—" I must not mention his name again, because it won't do to excite her ; but he is out in the cold altogether, because he has never shown any heroism. No, no, he shan't come, *Jess*. He is locked up, for want of chivalry. Oh, Uncle Penniloe, there is one question I have long been wanting to ask you. Do you think it possible for even God to forgive the man—the brute, I mean—who slashed this little dear like that, for being so loving, and so true ?"

" My dear child," Mr. Penniloe replied; " I have just been saying to myself, how like your dear father you are growing—in goodness and kindness of face, I mean. But

when you look like that, the resemblance is quite lost. I
should never have thought you capable of such a ferocious
aspect."

"Ah, that is because you don't know what I can do."
But as she spoke, her arched brows were relaxing, and her
flashing eyes filled with their usual soft gleam. "You
forget that I am half a Spaniard still, or at any rate a
quarter one, and therefore I can be very terrible sometimes.
Ah, you should have seen me the other day. I let somebody
know who I am. He thought perhaps that butter wouldn't
melt in my mouth. Did not I astonish him, the impertinent
low wretch?"

"Why, Nicie, this is not at all like you! I always quote
you as a model of sweet temper. Who can have aroused
your angry passions thus?"

"Oh, never mind. I should like to tell you, and I want
to tell you very much. But I am not permitted, though I
don't know why. My mother has begged me particularly
not to speak of that man who came—gentleman, I suppose
he would call himself—but there, I am telling you all about
him! And mother is so different, and so much more humble
now. If she were still as unfair as she was, I should not be
so particular. But she seems to be so sad, and so mysterious
now, without accusing any one. And so I will not say a
word against her orders. You would not wish it, Uncle
Penniloe, I am sure."

"Certainly not, my dear. I will not ask another question.
I have noticed that your mother is quite different myself. I
hope she is not falling into really bad health."

"No, I don't think that. But into frightfully low spirits.
We have enough to account for that, haven't we, Uncle
Penniloe? To think of my dear father, all this time! What
can I do? I am so wretchedly helpless. I try to trust
in God, and to say to myself—' What does the earthly part
matter, after all? When the soul is with the Lord, or only
waiting for His time, and perhaps rewarded all the better
—because—because of wicked treatment here.' But oh, it
won't do, Uncle Penniloe, it won't, when I think how noble
and how good he was, and to be treated in that way! And
then I fall away, and cry, and sob, and there comes such a
pain—such a pain in my heart, that I have no breath left,

and can only lie down, and pray that God would take me to my father. Is it wicked? I suppose it is. But how am I to help it?"

"No, my dear, it is not wicked to give way sometimes." The Parson's voice was tremulous, at sight of her distress, and remembrance of his own, not so very long ago. "Sorrow is sent to all of us, and doubtless for our good; and if we did not feel it, how could we be at all improved by it? But you have borne it well, my child; and so has your good mother, considering how the first sad blow has been doubled and prolonged so strangely. But now it will be better for you, ever so much better, Nicie, with your dear brother home again."

"But when will that be? Perhaps not for years. We do not even know where he is. They were not likely to stay long in Malta. He may be at the Cape of Good Hope by this time, if the ship has had long enough to get there. Everything seems to be so much against us."

"Are you sure that you are right, my dear?" Mr. Penniloe asked with no little surprise. "From what your mother said just now, I hoped that I should see my old pupil very soon."

"I am afraid not, Uncle Penniloe. My dear mother seems to confuse things a little, or not quite understand them. Through her late illness, no doubt it is. We have not had a word from Tom, since that letter, which had such a wonderful effect, as I told you, when you were gone to London. And then, if you remember, he had no idea how long they were to be at Valetta. And he said nothing about their future movements very clearly. So full of his duties, no doubt, that he had no time to write long particulars. Even now he may never have heard of—of what has happened, and our sad condition. They may have been at sea, ever since he wrote. Soldiers can never tell where they may have to be."

"That has always been so, and is a part of discipline;" the Parson was thinking of the Centurion and his men. "But even if your letter should have gone astray, they must have seen some English newspapers, I should think."

"Tom is very clever, as you know, Uncle Penniloe; but he never reads a word, when he can help it. And besides

that, it is only fair to remember that he is under Government. And the Government never neglects an opportunity
of turning right into left, and the rest upside down. If all
the baggage intended for their draft, was sent to the West
Indies, because they were ordered to the East, it ought to
follow that their letters would go too. But the worst of it
is that one cannot be sure they will stick to a mistake, after
making it."

"It is most probable that they would; especially if it
were pointed out to them. Your dear father told me that
they never forgive anybody for correcting them. But how
then could your mother feel so sure about Tom's coming
home almost immediately?"

"It puzzles me, until I have time to think;" answered
Nicie, looking down. "She has never said a word to me
about it, beyond praying and hoping for Tom to come home.
Oh, I know, or at least I can guess, how! She may have
had a dream—she believes firmly in her dreams, and she
has not had time to tell me yet."

Mr. Penniloe had no right to seek further, and no inclination so to do. The meanest, mangiest, and most
sneaking understrapper of that recent addition to our liberal
institutions—the "Private Enquiry Firm"—could never
have suspected Nicie Waldron, after looking at her, of any
of those subterfuges, which he (like a slack-skin'd worm)
wriggles into. But on the other hand who could suppose
that Lady Waldron would endeavour to mislead her own
man of business by a trumpery deceit? And yet who was
that strange visitor, of whom her daughter was not allowed
to speak?

Unable to understand these things, the curate shortly
took his leave, being resolved, like a wise man, to think as
little as he could about them, until Time—that mighty
locksmith, at whom even Love rarely wins the latest laugh
—should bring his skeleton key to bear on the wards of
this enigma.

What else can a busy man do, when puzzled even by his
own affairs? And how much more must it be so, in the
business of other persons, which he doubts his right to
meddle with? Perhaps it would have been difficult to find
any male member of our race more deeply moved by the

haps and mishaps of his fellow-creatures than this Parson of
Perlycross; and yet he could take a rosier view for most
of them than they took for themselves. So when he left
the grounds of Walderscourt, he buttoned up his Spencer,
and stepped out bravely, swinging his stick vigorously, and
trusting in the Lord.

"What did 'e hat me vor, like that?" cried a voice of
complaint from a brambled ditch, outside a thick copse
known as Puddicombe Wood. Mr. Penniloe had not got
his glasses on, and was grieved to feel rather than to see,
although he was at the right end of his stick, that he had
brought it down (with strong emphasis of a passage in his
coming sermon) on the head of a croucher in that tangled
ditch.

"Oh I beg your pardon! I am so sorry. I had not the
least idea there was anybody there. I was thinking of the
Sower, and the cares that choke the seed. But get up, and
let me see what I have done. What made you hide yourself
down there? I am not the gamekeeper. Why, it is Sam
Speccotty! Poaching again, I am afraid, Sam. But I
hope I have not hurt you—so very much."

"Bruk' my head in two. That's what you have done,
Passon. Oh you can't goo to tell on me, after hatting me
on the brains with clubstick! Ooh, ooh, ooh! I be gooing
to die, I be."

"Speccotty, no lies, and no shamming!" Mr. Penniloe
put on his spectacles, for he knew his customer well enough,
—a notorious poacher, but very seldom punished, because
he was considered "a natural." "This is no clubstick, but
a light walking-stick; and between it and your head there
was a thick briar, as well as this vast mop of hair. Let me
see what you have got under that tree-root."

Sam had been vainly endeavouring to lead his Minister
away from his own little buried napkin, or rather sack of
hidden treasure. "Turn it out;" commanded the Parson,
surprised at his own austerity.

"A brace of cock-pheasants, a couple of woodcocks, two
couple of rabbits, and a leash of hares! Oh, Sam, Sam!
What have you done? Speccotty, I am ashamed of you."

"Bain't no oother chap within ten maile," said Speccotty,
regarding the subject from a different point of view; "as

could a' dooed that, since dree o'clock this marnin'; now Passon do 'e know of wan?"

"I am happy to say that I do not; neither do I wish for his acquaintance. Give up your gun, Sam. Even if I let you off, I insist upon your tools; as well as all your plunder."

"Han't a got no goon," replied the poacher, looking slyly at the Parson, through the rough shock of his hair. "Never vired a goon, for none on 'un. Knows how to vang 'un, wi'out thiccy."

"I can well believe that." Mr. Penniloe knew not a little of poachers, from his boyish days, and was not without that secret vein of sympathy for them, which every sportsman has, so long as they elude and do not defy the law. "But I must consider what I shall do. Send all this to my house to-night, that I may return it to the proper owners. Unless you do that, you will be locked up to-morrow."

"Oh Passon, you might let me have the Roberts. To make a few broth for my old moother."

"Not a hair, nor a feather shall you keep. Your mother shall have some honest broth—but none of your stolen rabbits, Speccotty. You take it so lightly, that I fear you must be punished."

"Oh don't 'e give me up, sir. Oh, my poor head do go round so! Don't 'e give me up, for God's sake, Passon. Two or dree things I can tell 'e, as 'e 'd give the buttons off thy coat to know on. Do 'e mind when the Devil wor seen on Hagdon Hill, the day avore the good lady varled all down the Harseshoe?"

"I do remember hearing some foolish story, Sam, and silly people being frightened by some strange appearances, very easily explained, no doubt."

"You volk, as don't zee things, can make 'un any colour to your own liking. But I tell 'e old Nick gooed into the body of a girt wild cat up there; and to this zide of valley, her be toorned to a black dog. Zayeth so in the Baible, don't 'un?"

"I cannot recall any passage, Sam, to that effect; though I am often surprised by the knowledge of those who use Holy Scripture for argument, much more freely than for guidance. And I fear that is the case with you."

"Whuther a' dooed it, or whuther a' did not, I be the ekal of 'un, that I be. When her coom to me, a'gapin' and a yawnin', I up wi' bill-hook, and I gie'd 'un zummat. If 'tis gone back to hell a' harth, a' wun't coom out again, I reckon, wi'out Sam Speccotty's mark on 'un. 'Twill zave 'e a lot of sarmons, Passon. Her 'ont want no more knockin' on the head, this zide of Yester, to my reckoning. Hor! Passon be gone a'ready; a' don't want to hear of that. Taketh of his trade away. Ah, I could tell 'un zomethin', if a' wadn't such a softie."

Mr. Penniloe had hastened on, and no longer swung his holly-stick; not through fear of knocking any more skulking poachers on the head, but from the sadness which always fell upon him, at thought of the dark and deadly blow the Lord had been pleased to inflict on him.

CHAPTER XXX.

FRANKLY SPEAKING.

SUPPOSING a man to be engaged—as he often must be even now, when the general boast of all things is, that they have done themselves by machinery—in the useful and interesting work of sinking a well, by his own stroke and scoop; and supposing that, when he is up to his hips, and has not got a dry thread upon him, but reeks and drips, like a sprawling jelly-fish—at such a time there should drop upon him half a teaspoonful of water from the bucket he has been sending up—surely one might expect that man to accept with a smile that little dribble, even if he perceives it.

Alas, he does nothing of the kind! He swears, and jumps, as if he were in a shower-bath of vitriol, then he shouts for the ladder, drags his drenched legs up, and ascends for the purpose of thrashing his mate, who has dared to let a drop slip down on him. Such is the case; and no ratepayer who has had to delve for his own water (after being robbed by sewage-works) will fail to perceive the force of it.

Even so (if it be lawful to compare small things with great), even so it has been, and must be for ever, with a

young man over head and ears in love, and digging in the
depths of his own green gault. He throws back his head,
and he shovels for his life ; he scorns the poor fellows who
are looking down upon him ; and he sends up bucketfuls of
his own spooning, perhaps in the form of gravelly verse.
The more he gets waterlogged the deeper is his glow, and
the bowels of the earth are as goldbeaters' skin to him.
But let anybody cast cold water, though it be but a drop,
on his fervid frozen loins, and up he comes with both fists
clenched.

These are the truths that must be cited, in explanation
of the sad affair next to be recorded—the quarrel between
two almost equally fine fellows,—Dr. Jemmy Fox to wit,
and Master Frank Gilham. These two had naturally good
liking for each other. There was nothing very marvellous
about either of them ; although their respective mothers
perceived a heavenful of that quality. But they might be
regarded as fair specimens of Englishmen—more wonderful
perhaps than admirable in the eyes of other races. If it
were needful for any one to make choice between them,
that choice would be governed more by points of liking,
than of merit. Both were brave, straightforward, stubborn,
sensible, and self-respecting fellows, a little hot-headed
sometimes perhaps, but never consciously unjust.

It seemed a great pity, that such a pair should fall away
from friendship, when there were so many reasons for
goodwill and amity ; not to mention gratitude—that flower
of humanity, now extinct, through the number of its
cuttings that have all damped off. Jemmy Fox indeed had
cherished a small slip of that, when Gilham stood by him
in his first distress ; but unhappily the slightest change
of human weather is inevitably fatal to our very miffy
plant.

Young as he was, Frank Gilham had been to market
already too many times, to look for offal value in gratitude,
and indeed he was too generous to regard it as his due ;
still his feelings of friendship, and of admiration for the
superior powers of the other, were a little aggrieved when
he found himself kept at a distance, and avoided, for reasons
which he understood too well. So when he heard that
young Dr. Fox had returned from that visit to his father,

he rode up to *Old Barn,* to call upon him, and place things upon a plainer footing.

Jemmy received him in a friendly manner, but with his mind made up to put a stop to any nonsense concerning his sister Christie, if Gilham should be fool enough to afford him any opening. And this the young yeoman did without delay, for he saw no good reason why he should be made too little of.

"And how did you leave Miss Fox?" he asked, as they took their chairs opposite the great fireplace, in the bare room, scientific with a skull or two, and artistic with a few of Christie's water-colour sketches.

"I had no difficulty in leaving her," Jemmy answered, with a very poor attempt at wit, which he intended to be exasperating.

"How was she, I mean? I dare say you got away, without thinking much of anybody but yourself." Frank Gilham was irritated, as he deserved to be.

"Thank you; well, I think upon the whole," Jemmy Fox drawled out his words, as if his chin were too slack to keep them going, and he stroked it in a manner which is always hateful; "yes, I think I may say upon the whole, that she was quite as well as can be expected. I hope you can say the same of your dear mother."

Frank Gilham knew that he was challenged to the combat; and he came forth, as the duty is, and the habit of an Englishman.

"This is not the first time you have been rude to me;" he said. "And I won't pretend not to know the reason. You think that I have been guilty of some presumption, in daring to lift my eyes to your sister."

"To tell you the truth," replied Fox getting up, and meeting his steadfast gaze steadfastly; "you have expressed my opinion, better than I could myself have put it."

"It is not the sort of thing one can argue about," said the other, also rising; "I know very well that she is too good for me, and has the right to look ever so much higher. But for all that, I have a perfect right to set my heart upon her; especially considering—considering, that I can't help it. And if I do nothing to annoy her, or even to let

her know of my presumption, what right have you to make
a grievance of it?"

"I have never made a grievance of it. I simply wish
you to understand, that I do not approve of it."

"You have a perfect right to disapprove; and to let me
know that you do so. Only it would have been more to
your credit, if you had done it in an open manner, and in
plain English; instead of cutting me, or at any rate
dropping my acquaintance. I don't call that straightforward."

"The man is a jackass. What rot he talks! Look
here, my fine fellow. How could I speak to you about it,
before you acknowledged your infatuation? Could I come
up to you in the street, and say—'Hi there! You are in
love with my sister, are you? If you want to keep a sound
skin, you'll haul off.' Is that the straightforward course I
should have taken?"

"Well, there may be something in the way you put it.
But I would leave it to anybody, whether you have acted
fairly. And why should I haul off, I should like to know.
I won't haul off, for fifty of you. Because I have got no
money, I suppose! How would you like to be ordered to
haul off from Miss Waldron, in case you were to lose your
money, or anything went against you? Instead of hauling
off, I'll hold on—in my own mind, at any rate. I don't
want a farthing of the money of your family. I would
rather not have it,—dirty stuff, what good is it? But I
tell you what—if your dear sister would only give me one
good word, I would snap my fingers at you, and everybody.
I know I am nothing at all. However, I am quite as good
as you are; though not to be spoken of, in the same week
with her. I tell you, I don't care twopence for any man,
or all the men in the world put together—if only your
sister thinks well of me. So now, you know what you may
look out for."

"All this is very fine; but it won't do, Gilham." Fox
thought he saw his way to settle him. "Surely you are
old enough to see the folly of getting so excited. My
sister will very soon be married to Sir Henry Haggerstone
—a man of influence, and large fortune. And you—, well
to some lady, who can see your value, through a ball of

glass, as you do. That power is not given to all of us; but on no account would I disparage you. And when this little joke is over, you will come, and beg my pardon; and we shall be hearty friends again."

"Sir Henry Haggerstone!" Gilham replied, in a tone of contempt, which would justly have astonished that exemplary baronet. "Not she! Why, that's the old codger that has had three wives—fiddles, and fiddlesticks, I'm not afraid of him! But just tell me one thing now, upon your honour. Would you object to me, if she liked me, and I had a hundred thousand pounds?"

"Well, no, I don't know that I should, Mr. Gilham."

"Then, Dr. Fox, you would sell your sister, for a hundred thousand pounds. And if she likes to put a lower price upon herself, what right have you to stop her?"

"I tell you, Gilham, all this is childish talk. If Christie has been fool enough to take a fancy to you, it is your place, as a man of honour, to bear in mind how young she is; and to be very careful that you do nothing to encourage it."

"But there is no chance of such luck. Has it ever seemed likely to you, my dear Jemmy, that she—that she even had any idea——"

"A great deal too much, I am afraid. At least, I don't mean to say that exactly—but at any rate—well, enough to place you on your honour."

"And upon my honour I will be—not to neglect any shadow of a chance, that turns up in my favour. But I can never believe it, Jemmy; she is ever so much too lofty, and too lovely, and too clever—did anybody ever see such fingers, and such eyes, and such a smile, and such a voice? And altogether——"

"Altogether a pack of rubbish. The sooner you order your horse, the better. I can't have you raving here, and fetching all the parish up the hill."

"I am a sensible man, Jemmy Fox. I know a noble thing, when I see it. You are too small of nature, and too selfish for such perception. But you may abuse me, to your heart's content. You will never get a harsh word in reply; after what you have told me. Because there must be good in you, or you would never have such a sister. I shall take my own course now; without the smallest consideration for your crotchets. Now don't make any mistake about that. And as for honour—clearly understand, that I shall pitch it to the Devil."

" Well, don't come here with any more of your raving. And don't expect me to encourage you. You have been a good fellow—I don't mind saying that—until you took this infernal craze."

"Oh, I won't trouble you; never you fear. You are doing what you think right, no doubt; and you are welcome to do your worst. Only there is one thing I must say. I know that you are too much of a man, to belie me to your sister, or run me down, behind my back. Shake hands, Jemmy, before I go; perhaps we shall never shake hands again."

"Get somebody to leave you that hundred thousand pounds," said Fox, as he complied with this request; "and then we'll shake hands all day long, instead of shaking fists at each other."

"Jem Crow said to his first wife's mother,
What right have you to be anybody's brother?"

Gilham responded, being in high spirits, with this quotation from that piece of negro doggerel, with which all England was at that time crazed. And thus they parted, with a neutral smile; and none the less perhaps, for that each of them perceived that the parting would prove a long one.

" What will Nicie have to say about all this? I shall not be contented until I know;" said Fox to himself, when his visitor was gone; " I have a great mind to go and get my riding gaiters. That blessed mother of hers can scarcely growl at me, if I call to-day; considering how long I have been away. I seem to knock under to everybody now. I can't think what has come over me."

When a man begins to think that of himself, it shows that he is getting pugnacious, and has not found his proper outlet. The finest thing for him is a long ride then; or a long walk, if he has only two legs. Fox was shaking down upon his merits, but still a little crusty with himself, and therefore very much so with every one outside it, when his

x

pretty mare pulled up, to think about the water she was
bound to walk through at Priestwell.

This is one of the fairest hamlets to be found in England.
There are houses enough to make one think of the other
people that live in them; but not so many as to make it
certain that a great many people will be nasty. You might
expect, if you lived there, to know something about everybody in the place; and yet only to lift up your hands, and
smile, when they did a thing you were too wise to do. The
critical inhabitant in such a place—unless he is very
wicked—must be happy. He falls into a habitude of small
smiles; "many a mickle makes a muckle"—if that be the
right way to quote it, which it isn't—however, the result is
all the same, he knows what he is about, and it leads him to
smile twenty times, for one smile he would have had in town.

All these things were producing a fine effect upon the
character of Dr. Gronow. By head and shoulders, without
standing up for himself for a single moment, he was the
biggest man at Priestwell; in knowledge of the world, in
acquaintance with books, in power to give good advice, and
to help the people who took it—the largest. And after the
many hot contentions of his life, and the trouble in being
understood (where the game never pays for the candle)
here he was taken at his own appraisement, after liberal
prepayment.

He was not a bad man, take him all in all; though
inclined by nature to be many-angled, rather than many-
sided. And now, as he stood on the plank that goes over the
brook where the road goes under it, he was about as happy as
the best of men can be. The old Doctor in truth was as full
of delight—though his countenance never expressed it—as
the young Doctor was of dejection. And why? For the
very noble reason, that the wiser man now had his fly-rod
in hand, fly-book in pocket, creel on back, and waterproof
boots upon stiff but sturdy legs. And, main point of all
—he was just setting forth; his return must be effected
perhaps in quite another pair of shoes.

The Priestwell water flows into the Perle from the north,
some half mile higher up than the influx of Susscot brook
from the south, and it used to be full of bright stickles and
dark hovers, peopled with many a bouncing trout. For a

trout of a pound is a bouncer there ; and a half-pounder even is held a comely fish ; and sooth to say, the angler is not so churlish as to fail of finding joy in one of half that size. Not a sign of Spring was on the earth as yet, and very little tidings of it in the air ; but any amount was in the old man's heart, as he listened to the warbling of the brook, and said to himself that he should catch, perhaps, a fish. He was going to fish downwards, as he always did, for he never liked to contradict the water. At the elbow of the stream was his own willow-tree, at the bottom of his lawn, and there a big fish lived—the Dr. Gronow of the liquid realm, who defied the Dr. Gronow of the dry land. Ha, why not tackle him this very afternoon, and ennoble the opening day thereby ; for the miserable floods, and the long snow-time, and the shackling of the stream is over ; no water-colour artist could have brought the stickles to a finer fishing tint ; and lo, there is a trout upon the rise down there, tempted by the quiver of a real iron-blue !

With these thoughts glowing in his heart, and the smoke of his pipe making rings upon the naked alder-twigs, he was giving his flies the last titivating touch—for he always fished with three, though two were one too many—when he heard a voice not too encouraging.

" I say, Doctor, if you don't look out, you'll be certain to get bogged, you know."

" Don't care if I do ;" replied the Doctor, whisking his flies around his head, and startling *Perle* with the flash of his rod.

" You had better go home," continued Jemmy, " and let the banks dry up a bit, and some of your fish have time to breed again. Why, the floods must have washed them all down into the Perle ; and the Perle must have washed them all down into the sea."

" That shows how much you know about it. I have got a most splendid patent dodge, at the bottom of my last meadow. I'll show it to you some fine day, if you are good. It is so constructed that it keeps all my trout from going down into the Perle, and yet it lets all the Perle trout come up to me ; and when they are up, they can't get back again of course. And the same thing reversed, at the top of my grounds. I expect to have more fish than pebbles in my brook. And nobody can see it, that's the beauty of it. But mind, you mustn't say a word about it, Jemmy. People are so selfish ! "

"Of course, I won't; you may trust me. But when you have got everybody else's fish in your water, can you get them out of it ? I know nothing at all about it. But to make any hand at angling, is it not the case that you must take to it in early life ? Look at Pike, for instance. What a hand he is ! Never comes home without a basketful. He'll be here again next week, I believe."

Fox knew well enough that Dr. Gronow hated the very name of Pike.

"I am truly sorry to hear it. I am sure it must be high time for that lad to go to College. Penniloe ought to be sent to prison, for keeping such a poacher. But as for myself, if I caught too many, I should not enjoy it half so much, because I should think there was no skill in it."

"Well, now, I never thought of that. And *pari ratione* if we save too many of our patients, we lay ourselves open to the charge of luck."

"No fear for you, Jemmy. You are not a lucky fellow. Come in and have a talk with me, by and by. I want to hear the last news, if there is any."

"Yes, there is some. But I must tell you now, or never. For I have to ride round through Pumpington. And I came this way on purpose, to get the benefit of your opinion."

"But, my dear fellow, it gets dark so soon ;" Dr. Gronow looked wistfully at his flies. "Well, if you won't be more than five minutes, I will put an iron-blue on, instead of a Half-Kingdon. But don't be longer than you can help. You are the only man in the parish I would stop for."

Omitting all description, except of persons, Fox told the elder doctor what he had learned at the mouth of the Mendip mine, and at the *Smoking Limekiln*, as well as what he knew of Harvey Tremlett from Mr. Penniloe's account, reminding him also of Joe Crang's description, and showing how well it tallied.

"My advice can be given in a word ; and that is 'Not a word ;' " answered Gronow, forgetting his flies for the moment. "Not a word to any one, but Mockham the

magistrate ; and not even to him, until needful. Shrove-
Tuesday, you say, is the date of the Fair. Don't apply for your
warrant, until that morning, if you can get it then without
delay. Only you must make sure that Mockham will be at
home to issue it, and you must have Joe Crang there quietly,
and gag him somewhere for the rest of the day—perhaps a
little opiate in his beer. You see it is of the first importance that not a word should leak out about your intention of nabbing those fellows at the Fair, until you are
down upon them ; for your birds would never come near
the trap. It is perfectly amazing how such things spread,
faster than any bird can fly ; for the whole world seems
to be in league against the law. There is plenty of time for
us to talk it over, between this and then, if you only keep it
close. Of course you have not mentioned it to anybody
yet."

" Not to a soul. I had sense enough for that. But I
might have done so before long, if I had missed meeting
you to-day. Shall I not tell even Penniloe? He has
known everything hitherto."

" Certainly not yet. He is quite safe of course, so
far as mere intention goes ; but he might make a slip,
and he is a nervous man. For his own sake, he had
better not have this upon his mind. And his ideas are
so queer. If he were questioned, I feel sure that he
would not even tell a white lie ; but be frightfully
clumsy, and say, 'I refuse to answer.' Better tell the
whole truth than do that ; for suspicion is shrewder than
certainty."

" But I don't like concealing it from him at all. I fear
he will be hurt, when he comes to know it ; because we
have acted together throughout, and the matter so closely
concerns his parish."

" Have no fear, Jemmy. I'll make that all right. We will
tell him about it on the day of action, and let him know
that for his own sake only, I persuaded you to keep it from
him. Why, that fellow's daughter is in his house, and a
wonderfully clever imp, they say. And I am not at all
sure that he would not preach about it. He thinks so much
more of people's souls, than of their parts that are
rational."

" Very well then, for his own sake, I won't say a word
to him about it. You are right; it would make him
miserable to have such a shindy so long in prospect. For
it will be a rare fight, I can tell you. The fellow is as big
as an elephant almost ; and my namesake, Jem Kettel, is
a stuggy young chap, very likely to prove a tough customer.
And then there will be Timberlegs, whoever he may be."

" All right, Jemmy, we will give a good account of them.
Mind v. Matter always wins the verdict. But let me congratulate you upon your luck. We must get to the bottom
of this strange affair now, if we can only nab those
fellows."

" I should hope so. But how do you think it will prove ?
Who will be detected as the leading villain ? For these
rogues have only been hired of course."

" Well, I own myself puzzled, Jemmy, worse than ever.
Until this last news of yours, I was inclined to think that
there had been some strange mistake all through, while the
good Colonel slept still undisturbed. But now it appears
that I must have been wrong. And I hardly like to tell
you my last idea, because of your peculiar position."

" I know what you mean, and I thank you for it ;" Fox
replied with a rapid glance. " But to my mind that seems
the very reason why I should know everything."

" Well, if you take it so, friend Jemmy, as my first
theory is now proved wrong, my second one is that Lady
Waldron knows more about this matter than anybody else.
She has always shown herself hostile to you, so that my
idea cannot shock you, as otherwise it might. Are you
angry with me ? "

" Not in the least ; though I cannot believe it, thereby
returning good for evil ; for she was quick enough to
believe it—or feign to do so—about me. There are things
that tend towards your conclusion. I am sorry to acknowledge that there are. And yet, until it is positively proved,
I will not think it possible. She is no great favourite of
mine, you know, any more than I am of hers. Also, I am
well aware that women do things a man never would
believe ; and some women don't mind doing anything. But
I cannot persuade myself that she is one of that sort. She
has too much pride to be a hypocrite."

"So I should have thought. But against facts, where are you? Shrove Tuesday will tell us a thing or two however. That is a very nice mare of yours. I know nothing of horses, but judge them by their eyes; though their legs are the proper study. Good-bye, my boy! Perhaps I shall amaze you with a dish of trout to-morrow. They are always in very fine condition here."

CHAPTER XXXI.

A GREAT PRIZE.

ONE of the beauties of this world is, for the many who are not too good for it, that they never can tell what may turn up next, and need not over-exert themselves in the production of novelty, because somebody will be sure to do it for them. And those especially who have the honour and pleasure of dealing with the gentler sex are certain, without any effort of their own, to encounter plenty of vicissitude.

Such was the fortune of Dr. Fox, when he called that day at Walderscourt. He found his sweet Nicie in a sad condition, terribly depressed, and anxious, in consequence of a long interview with her mother, which had been as follows.

For the last fortnight, or three weeks, Lady Waldron had not recovered strength, but fallen away even more, declining into a peculiar and morbid state. Sometimes gloomy, downcast, and listless, secluding herself, and taking very little food, and no exercise whatever ; at other times bewildered, excited, and restless, beginning a sentence and breaking it off, laughing about nothing, and then morose with every one. Pretty Tamar Haddon had a great deal to put up with, and probably would not have shown the needful patience, except for handsome fees lightly earned by reports collected in the village. But Sergeant Jakes being accessible no more—for he had cast off the spell in the Abbey, that Sunday—poor Lady Waldron's anxiety was fed with tales of very doubtful authority. And the strange point was that she showed no impatience at the tardiness of the enquiry now, but rather a petulant displeasure at its long continuance.

Now that very morning, while Fox was on the road to
call upon his beloved, she was sent for suddenly by her
mother, and hastened with some anxiety to the room which
the widow now left so seldom. Inez had long been familiar
with the truth that her mother's love for her was not too
ardent; and she often tried—but without much success—
to believe that the fault was on her part. The mother
ascribed it very largely to some defect in her daughter's
constitution. "She has not one drop of Spanish blood in
her. She is all of English, except perhaps her eyes; and
the eyes do not care to see things of Spain." Thus she
justified herself, unconscious perhaps that jealousy of the
father's love for this pet child had been, beyond doubt, the
first cause of her own estrangement.

This terribly harassed and lonely woman (with no one
but God to comfort her, and very little sense of any consolation thus) was now forsaken by that support of pride
and strength of passion, which had enabled her at first to
show a resolute front to affliction. Leaning back upon a
heavy couch, she was gazing without much interest at the
noble ivory crucifix, which had once so strongly affected her,
but now was merely a work of art, a subject for admiration
perhaps, but not for love or enthusiasm. Of these there was
no trace in her eyes, only apathy, weariness, despondence.

"Lock the outer door. I want no spies," she said in a
low voice which alarmed her daughter; "now come and sit
close to me in this chair. I will speak in my own language.
None but you and I understand it here now."

"It is well, mother mine," replied her daughter, speaking
also in Spanish; "but I wish it were equally well with
you."

"It will never be well with me again, and the time will
be long before it can be well with you. I have doubted
for days about telling you, my child, because I am loth to
grieve you. But the silence upon this matter is very bitter
to me; moreover it is needful that you should know, in
case of my obtaining the blessed release, that you also be
not triumphed over. It is of that unholy outrage I must
speak. Long has it been a black mystery to us. But I
understand it now—alas, I cannot help understanding it!"

Inez trembled exceedingly; but her mother, though

deadly pale, was calm. Both face and voice were under stern control, and there were no dramatic gestures.

"Never admit him within these doors, if I am not here to bar them. Never take his hand, never listen to his voice, never let your eyes rest upon his face. Never give him a crust, though he starve in a ditch; never let him be buried with holy rites. As he has treated my dear husband, so shall God treat him, when he is dead. It is for this reason that I tell you. If you loved your father, remember it."

"But who is it, mother? What man is this, who has abandoned his soul to the Evil One? Make me sure of his name, that I may obey you."

"The man who has done it is my own twin-brother, Rodrigo, Count de Varcas : Rodrigo, the accursed one."

The Spanish lady clasped her hands, and fell back against the wall, and dropped her eyes; as if the curse were upon her also, for being akin to the miscreant. Her daughter could find no words, and was in doubt of believing her own ears.

"Yes, I know well what I am saying;" Lady Waldron began again with some contempt. "I am strong enough. Offer me nothing to smell. Shall I never die? I ought to have died, before I knew this, if there were any mercy in Heaven. That my twin-brother, my own twin-brother, the one I have loved and laboured for, and even insulted my own good husband, because he would not bow down to him —not for any glory, revenge, or religion, but for the sake of grovelling money—oh Inez, my child, that he should have done this!"

"But how do you know that he has done it? Has he made any confession, mother? Surely it is possible to hope against it, unless he himself has said so."

"He has not himself said so. He never does. To accuse himself is no part of his habits, but rather to blame every other. And such is his manner that every one thinks he must be right and his enemies wrong. But to those who have experience of him, the question is often otherwise. You remember that very—very faithful gentleman, who came to us, about a month ago?"

"Mother, can you mean that man, arrogant but low,

who consumed all my dear father's boxes of cigars, and
called himself Señor José Quevedo, and expected even me
to salute him as of kin?"

"Hush, my child! He is your Uncle's foster-brother,
and trusted by him in everything. You know that I have
in the Journals announced my desire to hear from my
beloved brother—beloved alas too much, and vainly. I
was long waiting, I was yearning, having my son in the
distance, and you who went against me in everything, to
embrace and be strengthened by my only brother. What
other friend had I on earth? And in answer to my
anxiety arrives that man, sedate, mysterious, not to be
doubted, but regarded as a lofty cavalier. I take him in,
I trust him, I treat him highly, I remember him as with
my brother always in the milky days of childhood, although
but the son of a well-intentioned peasant. And then I
find what? That he has come for money—for money,
which has always been the bane of my only and well-born
brother, for the very dismal reason that he cannot cling to
it, and yet must have both hands filled with it for ever.
Inez, do you attend to me?"

"Mother, I am doing so, with all my ears; and with all
my heart as well I heed. But these things surprise me
much, because I have always heard from you that my
Uncle Rodrigo was so noble, so chivalrous, so far above all
Englishmen, by reason of the grandeur of his spirit."

"And in that style will he comport himself, upon most
of life's occasions, wherein money does not act as an im-
pediment. Of that character is he always, while having
more than he can spend of it. But let him see the necessity,
and the compulsion to deny himself, too near to him
approaching, and he will not possess that loftiness of spirit,
and benevolence universal. Departing from his larger
condition of mind, he will do things which honour does not
authorise. Things unworthy of the mighty Barcas, from
whom he is descended. But the Barcas have often been
strong and wicked; which is much better than weak and
base."

Her ladyship paused, as in contemplation of the sterling
nobility of her race, and apparently derived some comfort
from the strong wickedness of the Barcas.

"Mother, I hope that it is not so." Nicie's view of excellence was milder. "You are strong but never wicked. I am not strong ; but on the other hand, I trust, that I am not weak and base."

"You never can tell what you can do. You may be most wicked of the wicked yet. Those English girls, that are always good, are braised vegetables without pepper. The only one I ever saw to approve, was the one who was so rude to me. How great her indignation was ! She is worthy to be of Andalusia."

"But why should so wicked a thing be done—so horrible even from a stranger ?" The flashing of Nicie's dark eyes was not unworthy of Andalusia. "How could the meanest greed of money be gratified by such a deed ?"

"In this manner, if I understand aright. During the time of the French invasion, just before our marriage, the Junta of our City had to bear a great part of the burden of supporting and paying our brave troops. They fell into great distress for money, which became scarcer and scarcer, from the terrible war, and the plundering. All lovers of their country came with both hands full of treasure ; and among them my father contributed a loan of noble magnitude, which has impaired for years to come the fortunes of our family. For not a *peseta* will ever be repaid, inasmuch as there was no security. When all they could thus obtain was spent, and the richest men would advance no more, without prospect of regaining it, the Junta (of which my father was a member) contrived that the City should combine with them in pledging its revenues, which were large, to raise another series of loans. And to obtain these with more speed, they appealed to the spirit of gambling ; which is in the hearts of all men, but in different forms and manners.

"One loan that was promulgated thus amounted to 100,000 dollars, contributed in twenty shares of 5,000 dollars each : and every share was to have a life of not less than fifteen years in age appointed to represent it. No money was to be repaid ; but the interest to accumulate, until nineteen out of those twenty lives became extinct, and thereupon the whole was to go to the last survivor, and by that time it would be a very large sum. I believe that the scheme came from the French, who are wonderfully

clever in such calculations; whereas finance is not of us.
Do you seem to yourself to understand it?"

"Not very much, but to some extent. I have read of a
wheel of life; and this appears to me to be a kind of wheel
of death."

"So it is, my child. You can scarcely be so stupid, as
you have been described to me. I am not too strong of the
arithmetic science, though in other ways not wanting.
You will see, that there was a royal treasure thus, increasing for the one who should deserve it, by having more of
life than the nineteen others, and acquiring it thus, for the
time he had to come. That kind of lottery, coming from
Paris, was adopted by other Governments, under the title
of *Tontine*, I think. My dear father, who was a warm
patriot, but unable to contribute more without hope of
return, accepted two of those five thousand dollar shares,
and put into one the name of my brother, and into the
other that of my dear husband, then about to be: because
those two were young, while himself was growing old.
Your father has spoken to me of his share, several times,
as it became of greater value; and he provided for it in his
will, supposing that he should ever become the possessor,
although he approved not of any kind of gambling.

"If you can represent to yourself that scheme, you will
see that each share was enlarged in prospect, as the others
failed of theirs by death; and, of the twenty lives appointed,
the greater part vanished rapidly; many by war, and some
by duels, and others by accident and disease; until it
appears—though we knew it not—that your father and your
Uncle Rodrigo were the sole survivors. Your father and I
kept no watch upon it, being at such a distance; but now
I have learned that your Uncle has been exceedingly acute
and vigilant, having no regard for your dear father, and
small affection, I fear, for me; but a most passionate
devotion to the huge treasure now accumulated upon heavy
interest, and secured by the tolls of the City.

"I am grieved by discovering from this man Quevedo,
that your Uncle has been watching very keenly everything
that has happened here; he has employed an agent, whose
name I could not by any means extort from Quevedo, and
not contented with his reports, but excited by the tidings

of your father's ill-health, he has even been present in these parts himself, to reconnoitre for himself; for he is capable of speaking English, even better than I do. Quevedo is very cautious; but by plying him with Spanish wine, such as he cannot procure in Spain, feigning also to be on his side, I extorted from him more than he wished to part with. No suspicion had I, while he was here, that his master was guilty of the black disgrace thus inflicted upon us: or can you imagine that I would allow that man to remain in the house of the outraged one? And Quevedo himself either feigns, or possesses, total ignorance of this vile deed."

"But, mother dear, how did this suspicion grow upon you? And for what purpose—if I may inquire—was that man Quevedo sent to you?"

"He was sent with two objects. To obtain my signature to an attested declaration as to the date of your father's death; and in the second place to borrow money for the support of your Uncle's claim. It could not be expected that the City would discharge so vast a sum (more than five hundred thousand crowns they say) without interposing every possible obstacle and delay; and our family, through your Uncle's conduct, has lost all the influence it possessed when I was young. I am pleased to think now that he must be disappointed with the very small sum which I advanced, in my deep disgust at discovering, that at the very time when I was sighing and languishing for his support, he was at my very doors, but through his own selfish malignity avoided his twin-sister. Quevedo meant not to have told me that. But alas! I extorted it from him, after a slip of his faithful tongue. For you know, I believe, that your father and uncle were never very friendly. My brother liked not that I should wed an Englishman; all men of this nation he regarded with contempt, boasting as they did in our country, where we permitted them to come and fight. But you have never been told, my child, that the scar upon your dear father's face was inflicted by your Uncle's sword, employed (as I am ashamed to confess) in an unfair combat. Upon recovering from the stealthy blow, your father in his great strength could have crushed him to death, for he was then a stripling; but for my sake he forbore. It has been concealed from you. There is no concealment now."

"Oh, mother, how savage and ignominious also! I wonder that you ever could desire to behold such a man again; and that you could find it in your heart to receive his envoy kindly."

"Many years have passed since then, my child. And we have a saying, 'To a fellow-countryman forgive much, and to a brother everything.' Your father had forgiven him, before the wound was healed. Much more slowly did I forgive. And, but for this matter, never would I have spoken."

"Oh, mother dear, you have had much sorrow! I have never considered it, as I should have done. A child is like an egg, as you say in Spain, that demands all the warmth for itself, and yields none. Yet am I surprised, that knowing so much of him, you still desired his presence, and listened to the deceits of his messenger. But you have wisdom; and I have none. Tell me then what he had to gain, by an outrage hateful to a human being, and impossible to a Christian."

"It is not clear, my child, to put it to your comprehension. The things that are of great power with us are not in this Country so copious. We are loftier. We are more friendly with the Great Powers that reside above. In every great enterprise, we feel what would be their own sentiments; though not to be explained by heretical logic. Your Uncle has never been devoted to the Church, and has profited little by her teaching; but he is not estranged from her so much, that he need in honour hesitate to have use and advantage from her charitable breast. For she loves every one, even those who mock her, with feeble imitation of her calls."

"Mother, but hitherto you have cared little or nothing for Holy Church. You have allowed me to wander from her; and my mind is the stronger for the exercise. Why then this new zeal and devotion?"

"Inez, the reason is very simple; although you may not understand it yet. We love the Institutions that make much of us, even when we are dead, and comfort our bodies with ceremonies, and the weepers with reasons for smiling. This heretic corporation, to which Mr. Penniloe belongs, has many good things imitated from us; but does not understand itself. Therefore, it is not a power in the land, to govern the law, or to guide great actions of property and of behaviour, as the Holy Catholic Church can do, in the lands where she has not been deposed. Knowing how such things are with us, your Uncle (as I am impelled to believe), having plenty of time for preparation, had arranged to make one master-stroke, towards this great object of his life. At once to bring all the Ecclesiastics to his side with fervour, and before the multitude to prove his claim in a manner the most dramatic.

"Behold it thus, as upon a stage! The whole City is agitated with the news, and the immensity of his claim. The young men say that it is just to pay it, if it can be proved, for the honour of the City. But the old men shake their heads, and ask where is the money to come from; what new tolls can be imposed; and who can believe a thing, that must be proved by the oaths of foreign heretics?

" Lo there appears the commanding figure of the Count de Varcas before the great Cathedral doors; behind him a train of sailors bear the body of the great British warrior, well-known among the elder citizens by his lofty stature and many wounds, renowned among the younger as a mighty hero. The Bishop, Archbishop, and all powers of the Church (being dealt with privately beforehand) are moved to tears by this Act of Grace, this manifest conversion of a noble Briton, claiming the sacred rites of *Campo Santo*, and not likely to enjoy them without much munificence, when that most righteous claim upon the Seculars is paid. Dares any one to doubt identity? Behold, upon the finger of the departed one, is the very ring with which the City's benefactor sealed his portion of the covenant; and which he presented to his son-in-law, as a holy relic of his ancient family, upon betrothal to his daughter.

"Thereupon arises the universal cry—'redeem the honour of the City.' A few formalities still remain; one of which is satisfied by the arrival of Quevedo with my deposition. The noble Count, the descendant of the Barcas, rides in a chariot extolled by all, and scatters a few *pesetas* of his half a million dollars. It was gained by lottery, it goes by gambling; in six months he is penniless again. He has robbed his brother's grave in vain. For another hundred dollars, he would rob his twin-sister's."

"Oh, mother, it is horrible! Too horrible to be true. And yet how it clears up everything! And even so, how much better it is, than what we supposed, and shuddered at! But have you any evidence beyond suspicion? If it is not unbecoming, I would venture to remind you, that you have already in your mind condemned another, whose innocence is now established."

"Nay, not established, except to minds that are, like mine, full of charity. It is not impossible, that he may have joined my brother—oh that I should call him so!—in this abominable enterprise. I say it not, to vex you in your lofty faith. But it would have made that enterprise far easier to arrange. And if a noble Spaniard can stoop thus, why should not a common Englishman?"

"Because he is a gentleman;" cried Nicie, rising with a flash of indignation, "which a nobleman sometimes is not. And since you have spoken thus, I doubt the truth of your other accusation. But that can very soon be put to the test, by making enquiry on the spot. If what you suppose has happened at all, it must be of public knowledge there. Have you sent any one to enquire about it?"

"Not yet. I have not long seen things clearly. Only since that Quevedo left, it has come upon me by reasoning. Neither do I know of any trusty person. It must be one faithful to the family, and careful of its reputation; for the disgrace shall never be known in this cold England. Remember therefore, I say, that you speak no word, not even to Mr. Penniloe, or Dr. Fox, of this conclusion forced upon me. If in justice to others we are compelled to avow that the deed was of the family, we must declare that it was of piety and high religious feeling, and strictly conceal that it was of sordid lucre."

"But mother, they may in the course of their own enquiries discover how it was at last. The last things ascertained tend that way. And if they should find any trace of ship——"

"I have given orders to drop all further searches. And you must use your influence with—with all you have any sway upon, that nothing more shall be done at present. Of course you will not supply the reason; but say that it has been so arranged. Now go, my child; I have talked too long. My strength is not as it was, and I dwell most heavily on the better days. But one thing I would enjoin upon you. Until I speak again of that which I have seen in my own mind, to its distress and misery, ask me no more about it, neither in any way refer to it. The Lord,—who is not of this Church, or that, but looks down upon us from the Crucifix,—He can pity and protect us. But you will be glad that I have told you this; because it will devour me the less."

CHAPTER XXXII.

PLEADINGS.

"But it will devour me the more. My mother cannot love me;" the poor girl was obliged to think, as she sat in her lonely room again. "She has laid this heavy burden on me; and I am to share it with no one. Does she suppose that I feel nothing, and am wholly absorbed in love-proceedings, forgetting all duty to my father? Sometimes I doubt almost whether Jemmy Fox is worthy of my affection. I am not very precious. I know that—the lesson is often impressed upon me—but I know that I am simple, and loving, and true; and he takes me too much for granted. If he were noble, and could love with all his heart, would he be so hard upon his sister, for liking a man, who is her equal in everything but money? The next time I see him, I will try him about that. If a man is noble, as I understand the word, he will be noble for others, as well as for himself. Uncle Penniloe is the only real nobleman I know; because to him others are equal to himself."

This was only a passing mood, and not practical enough to be permanent. However it was the prevailing one, when in came Jemmy Fox himself. That young doctor plumed himself upon his deep knowledge of the fairer sex; and yet like the rest of mankind who do so, he showed little of that knowledge in his dealings with them.

In the midst of so many doubts and fears, and with a

Y

miserable sense of loneliness, Miss Waldron was in "a high-strung condition "—as ladies themselves describe it—though as gentle and affectionate as ever. She was gazing at little pet *Pixie*, and wondering in her self-abasement, whether there is any human love so deep, devoted, and everlasting (while his little life endures) as that of an ordinary dog. *Pixie*, the pug-dog, sitting at her feet was absorbed in wistful watching, too sure that his mistress was plunged in trouble, beyond the reach of his poor mind, but not perhaps beyond the humble solace of such a yearning heart.

In this interchange of tender feelings, a still more tender vein was touched. "Squeak!" went *Pixie*, with a jump, and then a long eloquence of yelp and howl proved that he partook too deeply of the woe he had prayed to share. A heavy riding-boot had crushed his short but sympathetic tail—the tail he was so fond of chasing as a joyful vision, but now too mournfully and materially his own!

Dr. Fox, with a cheerful smile, as if he had done something meritorious, gazed into Nicie's sparkling eyes. Perhaps he expected a lovely kiss, after his long absence.

"Why, you don't seem to care a bit for what you have done!" cried the young girl, almost repelling him. "Allow me to go to my wounded little dear. Oh you poor little persecuted pet, what did they do to you? Was his lovely taily broken? Oh the precious little martyr, that he should have come to this! Did a monstrous elephant come, and crush his darling life out? Give his Missy a pretty kiss, with the great tears rolling on his cheek."

"Well, I wish you'd make half as much fuss about me;" said Fox, with all the self-command that could well be expected. "You haven't even asked me how I am!"

"Oh, I beg your pardon then;" she answered, looking up at him, with the little dog's nose cuddled into her neck, and his short sobs puffing up the golden undergrowth of her darkly-clustering hair. "Yes, to be sure, I should have asked that. It was very forgetful of me. But his poor tail seems to be a little easier now; and the vigour of your step shows how well you have come back to us."

"Well, more than welcome, I am afraid. I can always make allowance for the humours of young ladies; and I know how good and sweet you are. But I think you might have been glad to see me."

"Not when you tread upon my dear dog's tail, and laugh in my face afterwards, instead of being very sorry. I should have begged pardon, if I had been so clumsy as to tread upon a dog of yours."

"Dogs are all very well, in their way; but they have no right to get into our way. This poor little puggie's tail is all right now. Shake hands, Puggie. Why, look! He has forgiven me."

"That shows how wonderfully kind he is, and how little he deserves to be trodden on. But I will not say another word about that; only you might have been sorrier. Their consciences are so much better than ours. He is licking your hand, as if he had done the wrong. Your sister agreed with me about their nobility. How is darling Christie?"

"Everybody is a darling, except me to-day! Christie is well enough. She always is; except when she goes a cropper out of a trap, and knocks young men's waistcoat-buttons off."

"How coarsely you put it, when you ought to be most thankful to the gentleman who rescued her, when you left her at the mercy of a half-wild horse!"

"I don't know what to make of you to-day, Miss Waldron. Have I done anything to offend you? You are too just and sensible, and—gentle, I should like to say—not to know that you have put an entirely wrong construction upon that little accident with Farrant's old screw. It was Christie's own fault, every bit of it. She thought herself a grand whip, and she came to grief; as girls generally do, when they are bumptious."

"You seem to have a great contempt for girls, Dr. Fox. What have the poor things done to offend you so?"

"Somebody must have been speaking against me. I'd give a trifle to know who it is. I have always been accustomed to reasonable treatment."

"There now, his dear little tail is better! Little *Pixie* loves me so. Little *Pixie* never tells somebody that she is an unreasonable creature. Little *Pixie* is too polite for that."

"Well, I think I had better be off for the day. I have

Y 2

heard of people getting out of bed the wrong side ; and you can't make it right all the day, when that has happened. Miss Waldron, I must not go away without saying that my sister sends you her very best love. I was to be sure to remember that."

"Oh, thank you, Dr. Fox! Your sister is always so very sweet and considerate. And I hope she has also been allowed to send it where it is due, a thousand times as much as here."

"Where can that be? At the rectory, I suppose. Yes, she has not forgotten Mr. Penniloe. She is not at all fickle in her likings."

"Now that is a very fine quality indeed, as well as a very rare one. And another she has, and will not be driven from it ; and I own that I quite agree with her. She does not look down upon other people, and think that they belong to another world, because they are not so well off in this one as she is. A gentleman is a gentleman, in her judgment, and is not to be cast by, after many kind acts, merely because he is not made of money."

"Ah, now I see what all this comes to !" exclaimed Fox, smiling pleasantly. "Well, I am quite open to a little reasoning there, because the whole thing is so ridiculous. Now put it to yourself ; how would you like to be a sort of son-in-law to good Mother Gilham's green coal-scuttle? A coal-scuttle should make one grateful, you will say. Hear, hear ! not at all a bad pun that ; though quite involuntary."

"The bonnet may be behind the age, or in front of it, I know not which ;" said Nicie, very resolute to show no smile ; "but a better and sweeter old face never looked——"

"A better horse never looked out of a bridle. It is bridle, and blinkers, and saddle, all in one."

"It is quite useless trying to make me laugh." Her voice however belied her ; and *Pixie* watching her face began to wag the wounded tail again. "Your sister, who knows what bonnets are, to which you can have no pretension, is well acquainted with the sterling value——"

"Oh come, I am sure it would not fetch much now, though it may have cost two guineas, or more, in the days before ' my son Frank ' was born."

"Really, Jemmy, you are too bad, when I want to talk seriously."

"So long as I am 'Jemmy' once more, I don't care how bad I am."

"That was a slip. But you must listen to me. I will not be laughed off from saying what I think. Do you suppose that it is a joking matter for poor Frank Gilham?"

"I don't care a copper for his state of mind, if Chris is not fool enough to share it. The stupid fellow came to me this morning, and instead of trying to smoothe me down, what does he do but blow me up sky-high! You should have heard him. He never swore at all, but gave utterance to the noblest sentiments—just because they were in his favour."

"Then I admire him for it. It was very manly of him. Why were all large ideas in his favour? Just because the small ones are on your side. I suppose, you pretend to care for me?"

"No pretence about it. All too true. And this is what I get done to me?"

"But how would you like my brother to come and say—'I disapprove of Dr. Fox. I forbid you to say another word to him'? Would you recognize his fraternal right in the matter, and go away quietly?"

"Hardly that. I should leave it to you. And if you held by me, I should snap my fingers at him."

"Of course you would. And so would anybody else; Frank Gilham among the number. And your sister—is she to have no voice, because you are a roaring lion? Surely her parents, and not her brother, should bar the way, if it must be barred. Just think of yourself, and ask yourself how your own law would fit you."

"The cases are very different, and you know it as well as I do. Frank Gilham is quite a poor man; and, although he is not a bad kind of fellow, his position in the world is not the same as ours."

"That may be so. But if Christie loves him, and is quite content with his position in the world, and puts up with the coal-scuttle—as you call it—and he is a good man and true, and a gentleman, are they both to be miserable, to please you? And more than that—you don't know

Christie. If Frank Gilham shows proper courage, and is not afraid of mean imputations, no one will ask your leave, I think."

"Well, I shall have done my best; and if I cannot stop it, let them rue the day. Her father and mother would never allow it; and as I am responsible for the whole affair, and cannot consult them, as things are now, I am bound to act in their place, I think. But never mind that. One may argue for ever, and a girl in a moment can turn the tables on the cleverest man alive. Let us come back to our own affairs. I have some news which ought to please you. By rare good luck I have hit upon the very two men who were employed upon that awful business. I shall have them soon, and then we shall know all about this most mysterious case. By George, it shall go hard indeed with the miscreant who plotted it."

"Oh don't—oh don't! What good can it be?" cried Nicie, trembling, and stammering. "It will kill my mother; I am sure it will. I implore you not to go on with it."

"What!" exclaimed Fox with amazement. "You to ask me, you his only daughter, to let it be so—to hush up the matter—to submit to this atrocious wrong! And your father—it is the last thing I ever should have thought to hear."

In shame and terror she could not speak, but quailed before his indignant gaze, and turned away from him with a deep low sob.

"My darling, my innocent dear," he cried in alarm at her bitter anguish; "give me your hand; let me look at your face. I know that no power on earth would make you do a thing that you saw to be shameful. I beg your pardon humbly, if I spoke too harshly. You know that I would not vex you, Inez, and beyond any doubt you can explain this strange—this inconceivable thing. You are sure to have some good reason for it."

"Yes, you would say so if you knew all. But not now—I dare not; it is too dreadful. It is not for myself. If I had my own way—but what use? I dare not even tell you that. For the present, at least for the present, do nothing. If you care about me at all, I beg you not to do what would never be forgiven. And my mother is in such a miserable state, so delicate, so frail, and helpless! Do for my sake, do show this once, that you have some affection for me."

Nicie put her soft hand on his shoulder, and pleaded her cause with no more words, but a gaze of such tenderness and sweet faith, that he could not resist it. Especially as he saw his way to reassure her, without departing from the plan he had resolved upon.

"I will do anything, my pretty dove," he said with a noble surrender; "to relieve your precious and trustful heart. I will even do this, if it satisfies you—I will take no steps for another month, an entire month from this present time. I cannot promise more than that, now can I, for any bewitchment? And in return, you must pledge yourself to give your mother not even a hint of what I have just told you. It would only make her anxious, which would be very bad for her health, poor thing; and she has not the faith in me, that you have. She must not even dream that I have heard of those two villains."

This was a bright afterthought of his; for if Lady Waldron should know of his discovery, she might contrive to inform them, that he had his eye upon them.

"Oh, how good you are!" cried Nicie. "I can never thank you enough, dear Jemmy; and it must appear so cruel of me, to ask you to forego so long the chance of shaming those low people, who have dared to belie you so."

"What is a month, compared to you?" Jemmy asked, with real greatness. "But if you feel any obligation, you know how to reward me, dear."

Nicie looked at him, with critical eyes; and then as if reckless of anything small, flung both arms round his neck, and kissed him.

"Oh it is so kind, so kind of him!" she declared to herself, to excuse herself; while he thought it was very kind of her. And she, being timid of her own affection, loved him all the more for not encroaching on it.

Jemmy rode away in a happy frame of mind. He loved that beautiful maiden, and he was assured of her love for him. He knew that she was far above him, in the gifts of nature, and the bloom that beautifies them—the bloom that is not of the cheeks alone, but of the gentle dew of kind-

ness, and the pearl of innocence. Fox felt a little ashamed
of himself, for a trifle of sharp practice; but his reason soon
persuaded him, that his conscience was too ticklish. And
that is a thing to be stopped at once.

While jogging along in this condition, on the road towards
Pumpington, he fell in with another horseman less inclined
to cheerfulness. This was Farmer Stephen Horner, a
younger brother of Farmer John, a less substantial, and
therefore perhaps more captious agriculturist. He was
riding a very clever cob, and looked both clever and smart
himself, in his bottle-green cutaway coat, red waistcoat,
white cord breeches and hard brown hat. Striking into the
turnpike road from a grass-track skirting the Beacon Hill,
he hailed the Doctor, and rode beside him.

"Heard the news, have 'e?" asked Farmer Steve, as his
fat calves creaked against the saddle-flaps within a few
inches of Jemmy's, and their horses kept step, like a dealer's
pair. "But there—come to think of it, I be a fool for
asking, and you always along of Passon so?"

"Only came home yesterday. Haven't seen him yet,"
the Doctor answered briskly. "Haven't heard anything
particular. Nothing the matter with him, I hope?"

"Not him, sir, so much as what he've taken up. Hath
made up his mind, so people say, to abolish our old Fair
to Perlycross." Farmer Steve watched the Doctor's face.
He held his own opinion, but he liked to know the other's
first. Moreover he owed him a little bill.

"But surely he cannot do that;" said Fox, who cared
not a jot about the fair, but thought of his own concern
with it. "Why, it was granted by charter, I believe,
hundreds of years ago; when Perlycross was a much larger
place, and the main road to London passed through it, as
the pack-saddle teams do still sometimes."

"So it were, sir, so it were. Many's the time when I
were a boy, I have read of Magner Charter, and the time
as they starved the King in the island, afore the old yew-tree
come on our old tower. But my brother John, he reckoneth
as he knoweth everything; and he saith our market-place
belongeth to the Dean and Chapter, and Fair was granted
to Church, he saith, and so Church can abolish it. But I
can't see no sense in that. Why, it be outside of Church

railings altogether Now you are a learned man, Doctor Fox. And if you'll give me your opinion, I can promise 'e, it shan't go no further."

"The plain truth is," replied Jemmy, knowing well that if his opinion went against the Parson, it would be all over the parish by supper-time, "I have never gone into the subject, and I know nothing whatever about it. But we all know the Fair has come down to nothing now. There has not been a beast there for the last three years, and nothing but a score of pigs, and one pen of sheep last year. It has come to be nothing but a pleasure-fair, with a little show of wrestling, and some singlestick play, followed by a big bout of drinking. Still I should have thought there would be at least a twelvemonth's notice, and a public proclamation."

"So say I, sir; and the very same words I used to my brother John, last night. John Horner is getting a'most too big, with his Churchwarden, and his hundred pounds, he had better a' kept for his family. Let 'un find out who have robbed his own Churchyard, afore 'a singeth out again' a poor man's glass of ale. I don't hold with John in all things; though a' hath key pianner for's dafters, and addeth field to field, same as rich man in the Bible laid up treasure for his soul this night. I tell you what, Doctor, and you may tell John Horner—I likes old things, for being old; though there may be more bad than good in them. What harm, if a few chaps do get drunk, and the quarrelsome folks has their heads cracked? They'd only go and do it somewhere else, if they was stopped of our place. Passon be a good man as ever lived, and wonnerful kind to the poor folk. But a' beginneth to have his way too much; and all along of my brother John. To tell you the truth, Doctor, I couldn't bear the job about that old tombstone, to memory of Squire Jan Toms, and a fine piece of poetry it were too. Leap-frogged it, hundreds and hundreds of times, when I were a boy, I have; and so has my father and grandfather afore me; and why not my sons, and my grandsons too, when perhaps my own standeth 'longside of 'un? I won't believe a word of it, but what thic old ancient stone were smashed up a' purpose, by order of Passon Penniloe. Tell 'e what, Doctor, thic there channging of every mortial thing, just for the sake of channging, bain't the right way for to fetch folks to church; 'cordin' at least to my mind. Why do us go to church? Why, because can't help it; 'long of wives and children, when they comes, and lookin' out for 'un, when the children was ourselves. Turn the bottom up, sir, and what be that but custom, same as one generation requireth from another? And to put new patches on it, and be proud of them, is the same thing as tinker did to wife's ham-boiler—drawed the rivets out, and made 'un leak worse than ever. Not another shilling will they patchers get from me."

Farmer Steve sat down in his saddle, and his red waist-coat settled down upon the pommel. His sturdy cob also laid down his ears, and stubborn British sentiment was in every line of both of them.

"Well, I won't pretend to say about the other matters;" said Fox, who as an Englishman could allow for obstinacy. "But, Farmer, I am sure that you are wrong about the tombstone. Parson did not like it, and no wonder. But he is not the man to do things crookedly. He would have moved it openly, or not at all. It was quite as much an accident, as if your horse put his foot upon a nut and cracked it."

"Well, sir, well, sir, we has our own opinions. Oh, you have paid the pike for me! Thank 'e, Doctor. I'll pay yours, next time we come this way together."

The story of the tombstone was simply this. John Toms, a rollicking Cavalier of ancient Devonshire lineage, had lived and died at Perlycross, nearly two centuries agone. His grave was towards the great southern porch, and there stood his headstone large and bold, confronting the faithful at a corner where two causeways met. Thus every worshipper, who entered the House of Prayer by its main approach, was invited to reflect upon the fine qualities of this gentleman, as recorded in large letters. To a devout mind this might do no harm; but all Perlycross was not devout, and many a light thought was suggested, or perhaps an untimely smile produced, by this too sprightly memorial. "A spirited epitaph that, sir," was the frequent remark of visitors. "But scarcely conceived in a proper spirit," was the Parson's general reply.

The hideous western gallery, the parish revel called the Fair, and this unseemly tombstone, had been sore tribulations to the placid mind of Penniloe ; and yet he durst not touch that stone, sacred not to memory only, but to vested rights, and living vein of local sentiment. However the fates were merciful.

"Very sad accident this morning, sir. I do hope you will try to forgive us, Mr. Penniloe," said Robson Adney, the manager of the works, one fine October morning, and he said it with a stealthy wink ; "seven of our chaps have let our biggest scaffold-pole, that red one, with a butt as big as a milestone, roll off their clumsy shoulders, and it has smashed poor Squire Toms' old tombstone into a thousand pieces. Never read a word of it again, sir—such a sad loss to the churchyard ! But quite an accident, sir, you know ; purely a casual accident."

The Curate looked at him, but he "smiled none"—as another tombstone still expresses it ; and if charity compelled Mr. Penniloe to believe him, gratitude enforced another view ; for Adney well knew his dislike of that stone, and was always so eager to please him.

But that every one who so desires may judge for himself, whether Farmer Steve was right, or Parson Penniloe, here are the well-remembered lines that formed the preface to Divine worship in the parish of Perlycross.

> "'Halloa! who lieth here?'
> 'I, old Squire Jan Toms.'
> 'What dost lack?' 'A tun of beer,
> For a tipple with them fantoms.'"

CHAPTER XXXIII.

THE SCHOOLMASTER ABROAD.

"Boys, here's a noise ! "

Sergeant Jakes strode up and down the long schoolroom on Friday morning, flapping his empty sleeve, and swinging that big cane with the tuberous joints, whose taste was none too saccharine. That well-known ejaculation, so expressive of stern astonishment, had for the moment its due effect. Curly heads were jerked back, elbows squared, sniggers were hushed, the munch of apples (which had been as of milching kine) stuck fast, or was shunted into bulging cheek; never a boy seemed capable of dreaming that there was any other boy in the world besides himself. Scratch of pens, and grunts of mental labour, were the only sounds in this culmination of literature, known as "Copy-exercise." As Achilles, though reduced to a ghost, took a longer stride at the prowess of his son; and as deep joys, on a similar occasion, pervaded Latona's silent breast; even so High-Jarks sucked the top of his cane, and felt that he had not lived in vain. There are many men still hearty—though it is so long ago—who have led a finer life, through that man's higher culture.

But presently—such is the nature of human nature, in its crude probation—the effect of that noble remonstrance waned. Silence (which is itself a shadow, cast by death upon life perhaps) began to flicker—as all dulness should—with the play of small ideas moving it. Little timid whispers, a cane's length below the breath, and with the heart shuffling out of all participation; and then a tacit grin that was afraid to move the molars, and then a cock of eye, that was intended to involve (when a bigger eye was turned away) its mighty owner; and then a clink of marbles in a pocket down the leg; and then a downright joke, of such very subtle humour, that it stole along the bench through funnel'd hands; and then alas, a small boy of suicidal levity sputtered out a laugh, which made wiser wigs stand up!

His crime was only deepened by ending in sham cough; and sad to say, the very boy who had made the fatal joke (instead of being grateful for reckless approbation) stood up and pointed an unmanly finger at him. The Sergeant's keen eye was upon them both; and a tremble ran along the oak, that bore many tempting aptitudes for the vindication of ethics. But the Sergeant bode his time. His sense of justice was chivalrous. Let the big boy make another joke.

"Boys, here's a noise, again!"

Those who have not had the privilege of the Sergeant's lofty discipline can never understand—far less convey—the significance of his second shout. It expressed profound amazement, horror at our fallen state, incredulity of his own ears, promptitude to redress the wrong, and yet a pathetic sorrow at the impending grim necessity. The boys knew well that his second protest never ascended to heaven in vain ; and the owners of tender quarters shrank, and made ready to slide beneath the protection of their bench. Other boys, with thick corduroys, quailed for the moment, and closed their mouths ; but what mouth was ever closed permanently, by the opening of another ?

" Now you shall have it, boys," the Sergeant thundered, as the uproar waxed beyond power of words. " Any boy slipping out of stroke shall have double cuts for cowardice. Stop the ends up. All along both rows of benches ; I am coming, I am coming ! "

" Oh sir, please sir, 'twadn' me, sir ! 'Twor all along o' Bill Cornish, sir."

He had got this trimmer by the collar, and his cane swung high in air, when the door was opened vigorously, and a brilliant form appeared. Brilliant, less by its own merits, than by brave embellishment, as behoves a youth ascending stairs of state from page to footman, and mounting upward, ever upward, to the vinous heights of Butlerhood. For this was Bob Cornish, Bill's elder brother ; and he smiled at the terrors of the hurtling cane, compulsive but a year ago, of tears.

With a dignity already imbibed from Binstock, this young man took off his hat, and employing a spare slate as a tray, presented a letter with a graceful bow. He was none too soon, but just in time. The weapon of outraged law came down, too lightly to dust a jacket ; and the smiter, wonder-smitten, went to a desk, and read as follows.

" Lady Waldron will be much obliged if Sergeant Jakes will come immediately in the vehicle sent with the bearer of this letter. Let no engagement forbid this. Mr. Penniloe has kindly consented to it."

The roof resounded with shouts of joy, instead of heavy wailing, as the Sergeant at once dismissed the school ; and in half an hour he entered the business-room at Walderscourt, and there found the lady of the house, looking very resolute, and accompanied by her daughter.

"Soldier Jakes will take a chair. See that the door is closed, my child, and no persons lingering near it. Now, Inez, will you say to this brave soldier of your father's regiment, what we desire him to undertake, if he will be so faithful ; for the benefit of his Colonel's family ; also for the credit of this English country."

This was clever of my lady. She knew that the veteran's liking was not particularly active for herself, or any of the Spanish nation ; but that he had transferred his love and fealty of so many years, to his Officer's gentle daughter. Any request from Nicie would be almost as sacred a command to him, as if it had come from her father. He stood up, made a low bow followed by a military salute, and gazed at the sweet face he loved so well.

"It is for my dear father's sake ; and I am as sure as he himself would be," Miss Waldron spoke with tears in her eyes, and a sad smile on her lips that would have moved a heart much harder than this veteran's, "that you will not refuse to do us a great, a very great service, if you can. And we have nobody we can trust like you ; because you are so true, and brave."

The Sergeant rose again, and made another bow even deeper than the former one ; but instead of touching his grizzled locks he laid his one hand on his heart ; and although by no means a gushing man, he found it impossible to prevent a little gleam, like the upshot of a well, quivering under his ferny brows.

"We would not ask you even so," continued Nicie, with a grateful glance, "if it were not that you know the place, and perhaps may find some people there still living to remember you. When my father lay wounded at the house of my grandfather, and was in great danger of his life, you, being also disabled for a time, were allowed at his request to remain with him, and help him. Will you go to that place again, to do us a service no one else can do ?"

"To the end of the world, Miss, without asking why. But the Lord have mercy on all them boys ! Whatever will they do without me ?"

"We will arrange about all that, with Mr. Penniloe's consent. If that can be managed, will you go, at once, and at any inconvenience to yourself ?"

"No ill-convenience shall stop me, Miss. If I thought of that twice, I should be a deserter, afore the lines of the enemy. To be of the least bit of use to you, is an honour as well as a duty to me."

"I thought that you would; I was sure that you would." Inez gave a glance of triumph at her less trustful mother. "And what makes us hurry you so, is the chance that has suddenly offered for your passage. We heard this morning, by an accident almost, that a ship is to sail from Topsham to-morrow, bound direct for Cadiz. Not a large ship, but a fast-sailing vessel—a schooner I think they call it, and the Captain is one of Binstock's brothers. You would get there in half the time it would take to go to London, and wait about for passage, and then come all down the Channel. And from Cadiz you can easily get on. You know a little Spanish, don't you?"

"Not reg'lar, Miss. But it will come back again. I picked up just enough for this—I couldn't understand them much; but I could make them look as if they understanded me."

"That is quite sufficient. You will have letters to three or four persons who are settled there, old servants of my grandfather. We cannot tell which of them may be alive, but may well hope that some of them are so. The old house is gone, I must tell you that. After all the troubles of the war, there was not enough left to keep it up with."

"That grand old house, Miss, with the pillars, and the carrots, and the arches, the same as in a picture! And everybody welcome; and you never knew if there was fifty, or a hundred in it——"

"Sergeant, you describe it well;" Lady Waldron interrupted. "There are no such mansions in this country. Alas, it is gone from us for ever, because we loved our native land too well!"

"Not only that," said the truthful Inez; "but also because the young Count, as you would call him, has wasted the relics of his patrimony. And now I will explain to you the reasons for our asking this great service of you."

The veteran listened with close attention, and no small astonishment, to the young lady's clear account of that great public lottery, and the gorgeous prize accruing on the death of Sir Thomas Waldron. This was enough to tempt a ruined man to desperate measures; and Jakes had some knowledge in early days of the young Count's headstrong character. But if it should prove so, if he were guilty of the crime which had caused so much distress and such prolonged unhappiness, yet his sister could not bear that the sordid motive should be disclosed, at least in this part of the world. For the sake of others, it would be needful to denounce the culprit; but if the detection were managed well, no motive need be assigned at all. Let every one form his own conclusion. Spanish papers, and Spanish news, came very sparely to Devonshire; and the English public would be sure (in ignorance of that financial scheme, whose result supplied the temptation) to ascribe the assault upon Protestant rites to Popish contempt and bigotry.

"I should tell the whole, if I had to decide it;" said Nicie with the candour and simplicity of youth. "If he has done it, for the sake of nasty money, let everybody know what he has done it for."

But the Sergeant shook his head, and quite agreed with Lady Waldron. The world was quite quick enough at bad constructions, without receiving them ready-made.

"Leave busy-bodies to do their own buzzing;" was his oracular suggestion. "'Tis a grand old family, even on your mother's side, Miss;" Nicie smiled a little, as her mother stared at this new comparative estimate. "And what odds to our clodhoppers what they do? A Don don't look at things the same as a dung-carter; and it takes a man who knows the world to make allowance for him. The Count may have done it, mind. I won't say no, until such time as I can prove it. But after all, 'tis comforting to think that it was so, compared to what we all was afraid of. Why, the dear old Colonel would be as happy as a King, in the place he was so nigh going to after the battle of Barosa; looking down over the winding of the river, and the moon among the orange-trees, where he was a' making love!"

"Hush!" whispered Nicie, as her mother turned away, with a trembling in her throat; and the old man saw that the memory of the brighter days had brought the shadows also.

" Saturday to-morrow. Boys will do very well, till Monday ; " he came out with this abruptly, to cover his confusion. " By that time, please God, I shall be in the Bay of Biscay. This is what I'll do, Miss, if it suits you and my lady. I'll come again to-night at nine o'clock, with my kit slung tidy, and not a word to anybody. Then I can have the letters, Miss, and my last orders. Ship sails at noon to-morrow, name of *Montilla*. Mail-coach to Exeter passes White Post, a little after half-past ten to-night. Be aboard easily, afore daylight. No, Miss, thank you, I shan't want no money. Passage paid to and fro. Old soldier always hath a shot in the locker."

" As if we should let you go, like that ! You shall not go at all, unless you take this purse."

That evening he received his last instructions, and the next day he sailed in the schooner *Montilla*.

Even after the many strange events, which had by this time caused such a whirl of giddiness in Perlycross, that if there had been a good crack across the street, every man and woman would have fallen headlong into it ; and even before there had been leisure for people to try to tell them anyhow, to one another—much less discuss them at all as they deserved—this sudden break-up of the school, and disappearance of High Jarks, would have been absolutely beyond belief, if there had not been scores of boys, too loudly in evidence everywhere. But when a chap, about four feet high, came scudding in at any door that was open, and kicking at it if it dared to be shut, and then went trying every cupboard-lock, and making sad eyes at his mother if the key was out ; and then again, when he was stuffed to his buttons—which he would be, as sure as eggs are eggs—if the street went howling with his playful ways, and every corner was in a jerk with him, and no elderly lady could go along without her umbrella in front of her— how was it possible for any mother not to feel herself guilty of more harm than good ?

In a word, " High Jarks " was justified (as all wisdom is) of his children ; and the weak-minded women, who had complained that he smote too hard, were the first to find fault with the feeble measures of his substitute, Vickary Toogood of Honiton. This gentleman came into office on

z

Monday, smiling in a very superior manner at his predecessor's arrangements.

"I think we may lock up that," he said, pointing to the
Sergeant's little tickler; "we must be unworthy of our
vocation, if we cannot dispense with such primitive tools."
A burst of applause thrilled every bench; but knowing the
boys of his parish so well, Mr. Penniloe shook his head
with dubious delight.

And truly before the week was out, many a time would
he murmur sadly—"Oh for one hour of the Sergeant!" as
he heard the Babel of tongues outside, and entering saw
the sprawling elbows, slouching shoulders, and hands in
pockets, which the "Apostle of Moral force"—*Moral farce*
was its sound and meaning here—permitted as the attitude
of pupilage.

"Sim'th I be quite out in my reckoning;" old Channing
the Clerk had the cheek to say, as he met the Parson outside the school-door; "didn't know it were Whit-Monday
yet."

Mr. Penniloe smiled, but without rejoicing; he understood the reference too well. Upon Whit-Monday the two
rival Benefit-clubs of the village held their feast, and did
their very utmost from bridge to Abbey, to out-drum, out-
fife, and out-trumpet one another. Neither in his house
was his conscience left untouched.

"I think Lady Waldron might have sent us a better man
than that is;" Mrs. Muggridge observed one afternoon,
when the uproar came across the road, and pierced the
rectory windows. "I am not sure but what little Master
Mike could keep better order than that is. Why, the
beating of the bounds was nothing to it. What could you
be about, sir, to take such a man as that?" Thyatira had
long established full privilege of censure.

"Certainly there is a noise;" the Curate was always
candid. "But he brought the very highest credentials
from the Institute. We have scarcely given him fair trial
yet. The system is new, you see, Mrs. Muggridge; and it
must be allowed some time to take effect. No physical
force, the moral sense appealed to, the higher qualities
educed by kindness, the innate preference of right promoted
and strengthened by self-exertion, the juvenile faculties to

be elevated, from the moment of earliest development, by a perception of their high responsibility, and, and—well I really forget the rest, but you perceive that it amounts to——"

"Row, and riot, and roaring rubbish. That's what it amounts to, sir. But I beg your pardon, sir; excuse my boldness, for speaking out, upon things so far above me. But when they comes across the road, at ten o'clock in the morning, to beg for a lump of raw beefsteak, by reason of two boys getting four black eyes, in fighting across the Master's desk, the new system seem not Apostolical. An Apostle, about as much as I am! My father was above me, and had gifts, and he put himself back, when not understanded, to the rising generation; but he never would demean himself, to send for raw beefsteak for their black eyes."

"And I think he would have shown his common sense in that. What did you do, my good Thyatira?" Mr. Penniloe had a little spice of mischief in him, which always accompanies a sub-sense of humour.

"This was what I did, sir. I looked at him, and he seemed to have been in the wars himself, and to have come across, perhaps to get out of them, being one of the clever ones, as true Schoolmaster sayeth, and by the same token not so thick of head; and he looked up at me, as if he was proud of it, to take me in; while the real fighting boys look down, as I know by my brother who was guilty of it; and I said to him, very quiet like—'No steak kept here for moral-force black-eyes-boys. You go to Robert Jakes, the brother of a man that understands his business, and tell him to enter in his books, half a pound prime-cut, for four black eyes, to the credit of Vickary Toogood.'"

It was not only thus, but in many other ways, that the village at large shed painful tears (sadly warranted by the ears), and the Church looked with scorn at the children straggling in, like a lot of Dissenters going anyhow; and the Cross at the meeting of the four main roads, which had been a fine stump for centuries, lost its proper coat of whitewash on Candlemas-day; and the crystal Perle itself began to be threaded with red from pugnacious noses. For the lesson of all history was repeated, that softness

z 2

universal, and unlimited concession, set off very grandly, but come home with broken heads, to load their guns with grapnel.

And what could Mr. Penniloe do, when some of the worst belligerents were those of his own household; upon one frontier his three pupils, and upon another, Zip Tremlett? Pike, Peckover, and Mopuss, the pupils now come back again, were all very decent and law-abiding fellows, but had drifted into a savage feud with the factory boys at the bottom of the village. As they were but three against three score, it soon became unsafe for them to cross Perlebridge, without securing their line of retreat. Of course they looked down from a lofty height upon "cads who smelled of yarn, and even worse;" but what could moral, or even lineal excellence, avail them against the huge disparity of numbers? Each of them held himself a match for any three of the enemy, and they issued a challenge upon that scale; but the paper-cap'd host showed no chivalry. On one occasion, this noble trio held the bridge victoriously against the whole force of the enemy, inflicting serious loss, and even preparing for a charge upon the mass. But the cowardly mass found a heap of road-metal, and in lack of their own filled the air with it, and the Pennilovian heroes had begun to bite the dust, when luckily Farmer John rode up, and saved the little force from annihilation by slashing right and left through the Operative phalanx.

When Mr. Penniloe heard of this pitched battle, he was deeply grieved; and sending for his pupils administered a severe rebuke to them. But John Pike's reply was a puzzler to him.

"If you please, sir, will you tell us what to do, when they fall upon us?"

"Endeavour to avoid them;" replied the Clergyman, feeling some want of confidence however in his counsel.

"So we do, sir, all we can;" Pike made answer, with the aspect of a dove. "But they won't be avoided, when they think they've got enough cads together to lick us."

"I should like to know one thing," enquired the Hopper, striking out his calves, which were now becoming of commanding size; "are we to be called 'Latin tay-kettles,' and 'Parson's pups,' andthen do nothing but run away?"

"My father says that the road is called the King's Highway;" said Mopuss, who was a fat boy, with great deliberation, "because all his subjects have a right to it, but no right to throw it at one another."

"I admit that a difficulty arises there;" replied Mr Penniloe as gravely as he could, for Mopuss was always quoting his papa, a lawyer of some eminence. "But really, my lads, we must not have any more of this. There is fault upon both sides, beyond all doubt. I shall see the factory manager to-morrow, and get him to warn his pugnacious band. I am very unwilling to confine you to these premises; but if I hear of any more pitched battles, I shall be compelled to do so, until peace has been proclaimed."

Here again was Jakes to seek; for the fear of him lay upon the factory boys, as heavily as upon his own school-children. And perhaps as sore a point as any was that he should have been rapt away, without full reason rendered.

CHAPTER XXXIV.

LOYALTY.

"I do not consider myself at all an inquisitive man," Mr. Penniloe reflected, and here the truth was with him; "nevertheless it is hard upon me to be refused almost the right to speculate upon this question. They have told me that it is of the last importance, to secure this great disciplinarian — never appreciated while with us, but now deplored so deeply—for a special service in the south of Spain. What that special service is, I am not to know, until his return; possibly not even then. And Mr. Webber has no idea what the meaning of it is. But I know that it has much to do—all to do, I might even say—with that frightful outrage of last November—three months ago, alas, alas, and a sad disgrace upon this parish still! Marvellous are the visitations of the Lord. Practically speaking, we know but little more of that affair now, than on the day it was discovered. If it were not for one thing, I should even be driven at last to Gowler's black conclusion; and my faith in the true love of a woman, and in the honesty of a proud brave woman would be shattered, and leave me miserable. But now it is evident that good and gentle Nicie is acting entirely with her mother ; and to imagine that she would wrong her father is impossible. Perhaps I shall even get friend Gowler's hundred pounds. What a triumph that would be ! To obtain a large sum for the Service of God from an avowed— ah well, who am I to think harshly of him ? But the money might even be blest to himself ; which is the first thing to consider. It is my duty to accept it therefore, if I can only get it.

"And here again is Jemmy Fox, not behaving at all as he used to do. Concealing something from me—I am almost sure of it by his manner—and discussing it, I do believe, with Gronow—an intimacy that cannot be good for him. I wish I could perceive more clearly, in what points I have neglected my duty to the parish ; for I seem to be losing hold upon it, which must be entirely my own fault. There must be some want of judgment somewhere—what else could lead to such very sad fighting ? Even Zip, a little girl, disgracing us by fighting in the streets ! That at any rate I can stop, and will do so pretty speedily."

This was a lucky thought for him, because it led to action, instead of brooding, into which miserable condition he might otherwise have dropped. And when a man too keen of conscience hauls himself across the coals, the Governor of a hot place takes advantage to peep up between them. Mr. Penniloe rang the bell, and begged Mrs. Muggridge to be good enough to send Miss Zippy to him.

Zip, who had grown at least two inches since the death of her grandmother—not in length perhaps so much as in the height she made of it—came shyly into the dusky book-room, with one of her long hands crumpling the lower corner of her pinafore into her great brown eyes. She knew she was going to catch it, and knew also the way to meet it, for she opened the conversation with a long-drawn sob.

"Don't be frightened, my dear child ;" said the Parson with the worst of his intention waning. "I am not going to scold you much, my dear."

"Oh, I was so terrible afraid, you was." The little girl crept up close to him, and began to play with his button-hole, curving her lissome fingers in and out, like rosebuds in a trellis, and looking down at the teardrops on her pinny. "Plaise sir, I knows well enough as I desarves a bit of it." " Then why did you do it, my dear child ? But I am glad that you feel it to be wrong."

The clergyman was sitting in the deep square chair, where most of his sermons came to him, and he brought his calm face down a little, to catch the expression of the young thing's eyes. Suddenly she threw herself into his arms, and kissed his lips, and cheeks, and forehead, and stroked his silvery hair, and burst into a passionate wail ; and then slid down upon a footstool, and nursed his foot.

" Do 'e know why I done that ?" she whispered, looking up over his knees at him. "Because there be nobody like 'e, in the heavens, or the earth, or the waters under the earth. Her may be as jealous as ever her plaiseth ; but I tell 'e, I don't care a cuss."

" My dear little impetuous creature," Mr. Penniloe knew that his darling Fay was the one defied thus recklessly ; " I am sure that you are fond of all of us. And to please me, as well as for much higher reasons, you must never use bad words. Bad deeds too I have heard of, Zip, though I am not going to scold much now. But why did you get into conflict with a boy ?"

Zip pondered the meaning of these words for a moment, and then her conscience interpreted.

" Because he spoke bad of 'e, about the Fair." She crooked her quick fingers together as she spoke, and tore them asunder with vehemence.

" And what did you do to him ? Eh Zip ? Oh Zip !"

" Nort, for to sarve 'un out, as a' desarved. Only pulled most of 's hair out. His moother hurned arter me ; but I got inside the ge-at."

" A nice use indeed for my premises—to make them a refuge, after committing assault and battery ! Well, what shall we come to next ?"

" Plaise sir, I want to tell 'e zummut ;" said the child, looking up very earnestly. "Bain't it Perlycrass Fair, come Tuesday next ?"

" I am sorry to say that it is. A day of sad noise and uproar. Remember that little Zip must not go outside the gates, that day."

" Nor Passon nayther ; " the child took hold of his hand, as if she were pulling him inside the gate, for her nature was full of gestures ; and then she gazed at him with a sage smile of triumph—"and Passon mustn't go nayther."

Mr. Penniloe took little heed of this (though he had to think of it afterwards) but sent the child to have her tea, with Muggridge and the children.

But before he could set to his work in earnest, although he had discovered much to do, in came his own child, little Fay, looking round the room indignantly. With her lady-like style, she was much too grand to admit a suspicion of jealousy, but she smoothed her golden hair gently back, and just condescended to glance round the chairs. Mr. Penniloe said nothing, and feigned to see nothing, though getting a little afraid in his heart ; for he always looked on Fay as representing her dear mother. He knew that the true way to learn a child's sentiments, is to let them come out of their own accord. There is nothing more jealous than a child, except a dog.

"Oh, I thought Darkie was here again !" said Fay, throwing back her shoulders, and spinning on one leg. "This room belongs to Darkie now altogether. Though I can't see what right she has to it."

Mr. Penniloe treated this soliloquy, as if he had not heard it ; and went on with his work, as if he had no time to attend to children's affairs just now.

"It may be right, or it may be wrong," said Fay, addressing the room in general, and using a phrase she had caught up from Pike, a very great favourite of hers ; " but I can't see why all the people of this house should have to make way for a Gipsy."

This was a little too much for a father and clergyman to put up with. "Fay !" said Mr. Penniloe in a voice that made her tremble ; and she came and stood before him, contrite and sobbing, with her head down, and both hands behind her back. Without raising her eyes the fair child listened, while her father spoke impressively ; and then with a reckless look, she tendered full confession.

" Father, I know that I am very wicked, and I seem to get worse every day. I wish I was the Devil altogether ; because then I could not get any worse."

"My little child," said her father with amazement; "I can scarcely believe my ears. My gentle little Fay to use such words!"

"Oh, *she* thinks nothing of saying that! And you know how fond you are of her, papa. I thought it might make you fond of me."

"This must be seen to at once," thought Mr Penniloe, when he had sent his jealous little pet away; "but what can I do with that poor deserted child? Passionate, loving, very strong-willed, grateful, fearless, sensitive, inclined to be contemptuous, wonderfully quick at learning, she has all the elements of a very noble woman—or of a very pitiable wreck. Quite unfit to be with my children, as my better judgment pronounced at first. She ought to be under a religious, large-minded, firm, but gentle woman—a lady too, or she would laugh at her. Though she speaks broad Devonshire dialect herself, she detects in a moment the mistakes of others, and she has a lofty contempt for vulgarity. She is thrown by the will of God upon my hands, and I should be a coward, or a heartless wretch, if I shirked the responsibility. It will almost break her heart to go from me; but go she must for her own sake, as well as that of my little ones."

"How are you, sir?" cried a cheerful voice. "I fear that I interrupt you. But I knocked three or four times, and got no answer. Excuse my coming in like this. Can I have a little talk with you?"

"Certainly, Dr. Fox. I beg your pardon; but my mind was running upon difficult questions. Let us have the candles, and then I am at your service."

"Now," said Jemmy when they were alone again; "I dare say you think that I have behaved very badly, in keeping out of your way so long."

"Not badly, but strangely;" replied the Parson, who never departed from the truth, even for the sake of politeness. "I concluded that there must be some reason; knowing that I had done nothing to cause it."

"I should rather think not. Nothing ever changes you. But it was for your sake. And now I will enlighten you, as the time is so close at hand. It appears that you have not succeeded in abolishing the Fair."

"Not for this year. There were various formalities. But this will be the last of those revels, I believe. The proclamation will be read on Tuesday morning. After this year, I hope, no more carousals prolonged far into the Penitential day. It will take them by surprise; but it is better so. Otherwise there would have been preparations for a revel more reckless, as being the last."

"I suppose you know, sir, what bitter offence you are giving to hundreds of people all around?"

"I am sorry that it should be so. But it is my simple duty."

"Nothing ever stops you from your duty. But I hope you will do your duty to yourself and us, by remaining upon your own premises that day."

"Certainly not. If I did such a thing, I should seem to be frightened of my own act. Please God, I shall be in the market-place, to hear the proclamation read, and attend to my parish-work afterwards."

"I know that it is useless to argue with you, sir. None of our people would dare to insult you; but one cannot be sure of outsiders. At any rate, do keep near the village, where there are plenty to defend you."

"No one will touch me. I am not a hero; and I can't afford to get my new hat damaged. I shall remain among the civilized, unless I am called away."

"Well, that is something; though not all that I could wish. And now I will tell you why I am glad, much as I dislike the Fair, that for this year at least it is to be. It is a most important date to me, and I hope it will bring you some satisfaction also. Unless we manage very badly indeed, or have desperately bad luck, we shall get hold of the villains who profaned your churchyard, and through them of course find the instigator."

With this preface, Fox told his tale to Mr. Penniloe, and quite satisfied him about the reasons for concealing it so long, as well as made him see that it would not do to preach upon the subject yet.

"My dear young friend, no levity, if you please;" said the Parson, though himself a little, a very little, prone to it on the sly, among people too solid to stumble. "I draw my lessons from the past, or present. Better men than

myself insist upon the terrors of the future, and scare
people from looking forward., But our Church, according
to my views, is a cheerful and progressive mother, encouraging her children, and fortifying——"

"Quite so;" said Jemmy Fox, anticipating too much
on that head; "but she would not fortify us with such
a Lenten *fare* as this. Little pun, sir, not so very bad.
However, to business. I meant to have told you nothing
of this till Monday or Tuesday, until it struck me that you
would be hurt perhaps, if the notice were so very short.
The great point is that not a word of our intentions should
get abroad, or the rogues might make themselves more
scarce than rogues unluckily are allowed to be. This is
why we have put off our application to Mockham, until
Tuesday morning; and even then we shall lay our information as privately as possible. But we must have a powerful
posse, when we proceed to arrest them; for one of the men,
as I told you, is of tremendous bulk and stature, and the
other not a weakling. And perhaps the third, the fellow
they come to meet, will show fight on their behalf. We
must allow no chance of escape, and possibly they may
have fire-arms. We shall want at least four constables, as
well as Gronow, and myself."

" But all good subjects of the King are bound to assist,
if called upon in the name of His Majesty, at the execution
of a warrant."

"So they are; but they never do it, even when there is
no danger. In the present case, they would boldly run
away. And more than that, by ten o'clock on Fair-night,
how will His Majesty's true lieges be? Unable to keep
their own legs, I fear. The trouble will be to keep our own
force sober. But Gronow has undertaken to see to that.
If he can do it, we shall be all right. We may fairly
presume that the enemy also will not be too steady upon
their pins. The only thing I don't like is that a man of
Gronow's age should be in the scuffle. He has promised to
keep in the background; but if things get lively, can I
trust him?"

" I should think it very doubtful. He looks an uncommonly resolute man. If there is a conflict, he will be in it.
But do you think that the big man Harvey really is our

Zippy's father? If so, I am puzzled by what his mother said ; and I think the old lady was truthful. So far as I could understand what she said, her son had never been engaged in any of the shocking work we hear so much of now. And she would not have denied it from any sense of shame, for she confessed to even worse things, on the part of other sons."

" She may not have known it. He has so rarely been at home. A man of that size would have been notorious throughout the parish, if he had ever lived at home ; whereas nobody knows him, not even Joe Crang, who knows every man and horse for miles around. But the Whetstone people are a tribe apart, and keep all their desolate region to themselves."

" The district is extra-parochial, a sort of No-man's land almost," Mr. Penniloe answered thoughtfully. "An entire parish intervenes between their hill and Hagdon ; so that I cannot go among them, without seeming to intrude upon a neighbour's duties. Otherwise it is very sad to think that a colony almost of heathens should be permitted in the midst of us. I hear that there is a new landowner now, coming from your father's part of the country, who claims seigniorial rights over them, which they intend to resist with all their might."

" To be sure. Sir Henry Haggerstone is the man, a great friend of mine, and possibly something nearer before long. He cares not a pin for the money ; but he is not the man to forego his rights, especially when they are challenged. I take a great interest in those people. Sir Henry promised me an introduction, through his steward, or whoever it is ; and but for this business I should have gone over. But as these two fellows have been among them, I thought it wiser to keep away. I intend to know more of them, when this is over. I rather like fellows who refuse to pay."

" You have plenty of experience of them, doctor, without going over to the Whetstone. Would that we had a few gratuitous Church-builders, as well as a gratuitous doctor in this parish ! But I sadly fear that your services will be too much in demand after this arrest. You should have at least six constables, if our people will not help you.

Supposing that the Whetstone men are there, would they
not attempt a rescue ? "

" No sir ; they will not be there ; it is not their custom.
I am ashamed, as it is, to take four men against two, and
would not, except for the great importance of it. But I
am keeping you too long. I shall make a point of behold-
ing you no more, until Wednesday morning ; except of
course in church on Sunday. You must be kept out of it
altogether. It is not for me to tell you what to do ; but I
trust that you will not add to our anxieties, by appearing
at all in the matter. Your busiest time of the year is at
hand ; and I scarcely know whether I have done right, in
worrying you at all about this affair."

" Truly the time is appointed now for conflict with the
unseen powers, rather than those of our own race. But
why are we told to gird our loins—of which succincture the
Spencer is expressive, and therefore curtly clerical—unless
we are also to withstand evil-doers, even in the market-
place ? Peace is a thing that we all desire ; but no man
must be selfish of it. If every man stuck to his own
corner only, would there ever be a dining-table ? Be not
surprised then, Master Jemmy Fox, if I should appear
upon the warlike scene. As the Statesmen of the age say
—when they don't know what to say—I reserve my right
of action."

Fox was compelled to be satisfied with this because he
could get no better. Yet he found it hard to be comfortable about the now urgent outlook. Beyond any doubt,
he must go through with the matter in hand, and fight it
well out. But where would he be, if the battle left him,
with two noble heroes disabled, and both of them beyond
the heroic time of life. As concerned himself, he was quite
up for the fight, and regarded the prospect with pleasure,
as behoves a young man, who requires a little change, and
has a lady-love who will rejoice in his feats. Moreover he
knew that he was very quick of foot, and full of nimble
dodges ; but these elderly men could not so skip away, even
if their dignity allowed it. After much grim meditation,
when he left the rectory, he made up his mind to go
straight to Squire Mockham ; and although it was a
doubtful play of cards, to consult thus informally the

Justice, before whom the information was soon to be laid, it seemed to him, on the whole, to be the proper course. On Tuesday it would be too late to receive any advice upon the subject.

But Mr. Mockham made no bones of it. Whether he would grant the warrant or not, was quite another question, and must depend upon the formal depositions when received. The advice that he gave was contingent only upon the issue of the warrant, as to which he could say nothing yet. But he did not hesitate, as the young man's friend, to counsel him about his own share in the matter.

"Keep all your friends out of it. Let none of them be there. The execution of a warrant is the duty of the Authorities, not of amateurs and volunteers. Even you yourself should not appear, unless it be just to identify; though afterwards you must do so, of course, when the charge comes to be heard. Better even that criminals should escape, than that non-official persons should take the business on themselves. As a magistrate's son, you must know this."

"That is all very well, in an ordinary case," said Fox, who had got a great deal more than he wanted. "But here it is of such extreme importance to get to the bottom of this matter; and if they escape, where are we?"

"All very true. But if you apply to the law, you must let the law do its own work, and in its own way, though it be not perfect. All you can do, is to hope for the best."

"And probably get the worst," said Jemmy, with a grin of resignation. "But I suppose I may be at hand, and ready to give assistance, if called upon?"

"Certainly," answered Mr. Mockham, rubbing his hands gently; "that is the privilege of every subject, though not claimed very greedily. By-the-by, I was told that there is to be some sort of wrestling at your Fair this year. Have you heard anything about it?"

"Well, perhaps a little." The young man looked slyly at the Magistrate, for one of the first things he had heard was that Mockham had started the scheme by giving ten guineas towards the prize-fund. "Among other things I heard that Polwarth is coming, the Cornish champion, as they call him."

"And he holds the West of England belt. It is too bad," said the Magistrate, "that we should have no man to redeem it. When I was a boy, we should all have been mad, if the belt had gone over the border long. But who is there now? The sport is decaying, and fisticuffs (far more degrading work) are ousting it altogether. I think you went to see the play last year."

"I just looked in at it, once or twice. It did not matter very much to me, as a son of Somerset; but it must have been very grievous to a true Devonian, to see Cornwall chucking his countrymen about, like a lot of wax-headed ninepins. And no doubt he will do the same thing this year. You can't help it—can you, Squire?"

"Don't be too sure of that, my friend. A man we never heard of has challenged for the belt, on behalf of Devon. He will not play in the standards, but have best of three backs with the Cornishman, for the belt and a special prize raised by subscription. When I was a lad I used to love to see it, ay, and I knew all the leading men. Why, all the great people used to go to see it then. The Lord Lieutenant of the county would come down from Westminster for any great match; and as for Magistrates—well, the times are changed."

"You need not have asked me the news, I see. To know all about it, I must come to you. I should have been glad to see something of it, if it is to be such a big affair. But that will be impossible on account of this job. Good night, sir. Twelve o'clock, I think you said, will suit for our application?"

"Yes, and to stop malicious mouths—for they get up an outcry, if one knows anybody—I shall get Sir Edwin Sanford to join me. He is in the Commission for Somerset too; and so we can arrange it—if issued at all, to hold good across the border."

CHAPTER XXXV.

A WRESTLING BOUT.

VALENTINE'S DAY was on Sunday that year, and a violent gale from the south and west set in before daylight, and lasted until the evening, without bringing any rain. Anxiety was felt about the Chancel roof, which had only been patched up temporarily, and waterproofed with thick tarpaulins ; for the Exeter builders had ceased work entirely during that December frost, and as yet had not returned to it. To hurry them, while engaged elsewhere, would not have been just, or even wise, inasmuch as they might very fairly say, "let us have a little balancing of books first, if you please."

However, the old roof withstood the gale, being sheltered from the worst of it, and no further sinking of the wall took place ; but at the Abbey, some fifty yards eastward, a very sad thing came to pass. The south-western corner and the western end (the most conspicuous part remaining) were stripped, as if by a giant's rip-hook, of all their dark mantle of ivy. Like a sail blown out of the bolt-ropes, away it all went bodily, leaving the white flint rough and rugged, and staring like a suburban villa of the most choice effrontery. The contrast with the remainder of the ruins and the old stone church was hideous ; and Mr. Penniloe at once resolved to replace and secure afresh as much of the fallen drapery as had not been shattered beyond hope of life. Walter Haddon very kindly offered to supply the ladders, and pay half the cost ; for the picturesque aspect of his house was ruined by this bald background. This job was to be put in hand on Thursday ; but worse things happened before that day.

"Us be going to have a bad week of it," old Channing, the clerk, observed on Monday, as he watched the four vanes on the tower (for his eyes were almost as keen as ever) and the woodcock feathers on the western sky ; "never knowed a dry gale yet, but were follered by a wet one twice as bad ; leastways, if a' coom from the Dartmoor mountains."

However, things seemed right enough on Tuesday morning, to people who seldom think much of the sky ; and the rustics came trooping in to the Fair, as brave as need be, and with all their Sunday finery. A prettier lot of country girls no Englishman might wish, and perhaps no other man might hope to see, than the laughing, giggling, blushing, wondering, simpering, fluttering, or bridling maidens, fresh from dairy, or churn, or linhay, but all in very bright array, with love-knots on their breasts, and lavender in their pocket-handkerchiefs. With no depressing elegance perhaps among them, and no poetic sighing for impossible ideals ; and probably glancing backwards, more than forwards on the path of life, because the rule and the practice is, for the lads of the party to walk behind.

Louts are these, it must be acknowledged, if looked at from too high a point ; and yet, in their way, not by any means so low, as a topper on the high horse, with astral spurs, and a banner of bad Latin, might condemn them for to be. If they are clumsy, and awkward, and sheepish, and can only say—"Thank 'e, sir ! Veyther is quite well," in answer to "How are you to-day, John ?"—some of it surely is by reason of a very noble quality, now rarer than the great auk's egg ; and known, while it was a noun still substantive, as modesty. But there they were, and plenty of them, in the year 1836 ; and they meant to spend their money in good fairing, if so be their girls were kind.

Mr. Penniloe had a lot of good heart in him ; and when he came out to stand by the bellman, and trumpeter who thrilled the market-place, his common sense, and knowledge of the darker side, had as much as they could do to back him up against the impression of the fair young faces, that fell into the dumps, at his sad decree. The strong evil-doers were not come yet, their time would not begin till the lights began to flare, and the dark corners hovered with temptation. Silence was enjoined three times by ding-dong of bell and blare of trump, and thrice the fatal document was read with stern solemnity and mute acceptance of every creature except ducks, whom nothing short of death can silence, and scarcely even that when once their long valves quiver with the elegiac strain.

The trumpeter from Exeter, with scarlet sash and tassel,

2 A

looked down from an immeasurable height upon the village bellman, and a fiddler in the distance, and took it much amiss that he should be compelled to time his sonorous blasts by the tinkle tinkle of old nunks.

"Truly, I am sorry," said the Curate to himself, while lads and lasses, decked with primrose, and the first white violets, whispered sadly to one another—" no more fairing after this "—" I am sorry that it should be needful to stop all these innocent enjoyments."

"Then why did you send for me, sir?" asked the trumpeter rather savagely, as one who had begged at the rectory for beer, to medicate his lips against the twang of brass, but won not a drop from Mrs. Muggridge.

Suddenly there came a little volley of sharp drops—not of the liquid he desired—dashed into the trumpeter's red face, and against the back of the Parson's hat—the first skit of rain, that seemed rather to rise, as if from a blow-pipe, than fall from the clouds. Mr. Penniloe hastened to his house close by, for the market-place was almost in a straight line with the school, and taking his old gingham umbrella, set off alone for a hamlet called Southend, not more than half a mile from the village. Although not so learned in the weather as his clerk, he could see that the afternoon was likely to prove wet, and the longer he left it the worse it would be, according to all indications. Without any thought of adversaries, he left the village at a good brisk pace, to see an old parishioner of whose illness he had heard.

Crossing a meadow on his homeward course he observed that the footpath was littered here and there with strips and patches of yellow osier peel, as if, since he had passed an hour or so ago, some idle fellow had been "whittling" wands from a withy-bed which was not far off. For a moment he wondered what this could mean; but not a suspicion crossed his mind of a rod in preparation for his own back.

Alas, too soon was this gentleman enlightened. The lonely footpath came sideways into a dark and still more lonesome lane, deeply sunk between tangled hedges, except where a mouldering cob wall stood, sole relic of a worn-out linhay. Mr. Penniloe jumped lightly from the treddled stile into the mucky and murky lane, congratulating himself upon shelter here, for a squally rain was setting in; but the leap was into a den of wolves.

From behind the cob wall, with a yell, out rushed four hulking fellows, long of arm and leg, still longer of the weapons in their hands. Each of them bore a white withy switch, flexible, tough, substantial, seemly instrument for a pious verger—but what would pious vergers be doing here, and why should their faces retire from view? Each of them had tied across his most expressive, and too distinctive part, a patch of white muslin, such as imparts the sweet sense of modesty to a chamber-window; but modesty in these men was small.

Three of them barred the Parson's road, while the fourth cut off his communications in the rear; but even so did he not perceive the full atrocity of their intentions. To him they appeared to be inditing of some new form of poaching, or some country game of skill perhaps, or these might be rods of measurement.

"Allow me to pass, my friends," he said; "I shall not interfere with your proceedings. Be good enough to let me go by."

"Us has got a little bit o' zummat," said the biggest of them, with his legs astraddle, "to goo with 'e, Passon, and to 'baide with 'e a bit. A choice bit of fairing, zort o' peppermint stick, or stick lickerish."

"I am not a fighting man; but if any man strikes me, let him beware for himself. I am not to be stopped on a public highway, like this."

As Mr. Penniloe spoke, he unwisely closed his umbrella, and holding it as a staff of defence, advanced against the enemy.

One step was all the advance he made, for ere he could take another, he was collared, and tripped up, and cast forward heavily upon his forehead. There certainly was a great stone in the mud; but he never knew whether it was that, or a blow from a stick, or even the ebony knob of his own umbrella, that struck him so violently as he fell; but the effect was that he lay upon his face, quite stunned, and in danger of being smothered in the muck.

"Up with's coat-tails! Us'll dust his jacket. Ring the bull on 'un—one, two, dree, vour."

The four stood round, with this very fine Christian, ready
—as the Christian faith directs, for weak members, not
warmed up with it,—ready to take everything he could not
help; and the four switches hummed in the air with delight,
like the thirsty swords of Homer; when a rush as of many
winds swept them back to innocence. A man of great
stature, and with blazing eyes, spent no words upon them,
but lifted up the biggest with a chuck below his chin, which
sent him sprawling into the ditch, with a broken jaw, then
took another by the scruff of his small clothes, and hefted
him into a dog-rose stool, which happened to stand on the top
of the hedge with shark's teeth ready for their business;
then he leaped over the prostrate Parson, but only smote
vacant air that time. "The devil, the devil, 'tis the devil
himself!" cried the two other fellows, cutting for their
very lives.

"Reckon, I were not a breath too soon;" said the man
who had done it, as he lifted Mr. Penniloe, whose lips were
bubbling and nose clotted up; "why, they would have killed
'e in another minute, my dear. D—d if I bain't afeared
they has done it now."

That the clergyman should let an oath pass unrebuked,
would have been proof enough to any one who knew him
that it never reached his mind. His silver hair was clogged
with mud, and his gentle face begrimed with it, and his
head fell back between the big man's knees, and his blue
eyes rolled about without seeing earth or heaven.

"That doiled Jemmy Fox, we wants 'un now. Never
knowed a doctor come, when a' were wanted. Holloa, you
be moving there, be you? You dare stir, you murderer!"
It was one of the men lately pitched into the hedge; but
he only groaned again, at that great voice.

"Do 'e veel a bit better now, my dear? I've a girt
mind to kill they two hosebirds in the hedge; and what's
more, I wull, if 'e don't came round pretty peart."

As if to prevent the manslaughter threatened, the Parson
breathed heavily once or twice, and tried to put his hand to
his temples; and then looked about with a placid amazement.

"You 'bide there, sir, for a second," said the man, setting
him carefully upon a dry bank with his head against an

ash-tree. "Thy soul shall zee her desire of thine enemies, as I've a'read when I waz a little buy."

To verify this promise of Holy Writ, he took up the stoutest of the white switches, and visiting the ditch first, and then the hedge-trough, left not a single accessible part of either of those ruffians without a weal upon it as big as his thumb, and his thumb was not a little one. They howled like a couple of pigs at the blacksmith's, when he slips the ring into their noses red-hot; and it is lawful to hope that they felt their evil deeds.

"T'other two shall have the very same, bumbai; I knows where to put hands on 'em both;" said the operator, pointing towards the village; and it is as well to mention that he did it.

"Now, sir, you come along of I." He cast away the fourth rod, having elicited their virtues, and taking Mr. Penniloe in his arms, went steadily with him to the nearest house. This stood alone in the outskirts of the village; and there two very good old ladies lived, with a handsome green railing in front of them.

These, after wringing their hands for some minutes, enabled Mr. Penniloe to wash his face and head, and gave him some red currant wine, and sent their child of all work for Mrs. Muggridge. Meanwhile the Parson began to take a more distinct view of the world again, his first emotion being anxiety about his Sunday beaver, which he had been wearing in honour of the Proclamation—the last duty it was ever destined to discharge. But the "gigantic individual," as the good ladies called him, was nowhere to be seen, when they mustered courage to persuade one another to peep outside the rails.

By this time the weather was becoming very bad. Everybody knows how a great gale rises; not with any hurry, or assertion of itself, (as a little squall does, that is limited for time) but with a soft hypocritical sigh, and short puffs of dissimulation. The solid great storm, that gets up in the south, and means to make every tree in England bow, to shatter the spray on the Land's-end cliffs while it shakes all the towers of London, begins its advance without any broad rush, but with many little ticklings of the space it is to sweep. A trumpery frolic where four roads meet, a woman's umbrella turned inside out, a hat tossed into a horse-pond perhaps, a weather-cock befooled into chace of head with tail, and a clutch of big raindrops sheafed into the sky and shattered into mist again—these, and a thousand other little pranks and pleasantries, are as the shrill admonitions of the fife, in the vanguard of the great invasion of the heavens.

But what cares a man, with his money in his pockets, how these larger things are done? And even if his money be yet to seek, still more shall it preponderate. A tourney of wrestlers for cash and great glory was crowding the courtyard of the *Ivy-bush* with every man who could raise a shilling. A steep roof of rick-cloth and weatherproof canvas, supported on a massive ridge-pole would have protected the enclosure from any ordinary storm; but now the tempestuous wind was tugging, whistling, panting, shrieking, and with great might thundering, and the violent rain was pelting, like the rattle of pebbles on the Chessil beach, against the strained canvas of the roof; while the rough hoops of candles inside were swinging, with their crops of guttering tallow welted, like sucked stumps of Asparagus. Nevertheless the spectators below, mounted on bench, or stool, or trestle, or huddled against the rope-ring, were jostling, and stamping, and craning their necks, and digging elbows into one another, and yelling, and swearing, and waving rotten hats, as if the only element the Lord ever made was mob.

Suddenly all jabber ceased, and only the howls of the storm were heard, and the patter from the sodden roof, as Polwarth of Bodmin, having taken formal back from Dascombe of Devon, (the winner of the Standards, a very fine player, but not big enough for him) skirred his flat hat into the middle of the sawdust, and stood there flapping his brawny arms, and tossing his big-rooted nose, like a bull. In the flare of the lights, his grin looked malignant, and the swing of his bulk overweening; and though he said nothing but "Cornwall for ever!" he said it as if it meant— "Devonshire be d—d!"

After looking at the company with mild contempt, he swaggered towards the umpires, and took off his belt, with the silver buckles and the red stones flashing, and hung it upon the cross-rail for defiance. A shiver and a tremble of silence ran through the hearts, and on the lips of three hundred sad spectators. Especially a gentleman who sate behind the umpires, dressed in dark riding-suit and a flapped hat, was swinging from side to side with strong feeling.

"Is there no man to try a fall for Devonshire? Won't kill him to be beaten. Consolation money, fifty shillings." The chairman of the Committee announced; but nobody came forward.

A deep groan was heard from old Channing the Clerk, who had known such very different days; while the Cornishman made his three rounds of the ring, before he should buckle on the belt again; and snorted each time, like Goliath. Gathering up the creases of his calves, which hung like the chins of an Alderman, he stuck his heels into the Devonshire earth, to ask what it was made of. Then. with a smile, which he felt to be kind, and heartily large to this part of the world, he stooped to pick up the hat gay with seven ribbons, wrung from Devonshire button-holes.

But behold, while his great hand was going to pick it up thus carelessly, another hat struck it, and whirled it away, as a quoit strikes a quoit that appears to have won.

"Devon for ever! And Cornwall to the Devil!" A mighty voice shouted, and a mighty man came in, shaking the rain and the wind from his hair. A roar of hurrahs overpowered the gale, as the man taking heed of nobody, strode up to the belt, and with a pat of his left hand, said —"I wants this here little bit of ribbon."

"Thee must plai for 'un fust," cried the hero of Cornwall.
"What else be I come for?" the other enquired.

When formalities had been satisfied, and the proper clothing donned, and the champions stood forth in the ring, looking at one another, the roof might have dropped, without any man heeding, until it came across his eyes.

The challenger's name had been announced—"Harvey Tremlett, of Devonshire"—but only one or two besides old Channing had any idea who he was; and even old Channing was not aware that the man had been a wrestler from early youth, so seldom had he visited his native place.

"A' standeth like a man as understood it," "A' be bigger

in the back than Carnishman," "Hope 'a hath trained, or 's
wind won't hold;" sundry such comments of critical power
showed that the public, as usual, knew ten times as much
as the performers.

These, according to the manner of the time, were clad
alike, but wore no pads, for the brutal practice of kicking
was now forbidden at meetings of the better sort. A jacket,
or jerkin, of tough sail-cloth, half-sleeved and open in front
afforded firm grasp, but no clutch for throttling; breeches
of the stoutest cord, belted at waist and strapped at knee,
red worsted stockings for Devonshire, and yellow on behalf
of Cornwall, completed their array; except that the
Cornishman wore ankle-boots, while the son of Devon, at
his own request, was provided only with sailor's pumps.
The advantage of these, for lightness of step and pliancy of
sole, was obvious; but very few players would venture upon
them, at the risk of a crushed and disabled foot. "Fear
he bain't nim' enough for they pea-shells. They be all very
well for a boy;" said Channing.

The Cornishman saw that he had found his match,
perhaps even his master in bodily strength, if the lasting
power could be trusted. Skill and endurance must decide
the issue, and here he knew his own pre-eminence. He
had three or four devices of his own invention, but of very
doubtful fairness; if all other powers failed, he would have
recourse to them.

For two or three circuits of the ring, their mighty frames
and limbs kept time and poise with one another. Each
with his left hand grasped the other by the shoulder lappet;
each kept his right hand hovering like a hawk, and the
fingers in ply for a dash, a grip, a tug. Face to face, and
eye to eye, intent upon every twinkle, step for step they
marched sideways, as if to the stroke of a heavy bell, or the
beating of slow music. Each had his weight thrown
slightly forwards, and his shoulders slouched a little,
watching for one unwary move, and testing by some subtle
thrill the substance of the other, as a glass is tilliped to try
its ring.

By a feint of false step, and a trick of eye, Polwarth got
an opening. In he dashed, the other's arm flew up, and the
Cornish grip went round him. In vain he put forth his

mighty strength, for there was no room to use it. Down
he crashed, but turned in falling, so that the back was
doubtful.

"Back"! "Fair back"! "No back at all." "Four
pins." "Never, no, three pins." "See where his arm
was?" "Foul, foul, foul!" Shouts of wrath, and even
blows ensued; for a score or two of Cornishmen were there.
"Hush for the Umpires!" "Hold your noise." "Thee be
a liar." "So be you." The wind and the rain were well
out-roared, until the Umpires, after some little consultation
gave award.

"We allow it true back, for Cornwall. Unless the fall
claims foul below belt. If so, it will be for Referee."
Which showed that they differed upon that point.

"Let 'un have it. I won't claim no foul. Let 'un do it
again, if 'a can." Thus spake the fallen man, striding up to
the Umpires' post. A roar of cheers rang round the tent,
though many a Devonshire face looked glum, and a few
groans clashed with the frank hurrahs.

The second bout was a brief one, but afforded much
satisfaction to all lovers of fair play, and therefore perhaps
to the Cornishmen. What Tremlett did was simply this.
He feigned to be wholly absorbed in guarding against a
repetition of the recent trick. The other expecting nothing
more than tactics of defence was caught, quite unawares,
by his own device, and down he went—a very candid four-
pin fall.

Now came the final bout, the supreme decision of the tie,
the crowning struggle for the palm. The issue was so
doubtful, that the oldest and most sage of all palæstric
oracles could but look,—and feared that voice might not
prove—wise. Skill was equally divided, (setting dubious
tricks aside), strength was a little in favour of Devon, but
not too much turn of the balance, (for Cornwall had not
produced a man of such magnitude for many years)
experience was on Cornwall's side; condition, and lasting
power, seemed to be pretty fairly on a par. What was to
settle it? Devonshire knew.

That is to say, the fair County had its hopes,—though
always too modest and frugal to back them—that something
which it produces even more freely than fair cheeks and

kind eyes, and of which the corner land is not so lavish—to wit fine temper, and tranquillity of nature, might come to their mother's assistance. Even for fighting, no man is at the best of himself, when exasperated. Far less can he be so in the gentler art.

A proverb of large equity, and time-honoured wisdom, declares (with the bluntness of its race) that "sauce for the goose is sauce for the gander." This maxim is pleasant enough to the goose; but the gander sputters wrathfully when it comes home to his breast. Polwarth felt it as a heinous outrage, that he had been the victim of his own device. As he faced his rival for the last encounter, a scowl came down upon his noble knobby forehead, his keen eyes glowered as with fire in his chest, and his wiry lips closed viciously. The Devonshire man, endowed with larger and less turbid outlook, perceived that the other's wrath was kindled, and his own duty was to feed the flame.

Accordingly, by quiet tricks, and flicks, such as no man would even feel unless already too peppery, he worked the moral system hard, and roused in the other's ample breast —or brain, if that be the combative part—a lofty disdain of discretion. Polwarth ground his teeth, and clenched his fist, spat fire—and all was up with him. One savage dash he made, which might have swept a milestone backward, breast clashed on breast, he swung too high, the great yellow legs forsook the earth, and the great red ones flashed between them, then the mighty frame span in the air like a flail, and fell flat as the blade of a turf-beater's spade.

"All over! All up! Needn't ask about that. Three times three for Devonshire! Again, again, again! Carnies, what can 'e say to that now?"

Wild triumph, fierce dejection, yearning to fight it out prevailed; every man's head was out of the government of his neck—when these two leading Counties were quenched alike. The great pole of red pine, fit mast for an Admiral, bearing all the structure overhead, snapped, like a carrot, to a vast wild blast. In a weltering squash lay victor and vanquished, man with his fists up, and man eager to go at him, hearts too big to hold themselves for exultation, and hearts so low that wifely touch was needed to encourage them, glorious head that had won fifty shillings, and poor

numskull that had lost a pot of beer. Prostrate all, with
mouths full of tallow, sawdust, pitch, and another fellow's
toes. Many were for a twelvemonth limpers; but nobody
went to Churchyard.

CHAPTER XXXVI.

A FIGHTING BOUT.

AFTER that mighty crash, every body with any sense left
in its head went home. There was more to talk about than
Perlycross had come across in half a century. And the
worst of it was, that every blessed man had his own troubles
first to attend to; which is no fun at all, though his
neighbour's are so pleasant. The Fair, in the covered
market-place, had long been a dreary concern, contending
vainly against the stronger charm of the wrestling booth,
and still more vainly against the furious weather. Even
the biggest and best fed flares—and they were quite as
brisk in those days as they are now—gifted though they
might be with rage and vigour, lost all self-control, and
dashed in yellow forks, here there and everywhere, singeing
sometimes their own author's whiskers. Like a man who
lives too fast, they killed themselves; and the poor Cheap-
Jacks, the Universal Oracles, the Benevolent Bounty-men,
chucking guineas right and left, the Master of Cupid's
bower, who supplied every lass with a lord, and every lad
with a lady having a lapful of a hundred thousand pounds
—sadly they all strapped up, and lit their pipes, and
shivered at that terrible tramp before them, cursing the
weather, and their wives, and even the hallowed village of
Perlycross.

Though the coaches had forsaken this ancient track from
Exeter to London, and followed the broader turnpike roads,
there still used to be every now and then a string of pack-
horses, or an old stage-waggon, not afraid of hills and
making no fuss about time, but straggling at leisure
through the pristine thoroughfares, thwarted less with
toll-bars.

Notably, old Hill's *God-be-with-us* van left Exeter on

Tuesdays, with the goodwill of three horses, some few hours
in the afternoon, and might be trusted to appear at
Perlycross according to the weather and condition of the
roads. What more comfortable course of travel could there
be for any one who understood it, and enjoyed sound sleep,
and a good glass of ale at intervals, with room enough to
dine inside if he thought fit, than the *God-be-with-us* van
afforded? For old Hill was always in charge of it himself,
and expected no more than a penny a mile, and perhaps the
power to drink the good health of any peaceful subject of
the King, who might be inclined to come along with him,
and listen to his moving tales. The horses were fat, and
they rested at night, and took it easily in the daytime; and
the leader had three little bells on his neck, looking, when
you sat behind him, like a pair of scales; and without them
he always declined to take a step, and the wheelers backed
him up in that denial. For a man not bound to any domineer-
ing hour, or even to a self-important day, the broad-wheeled
waggon belonging to old Hill—"Old-as-the-Hills" some
flippant younkers called him—was as good an engine as need
be, for crossing of the country, when it wanted to be crossed,
and halting at any town of hospitable turn.

That same Shrove-Tuesday,—and it is well to mark the
day, because Master Hill was so superior to dates—this
man who asserted the dignity of our race, by not allowing
matter to disturb him, was coming down hill with his heavy
drag on, in a road that was soft from the goodness of the
soil; when a man with two legs made of better stuff than
ours, either came out of a gate across the van, or else fairly
walked it down by superior speed behind. "Ship ahoy!"
he shouted; and old Hill was wide awake, for he had two
or three barrels that would keep rolling into the small of
his back—as he called it, with his usual oblivion of chronology—and so he was enabled to discern this man, and begin
at his leisure to consider him.

If the man had shouted again, or shown any other
symptom of small hurry, the driver—or properly speaking
the drifter, for the horses did their own driving—would
have felt some disappointment in him, as an inferior fellow-
creature. But the man on foot, or at least on stumps, was
in no more hurry than old Hill himself, and steadfastly

trudged to the bottom of the hill, looking only at the horses
—a very fine sign.

The land being Devon, it is needless to say that there was
no inconsistency about it. Wherever one hill ends, there
another begins, with just room enough between them for a
horse to spread his legs, and shake himself with self-appro-
bation. And he is pretty sure to find a crystal brook,
purling across the road, and twinkling bright temptation
to him.

"Hook up skid, and then 'e can jump in ; " said old Hill
in the hollow where the horses backed, and he knew by the
clank that it had been done, and then by a rattle on the
floor behind him, that the stranger had embarked by the
chains at the rear. After about a mile or so of soft low
whistling, in which he excelled all Carriers, old Hill turned
round with a pleasant grin, for there was a great deal of
good about him.

"Going far ? " He asked, as an opening of politeness,
rather than of curiosity.

"Zort of a place, called Perlycrass ; " replied the wooden-
leg'd man, who was sitting on a barrel. Manifestly an
ancient sailor, weather-beaten, and taciturn, the residue of
a strong and handsome man.

The whole of this had been as nearly to the Carrier's
liking, as the words and deeds of any man can be to any
other's. Therefore before another mile had been travelled,
old Hill turned round again, with a grin still sweeter.

"Pancake day, bain't it ? " was his very kind enquiry.

" B'lieve it be ; " replied the other, in the best and truest
British style. After this no more was lacking to secure old
Hill's regard than the very thing the sailor did. There
was a little flap of canvas, like a loophole in the tilt, fitted
for the use of chawers, and the cleanliness of the floor.
Timberlegs after using this, with much deliberation and great
skill, made his way forward, and in deep silence poked old
Hill with his open tobacco-box. If it were not silver, it
was quite as good to look at, and as bright as if it held the
freedom of the City ; the tobacco, moreover, was of goodly
reek, and a promise of inspiration such as never flows through
Custom-house.

" Thank 'e, I'll have a blade bumbai. Will 'e zit upon that

rope of onions?" The sailor shook his head; for the rim of
a barrel, though apt to cut, cuts evenly like a good schoolmaster.

"'Long of Nelson?" Master Hill enquired, pointing to
the places where the feet were now of deputy. The old Tar
nodded; and then with that sensitive love of accuracy which
marks the Tar, growled out, "Leastways, wan of them."

"And what come to t'other wan?" Master Hill was
capable of really large human interest.

"Had 'un off, to square the spars, and for zake of vamily."
He had no desire to pursue the subject, and closed it by a
big squirt through the flap.

Old Hill nodded with manly approbation. Plymouth
was his birthplace; and he knew that other sons of Nelson
had done this; for it balanced their bodies, and composed
their minds with another five shillings a week for life, and
the sale of the leg covered all expenses.

"You'm a very ingenious man;" he glanced as he spoke,
at the sailor's jury-rig; "I'll war'n no doctor could a'
vitted 'e up, like thiccy."

"Vitted 'un myself with double swivel. Can make four
knots an hour now. They doctors can undo 'e; but 'em
can't do 'e up. A cove can't make sail upon a truck-head."

"And what do 'e say to the weather, Cap'n?" Master
Hill enquired of his passenger, when a few more compliments
had passed, and the manes of the horses began to ruffle, and
the tilt to sway and rattle with the waxing storm.

"Think us shall have as big a gale of wind as ever come
out of the heavens," the sailor replied, after stumping to the
tail of the van, and gazing windwards; "heave to pretty
smart, and make all snug afore sunset, is my advice. Too
much sail on this here little craft, for such a blow as us
shall have to-night."

"Can't stop short of Taunton town." Old Hill was
famed for his obstinacy.

"Can 'e take in sail? Can 'e dowse this here canvas?
Can 'e reef it then somehow?" The old man shook his
head. "Tell 'e what then, shipmate—if 'e carry on for six
hours more, this here craft will be on her beam-ends, wi'out
mainsail parteth from his lashings, sure as my name is Dick
Herniman."

This Tar of the old school, better known as "timber-leg'd
Dick," disembarked from the craft, whose wreck he had
thus predicted, at a turning betwixt Perliton and Perlycross, and stumped away up a narrow lane, at a pace quite
equal to that of the *God-be-with-us* van. The horses looked
after him, as a specimen of biped hitherto beyond their
experience; and old Hill himself, though incapable of
amazement (which is a rapid process) confessed that there
were some advantages in this form of human pedal, as well
as fine economy of cloth and leather.

"How 'a doth get along, nimbler nor I could!" the
Carrier reflected, as his nags drove on again. "Up to
zummat ratchety, I'll be bound he be now. A leary old
salt as ever lived. Never laughed once, never showed a
smile, but gotten it all in his eyes he have: and the eyes be
truer folks than the lips. Enough a'most to tempt a man
to cut off 's own two legses."

Some hours later than this, and one hour later than the
downfall of the wrestler's roof, the long market-place,
forming one side of the street—a low narrow building set
against the churchyard wall, between the school and the
lych-gate, looked as dismal, and dreary, and deserted, as the
bitterest enemy of Fairs could wish. The torrents of rain,
and fury of the wind, had driven all pleasure-seekers, in a
grievously drenched and battered plight, to seek for wiser
comfort; and only a dozen or so of poor creatures, either
too tipsy to battle with the wind, or too reckless in their
rags to care where they were, wallowed upon sacks, and
scrabbled under the stanchion-boards, where the gaiety had
been. The main gates, buckled back upon their heavy
hinges, were allowed to do nothing in their proper line of
business, until the Church-clock should strike twelve, for
such was the usage; though as usual nobody had ever heard
who ordained it. A few oil-lamps were still in their duty,
swinging like welted horn-poppies in the draught, and
shedding a pale and spluttering light.

The man who bore the keys had gone home three times,
keeping under hele with his oil-skins on, to ask his wife—
who was a woman of some mark—whether he might not
lock the gates, and come home and have his bit of bacon.
But she having strong sense of duty, and a good log blazing,

and her cup of tea, had allowed him very generously to warm his hands a little, and then begged him to think of his family. This was the main thing that he had to do; and he went forth again into the dark, to do it.

Meanwhile, without anybody to take heed (for the Sergeant, ever vigilant, was now on guard in Spain), a small but choice company of human beings, was preparing for action in the old school-porch, which stood at the back of the building. Staffs they had, and handcuffs too, and supple straps, and loops of cord; all being men of some learning in the law, and the crooked ways of people out of harmony therewith. If there had been light enough to understand a smile, they would have smiled at one another, so positive were they that they had an easy job, and so grudgeful that the money should cut up so small. The two worthy constables of Perlycross felt certain that they could do it better by themselves; and the four invoked from Perliton were vexed, to have to act with village lubbers. Their orders were not to go nigh the wrestling, or show themselves inside the market-place, but to keep themselves quiet, and shun the weather, and what was a great deal worse, the beer. Every now and then, the ideas of jolly noises, such as were appropriate to the time, were borne upon the rollicking wings of the wind into their silent vestibule, suggesting some wiping of lips, which, alas, were ever so much too dry already. At a certain signal, they were all to hasten across the corner of the churchyard, at the back of the market-place, and enter a private door at the east end of the building, after passing through the lych-gate.

Suddenly the rain ceased, as if at sound of trumpet; like the mouth of a cavern the sky flew open, and the wind, leaping three points of the compass, rushed upon the world from the chambers of the west. Such a blast, as had never been felt before, filled the whole valley of the Perle, and flung mowstack, and oakwood, farmhouse, and abbey, under the sweep of its wings as it flew. The roar of the air overpowered the crash of the ruin it made, and left no man the sound of his own voice to himself.

These great swoops of wind always lighten the sky; and as soon as the people blown down could get up, they were able to see the church-tower still upright, though many men

swore that they heard it go rock. Very likely it rocked,
but could they have heard it?

In the thick of the din of this awful night, when the
church-clock struck only five instead of ten—and it might
have struck fifty, without being heard—three men managed,
one by one, and without any view of one another, to creep
along the creases of the storm, and gain the gloomy shelter
of the market-place. "Every man for himself," is the
universal law, when the heavens are against the whole race
of us. Not one of these men cared to ask about the condition of the other two, nor even expected much to see
them, though each was more resolute to be there himself,
because of its being so difficult.

" Very little chance of Timberlegs to-night," said one to
another, as two of them stood in deep shadow against the
back wall, where a voice could be heard if pitched in the
right direction; "he could never make way again' a starm
like this."

"Thou bee'st a liar," replied a gruff voice, as the clank of
metal on the stone was heard. "Timberlegs can goo, where
flesh and bone be mollichops." He carried a staff like a
long handspike, and prodded the biped on his needless feet,
to make him wish to be relieved of them.

" Us be all here now," said the third man, who seemed in
the wavering gloom to fill half the place. "What hast
thou brought us for, Timber-leg'd Dick?"

" Bit of a job, same as three months back. Better than
clam-pits, worn't it now? Got a good offer for thee too,
Harvey, for that old ramshackle place. Handy hole for a
louderin' job, and not far from them clam-pits."

"Ay, so a' be. Never thought of that. And must have
another coney, now they wise 'uns have vound out Nigger's
Nock. Lor' what a laugh we had, Jem and I, at they fules
of Perlycrass!"

"Then Perlycross will have the laugh at thee. Harvey
Tremlett, and James Kettel, I arrest 'e both, in the name
of His Majesty the King."

Six able-bodied men (who had entered, unheard in the
roar of the gale, and unseen in the gloom), stood with
drawn staffs, heels together, and shoulder to shoulder, in a
semi-circle, enclosing the three conspirators.

2 B

"Read thy warrant aloud," said Dick Herniman, striking his handspike upon the stones, and taking command in right of intellect; while the other twain laid their backs against the wall, and held themselves ready for the issue.

Dick had hit a very hard nail on the head. None of these constables had been young enough to undergo Sergeant Jakes, and thenceforth defy the most lofty examiner.

"Didn't hear what 'e zed," replied head-constable, making excuse of the wind, which had blown him but little of the elements. But he lowered his staff, and held consultation.

"Then I zay it again," shouted Timber-leg'd Dick, stumping forth with a power of learning, for he had picked up good leisure in hospitals; "if thou representest the King, read His Majesty's words, afore taking his name in vain."

These six men were ready, and resolute enough, to meet any bodily conflict; but the literary crisis scared them. "Can e' do it, Jack?" "Don't know as I can." "Wish my boy Bill was here." "Don't run in my line"—and so on.

"If none on 'e knows what he be about," said the man with the best legs to stand upon, advancing into the midst of them, "I know a deal of the law; and I tell 'e, as a friend of the King, who hath lost two legs for 'un, in the Royal Navy, there can't be no lawful arrest made here. And the liberty of the subject cometh in, the same as a' doth again' highwaymen. Harvey Tremlett, and Jem Kettel, the law be on your side, to 'protect the liberty of the subject.'"

This was enough for the pair who had stood, as law-abiding Englishmen, against the wall, with their big fists doubled, and their great hearts doubting. "Here goo'th for the liberty of the subject," cried Harvey Tremlett, striding forth; "I shan't strike none as don't strike me. But if a' doth, a' must look out."

The constables wavered, in fear of the law, and doubt of their own duty; for they had often heard that every man had a right to know what he was arrested for. Unluckily one of them made a blow with his staff at Harvey Tremlett; then he dropped on the flags with a clump in his ear, and the fight in a moment was raging.

Somebody knocked Jemmy Kettel on the head, as being more easy to deal with; and then the blood of the big man rose. Three stout fellows fell upon him all together, and heavy blows rung on the drum of his chest, from truncheons plied like wheel-spokes. Forth flew his fist-clubs right and left, one of them meeting a staff in the air, and shattering it back into its owner's face. Never was the peace of the King more broken; no man could see what became of his blows, legs and arms went about like windmills, substance and shadow were all as one, till the substance rolled upon the ground, and groaned.

This dark fight resembled the clashing of a hedgerow in the fury of a midnight storm; when the wind has got in and cannot get out, when ground-ash, and sycamore, pole, stub, and saplin, are dashing and whirling against one another, and even the sturdy oak-tree in the trough is swaying, and creaking, and swinging on its bole.

"Zoonder not to kill e'er a wan of 'e, I 'ood. But by the Lord, if 'e comes they byses"—shouted Harvey Tremlett, as a rope was thrown over his head from behind, but cut in half a second by Herniman—"more of 'e, be there?" as the figures thickened—"have at 'e then, wi' zummat more harder nor vistics be!"

He wrenched from a constable his staff, and strode onward, being already near the main gate now. As he whirled the heavy truncheon round his head, the constables hung back, having two already wounded, and one in the grip of reviving Jem, who was rolling on the floor with him. "Zurrender to His Majesty;" they called out, preferring the voluntary system.

"A varden for the lot of 'e!" the big man said, and he marched in a manner that presented it.

But not so did he walk off, blameless and respectable. He had kept his temper wonderfully, believing the law to be on his side, after all he had done for the County.

Now his nature was pressed a little too hard for itself, when just as he had called out—"coom along, Jem; there be nort to stop 'e, Timberlegs;" retiring his forces with honour—two figures, hitherto out of the moil, stood across him at the mouth of exit.

"Who be you?" he asked, with his anger in a flame; for they showed neither staff of the King, nor warrant. "Volunteers, be 'e? Have a care what be about."

"Harvey Tremlett, here you stop." Said a tall man, square in front of him. But luckily for his life, the lift of the sky showed that his hair was silvery.

"Never hits an old man. You lie there;" Tremlett took him with his left hand, and laid him on the stones. But meanwhile the other flung his arms around his waist.

"Wult have a zettler? Then thee shall," cried the big man, tearing him out like a child, and swinging his truncheon, for to knock him on the head, and Jemmy Fox felt that his time was come.

Down came the truncheon, like a paviour's rammer, and brains would have weltered on the floor like suds, but a stout arm dashed across, and received the crash descending.

"Pumpkins!" cried the smiter, wondering much what he had smitten, as two bodies rolled between his legs and on the stones. "Coom along, Jemmy boy. Nare a wan to stop 'e."

The remnant of the constables upon their legs fell back. The Lord was against them. They had done their best. The next job for them was to heal their wounds, and get an allowance for them, if they could.

Now the human noise was over, but the wind roared on, and the rushing of the clouds let the stars look down again. Tremlett stood victorious in the middle of the gateway. Hurry was a state of mind beyond his understanding. Was everybody satisfied? Well, no one came for more. He took an observation of the weather, and turned round.

"Shan't bide here no longer," he announced. "Dick, us'll vinish up our clack to my place. Rain be droud up, and I be off."

"No, Harvey Tremlett, you will not be off. You will stay here like a man, and stand your trial."

Mr. Penniloe's hand was upon his shoulder, and the light of the stars, thrown in vaporous waves, showed the pale face firmly regarding him.

"Well, and if I says no to it, what can 'e do?"

"Hold you by the collar, as my duty is." The Parson set his teeth, and his delicate white fingers tightened their not very formidable grasp.

"Sesh!" said the big man, with a whistle, and making

as if he could not move. " When a man bo baten, a'
must gie in. Wun't 'e let me goo, Passon? Do 'e let
me goo."

" Tremlett, my duty is to hold you fast. I owe it to a
dear friend of mine, as well as to my parish."

" Well, you be a braver man than most of 'em, I
zimmeth. But do 'e tell a poor chap, as have no chance at
all wi' 'e, what a' hath dooed, to be lawed for 'un so crule
now."

" Prisoner, as if you did not know. You are charged
with breaking open Colonel Waldron's grave, and carrying
off his body."

" Oh Lord ! Oh Lord in Heaven !" shouted Harvey
Tremlett. " Jem Kettel, hark to thiccy ! Timberlegs, do
'e hear thic? All they blessed constables, as has got their
bellyful, and ever so many wise gen'lemen too, what do 'e
think 'em be arter us for? Arter us for resurrectioneering !
Never heered tell such a joke in all my life. They hosebirds to *Ivy-bush* cries ' Carnwall for ever !' But I'm blest
if I don't cry out ' Perlycrass for ever !' Oh Lord, oh
Lord ! Was there ever such a joke? Don't 'e hold me,
sir, for half a minute, just while I has out my laugh—fear
I should throw 'e down with shaking so."

Timber-leg'd Dick came up to his side, and not being of
the laughing kind, made up for it by a little hornpipe in
the lee; his mental feet striking, from the flints pitched
there, sparks enough to light a dozen pipes ; while Kettel,
though damaged severely about the mouth, was still able
to compass a broad and loud guffaw.

" Prisoners," Mr. Penniloe said severely, for he misliked
the ridicule of his parish ; " this is not at all a matter to
be laughed at. The evidence against you is very strong, I
fear."

" Zurrender, zurrender, to His Majesty the King !"
cried Tremlett, being never much at argument. " Constables, if 'ee can goo, take charge. But I 'out have no
handicuffs, mind. Wudn't a gie'd 'ee a clout, if I had
knawed it. Zarve 'ee right though, for not radlug of thic
warrant-papper. Jemmy boy, you zurrender to the King ;
and I be Passon's prisoner. Honour bright fust though
—nort to come agin' us, unless a' be zet down in warrant-

papper. Passon, thee must gi'c thy word for that. Timberlegs, coom along for layyer."

"Certainly, I give my word, as far as it will go, that no other charge shall be brought against you. The warrant is issued for that crime only. Prove yourselves guiltless of that, and you are free."

"Us won't be very long in prison then. A day or two bain't much odds to we."

CHAPTER XXXVII.

GENTLE AS A LAMB.

OF the nine people wounded in that Agonaic struggle, which cast expiring lustre on the Fairs of Perlycross, every one found his case most serious to himself, and still more so to his wife; and even solemn, in the presence of those who had to settle compensation. Herniman had done some execution, as well as received a nasty splinter of one leg, which broke down after his hornpipe; and Kettel had mauled the man who rolled over with him. But, as appeared when the case was heard, Tremlett had by no means done his best; and his lawyer put it touchingly and with great effect, that he was loth to smite the sons of his native county, when he had just redeemed their glory, by noble discomfiture of Cornwall.

One man only had a parlous wound; and as is generally ordained in human matters, this was the one most impartial of all, the one who had no interest of his own to serve, the one who was present simply out of pure benevolence, and a Briton's love of order. So at least his mother said; and every one acknowledged that she was a woman of high reasoning powers. Many others felt for him, as who would have done the same, with like opportunity.

For only let a healthy, strong, and earnest-minded Englishman—to use a beloved compound epithet of the day —hear of a hot and lawful fight impending, with people involved in it, of whom he has some knowledge, and we may trust him heartily to be there or thereabouts, to see— as he puts it to his conscience—fair play. But an if he chance to be in love just then, with a very large percentage of despair to reckon up, and one of the combatants is in the count against him, can a doubt remain of his eager punctuality?

This was poor Frank Gilham's case. Dr. Gronow was a prudent man, and liked to have the legions on his side. He perceived that young Frank was a staunch and stalwart fellow, sure to strike a good blow on a friend's behalf. He was well aware also of his love for Christie, and could not see why it should come to nothing. While Jemmy Fox's faith in the resources of the law, and in his own prowess as a power in reserve, were not so convincing to the elder mind. "Better make sure, than be too certain," was a favourite maxim of this shrewd old stager; and so without Jemmy's knowledge he invited Frank, to keep out of sight unless wanted.

This measure saved the life of Dr. Fox, and that of Harvey Tremlett too, some of whose brothers had adorned the gallows. Even as it was, Jemmy Fox lay stunned, with the other man's arm much inserted in his hat. Where he would have been without that arm for buffer, the Cherub, who sits on the chimney-pots of Harley Street, alone can say. Happily the other doctor was unhurt, and left in full possession of his wits, which he at once exerted. After examining the wounded yeoman, who had fainted from the pain and shock, he borrowed a mattress from the rectory, a spring-cart and truss of hay from Channing the baker, and various other appliances; and thus in spite of the storm conveyed both patients to hospital. This was the *Old Barn* itself, because all surgical needs would be forthcoming there more readily, and so it was wiser to decline Mr. Penniloe's offer of the rectory.

With the jolting of the cart, and the freshness of the air, Fox began to revive ere long; and though still very weak and dizzy, was able to be of some service at his own dwelling-place; and although he might not, when this matter first arose, have shown all the gratitude which the sanguine do expect, in return for Frank Gilham's loyalty, he felt very deep contrition now, when he saw this frightful fracture, and found his own head quite uncracked.

The six constables, though they had some black eyes,

bruised limbs, and broken noses, and other sources of regret,
were (in strict matter of fact, and without any view to
compensation) quite as well as could be expected. And as
happens too often, the one who groaned the most had the
least occasion for it. It was only the wick of a lamp, that
had dropped, without going out, on this man's collar, and
burned a little hole in his *niddick*, as it used to be called in
Devonshire.

Tremlett readily gave his word that no escape should be
attempted; and when Mrs. Muggridge came to know that
this was the man who had saved her master, nothing could
be too good for him. So constables and prisoners were fed
and cared for, and stowed for the night in the long school-
room, with hailstones hopping in the fireplace.

In the morning, the weather was worse again; for this
was a double-barrel'd gale, as an ignorant man might term
it; or rather perhaps two several gales, arising from some
vast disturbance, and hitting into one another. Otherwise,
why should it be known and remembered even to the present
day, as the great Ash-Wednesday gale, although it began
on Shrove-Tuesday, and in many parts raged most fiercely
then? At Perlycross certainly there was no such blast
upon the second day, as that which swept the Abbey down:
when the wind leaped suddenly to the west, and the sky
fell open, as above recorded.

Upon that wild Ash-Wednesday forenoon, the curate
stood in the churchyard mourning, even more than the
melancholy date requires. Where the old Abbey had stood
for ages (backing up the venerable church with grand dark-
robed solemnity, and lifting the buckler of ancient faith above
many a sleeping patriarch) there was nothing but a hideous
gap, with murky clouds galloping over it. Shorn of its
ivy curtain by the tempest of last Sunday, the mighty
frame had reeled, and staggered, and with one crash
gone to ground last night, before the impetuous welkin's
weight.

"Is all I do to be always vain, and worse than vain—
destructive, hurtful, baneful, fatal I might say, to the very
objects for which I strive? Here is the church, unfinished,
leaky, with one of its corners gone underground, and the
grand stone screen smashed in two; here is the Abbey, or

alas not here, but only an ugly pile of stones! Here is the
outrage to my dear friend, and the shame to the parish as
black as ever; for those men clearly know nothing of it.
And here, or at any rate close at hand, the sad drawback
upon all good works; for at Lady-day in pour the bills, and
my prayers (however earnest) will not pay them. It has
pleased the Lord, in His infinite wisdom, to leave me very
short of cash."

Unhappily his best hat had been spoiled, in that interview
with the four vergers; and in his humility he was not sure
that the one on his head was good enough even to go to
the Commination service. However it need not have felt
unworthy; for there was not a soul in the church to be
adjured, save that which had been under its own brim.
The clerk was off for Perliton, swearing—even at his time
of life!—that he had been subpœnaed, as if that could be
on such occasion; and as for the pupils, all bound to be in
church, the Hopper had been ordered by the Constables to
present himself to the Magistrates (though all the Constables
denied it) and Pike, and Mopuss, felt it their duty to go
with him.

In a word, all Perlycross was off, though services of the
Church had not yet attained their present continuity; and
though every woman, and even man, had to plod three
splashy miles, with head on chest, in the teeth of the gale
up the river. How they should get into the room, when
there, was a question that never occurred to them. There
they all yearned to be; and the main part, who could not
raise a shilling, or prove themselves Uncles, or Aunts, or
former sweethearts of the two Constables who|kept the door,
had to crouch under dripping shrubs outside the windows,
and spoiled all Squire Mockham's young crocuses.

That gentleman was so upright, and thoroughly impartial,
that to counteract his own predilections for a champion
wrestler, he had begged a brother-magistrate to come and
sit with him on this occasion; not Sir Edwin Sanford,
who was of the Quorum for Somerset, but a man of some
learning and high esteem, the well-known Dr. Morshead.
Thus there would be less temptation for any tattler to cry,
"hole and corner," as spiteful folk rejoice to do, while
keeping in that same place themselves. Although there

was less perhaps of mischief-making in those days than now; and there could be no more.

The Constables marched in, with puff and blow, like victors over rebels, and as if they had carried the prisoners captive, every yard of the way, from Perlycross. All of them began to talk at once, and to describe with more vigour than truth the conflict of the night before. But Dr. Morshead stopped them short, for the question of resistance was not yet raised. What the Bench had first to decide was whether a case could be made out for a *mittimus*, in pursuance of the warrant, to the next Petty Sessions on Monday; whence the prisoners would be remitted probably to the Quarter Sessions.

The two accused stood side by side (peaceful and decorous, as if they were accustomed to it); and without any trepidation admitted their identity. It was rather against their interests that the Official Clerk was absent—this not being a stated meeting, but held for special purpose—for Magistrates used to be a little nervous, without their proper adviser; and in fear of permitting the guilty to escape, they sometimes remanded upon insufficient grounds.

In the present case, there was nothing whatever to connect these two men with the crime, except the testimony of Joe Crang, and what might be regarded as their own admission, overheard by Dr. Fox. The latter was not in court, nor likely so to be; and as for the blacksmith's evidence, however positive it might seem, what did it amount to? And such as it was, it was torn to rags, through the quaking of the deponent.

For a sharp little lawyer started up, as lawyers are sure to do everywhere, and crossed the room to where Herniman sat, drumming the floor with metallic power, and looking very stolid. But a glance had convinced the keen Attorney, that here were the brains of the party, and a few short whispers settled it. " Guinea, if 'e gets 'em off'; if not, ne'er a farden." " Right!" said the lawyer, and announced himself.

" Blickson, for the defence, your Worships—Maurice Blickson of Silverton." The proper bows were interchanged; and then came Crang's excruciation. Already this sturdy and very honest fellow, was as he elegantly described it, in a "lantern-sweat" of terror. It is one thing to tell a tale to two friends in a potato-field, and another to narrate the same on oath, with four or five quills in mysterious march, two most worshipful signors bending brows of doubt upon you, and thirty or forty faces scowling at every word—"What a liar you be!" And when on the top of all this, stands up a noble gentleman, with keen eyes, peremptory voice, contemptuous smiles, and angry gestures, all expressing his Christian sorrow, that the Devil should have so got hold of you,—what blacksmith, even of poetic anvil (whence all rhythm and metre spring) can have any breath left in his own bellows?

Joe Crang had fallen on his knees, to take the oath; as witnesses did, from a holy belief that this turned the rungs of the gallows the wrong way; and then he had told his little tale most sadly, as one who hopes never to be told of it again. His business had thriven, while his health was undermined; through the scores of good people, who could rout up so much as a knife that wanted a rivet, or even a boy with one tooth pushing up another; and though none of them paid more than fourpence for things that would last them a fortnight to talk about, their money stayed under the thatch, while Joe spent nothing but a wink for all his beer.

But ah, this was no winking time! Crang was beginning to shuffle off, with his knuckles to his forehead; and recovering his mind so loudly that he got in a word about the quality of his iron—which for the rest of his life he would have cited, to show how he beat they Justesses—when he found himself recalled, and told to put his feet together. This, from long practice of his art, had become a difficulty to him, and in labouring to do it he lost all possibility of bringing his wits into the like position. This order showed Blickson to be almost a Verulam in his knowledge of mankind. Joe Crang recovered no self-possession, on his own side of better than a gallon strong.

"Blacksmith, what o'clock is it now?"

Crang put his ears up, as if he expected the Church-clock to come to his aid; and then with a rally of what he was hoping for, as soon as he got round the corner, replied—"Four and a half, your honour."

"I need not remind your Worships," said Blickson, when the laughter had subsided; "that this fellow's evidence, even if correct, proves nothing whatever against my Clients. But just to show what it is worth, I will, with your Worships' permission, put a simple question to him. He has sworn that it was two o'clock on a foggy morning, and with no Church-clock to help him, when he saw, in his night-mare this ghostly vision. Perhaps he should have said—'four and a half;' which in broad daylight is his idea of the present hour. Now, my poor fellow, did you swear, or did you not, on a previous occasion, that one of the men who so terrified you out of your heavy sleep, was Dr. James Fox—a gentleman, Dr. Morshead, of your own distinguished Profession? Don't shuffle with your feet, Crang, nor yet with your tongue. Did you swear that, or did you not?"

"Well, if I did, twadn't arkerate."

"In plain English, you perjured yourself on that occasion. And yet you expect their Worships to believe you now! Now look at the other man, the tall one. By which of his features do you recognize him now, at four and a half, in the morning?"

"Dun'now what veitchers be. Knows 'un by his size, and manner of standin'. Should like to hear's voice, if no object to you, layyer."

"My friend, you call me by your own name. Such is your confusion of ideas. Will your Worships allow me to assist this poor numskull? The great Cornish wrestler is here, led by that noble fraternal feeling, which is such a credit to all men distinguished, in any walk of life. Mr. Polwarth of Bodmin, will you kindly stand by the side of your brother in a very noble art?"

It was worth a long journey in bad weather (as Squire Mockham told his guests at his dinner-party afterwards, and Dr. Morshead and his son confirmed it) to see the two biggest growths of Devonshire and of Cornwall standing thus amicably side by side, smiling a little slyly at each other, and blinking at their Worships with some abashment, as if to say—"this is not quite in our line."

For a moment the audience forgot itself, and made itself audible with three loud cheers. "Silence!" cried their Worships, but not so very sternly.

"Reckon, I could drow 'e next time;" said Cornwall.

"Wun't zay but what 'e maight;" answered Devon courteously.

"Now little blacksmith," resumed the lawyer, though Joe Crang was considerably bigger than himself; "will you undertake to swear, upon your hope of salvation, which of those two gentlemen you saw, that night?"

Joe Crang stared at the two big men, and his mind gave way within him. He was dressed in his best, and his wife had polished up his cheeks and nose with yellow soap, which gleamed across his vision with a kind of glaze, and therein danced pen, ink, and paper, the figures of the big men, the faces of their Worships, and his own hopes of salvation.

"Maight 'a been Carnisher;" he began to stammer, with a desire to gratify his county; but a hiss went round the room from Devonian sense of Justice; and to strike a better balance, he finished in despair—"Wull then, it waz both on 'em."

"Stand down, sir!" Dr. Morshead shouted sternly, while Blickson went through a little panorama of righteous astonishment and disgust. All the audience roared, and a solid farmer called out—"Don't come near me, you infernal liar," as poor Crang sought shelter behind his top-coat. So much for honesty, simplicity, and candour, when the nervous system has broken down!

"After that, I should simply insult the intelligence of your Worships;" continued the triumphant lawyer, "by proceeding to address you. Perhaps I should ask you to commit that wretch for perjury; but I leave him to his conscience, if he has one."

"The case is dismissed," Dr. Morshead announced, after speaking for a moment to his colleague. "Unless there is any intention to charge these men with resisting or assaulting officers, in the execution of their warrant. It has been reported, though not formally, that some bystander was considerably injured. If any charge is entered on either behalf, we are ready to receive the depositions."

The constables, who had been knocked about, were beginning to consult together, when Blickson slipped among them, after whispering to Herniman, and a good deal of

nodding of heads took place, while pleasant ideas
were interchanged, such as, "handsome private compensation;" "twenty-five pounds to receive to-night, and such
men are always generous;" "a magnificent supper-party
at the least, if they are free. If not, all must come to
nothing."

The worthy constabulary—now represented by a still
worthier body, and one of still finer feeling—perceived the
full value of these arguments; and luckily for the accused, Dr
Gronow was not present, being sadly occupied at *Old Barn.*

"Although there is no charge, and no sign of any
charge, your Worships, and therefore I have no *locus
standi;*" Mr. Blickson had returned to his place, and
adopted an airy and large-hearted style; "I would
crave the indulgence of the Bench, for one or two
quite informal remarks; my object being to remove every
stigma from the characters of my respected Clients. On
the best authority I may state, that their one desire,
and intention, was to surrender, like a pair of lambs"—
at this description a grin went round, and the learned
Magistrates countenanced it—"if they could only realise the
nature of the charge against them. But when they demanded,
like Englishmen, to know why their liberty should be
suddenly abridged, what happened? No one answered
them! All those admirable men were doubtless eager to
maintain the best traditions of the law; but the hurricane
out-roared them. They laboured to convey their legal
message; but where is education, when the sky falls on its
head? On the other hand, one of these law-abiding men
had been engaged gloriously, in maintaining the athletic
honour of his county. This does not appear to have raised
in him at all the pugnacity, that might have been expected.
He strolled into the market-place, partly to stretch his poor
bruised legs, and partly perhaps, to relieve his mind; which
men of smaller nature would have done, by tippling.
Suddenly he is surrounded by a crowd of very strong men
in the dark. The Fair has long been over; the lights are
burning low; scarcely enough of fire in them to singe the neck
of an enterprising member of our brave Constabulary. In
the thick darkness, and hubbub of the storm, the hero who
has redeemed the belt, and therewith the ancient fame of

our county, supposes—naturally supposes, charitable as his
large mind is, that he is beset for the sake of the money,
which he has not yet received, but intends to distribute so
freely, when he gets it. The time of this honourable
Bench is too valuable to the public to be wasted over any
descriptions of a petty skirmish, no two of which are at all
alike. My large-bodied Client, the mighty wrestler, might
have been expected to put forth his strength. It is certain
that he did not do so. The man, who had smitten down
the pride of Cornwall, would strike not a blow against his
own county. He gave a playful push or two, a chuck
under the chin, such as a pretty milkmaid gets, when she
declines a sweeter touch. I marvel at his wonderful self-
control. His knuckles were shattered by a blow from a
staff; like a roof in a hailstorm his great chest rang—for
the men of Perliton can hit hard—yet is there anything to
show that he even endeavoured to strike in return? And
how did it end? In the very noblest way. The Pastor of the
village, a most saintly man, but less than an infant in
Harvey Tremlett's hands, appears at the gate, when there
is no other let or hindrance to the freedom of a Briton. Is
he thrust aside rudely? Is he kicked out of the way?
Nay, he lays a hand upon the big man's breast, the hand of
a Minister of the Cross. He explains that the law, by
some misapprehension, is fain to apprehend this simple-
minded hero. The nature of the sad mistake is explained;
and to use a common metaphor, which excited some
derision just now, but which I repeat, with facts to back
me,—gentle as a lamb, yonder lion surrenders !"

"The lamb is very fortunate in his shepherd ;" said Dr.
Morshead drily, as the lawyer sat down, under general
applause. "But there is nothing before the Bench, Mr.
Blickson. What is the object of all this eloquence?"

"The object of my very simple narrative, your Worships,
is to discharge my plain duty to my clients. I would ask
this Worshipful Bench, not only to dismiss a very absurd
application, but also to add their most weighty opinions,
that Harvey Tremlett, and James Fox—no, I beg pardon
that was the first mistake of this ever erroneous blacksmith
—James Kettel, I should say, have set a fine example of
perfect submission to the law of the land."

"Oh come, Mr. Blickson, that is out of the record. We pronounce no opinion upon that point. We simply adjudge that the case be now dismissed."

CHAPTER XXXVIII.

AN INLAND RUN.

"WON'ERFUL well, 'e doed it, sir. If ever I gets into Queer Street, you be the one to get me out."

This well-merited compliment was addressed by Dick Herniman to Attorney Blickson, at a convivial gathering held that same afternoon, to celebrate the above recorded triumph of Astræa. The festal party had been convoked at the Wheatsheaf Tavern in Perliton Square, and had taken the best room in the house, looking out of two windows upon that noble parallelogram, which Perliton never failed to bring with it, orally, when it condescended to visit Perlycross. The party had no idea of being too abstemious, the object of its existence being the promotion, as well as the assertion, of the liberty of the subject.

Six individuals were combining for this lofty purpose, to wit the two gentlemen so unjustly charged, and their shrewd ally of high artistic standing, that very able lawyer who had vindicated right; also Captain Timberlegs, and Horatio Peckover, Esquire; and pleasant it is as well as strange to add, Master Joseph Crang of Susscot, blacksmith, farrier, and engineer. For now little differences of opinion, charges of perjury and body-snatching, assault and battery, and general malfeasance, were sunk in the large liberality of success, the plenitude of John Barleycorn, and the congeniality of cordials.

That a stripling like the Hopper should be present was a proof of some failure of discretion upon his part, for which he atoned by a tremendous imposition; while the prudent Pike, and the modest Mopuss, had refused with short gratitude this banquet, and gone home. But the Hopper regarded himself as a witness—although he had not been called upon—in right of his researches at Blackmarsh, and declared that officially he must hear the matter out, for an explanation had been promised. The greater marvel was perhaps that Joe Crang should be there, after all the lash of tongue inflicted on him. But when their Worships were out of sight, Blickson had taken him by the hand, in a truly handsome manner, and assured him of the deep respect he felt, and ardent admiration, at his too transparent truthfulness. Joe Crang, whose heart was very sore, had shed a tear at this touching tribute, and was fain to admit, when the lawyer put it so, that he was compelled in his own art to strike the finest metal the hardest.

So now all six were in very sweet accord, having dined well, and now refining the firmer substances into the genial flow. Attorney Blickson was in the chair, for which nature had well qualified him; and perhaps in the present more ethereal age, he might have presided in a "syndicate" producing bubbles of gold and purple, subsiding into a bluer tone.

For this was a man of quick natural parts, and gifted in many ways for his profession. Every one said that he should have been a Barrister; for his character would not have mattered so much, when he went from one town to another, and above all to such a place as London, where they think but little of it. If he could only stay sober, and avoid promiscuous company, and make up his mind to keep his hand out of quiet people's pockets, and do a few other respectable things, there was no earthly reason that any one could see, why he should not achieve fifty guineas a day, and even be a match for Mopuss K. C., the father of Mr. Penniloe's fattest pupil.

"This honourable company has a duty now before it;" Mr. Blickson drew attention by rapping on the table, and then leaning back in his chair, with a long pipe rested on a bowl of punch, or rather nothing but a punch-bowl now. On his right hand sat Herniman, the giver of the feast— or the lender at least, till prize-money came to fist—and on the other side was Tremlett, held down by heavy nature from the higher flights of Bacchus, because no bowl was big enough to make him drunk; "yes, a duty, gentlemen, which I, as the representative of Law cannot see neglected. We have all enjoyed one another's 'good health,' in the way in which it concerns us most; we have also promoted, by

2 c

such prayers, the weal of the good Squire Mockham, and
that of another gentleman, who presented himself as *Amicus
curiæ*—gentlemen, excuse a sample of my native tongue—a
little prematurely perhaps last night, and left us to sigh for
him vainly to-day. I refer to the gentleman, with whom
another, happily now present, and the soul of our party,
and rejoicing equally in the Scriptural name of James,
was identified in an early stage of this still mysterious
history, by one of the most conscientious, truthful and self-
possessed of all witnesses, I have ever had the honour yet of
handling in the box. At least he was not in the box, because there was none; but he fully deserves to be kept in
a box. I am sorry to see you smile—at my prolixity I
fear; therefore I will relieve you of it. Action is always
more urgent than words. Duty demands that we should
have this bowl refilled. Pleasure, which is the fairer sex of
duty, as every noble sailor knows too well, awaits us next
in one of her most tempting forms, as an ancient Poet has
observed. If it is sweet to witness from the shore the
travail of another, how much sweeter to have his trials
brought before us over the flowing bowl, while we rejoice in
his success and share it. Gentlemen, I call upon Captain
Richard Herniman for his promised narrative of that great
expedition, which by some confusion of the public mind has
become connected with a darker enterprise. Captain
Richard Herniman to the fore!"

"Bain't no Cappen, and han't got no big words," said
Timber-leg'd Dick, getting up with a rattle, and standing
very staunchly; "but can't refuse this here gentleman,
under the circumstances. And every word as I says will
be true."

After this left-handed compliment, received with a cheer
in which the lawyer joined, the ancient salt promised that
among good friends, he relied on honour bright, that there
should be no dirty turn. To this all pledged themselves
most freely; and he trusting rather in his own reservations
than their pledge, that no harm should ever come of it,
shortly told his story, which in substance was as follows.
But some names which he omitted have been filled in, now
that all fear of enquiry is over.

In the previous September, when the nights were growing

long, a successful run across the Channel had been followed
by a peaceful, and well-conducted, landing at a lonely spot
on the Devonshire coast, where that pretty stream the Otter
flows into the sea. That part of the shore was very slackly
guarded then ; and none of the authorities got scent, while
scent was hot, of this cordial international transaction.
Some of these genuine wares found a home promptly and
pleasantly in the neighbourhood, among farmers, tradesmen,
squires, and others, including even some loyal rectors, and
zealous Justices of the Peace, or peradventure their wives
and daughters capable of minding their own keys. Some,
after dwelling in caves, or furze-ricks, barns, potato-buries,
or hollow trees, went inland, or to Sidmouth, or Seaton, or
anywhere else where a good tax-payer had plastered up his
windows, or put " Dairy " on the top of them.

But the prime of the cargo, and the very choicest goods,
such as fine Cognac, rich silk and rare lace, too good for
pedlars, and too dear for Country parsons still remained
stored away very snugly, in some old dry cellars beneath
the courtyard of a ruined house at Budleigh ; where nobody
cared to go poking about, because the old gentleman who
lived there once had been murdered nearly thirty years ago,
for informing against smugglers, and was believed to be in
the habit of walking there now. These shrewd men perceived how just it was that he should stand guard in the
spirit over that which in the flesh he had betrayed, especially as his treason had been caused by dissatisfaction
with his share in a very fine contraband venture. Much
was now committed to his posthumous sense of honour ;
for the free-traders vowed that they could make a thousand
pounds of these choice wares in any wealthy town, like
Bath, or Bristol, or even Weymouth, then more fashionable
than it is now.

But suddenly their bright hopes were dashed. Instead of
reflecting on the value of these goods, they were forced to
take hasty measures for their safety. A very bustling man,
of a strange suspicious turn, as dry as a mull of snuff, and
as rough as a nutmeg-grater ; in a word a Scotchman out of
sympathy with the natives, was appointed to the station at
Sidmouth, and before he unpacked his clothes began to rout
about, like a dog who has been trained to hunt for morels.

Very soon he came across some elegant French work, in cottages, or fishers' huts, or on the necks of milkmaids; and nothing would content him until he had discovered, even by such deep intriguery as the distribution of lollipops, the history of the recent enterprise.

"Let bygones be bygones," would have been the Christian sentiment of any new-comer at all connected with the district; and Sandy MacSpudder must have known quite well, that his curiosity was in the worst of taste, and the result too likely to cast discredit on his own predecessor, who was threatening to leave the world just then, with a large family unprovided for. Yet such was this Scotchman's pertinacity and push, that even the little quiet village of Budleigh, which has nothing to do but to listen to its own brook prattling to the gently smiling valley, even this rose-fringed couch of peace was ripped up by the slashing of this rude Lieutenant's cutlass. A spectre, even of the best Devonian antecedents, was of less account than a scare-crow to this matter-of-fact Lowlander. "A' can smell a rat in that ghostie," was his profane conclusion.

This put the spirited free-traders on their mettle. Fifty years ago, that Scotch interloper would have learned the restful qualities of a greener sod than his. But it is of interest to observe how the English nature softened, when the martial age had lapsed. It scarcely occurred to this gentler generation, that a bullet from behind a rock would send this spry enquirer to solve larger questions on his own account. Savage brutality had less example now.

The only thing therefore was to over-reach this man. He was watching all the roads along the coast, to east and west; but to guard all the tangles of the inward roads, and the blessed complexity of Devonshire lanes would have needed an army of pure natives. Whereas this busy foreigner placed no faith in any man born in that part of the world—such was his judgment—and had called for a draft of fellows having different vowels.

This being so, it served him right to be largely out-witted by the thick-heads he despised. And he had made such a fuss about it, at head-quarters, and promised such wonders if the case were left to him, that when he captured nothing but a string of worn-out kegs filled with diluted sheep-wash,

he not only suffered for a week from gastric troubles—
through his noseless hurry to identify Cognac—but also
received a stinging reprimand, and an order for removal to
a very rugged coast, where he might be more at home with
the language and the manners. And his predecessor's son
obtained that sunny situation. Thus is zeal rewarded
always, when it does not win the seal.

None will be surprised to hear that the simple yet
masterly stratagem, by means of which the fair western
county vindicated its commercial rights against northern
arrogance and ignoble arts, was the invention of a British
Tar, an old Agamemnon, a true heart of oak, re-membered
also in the same fine material. The lessons of Nelson had
not been thrown away; this humble follower of that great
hero first mis-led the adversary, and then broke his line.
Invested as he was by superior forces seeking access even
to his arsenal, he despatched to the eastward a lumbering
craft, better known to landsmen as a waggon, heavily laden
with straw newly threshed, under which was stowed a tier
of ancient kegs, which had undergone too many sinkings in
the sea (when a landing proved unsafe) to be trusted any
more with fine contents. Therefore they now contained
sheep-wash, diluted from the brook to the complexion of old
brandy. In the loading of this waggon special mystery was
observed, which did not escape the vigilance of the keen
lieutenant's watchmen. With a pair of good farm-horses,
and a farm-lad on the ridge of the load, and a heavy fellow
whistling not too loudly on the lade-rail, this harmless car
of fictitious Bacchus, crowned by effete Ceres, wended its
rustic way towards the lowest bridge of Otter, a classic and
idyllic stream. These two men, of pastoral strain and
richest breadth of language, carried orders of a simplicity
almost equal to their own.

No sooner was this waggon lost to sight and hearing in
the thick October night, and the spies sped away by the
short cuts to report it, than a long light cart, with a strong
out-stepping horse, came down the wooded valley to the
ghostly court. In half an hour, it was packed, and started
inland, passing the birthplace of a very great man, straight
away to Farringdon and Rockbear, with orders to put up at
Clist Hidon before daylight, where lived a farmer who

would harbour them securely. On the following night they
were to make their way, after shunning Cullompton, to the
shelter in Blackmarsh, where they would be safe from all
intrusion, and might await fresh instructions, which would
take them probably towards Bridgwater, and Bristol. By
friendly ministrations of the Whetstone men, who had some
experience in trade of this description, all this was managed
with the best success; Jem Kettel knew the country roads,
by dark as well as daylight, and Harvey Tremlett was not
a man to be collared very easily. In fact, without that sad
mishap to their very willing and active nag, they might
have fared through Perlycross, as they had through other
villages, where people wooed the early pillow, without a
trace or dream of any secret treasure passing.

Meanwhile at Sidmouth the clever Scotchman was enjoying
his own acuteness. He allowed that slowly rolling waggon
of the Eleusine dame to proceed some miles upon its course,
before his men stood at the horses' heads. There was
wisdom in this, as well as pleasure—the joy a cat pro-
longs with mouse—inasmuch as all these good things were
approaching his own den of spoil. When the Scotchmen
challenged the Devonshire swains, with flourish of iron, and
of language even harder, an interpreter was sorely needed.
Not a word could the Northmen understand that came from
the broad soft Southron tongues; while the Devonshire men
feigning, as they were bidden, to take them for highwaymen,
feigned also not to know a syllable of what they said.

This led, as it was meant to do, to very lavish waste of
time, and increment of trouble. The carters instead of
lending hand for the unloading of their waggon, sadly
delayed that operation, by shouting out "thaves!" at the
top of their voice, tickling their horses into a wild start now
and then, and rolling the Preventive men off at the tail.
MacSpudder himself had a narrow escape; for just when he
chanced to be between two wheels, both of them set off,
without a word of notice; and if he had possessed at all a
western body, it would have been run over. Being made of
corkscrew metal by hereditary right, he wriggled out as
sound as ever; and looked forward all the more to the
solace underlying this reluctant pile, as dry as any of his
own components.

Nothing but his own grunts can properly express the fattening of his self-esteem (the whole of which was home-fed) when his men, without a fork—for the Boreal mind had never thought of that—but with a great many chops of knuckles (for the skin of straw is tougher than a Scotch-man's) found their way at midnight, like a puzzled troop of divers, into the reef at bottom of the sheefy billows. Their throats were in a husky state, from chaff too penetrative, and barn-dust over volatile, and they risked their pulmonary weal, by opening a too sanguine cheer.

"Duty compels us to test the staple;" the Officer in command decreed; and many mouths gaped round the glow of his bullseye. "Don't 'ce titch none of that their wassh!" The benevolent Devonians exclaimed in vain Want of faith prevailed; every man suspected the verdict of his predecessor, and even his own at first swallow. If timber-leg'd Dick could have timed the issue, what a landing he might have made! For the Coast-guard tested staple so that twenty miles of coast were left free for fifty hours.

Having told these things in his gravest manner, Herniman, who so well combined the arts of peace and war, filled another pipe, and was open to enquiry. Every-body accepted his narrative with pleasure, and heartily wished him another such a chance of directing fair mer-chandise along the lanes of luck. The blacksmith alone had some qualms of conscience, for apparent back-slidings from the true faith of free-trade. But they clapped him on the back, and he promised with a gulp, that he never would peep into a Liberal Van again.

"There is one thing not quite clear to me;" said the Hopper, when the man of iron was settled below the table, whereas the youth had kept himself in trim for steeple-chasing. "What could our friend have seen in that vehicle of free-trade, to make him give that horrible account of its contents? And again, why did Mr. Harvey Tremlett carry off that tool of his, which I found in the water?"

With a wave of his hand—for his tongue had now lost, by one of nature's finest arrangements, the exuberance of the morning, whereas a man of sober silence would now have gushed into bright eloquence—the chairman deputed to Herniman, and Tremlett, the honour of replying to the Hopper.

"You see, sir," said the former, "it was just like this. We was hurried so in stowing cargo, that some of the finest laces in the world, such as they call *Valentines*, worth maybe fifty or a hundred pounds a yard, was shot into the hold anyhow, among a lot of silks and so on. Harvey, and Jemmy, was on honour to deliver goods as they received them; blacksmith seed some of this lace a'flappin' under black tarporly; and he knowed as your poor Squire had been figged out for 's last voyage with same sort of stuff, only not so good. A clever old 'ooman maketh some, to Perlycrass; Honiton lace they calls it here. What could a' think but that Squire was there? Reckon, Master Crang would a' told 'e this, if so be a' hadn't had a little drap too much."

"Thou bee'st a liar. Han't had half enough, I tell 'e." The blacksmith from under the table replied, and then rolled away into a bellowsful of snores.

"To be sure!" said Peckover. "I see now. Tamsin Tamlin's work it was. Sergeant Jakes told me all about it. With all the talk there had been of robbing graves, and two men keeping in the dark so, no wonder Crang thought what he did. Many people went to see that lace, I heard; and they said it was too good to go underground; though nothing could be too good for the Squire. Well now, about that other thing—why did Mr. Tremlett make off with *little Billy?*"

"Can't tell 'e, sir, very much about 'un;" the wrestler answered, with a laugh at the boy's examination. "Happen I tuk 'un up, a'veelin' of 'un, to frighten blacksmith maybe; and then I vancied a' maight come handy like, if nag's foot went wrong again. Then when nag gooed on all right, I just chucked 'un into a pool of watter, for to kape 'un out o' sight of twisty volk. Ort more to zatisfy this yung gent?"

"Yes. I am a twisty folk, I suppose. Unless there is any objection, I should like very much to know why Dr. Fox was sent on that fool's errand to the pits."

"Oh, I can tell 'e that, sir," replied Jem Kettel, for the spirit of the lad, and his interest in their doings, had made him a favourite with the present company. "It were one of my mates as took too much trouble. He were appointed to meet us at the cornder[of the four roads, an hour afore that! or more; and he got in a bit of a skear, it seems not knowing why we was so behindhand. But he knowed Dr. Vox, and thought 'un better out o' way, being such a sharp chap, and likely to turn meddlesome. He didn't want 'un to hang about up street, as a' maight with some sick 'ooman, and so he zent un' t'other road, to tend a little haxident. Wouldn't do he no harm, a' thought, and might zave us some bother. But, Lord! if us could have only knowed the toorn your volk would putt on it, I reckon us should have roared and roared, all droo the strates of Perlycrass. Vainest joke as ever coom to my hearin', or ever wull, however long the Lord kapeth me a'livin.' And to think of Jem Kettel being sworn to for a learned Doctor! Never had no teethache I han't, since the day I heered on it." A hearty laugh was held to be a sovereign cure for toothache then, and perhaps would be so still, if the patient could accomplish it.

"Well, so far as that goes, you have certainly got the laugh of us;" Master Peckover admitted, not forgetting that he himself came in for as much as any one. "But come now, as you are so sharp, just give me your good opinion. And you being all along the roads that night, ought to have seen something. Who were the real people in that horrid business?"

"The Lord in heaven knoweth, sir;" said Tremlett very solemnly. "Us passed in front of Perlycrass church, about dree o'clock of the morning. Nort were doing then, or us could scarcely have helped hearing of it. Even if 'em heered our wheels, and so got out of sight, I reckon, us must a' seed the earth-heap, though moon were gone a good bit afore that. And zim'th there waz no harse there. A harse will sing out a'most always to another harse at night, when a' heareth of him coming, and a' standeth lonely. Us coom athert ne'er chick nor cheeld from Perlycrass to Blackmarsh. As to us and Clam-pit volk, zoonder would us goo to gallows than have ort to say to grave-work. And gallows be too good for 'un, accardin' my opinion. But gen'lemen, afore us parts, I wants to drink the good health of the best man

I've a knowed on airth. Bain't saying much perhaps, for
my ways hath been crooked like. But maketh any kearless
chap belave in good above 'un, when a hap'th acrass a man
as thinketh nort of his own zell, but gi'eth his life to other
volk. God bless Passon Penniloe ! "

CHAPTER XXXIX.

NEEDFUL RETURNS.

Now it happened that none of these people, thus rejoicing in
the liberty of the subject, had heard of the very sad state
of things, mainly caused by their own acts, and now prevailing at *Old Barn*. Tremlett knew that he had struck a
vicious blow, at the head of a man who had grappled him,
but he thought he had missed it and struck something else,
a bag, or a hat, or he knew not what, in the pell mell scuffle
and the darkness. His turn of mind did not incline him to
be by any means particular as to his conduct, in a hot and
hard personal encounter ; but knowing his vast strength he
generally abstained from the use of heavy weapons, while
his temper was his own. But in this hot struggle, he had
met with a mutually shattering blow from a staff, as straight
as need be upon his right-hand knuckles ; and the pain
from this, coupled with the wrath aroused at the access of
volunteer enemies, had carried him—like the raging elements
outside—out of all remembrance of the true " sacredness
of humanity." He struck out, with a sense of not doing
the right thing, which is always strengthened afterwards ;
and his better stars being ablink in the gale, and the other
man's gone into the milky way, he hit him too hard ; which
is a not uncommon error.

Many might have reasoned (and before all others, Harvey
Tremlett's wife, if still within this world of reason ; and a
bad job it was for him that she was now outside it) that
nothing could be nobler, taking people as we find them—
and how else can we get the time to take them ?—than the
behaviour of this champion wrestler. But, without going
into such sweet logic of affinity, and rhetoric of friends
(whose minds have been made up in front of it) there was

this crushing fact to meet, that an innocent man's better arm was in a smash.

No milder word, however medical, is fit to apply to Frank Gilham's poor fore-arm. They might call it the *ulna*—for a bit of Latin is a solace, to the man who feels the pain in a brother Christian's member—and they might enter nobly into fine nerves of anatomy; but the one-sided difficulty still was there—they had got to talk about it; he had got to bear it.

Not that he made any coward outcry of it. A truer test of manliness (as has been often said, by those who have been through either trial), truer than the rush of blood and reckless dash of battle, is the calm, open-eyed, and firm-fibred endurance of long, ever-grinding, never-graduating pain. The pain that has no pang, or paroxysm, no generosity to make one cry out " Well done ! " to it, and be thankful to the Lord that it must have done its worst; but a fluid that keeps up a slow boil, by day and night, and never lifts the pot-lid, and never whirls about, but keeps up a steady stew of flesh, and bone, and marrow.

"I fear there is nothing for it, but to have it off," Dr. Gronow said, upon the third day of this frightful anguish. He had scarcely left the patient for an hour at a time; and if he had done harsh things in his better days, no one would believe it of him, who could see him now. " It was my advice at first, you know; but you would not have it, Jemmy. You are more of a surgeon than I am. But I doubt whether you should risk his life, like this."

" I am still in hopes of saving it. But you see how little I can do," replied Fox, whose voice was very low, for he was suffering still from that terrible concussion, and but for the urgency of Gilham's case, he would now have been doctoring the one who pays the worst for it. " If I had my proper touch, and strength of nerve, I never should have let it come to this. There is a vile bit of splinter that won't come in, and I am not firm enough to make it. I wish I had left it to you, as you offered. After all, you know much more than we do."

" No, my dear boy. It is your special line. Such a case as Lady Waldron's I might be more at home with. I should have had the arm off long ago. But the mother—the

mother is such a piteous creature? What has become of all
my nerve? I am quite convinced that fly-fishing makes a
man too gentle. I cannot stand half the things I once
thought nothing of. By-the-by, couldn't you counteract
her? You know the old proverb—

> 'One woman rules the men;
> Two makes them think again.'

It would be the best thing you could do."

"I don't see exactly what you mean," answered Jemmy,
who had lost nearly all of his sprightliness.

"Plainer than a pikestaff. Send for your sister. You
owe it to yourself, and her; and most of all to the man who
has placed his life in peril, to save yours. It is not a time
to be too finical."

"I have thought of it once or twice. She would be of
the greatest service now. But I don't much like to ask her.
Most likely she would refuse to come, after the way in
which I packed her off."

"My dear young friend," said Dr. Gronow, looking at
him steadfastly, "if that is all you have to say, you don't
deserve a wife at all worthy of the name. In the first
place, you won't sink your own little pride; and in the
next, you have no idea what a woman is."

"Young Farrant is the most obliging fellow in the
world," replied Fox, after thinking for a minute. "I will
put him on my young mare *Perle*, who knows the way;
and he'll be at Foxden before dark. If Chris likes to come,
she can be here well enough, by twelve or one o'clock
to-morrow."

"Like, or no like, I'll answer for her coming; and I'll
answer for her not being very long about it," said the senior
doctor; and on both points he was right.

Christie was not like herself, when she arrived, but pale,
and timid, and trembling. Her brother had not mentioned
Frank in his letter, doubting the turn she might take about
it, and preferring that she should come to see to himself,
which was her foremost duty. But young Mr. Farrant, the
Churchwarden's son, and pretty Minnie's brother, had no
embargo laid upon his tongue; and had there been fifty,
what could they have availed to debar such a clever young

lady? She had cried herself to sleep, when she knew all, and dreamed it a thousand times worse than it was.

Now she stood in the porch of the *Old Barn*, striving, and sternly determined to show herself rational, true to relationship, sisterly, and nothing more. But her white lips, quick breath, and quivering eyelids, were not altogether consistent with that. Instead of amazement, when Mrs. Gilham came to meet her, and no Jemmy, she did not even feign to be surprised, but fell into the bell-sleeves (which were fine things for embracing) and let the deep throbs of her heart disclose a tale that is better felt than told.

"My dearie," said the mother, as she laid the damask cheek against the wrinkled one, and stroked the bright hair with the palm of her hand, "don't 'e give way, that's a darling child. It will all be so different now you are come. It was what I was longing for, day and night, but could not bring myself to ask. And I felt so sure in my heart, my dear, how sorry you would be for him."

"I should think so. I can't tell you. And all done for Jemmy, who was so ungrateful! My brother would be dead, if your son was like him. There has never been anything half so noble, in all the history of the world."

"My dear, you say that, because you think well of our Frankie—I have not called him that, since Tuesday now. But you do think well of him, don't you now?"

"Don't talk to me of thinking well indeed! I never can endure those weak expressions. When I like people, I do like them."

"My dear, it reminds me quite of our own country, to hear you speak out so hearty. None of them do it up your way, much; according to what I hear of them. I feel it so kind of you, to like Frank Gilham."

"Well! am I never to be understood? Is there no meaning in the English language? I don't like him only. But with all my heart, I love him."

"He won't care if doctors cut his arm off now, if he hath one left to go round you."

The mother sobbed a little, with second fiddle in full view; but being still a mother, wiped her eyes, and smiled with content at the inevitable thing.

"One thing remember," said the girl, with a coaxing

domestic smile, and yet a lot of sparkle in her eyes; "if
you ever tell him what you twisted out of me, in a manner
which I may call—well, too circumstantial—I am afraid
that I never should forgive you. I am awfully proud, and
I can be tremendous. Perhaps he would not even care to
hear it. And then what would become of me? Can you
tell me that?"

"My dear, you know better. You know, as well as I do,
that ever since he saw you, he has thought of nothing else.
It has made me feel ashamed, that I should have a son
capable of throwing over all the world beside——"

"But don't you see, that is the very thing I like? Noble
as he is, if it were not for that, I—well, I won't go into it;
but you ought to understand. He can't think half so much
of me, as I do of him."

"Then there is a pair of you. And the Lord has made
you so. But never fear, my pretty. Not a whisper shall
he have. You shall tell him all about it, with your own
sweet lips."

"As if I could do that indeed! Why, Mrs. Gilham,
was that what you used to do, when you were young? I
thought people were ever so much more particular in those
days."

"I can hardly tell, my dear. Sometimes I quite forgot,
because it seems so long ago; and at other times I'm not
fit to describe it, because I am doing it over again. But
for pretty behaviour, and nice ways—nice people have them
in every generation; and you may take place with the best
of them. But we are talking, as if nothing was the matter.
And you have never asked even how we are going on!"

"Because I know all about it, from the best authority.
Coming up the hill we met Dr. Gronow, and I stopped the
chaise to have a talk with him. He does not think the arm
will ever be much good again; but he leaves it to younger
men, to be certain about anything. That was meant for
Jemmy, I suppose. He would rather have the pain, than
not, he says; meaning of course in the patient—not
himself. It shows healthy action—though I can't see how
—and just the proper quantity of inflammation, which I
should have thought couldn't be too little. He has come
round to Jemmy's opinion this morning, that if one—some-

thing or other—can be got to stay in its place, and not do something or other—the poor arm may be saved, after all ; though never as strong as it was before. He says it must have been a frightful blow. I hope that man will be punished for it heavily."

" I hope so too, with all my heart; though I am not revengeful. Mr. Penniloe was up here yesterday, and he tried to make the best of it. I was so vexed that I told him, he would not be quite such a Christian about it perhaps, if he had the pain in his own arm. But he has made the man promise to give himself up, if your brother, or my son, require it. I was for putting him in jail at once, but the others think it better to wait a bit. But as for his promise, I wouldn't give much for that. However, men manage those things, and not women. Did the doctor say whether you might see my Frankie ?"

" He said I might see Jemmy ; though Jemmy is very queer. But as for Frank, if I saw him through a chink in the wall, that would be quite enough. But he must not see me, unless it was with a telescope through a two-inch door. That annoyed me rather. As if we were such babies ! But he said that you were a most sensible woman, and that was the advice you gave him."

" What a story ! Oh my dear, never marry a doctor— though I hope you will never have the chance—but they really don't seem to care what they say. It was just the same in my dear husband's time. Dr. Gronow said to me —' if she comes when I am out, don't let her go near either of them. She might do a lot of mischief. She might get up an argument, or something.' And so, I said——"

" Oh, Mrs. Gilham, that is a great deal worse than telling almost any story. An argument ! Do I ever argue ? I had better have stayed away, if that is the way they think of me. A telescope and a two-inch door, and not be allowed perhaps to open my mouth ! There is something exceedingly unjust in the opinions men entertain of women."

" Not my Frank, my dear. That is where he differs from all the other young men in the world. He has the most correct and yet exalted views ; such as poets had, when there were any. If you could only hear him going on about you, before he got that wicked knock I mean, of course,—his opinions not only of your hair and face, nor even your eyes, though all perfectly true, but your mind, and your intellect, and disposition, and power of perceiving what people are, and then your conversation—almost too good for us, because of want of exercise—and then, well I really forget what came next."

" Oh, Mrs. Gilham, it is all so absurd ! How could he talk such nonsense ? I don't like to hear of such things ; and I cannot believe there could be anything, to come next."

" Oh yes, there was, my dear, now you remind me of it. It was about the small size of your ears, and the lovely curves inside them. He had found out in some ancient work,— for I believe he could hold his own in Greek and Latin, even with Mr. Penniloe,—that a well-shaped ear is one of the rarest of all feminine perfections. That made him think no doubt of yours, for men are quite babies when they are in love ; and he found yours according to the highest standard. Men seem to make all those rules about us, simply according to their own ideas ! What rules do we ever make about them ? "

" I am so glad that you look at things in that way," Christie answered, with her fingers going slyly up her hair, to let her ears know what was thought of them ; " because I was afraid that you were too much—well perhaps that thinking so much of your son, you might look at things one-sidedly. And yet I might have known from your unusual common sense—but I do believe Dr. Gronow is coming back ; and I have not even got my cloak off ! Wait a bit, till things come round a little. A telescope, and a two-inch door ! One had better go about in a coal-sack, and curl-papers. Not that I ever want such things,—curves enough in my ears perhaps. But really I must make myself a little decent. They have taken my things up to my old room, I suppose. Try to keep him here, till I come back. He says that I get up arguments. Let me get up one with him."

" My orders are as stern as they are sensible ; " Dr. Gronow declared, when she had returned, beautifully dressed and charming, and had thus attacked him with even more of blandishment than argument ; " Your brother you may see, but not to talk much at one time to him ; for his head is in a peculiar state, and he does much more than he ought to do. He insists upon doing everything, which means perpetual attention to his friend. But he does it all as if by instinct, apparently without knowing it; and that he should do it all to perfection, is a very noble proof of the thoroughness of his grounding. The old school, the old school of training—there is nothing like it after all. Any mere sciolist, any empiric, any smatterer of the new medical course—and where would Frank Gilham's arm be now? Not in a state of lenitive pain, sanative, and in some degree encouraging, but in a condition of incipient mortification. For this is a case of compound comminuted fracture; so severe that my own conviction was—however no more of that to you two ladies. Only feel assured that no more could be done for the patient in the best hospital in London. And talking of upstart schools indeed, and new-fangled education, have you heard what the boys have done at Perlycross? I heard the noise upstairs, and I was obliged to shut the window, although it is such a soft spring-day. I was going down the hill to stop it, when I met Miss Fox. It is one of the most extraordinary jokes I ever knew."

"Oh, do tell us. We have not heard a word about it. But I am beginning to think that this is not at all a common place. I am never surprised at anything that happens at Perlycross." This was not a loyal speech on the part of the fair Christie.

"From what I have heard of that Moral Force-man," Mrs. Gilham remarked, with slow shake of her head; "I fear that his system would work better in a future existence, than as we are now. From what my son told me, before his accident, I foresaw that it must lead up to something quite outrageous. Nothing ever answers long, that goes against all the wisdom of our ancestors."

"Excuse me for a minute; I must first see how things are going on upstairs. As soon as I am at liberty, I will tell you what I saw. Though I like the march of intellect, when discipline directs it."

Dr. Gronow, who was smiling, which he seldom was, except after whirling out a two-ounce trout, went gently upstairs and returned in a few minutes, and sat down to tell his little tale.

"Every thing there going on as well as can be. Your brother is delighted to hear that you are come. But the other patient must not hear a word about it yet. We don't want any rapid action of the heart. Well, what the young scamps have done is just this. The new schoolmaster has abolished canes, you know, and birches, and every kind of physical compulsion. He exclaims against coercion, and pronounces that boys are to be guided by their hearts, instead of being governed by their—pardon me, a word not acknowledged in the language of these loftier days. This gentleman seems to have abolished the old system of the puerile body and mind, without putting anything of cogency in its place. He has introduced novelties, very excellent no doubt, if the boys would only take to them, with intellects as lofty as his own. But that is the very thing the boys won't do. I am a Liberal—so far as feelings go, when not overpowered by the judgment—but I must acknowledge that the best extremes of life, the boyhood made of nature, and the age made of experience, are equally staunch in their Toryism. But this man's great word is—Reform. As long as the boys thought it meant their benches, and expected to have soft cushions on them, they were highly pleased, and looked forward to this tribute to a part which had hitherto been anything but sacred. Their mothers too encouraged it, on account of wear and tear; but their fathers could not see why they should sit softer at their books, than they had to do at their trenchers.

"But yesterday unluckily the whole of it came out. There arrived a great package, by old Hill the carrier, who has had his van mended that was blown over, and out rushed the boys, without asking any leave, to bring in their comfortable cushions. All they found was a great blackboard, swinging on a pillar, with a socket at the back, and a staple and chain to adjust it. Toogood expected them to be in raptures, but instead of that they all went into sulks; and the little fellows would not look at it, having heard of black magic and witchcraft. Toogood called it a 'Demonstration-table, for the exhibition of Object-lessons.'

"Mr. Penniloe, as you may suppose, had long been annoyed and unhappy about the new man's doings, but he is not supreme in the week-day school, as he is on Sunday; and he tried to make the best of it, till the right man should come home. And I cannot believe that he went away on purpose to-day, in order to let them have it out. But the boys found out that he was going, and there is nobody else they care twopence for.

"Everybody says, except their mothers, that they must have put their heads together over-night, or how could they have acted with such unity and precision? Not only in design but in execution, the accomplished tactician stands confessed. Instead of attacking the enemy at once, when many might have hastened to his rescue, they deferred operations until to-day, and even then waited for the proper moment. They allowed him to exhaust all the best of his breath in his usual frothy oration—for like most of such men he can spout for ever, and finds it much easier than careful teaching.

"Then as he leaned back, with pantings in his chest, and eyes turned up at his own eloquence, two of the biggest boys flung a piece of clothes-line round his arms from behind, and knotted it, while another slipped under the desk, and buckled his ankles together with a satchel-strap, before he knew what he was doing. Then as he began to shout and bellow, scarcely yet believing it, they with much panting and blowing, protrusion of tongues, and grunts of exertion, some working at his legs, and some shouldering at his loins, and others hauling on the clothes-line, but all with perfect harmony of action, fetched their preceptor to the Demonstration-board, and laying him with his back flat against it, strapped his feet to the pedestal; then pulling out the staple till the board was perpendicular, they secured his coat-collar to the shaft above it, and there he was—as upright as need be, but without the power to move, except at his own momentous peril. Then to make quite sure of him, a clever little fellow got upon a stool, and drew back his hair, bright red, and worn long like a woman's, and tied it with a book-tape behind the pillar. You may imagine how the poor preceptor looks. Any effort of his to release himself will crush him beneath the great Demonstration, like a mouse in a figure-of-four trap."

"But are we to believe, Dr. Gronow," asked Christie, "that you came away, and left the poor man in that helpless state?"

"Undoubtedly I did. It is no concern of mine. And the boys had only just got their pea-shooters. He has not had half enough to cure him yet. Besides, they had my promise; for the boys have got the keys, they are charging a penny for a view of this Reformer; but they won't let any one in without a promise of strict neutrality. I gave a shilling, for I am sure they have deserved it. Somebody will be sure to cast him loose, in plenty of time for his own good. This will be of the greatest service to him, and cure him for a long time of big words."

"But suppose he falls forward upon his face, and the board falls upon him and suffocates him. Why, it would be the death of Mr. Penniloe. You are wanted here of course, Dr. Gronow; but I shall put my bonnet on, and rush down the hill, to the release of the Higher Education."

"Don't rush too fast, Miss Fox. There's a tree blown down across the lane, after you turn out of the one you came by. We ought to have had it cleared, but they say it will take a fortnight to make some of the main roads passable again. I would not go, if I were you. Somebody will have set him free, before you get there. I'll go out and listen. With the wind in the north, we can hear their hurrah-ing quite plainly at the gate. You can come with me, if you like."

"Oh, it is no hurrah-ing, Dr. Gronow! How can you deceive me so? It is a very sad sound indeed;" said Christie, as they stood at the gate, and she held her pretty palms to serve as funnels for her much admired ears. "It sounds like a heap of boys weeping and wailing. I fear that something sadly vindictive has been done. One never can have a bit of triumph, without that."

She scarcely knew the full truth of her own words. It was indeed an epoch of Nemesis. This fourth generation of boys in that village are beginning to be told of it, on knees that shake, with time, as well as memory. And thus it befell.

"What, lock me out of my own school-door! Can't

come in, without I pay a penny! May do in Spain; but won't do here."

A strong foot was thrust into the double of the door, a rattle of the handle ran up the lock and timber, and conscience made a coward of the boy that took the pennies. An Odic Force, as the present quaky period calls it, permeated doubtless from the Master hand. Back went the boy, and across him strode a man, rather tall, wiry, torve of aspect, hyporrhined with a terse moustache, hatted with a vast sombrero. At a glance he had the whole situation in his eye, and his heart,—worst of all, in his strong right arm. He flung off a martial cloak, that might have cumbered action, stood at the end of the long desk, squared his shoulders and eyebrows, and shouted—

" Boys, here's a noise!"

As this famous battle-cry rang through the room, every mother's darling knew what was coming. Consternation is too weak a word. Grinning mouths fell into graves of terror, castaway pea-shooters quivered on the floor, fat legs rattled in their boots, and flew about, helter-skelter, anywhere, to save their dear foundations. Vain it was; no vanishing point could be discovered. Wisdom was come, to be justified of her children.

The schoolmaster of the ancient school marched with a grim smile to the door, locked it, and pocketed the key. Three little fellows, untaught as yet the expediency of letting well alone, had taken the bunch of keys, and brought forth, and were riding disdainfully the three canes dormant under the new dispensation. " Bring me those implements," commanded Sergeant Jakes, " perhaps they may do—to begin with." He arranged them lovingly, and then spoke wisely.

" My dear young friends, it is very sad to find, that while I have been in foreign parts, you have not been studying discipline. The gentleman, whom you have treated thus, will join me, I trust, by the time I have done, in maintaining that I do not bear the rod in vain. Any boy who crawls under a desk may feel assured that he will get it ten times worse."

Pity draws a mourning veil, though she keeps a place to peep through, when her highly respected cousin,

Justice, is thus compelled to assert herself. Enough that very few indeed of the highly cultured boys of Perlycross showed much aptitude that week for sedentary employment.

CHAPTER XL.

HOME AND FOREIGN.

SIX weeks was the average time allowed for the voyage to and fro of the schooner *Montilla* (owned by Messrs. Besley of Exeter) from Topsham to Cadiz, or wherever it might be; and little uneasiness was ever felt, if her absence extended to even three months. For Spaniards are not in the awkward habit of cracking whips at old Time, when he is out at grass, much less of jumping at his forelock; and Iberian time is nearly always out at grass. When a thing will not help to do itself to-day, who knows that it may not be in a kinder mood to-morrow? The spirit of worry, and unreasonable hurry, is a deadly blast to all serenity of mind and dignity of demeanour, and can be in harmony with nothing but bad weather. Thus the *Montilla's* period was a fluctuating numeral.

As yet English produce was of high repute, and the Continent had not been barb-wired by ourselves, against our fleecy merchandise. The Spaniards happened to be in the vein for working, and thus on this winter trip the good trader's hold was quickly cleared of English solids, and refilled with Spanish fluids; and so the *Montilla* was ready for voyage homeward the very day her passenger rejoined. This pleased him well, for he was anxious to get back, though not at all aware of the urgent need arising. Luckily for him and for all on board, the schooner lost a day in getting out to sea, and thus ran into the rough fringes only of the great storm that swept the English coast and channel. In fact she made good weather across the Bay of Biscay, and swang into her berth at Topsham, several days before she was counted due.

The Sergeant's first duty was, of course, to report himself at Walderscourt; and this he had done, before he made that auspicious re-entry upon his own domain. The ladies did not at all expect to see him, for days or even weeks to come, having heard nothing whatever of his doings; for the post beyond France was so uncertain then, that he went away with orders not to write.

When Jakes was shown into the room, Lady Waldron was sitting alone, and much agitated by a letter just received from Mr. Webber, containing his opinion of all that had happened at Perliton on Wednesday. Feeling her unfitness for another trial, she sent for her daughter, before permitting the envoy to relate his news. Then she strove to look calmly at him, and to maintain her cold dignity as of yore; but the power was no longer in her. Months of miserable suspense, perpetual brooding, and want of sleep, had lowered the standard of her pride; and nothing but a burst of painful sobs saved her from a worse condition.

The Sergeant stood hesitating by the door, feeling that he had no invitation to see this, and not presuming to offer comfort. But Miss Waldron seeing the best thing to do, called him, and bade him tell his news in brief.

"May it please your ladyship," the veteran began, staring deeply into his new Spanish hat, about which he had received some compliments; "all I have to tell your ladyship is for the honour of the family. Your ladyship's brother is as innocent as I be. He hath had nought to do with any wicked doings here. He hath not got his money, but he means to have it."

"Thank God!" cried Lady Waldron, but whether about the money, or the innocence, was not clear; and then she turned away, to have things out with herself; and Jakes was sent into the next room, and sat down, thanking the crown of his hat that it covered the whole of his domestic interests.

When feminine excitement was in some degree spent, and the love of particulars (which can never long be quenched by any depth of tears), was reviving, Sergeant Jakes was well received, and told his adventures like a veteran. A young man is apt to tell things hotly, as if nothing had ever come to pass before; but a steady-goer knows that the sun was shining, and the rain was raining, and the wind was blowing, ere he felt any one of them. Alike the whole must be cut short.

It appears that the Sergeant had a fine voyage out, and picked up a good deal of his lapsed Spanish lore, from two worthy Spanish hands among the crew. Besley of Exeter did things well—as the manner of that city is—victuals were good, and the crew right loyal, as generally happens in that case. Captain Binstock stood in awe of his elder brother, the butler, and never got out of his head its original belief that the Sergeant was his brother's schoolmaster. Against that idea chronology strove hazily, and therefore vainly. The Sergeant strode the deck with a stick he bought at Exeter, spoke of his experience in transports, regarded the masts as a pair of his own canes—in a word was master of the ship, whenever there was nothing to be done to her. A finer time he never had, for he was much too wiry to be sea-sick. All the crew liked him, whether present or absent, and never laughed at him but in the latter case. He corrected their English, when it did not suit his own, and thus created a new form of discipline. Most of this he recounted in his pungent manner, without a word of self-laudation; and it would have been a treat to Christie Fox to hear him; but his present listeners were too anxious about the result to enjoy this part of it.

Then he went to the city to which he was despatched, and presented his letters to the few he could find entitled to receive them. The greater part were gone beyond the world of letters, for twenty-five years make a sad gap in the post. And of the three survivors, one alone cared to be troubled with the bygone days. But that one was a host in himself, a loyal retainer of the ancient family, in the time of its grandeur, and now in possession of a sinecure post, as well as a nice farm on the hills, both of which he had obtained through their influence. He was delighted to hear once more of the beautiful lady he had formerly adored. He received the Sergeant as his guest, and told him all that was known of the present state of things, concerning the young Count—as he still called him—and all that was likely to come of it.

It was true that the Count had urged his claim, and brought evidence in support of it; but at present there seemed to be very little chance of his getting the money for years to come, even if he should do so in the end; and for that he must display, as they said, fresh powers of survivorship. He had been advised to make an offer of release and quit-claim, upon receipt of the sum originally advanced without any interest ; but he had answered sternly, "either I will have all, or none."

The amount was so large, that he could not expect to receive the whole immediately ; and he was ready to accept it by instalments; but the authorities would not pay a penny, nor attempt an arrangement with him, for fear of admitting their liability. In a very brief, and candid, but by no means honest manner, they refused to be bound at all by the action of their fathers. When that was of no avail, because the City-tolls were in the bond, they began to call for proof of this, and evidence of that, and set up every possible legal obstacle, hoping to exhaust the claimant's sadly dwindled revenues. Above all, they maintained that two of the lives in the assurance-deed were still subsisting, although their lapse was admitted in their own minutes, and registered in the record. And it was believed that in this behalf, they were having recourse to personation.

That scandalous pretext must be demolished, before it could become of prime moment to the Count to prove the decease of his brother-in-law ; and certain it was that no such dramatic incident had occurred in the City, as that which her ladyship had witnessed, by means of her imagination. With a long fight before him, and very scanty sinews of war to maintain it, the claimant had betaken himself to Madrid, where he had powerful friends, and might consult the best legal advisers. But his prospects were not encouraging ; for unless he could deposit a good round sum, for expenses of process, and long enquiry, and even counterbribing, no one was likely to take up his case, so strong and so tough were the forces in possession. Rash friends went so far as to recommend him to take the bull by the horns at once, to lay forcible hands upon the City-tolls, without any order from a law-court, for the Deed was so drastic that this power was conferred ; but he saw that to do this would simply be to play into the hands of the enemy. For thus he would probably find himself out-lawed, or perhaps cast into prison, with the lapse of his own life imminent; for the family of the Barcas were no longer supreme in the land, as they used to be.

"Ungrateful thieves! Vile pigs of burghers!" Lady Waldron exclaimed with just indignation. "My grandfather would have strung them up with straw in their noses, and set them on fire. They sneer at the family of Barca, do they? It shall trample them underfoot. My poor brother shall have my last penny to punish them; for that I have wronged him in my heart. Ours is a noble race, and most candid. We never deign to stoop ourselves to mistrust or suspicion: I trust Master Sergeant, you have not spoken so to the worthy and loyal Diego, that my brother may ever hear of the thoughts introduced into my mind concerning him?"

"No, my lady, not a word. Everything I did, or said, was friendly, straight-forward, and favourable to the honour of the family."

"You are a brave man; you are a faithful soldier. Forget that by the force of circumstances I was compelled to have such opinions. But can you recite to me the names of the two persons, whose lives they have replenished?"

"Yes, my lady. Señor Diego wrote them down in this book on purpose. He thought that your ladyship might know something of them."

"For one I have knowledge of everything; but the other I do not know," Lady Waldron said, after reading the names. "This poor Señorita was one of my bridesmaids, known to me from my childhood. *La Giralda* was her name of intimacy, what you call her nickname, by reason of her stature. Her death I can prove too well, and expose any imitation. But the Spanish nation—you like them much? You find them gentle, brave, amiable, sober, not as the English are, generous, patriotic, honourable?"

"Quite as noble and good, my lady, as we found them five and twenty years agone. And I hope that the noble Count will get his money. A bargain is a bargain—as we say here. And if they are so honourable——"

"Ah, that is quite a different thing. Inez, I must leave you. I desire some time to think. My mind is very much relieved of one part, although of another still more distressed. I request you to see to the good refreshment of this honourable and faithful soldier."

Lady Waldron acknowledged the Sergeant's low bow, with a kind inclination of her Andalusian head (which is something in the headway among the foremost) and left the room with a lighter step than her heart had allowed her for many a week.

"This will never do, Sergeant; this won't do at all," said Miss Waldron coming up to him, as soon as she had shut the door behind her lofty mother. "I know by your countenance, and the way you were standing, and the sideway you sit down again, that you have not told us everything. That is not the right way to go on, Sergeant Jakes."

"Miss Nicie!" cried Jakes, with a forlorn hope of frightening her, for she had sat upon his knee, many a time, ten or twelve years ago, craving stories of good boys and bad boys. But now the eyes, which he used to fill with any emotion he chose to call for, could produce that effect upon his own.

"Can you think that I don't understand you?" said Nicie, never releasing him from her eyes. "What was the good of telling me all those stories, when I was a little thing, except for me to understand you? When anybody tells me a story that is true, it is no good for him to try anything else. I get so accustomed to his way, that I catch him out in a moment."

"But my dear, my dear Miss Nicie," the Sergeant looked all about, as in large appeal, instead of fixing steady gaze; "if I have told you a single word that is not as true as Gospel—may I——"

"Now don't be profane, Sergeant Jakes. That was allowed perhaps in war-time. And don't be crooked—which is even worse. I never called in question any one thing you have said. All I know is that you have stopped short. You used to do just the same with me, when things I was too young to hear came in. You are easier to read than one of your own copies. What have you kept in the background, you unfaithful soldier?"

"Oh Miss, how you do remind me of the Colonel! Not that he ever looked half as fierce. But he used to say,

'Jakes what a deep rogue you are!' meaning how deeply he could trust me, against all his enemies. But Miss, I have given my word about this."

"Then take it back, as some people do their presents. What is the good of being a deep rogue, if you can't be a shallow one? I should hope you would rather be a rogue, to other people than to me. I will never speak to you again, unless you show now that you can trust me, as my dear father used to trust in you. No secrets from me, if you please."

"Well, Miss, it was for your sake, more than anybody else's. But you must promise, honour bright, not to let her ladyship know of it; for it might be the death of her. It took me by surprise, and it hath almost knocked me over; for I never could have thought there was more troubles coming. But who do you think I ran up against, to Exeter?"

"How can I tell? Don't keep me waiting. That kind of riddle is so hateful always."

"Master Tom, Miss Nicie! Your brother, Master Tom! 'Sir Thomas Waldron' his proper name is now. You know they have got a new oil they call *gas*, to light the public places of the big towns with, and it makes everything as bright as day, and brighter than some of the days we get now. Well, I was intending to come on last night by the Bristol mail, and wait about till you was up; and as I was standing with my knapsack on my shoulder, to see her come in from Plymouth, in she comes, and a tall young man dressed all in black, gets down slowly from the roof, and stands looking about very queerly.

"'Bain't you going no further, Sir?' says the Guard to him very civil, as he locked the bags in; 'only allows us three minutes and a half,'—for the young man seemed as if he did not care what time it was.

"'No. I can't go home;' says he, as if nothing mattered to him. I was handing up my things, to get up myself, when the tone of his voice took me all of a heap.

"'What, Master Tom!' says I, going up to him.

"'Who are you?' says he. 'Master Tom, indeed!' For I had this queer sort of hat on, and cloak, like a blessed foreigner.

" Well, when I told him who I was, he did not seem at all as he used to be, but as if I had done him a great injury ; and as for his luggage, it would have gone on with the coach, if the Guard had not called out about it.

" ' Come in here ; ' he says to me, as if I was a dog, him that was always so well-spoken and polite ! And he turned sharp into *The Old London Inn*, leaving all his luggage on the stones outside.

" ' Private sitting-room, and four candles ! ' he called out, marching up the stairs, and making me a sign to follow him. Everybody seemed to know him there, and I told them to fetch his things in.

" ' No fire ! Hot enough already. Put the candles down, and go ; ' said he to the waiter, and then he locked the door, and threw the key upon the table. It takes a good deal to frighten me, Miss. But I assure you I was trembling ; for I never saw such a pair of eyes—not furious, but so desperate ; and I should have been but a baby in his hands, for he is bigger than even his father was. Then he pulled out a newspaper, and spread it among the candles.

" ' Now, you man of Perlycross,' he cried, ' you that teach the boys, who are going to be grave-robbers,— is this true, or is it all a cursed lie ? ' Excuse me telling you, Miss, exactly as he said it. ' The Lord in heaven help me, I think I shall go mad, unless you can tell me it is all a wicked lie.' Up and down the room he walked, as if the boards would sink under him ; while I was at my wits' ends, as you may well suppose, Miss.

" ' I have never heard a word of any of this, Master Tom ; ' I said, as soon as I had read it ; for it was all about something that came on at Perliton before the Magistrates, last Wednesday. ' I have been away in foreign parts.'

" Miss Nicie, he changed to me from that moment. I had not said a word about how long I was away, or anything whatever to deceive him. But he looked at my hat that was lying on a chair, and my cloak that was still on my back, as much as to say—' I ought to have known it ; ' and then he said, ' Give me your hand, Old Jakes. I beg your pardon a thousand times. What a fool I must be, to think you would ever have allowed it !

" This put me in a very awkward hole; for I was bound to
acknowledge that I had been here, when the thing, he was
so wild about, was done.   But I let him go on, and have
his raving out.   For men are pretty much the same as boys ;
though expecting of their own way more, which I try to
take out of the young ones.   But a loud singing out, and
a little bit of stamping, brings them into more sense of what
they be.

" ' I landed at Plymouth this morning,' he said, ' after
getting a letter, which had been I don't know where, to tell
me that my dear father, the best man that ever lived, was
dead.   I got leave immediately, and came home to comfort
my mother and sister, and to attend to all that was needful.
I went into the coffee-room, before the coach was ready ;
and taking up the papers, I find this !   They talk of it, as
if it was a thing well known, a case of great interest in the
county ; a *mystery* they call it, a very lively thing to talk
about—*The great Perlycross Mystery*, in big letters, cried at
every corner, made a fine joke of in every dirty pot-house.
It seems to have been going on for months.   Perhaps it has
killed my mother and my sister.   It would soon kill me, if
I were there, and could do nothing.'

" Here I found a sort of opening ; for the tears rolled
down his face, as he thought of you, Miss Nicie, and your
dear Mamma ; and the rage in his heart seemed to turn
into grief, and he sat down in one of the trumpery chairs
that they make nowadays, and it sprawled and squeaked
under him, being such an uncommon fine young man in
trouble.   So I went up to him, and stood before him, and
lifted his hands from his face, as I had done many's the
time, when he was a little fellow, and broke his nose perhaps
in his bravery.   And then he looked up at me quite mild,
and said—

" ' I believe I am a brute, Jakes.   But isn't this enough
to make me one ? '

" I stayed with him all night, Miss ; for he would not go
to bed, and he wouldn't have nothing for to eat or drink ;
and I was afraid to leave him so.   But I got him at last to
smoke a bit of my tobacco ; and that seemed to make him look
at things a little better.   I told him all I knew, and what
1 had been to Spain for, and how you and her ladyship were

trying bravely to bear the terrible will of the Lord; and then I coaxed him all I could, to come along of me, and help you to bear it. But he said—' I might take him for a coward, if I chose; but come to Walderscourt he wouldn't, and face his own mother and sister he couldn't; until he had cleared off this terrible disgrace.' "

" He is frightfully obstinate, he always was ;" said Nicie, who had listened to this tale, with streaming eyes ; " but it would be such a comfort to us both, to have him here. What has become of him ? Where is he now ? "

" That is the very thing I dare not tell you, Miss ; because he made me swear to keep it to myself. By good rights, I ought to have told you nothing ; but you managed so to work it out of me. I would not come away from him, till I knew where he would be, because he was in such a state of mind. But I softened him down a good bit, I believe ; and he might take a turn, if you were to write, imploring of him. I will take care that he gets it, for he made me promise to write, and let him know exactly how I found things here, after being away so long. But he is that bitter against this place, that it will take a deal to bring him here. You must work on his love for his mother, Miss Nicie, and his pity for the both of you. That is the only thing that touches him. And say that it is no fault of Perlycross, but strangers altogether."

" You shall have my letter before the postman comes, so that you may send it with your own. What a good friend you have been to us, dear Jakes ! My mother's heart would break at last, if she knew that Tom was in England, and would not come first of all to her. I can scarcely understand it. To me it seems so unnatural."

" Well, Miss, you never can tell by yourself, how other people will take things—not even your own brother. And I think he will soon come round, Miss Nicie. According to my opinion, it was the first shock of the thing, and the way he got it, that drove him out of his mind a'most. Maybe, he judges you by himself, and fancies it would only make you worse, to see him, with this disgrace upon him. For that's what he can't get out of his head ; and it would be a terrible meeting for my lady, with all the pride she hath in him. I reckon 'tis the Spanish blood that does it ; Englishman as he is, all over. But never fear, Miss Nicie ; we'll fetch him here, between the two of us, afore we are much older. He hath always been loving in his nature ; and love will drive the anger out."

CHAPTER XLI.

THE PRIDE OF LIFE.

HARVEY TREMLETT kept his promise not to leave the neighbourhood, until the result of the grievous injury done to Frank Gilham should be known. Another warrant against him might be issued for that fierce assault, and he had made up his mind to stand a trial, whatever result might come of it. What he feared most, and would have fled from, was a charge of running contraband goods, which might have destroyed a thriving trade, and sent him and his colleagues across the seas. Rough and savage as he became, (when his violent temper was provoked) and scornful of home-life and quiet labour — these and other far from ex-emplary traits, were mainly the result of his roving habits, and the coarse and lawless company into which he had ever fallen. And it tended little to his edification, that he exercised lordship over them, in virtue of superior strength.

But his nature was rather wild than brutal ; in its depths were sparks and flashes of manly generosity, and even warmth of true affection for the few who had been kind to him, if they took him the right way of his stubborn grain. He loved his only daughter Zip, although ashamed of showing it ; and he was very proud of his lineage, and the ancient name of Tremlett. Thus Mr. Penniloe had taken unawares the straightest road to his good will, by adopting the waif as an inmate of his house, and treating her, not as a servant, but a child. That Zip should be a lady, as the daughters of that Norman race had been for generations, was the main ambition of her father's life. He had seen no possibility of it ; and here was almost a surety of it, unless she herself threw away the chance.

Rather a pretty scene was toward for those who are fond of humanity, at the ruined Tremlett mill, on the morning

of Saint David's day. Harvey had taken to this retreat—
and a very lonely home it was—for sundry good reasons of
his own; the most important of which was not entrusted
even to his daughter, or the revered and beloved Parson.
This was to prepare a refuge, and a store house for Free-
trade, more convenient, better placed, larger, and much
safer than the now notorious fastness of Blackmarsh. Here
were old buildings, and mazy webs of wandering; soft cliff
was handy, dark wood and rushing waters, tangled lanes,
furzy corners, nooks of overhanging, depths of in-and-out
hood-winks of nature, when she does not wish man to
know everything about her. The solid firm, directed by
Timber-leg'd Dick, were prepared to pay a fine price, as for a
paper mill, for this last feudal tenure of the Tremlett race.

But the last male member of that much discounted stock
(or at any rate the last now producible in Court, without
criminal procedure) had refused to consider the most liberal
offers, even of a fine run of Free-trade, all to himself—as
still it is—for the alienation in fee-simple of this last sod of
hereditament. For good consideration, he would grant a
lease, which Blickson might prepare for them; but he would
be—something the nadir of benediction—if he didn't knock
down any man, who would try to make him rob his daughter.
The league of Free-traders came into his fine feelings, and
took the mills and premises, on a good elastic lease. But
the landlord must put them into suitable condition.

This he was doing now, with technical experience, endeavouring at the same time to discharge some little of his
new parental duties. Jem Kettel found it very hard, that
though allowed to work, he was not encouraged (as he used
to be) to participate in the higher moments. "You clear
out, when my darter cometh. You be no fit company for
she." Jem could not see it, for he knew how good he was.

But the big man had taken a much larger turn. He was
not going to alter his own course of life. That was quite
good enough for him; and really in those days people heard
so much of "Reform! Reform!" dinged for ever in their
ears, that any one at all inclined to think for himself had
a tendency towards backsliding. None the less, must he
urge others to reform; as the manner has been of all ages.

Tremlett's present anxiety was to provide his daughter

2 E

with good advice, and principles so exalted, that there
might be no further peril of her becoming like himself.
From him she was to learn the value of proper pride and
dignity, of behaving in her new position, as if she had been
born to it, of remembering distant forefathers, but forgetting her present father, at any rate as an example. To
this end he made her study the great ancestral Bible—not
the Canonical books however, so much as the covers and
fly-leaves—the wholly uninspired records of the Tremlett
family. These she perused with eager eyes, thinking more
highly of herself, and laying in large store of pride—a bitter
stock to start with—even when the course of youth is fair.

But whether for evil or for good, it was pleasant to see
the rough man sitting, this first day of the Spring-time,
teaching his little daughter how sadly he and she had come
down in the world. Zip had been spared from her regular
lessons, by way of a treat, to dine with her father, before
going—as was now arranged—to the care of a lady at
Exeter. Jem Kettel had been obliged to dine upon inferior
victuals, and at the less fashionable hour of eleven a.m. ;
for it was not to be known that he was there, lest attention
should be drawn to the job they were about. Tremlett
had washed himself very finely, in honour of this great
occasion, and donned a new red woollen jacket, following
every curve and chunk of his bulky chest and rugged arms.
He had finished his dinner, and was in good spirits, with
money enough from his wrestling prize to last him until the
next good run, and a pipe of choice tobacco (such as could
scarcely be got at Exeter), issuing soft rings of turquoise
tint to the black oak beams above. The mill-wheel was
gone ; but the murmur of the brook, and the tinkle of the
trickle from the shattered trough, and the singing of birds
in their love-time came, like the waving of a branch that
sends the sunshine in.

The dark-haired child was in the window-seat, with her
Sunday frock on, and her tresses ribboned back, and her
knees wide apart to make a lap for the Bible, upon which
her great brown eyes were fixed. Puffs of the March wind
now and then came in, where the lozenges of glass were
gone, and lifted loose tussocks of her untrussed hair, and
set the sunshine dancing on the worn planks of the floor.

But the girl was used to breezes, and her heart was in her lesson.

"Hunderds of 'em, more than all the Kings and Queens of England!" she said, with her very clear voice trembling, and her pointed fingers making hop-scotch in and out the lines of genealogy. "What can Fay Penniloe show like that? But was any of 'em Colonels, father?"

"Maight a' been, if 'em would a' comed down to it. But there wasn't no Colonels, in the old times, I've a' heered. Us was afore that sort of thing were found out."

"To be sure. I might have knowed. But was any of 'em, Sirs, the same as Sir Thomas Waldron was?"

"Scores of 'em, when they chose to come down to it. But they kept that, most ways, for the younger boys among 'em. The father of the family was bound to be a Lord."

"Oh father! Real lords? And me to have never seed one! What hath become of the laws of the land? But why bain't you a real lord, the same as they was?"

"Us never cared to keep it up;" said the last of the visible Tremletts, after pondering over this difficult point. "You see, Zip, it's only the women cares for that. 'Tis no more to a man, than the puff of this here pipe."

"But right is right, father. And it soundeth fine. Was any of them Earls, and Marquises, and Dukes, and whatever it is that comes over that?"

"They was everything they cared to be. Barons, and Counts, and Dukes, spelled the same as Ducks, and Holy Empires, and Holy Sepulkers. But do 'e, my dear, get my baccy box."

What summit of sovereignty they would have reached, if the lecture had proceeded, no one knows; for as Zip, like a Princess, was stepping in and out among the holes of the floor, with her father's tin box, the old door shook with a sharp and heavy knock; and the child with her face lit up by the glory of her birth, marched away to open it. This she accomplished with some trouble, for the timber was ponderous and rickety.

A tall young man strode in, as if the place belonged to him, and said, "I want to see Harvey Tremlett."

"Here be I. Who be you?"

The wrestler sat where he was, and did not even nod his

head ; for his rule was always to take people, just as they chose to take him. But the visitor cared little for his politeness, or his rudeness.

"I am Sir Thomas Waldron's son. If I came in upon you rudely, I am sorry for it. It is not what I often do. But just now I am not a bit like myself."

"Sir, I could take my oath of that ; for your father was a gen'leman. Zippy, dust a cheer, my dear."

"No, young lady, you shall not touch it," said the young man, with a long stride, and a gentle bow to the comely child. "I am fitter to lift chairs than you are."

This pleased the father mightily ; and he became quite gracious, when the young Sir Thomas said to him, while glancing with manifest surprise at his quick and intelligent daughter—

"Mr. Tremlett, I wish to speak to you, of a matter too sad to be talked about, in the presence of young ladies."

This was not said by way of flattery or conciliation ; for Zip, with her proud step and steadfast gaze, was of a very different type from that of the common cottage lass. She was already at the door, when her father said—

"Go you down to the brook, my dear, and see how many nestesses you can find. Then come back and say good-bye to Daddy, afore go home to Passonage. Must be back afore dark, you know."

"What a beautiful child !" Young Waldron had been looking with amazement at her. "I know what the Tremletts used to be ; but I had no idea they could be like that. I never saw such eyes in all my life."

"Her be well enough," replied the father shortly. "And now, sir, what is it as I can do for you? I knows zummat of the troubles on your mind ; and if I can do 'e any good, I wull."

"Two things I want of you. First, your word of honour —and I know what you Tremletts have been in better days —that you had nothing to do with that cursed and devilish crime in our churchyard."

"Sir," answered Tremlett, standing up for the first time in this interview, "I give you my oath by that book yon'ner that I knows nort about it. We be coom low ; but us bain't zunk to that yet."

He met Sir Thomas Waldron, eye to eye, and the young
man took his plastered hand, and knew that it was not a
liar's.

"Next I want your good advice," said the visitor, sitting
down by him ; "and your help, if you will give it. I will
not speak of money because I can see what you are. But
first to follow it up, there must be money. Shall I tell you
what I shall be glad to do, without risk of offending you?
Very well; I don't care a fig for money, in a matter such
as this. Money won't give you back your father, or your
mother, or anybody, when they are gone away from you.
But it may help you to do your duty to them. At present,
I have no money to speak of; because I have been with my
regiment, and there it goes away, like smoke. But I can
get any quantity almost, by going to our lawyers. If you
like, and will see to it, I will put a thousand pounds in your
hands, for you to be able to work things up ; and another
thousand, if you make anything of it. Don't be angry with
me. I don't want to bribe you. It is only for the sake of
doing right. I have seen a great deal of the world. Can
you ever get what is right, without paying for it?"

"No, sir, you can't. And not always, if you do. But
you be the right sort, and no mistake. Tell you what, Sir
Thomas—I won't take a farden of your money, 'cos it
would be a' robbin' of you. I han't got the brains for
gooin' under other folk, like. Generally they does that to
me. But I know an oncommon sharp young fellow, Jemmy
Kettel is his name. A chap as can goo and come fifty
taimes, a'most, while I be a toornin' round wance; a'
knoweth a'most every rogue for fifty maile around. And
if you like to goo so far as a ten-pun' note upon him, I'll
zee that a' doth his best wi' un. But never a farden over
what I said."

"I am very much obliged to you. Here it is ; and
another next week, if he requires it. I hate the sight of
money, while this thing lasts ; because I know that money
is at the bottom of it. Tremlett, you are a noble fellow.
Your opinion is worth something. Now don't you agree
with me in thinking, that after all it comes to this—everything else has been proved rubbish—the doctors are at the
bottom of it?"

"Well, sir, I am afeared they be. I never knowed nort of 'em, thank the Lord. But I did hear they was oncommon greedy to cut up a poor brother of mine, as coom to trouble. I was out o' country then ; or by Gosh, I wud a' found them a job or two to do at home."

The young man closed his lips, and thought. Tremlett's opinion, although of little value, was all that was needed to clench his own. " I'll go and put a stop to it at once ; " he muttered ; and after a few more words with the wrestler, he set his long legs going rapidly, and his forehead frowning, in the direction of that Æsculapian fortress, known as the *Old Barn.*

By this time Dr. Fox was in good health again, recovering his sprightly tone of mind, and magnanimous self-confidence. His gratitude to Frank Gilham now was as keen and strong as could be wished ; for the patient's calmness, and fortitude, and very fine constitution had secured his warm affection, by affording him such a field for skill, and such a signal triumph, as seldom yet have rejoiced a heart at once medical and surgical. Whenever Dr. Gronow came, and dwelling on the ingenious structure designed and wrought by Jemmy's skill, poured forth kind approval and the precious applause of an expert, the youthful doctor's delight was like a young mother's pride in her baby. And it surged within him all the more, because he could not—as the mother does—inundate all the world with it. Wiser too than that sweet parent, he had refused most stubbornly to risk the duration of his joy, or imperil the precious subject, by any ardour of excitement or flutter of the system.

The patient lay, like a well-set specimen in the box of a naturalist, carded, and trussed, and pinned, and fibred, bound to maintain one immutable plane. His mother hovered round him with perpetual presence ; as a house-martin flits round her fallen nestling, circling about that one pivot of the world, back for a twittering moment, again sweeping the air for a sip of him.

But the one he would have given all the world to have a sip of, even in a dream he must not see. Such was the stern decree of the power, even more ruthless than that to which it punctually despatches us—Æsculapius, less man-suete to human tears than Æacus. To put it more plainly, and therefore better,—Master Frank did not even know that Miss Christie was on the premises.

Christie was sitting by the window, thrown out where the barn-door used to be,—where the cart was backed up with the tithe-sheaves golden, but now the gilded pills were rolled, and the only wholesome bit of metal was the sunshine on her hair—when she saw a large figure come in at the gate (which was still of the fine agricultural sort) and a shudder ran down her ,shapely back. With feminine speed of apprehension, she felt that it could be one man only, the man she had heard so much of, a monster of size and ferocity, the man who had "concussed" her brother's head, and shattered an arm of great interest to her. That she ran to the door, which was wide to let the Spring in, and clapped it to the post, speaks volumes for her courage.

"You can't come in here, Harvey Tremlett," she cried, with a little foot set, as a forlorn hope, against the bottom of the door, which (after the manner of its kind) refused to go home, when called upon; "you have done harm enough, and I am astonished that you should dare to imagine we would let you in."

"But I am not Harvey Tremlett, at all. I am only Tom Waldron. And I don't see why I should be shut out when I have done no harm."

The young lady was not to be caught with chaff. She took a little peep through the chink, having learned that art in a very sweet manner of late; and then she threw open the door, and showed herself, a fine figure of blushes.

"Miss Fox, I am sure," said the visitor, smiling and lifting his hat as he had learned to do abroad. "But I won't come in, against orders, whatever the temptation may be."

"We don't know any harm of you, and you may come in;" answered Chris, who was never long taken aback. "Your sister is a dear friend of mine. I am sorry for being so rude to you."

Waldron sat down, and was cheerful for awhile, greatly pleased with his young entertainer, and her simple account of the state of things there. But when she enquired for his mother and sister, the cloud returned, and he meant business.

" You are likely to know more than I do," he said, " for
I have not been home, and cannot go there yet. I will not
trouble you with dark things—but may I have a little
talk with your brother ? "

Miss Fox left the room at once, and sent her brother
down ; and now a very strange surprise befell the sprightly
doctor. Sir Thomas Waldron met him with much cordiality
and warmth, for they had always been good friends, though
their natures were so different ; and then he delivered this
fatal shot.

"I am very sorry, my dear Jemmy, but I have had to
make up my mind to do a thing you won't much like. I
know you have always thought a great deal of my sister,
Inez ; and now I am told, though I have not seen her, that
you are as good as engaged to her. But you must perceive
that it would never do. I could not wish for a better sort
of fellow, and I have the highest opinion of you. Really I
think that you would have made her as happy as the day is
long, because you are so clever, and cheerful, and good-
tempered, and—and in fact I may say, good all round. But
you must both of you get over it. I am now the head of the
family ; and I don't like saying it, but I must. I cannot
allow you to have Nicie ; and I shall forbid Nicie to think
any more of you."

" What, the deuce, do you mean, Tom ? " asked Jemmy,
scarcely believing his ears. " What's up now, in the name
of goodness ? What on earth have you got into your
precious noddle ? "

" Jemmy, my noddle—as you call it—may not be a
quarter so clever as yours ; and in fact I know it is not
over-bright, without having the benefit of your opinion.
But for all that, it has some common sense ; and it knows
its own mind pretty well ; and what it says, it sticks to.
You are bound to take it in a friendly manner, because
that is how I intend it ; and you must see the good sense
of it. I shall be happy and proud myself to continue our
friendship. Only you must pledge your word, that you
will have nothing more to say to my sister, Inez."

" But why, Tom, why ? " Fox asked again, with increasing
wonder. He was half inclined to laugh at the other's
solemn and official style, but he saw that it would be a

dangerous thing, for Waldron's colour was rising. "What objection have you discovered, or somebody else found out for you? Surely you are dreaming, Tom!"

"No, I am not. And I shall not let you. I should almost have thought that you might have known, without my having to tell you. If you think twice, you will see at once, that reason, and common sense, and justice, and knowledge of the world, and the feeling of a gentleman— all compel you to—to knock off, if I may so express it. I can only say that if you can't see it, everybody else can, at a glance."

"No doubt I am the thickest of the thick—though it may not be the general opinion. But do give me ever such a little hint, Tom; something of a twinkle in this frightful fog."

"Well, you are a doctor, aren't you now?"

"Certainly I am, and proud of it. Only wish I was a better one."

"Very well. The doctors have dug up my father. And no doctor ever shall marry his daughter."

The absurdity of this was of a very common kind, as the fallacy is of the commonest; and there was nothing very rare to laugh at. But Fox did the worst thing he could have done—he laughed till his sides were aching. Too late he perceived that he had been as scant of discretion, as the other was of logic.

"That's how you take it, is it, Sir?" young Waldron cried, ready to knock him down, if he could have done so without cowardice. "A lucky thing for you, that you are on the sick-list; or I'd soon make you laugh the other side of your mouth, you guffawing jackanapes. If you can laugh at what was done to my father, it proves that you are capable of doing it. When you have done with your idiot grin, I'll just ask you one thing—never let me set eyes on your sniggering, grinning, pill-box of a face again."

"That you may be quite sure you never shall do," answered Fox, who was ashy pale with anger; "until you have begged my pardon humbly, and owned yourself a thick-headed, hot-headed fool. I am sorry that your father should have such a ninny of a cad to come after him.

Everybody acknowledges that the late Sir Thomas was a gentleman."

The present Sir Thomas would not trust himself near such a fellow for another moment, but flung out of the house without his hat; while Fox proved that he was no coward, by following, and throwing it after him. And the other young man proved the like of himself, by not turning round and smashing him.

CHAPTER XLII.

HIS LAST BIVOUAC.

"HAVE I done wrong?" Young Waldron asked himself, as he strode down the hill, with his face still burning, and that muddy hat on. "Most fellows would have knocked him down. I hope that nice girl heard nothing of the row. The walls are jolly thick, that's one good thing; as thick as my poor head, I dare say. But when the fellow dared to laugh! Good Heavens, is our family reduced to that? I dare say I am a hot-headed fool, though I kept my temper wonderfully; and to tell me I am not a gentleman! Well, I don't care a rap who sees me now, for they must hear of this affair at Walderscourt. I think the best thing that I can do is to go and see old Penniloe. He is as honest as he is clear-headed. If he says I'm wrong, I'll believe it. And I'll take his advice about other things."

This was the wisest resolution of his life, inasmuch as it proved to be the happiest. Mr. Penniloe had just finished afternoon work with his pupils, and they were setting off; Pike with his rod to the long pool up the meadows, which always fished best with a cockle up it, Peckover for a long steeple-chase, and Mopuss to look for chalcedonies, and mosses, among the cleves of Hagdon Hill; for nature had nudged him into that high bliss, which a child has in routing out his father's pockets. The Parson, who felt a warm regard for a very fine specimen of hot youth, who was at once the son of his oldest friend, and his own son in literature—though Minerva sat cross-legged at that travail —he, Mr. Penniloe, was in a gentle mood, as he seldom

failed to be ; moreover in a fine mood, as behoves a man
who has been dealing with great authors, and walking as in
a crystal world, so different from our turbid fog.

To him the young man poured forth his troubles, deeper
than of certain Classic woes, too substantial to be laid by
any triple cast of dust. And then he confessed his flagrant
insult to a rising member of the great Profession.

"You have behaved very badly, according to your own
account ;" Mr. Penniloe said with much decision, knowing
that his own weakness was to let people off too easily, and
feeling that duty to his ancient friend compelled him to
chastise his son ; "but your bad behaviour to Jemmy Fox
has some excuse in quick temper provoked. Your conduct
towards your mother and sister is ten times worse ; because
it is mean."

"I don't see how you can make that out." Young
Waldron would have flown into a fury with any other man
who had said this. Even as it was, he stood up with a
doubtful countenance, glancing at the door.

"It is mean, in this way," continued the Parson, leaving
him to go, if he thought fit, "that you have thought more
of yourself than them. Because it would have hurt your
pride to go to them, with this wrong still unredressed, you
have chosen to forget the comfort your presence must have
afforded them, and the bitter pain they must feel at hearing
that you have returned and avoided them. In a like case,
your father would not have acted so."

Waldron sat down again, and his great frame trembled.
He covered his face with his hands, and tears shone upon
his warted knuckles ; for he had not yet lost all those
exuberances of youth.

"I never thought of that," he muttered ; "it never
struck me in that way. Though Jakes said something
like it. But he could not put it, as you do. I see that I
have been a cad, as Jemmy Fox declared I was."

"Jemmy is older, and he should have known better than
to say anything of the sort. He must have lost his temper
sadly ; because he could never have thought it. You have
not been what he calls a cad ; but in your haste and misery,
you came to the wrong decision. I have spoken strongly,
Tom, my boy ; more strongly perhaps than I should have

done. But your mother is in weak health now; and you are all in all to her."

"The best you can show me to be is a brute; and I am not sure that that is not worse than a cad. I ought to be kicked every inch of the way home; and I'll go there as fast as if I was."

"That won't do at all," replied the Curate smiling. "To go is your duty; but not to rush in like a thunderbolt, and amaze them. They have been so anxious about your return, that it must be broken very gently to them. If you wish it, and can wait a little while, I will go with you, and prepare them for it."

"Sir, if you only would—but no, I don't deserve it. It is a great deal too much to expect of you."

"What is the time? Oh, a quarter past four. At half past, I have to baptise a child well advanced in his seventh year, whose parents have made it the very greatest personal favour to me, to allow him to be 'crassed'—as they express it. And I only discovered their neglect, last week! Who am I to find fault with any one? If you don't mind waiting for about half-an-hour, I will come back for you, and meanwhile Mrs. Muggridge will make your hat look better; Master Jemmy must have lost his temper too, I am afraid. Good-bye for the moment; unless I am punctual to the minute, I know too well what will happen—they will all be off. For they 'can't zee no vally in it,' as they say. Alas, alas, and we are wild about Missions to Hindoos, and Hottentots!"

As soon as Mr. Penniloe had left the house, the youth, who had been lowered in his own esteem, felt a very strong desire to go after him. Possibly this was increased by the sad reproachful gaze of Thyatira; who, as an old friend, longed to hear all about him, but was too well-mannered to ask questions. Cutting all consideration short—which is often the best thing to do with it—he put on his fairly re-established hat, and cared not a penny whether Mrs. Channing, the baker's wife, was taking a look into the street or not; or even Mrs. Tapscott, with the rosemary over her window.

Then he turned in at the lych-gate, thinking of the day when his father's body had lain there (as the proper thing was for a body to do) and then he stood in the churchyard, where the many ways of death divided. Three main paths, all well-gravelled, ran among those who had toddled in the time of childhood down them, with wormwood and stock-gilly flowers in their hands; and then sauntered along them, with hands in pockets, and eyes for the maidens over tombstone-heads; and then had come limping along on their staffs; and now were having all this done for them, without knowing anything about it.

None of these ways was at all to his liking. Peace—at least in death—was there, green turf and the rounded bank, gray stone, and the un-household name, to be made out by a grandchild perhaps, proud of skill in ancient letters, prouder still of a pocket-knife. What a faint scratch on soft stone! And yet the character far and away stronger than that of the lettered times that follow it.

Young Waldron was not of a morbid cast, neither was his mind introspective; as (for the good of mankind) is ordained to those who have the world before them. He turned to the right by a track across the grass, followed the bend of the churchyard wall, and fearing to go any further, lest he should stumble on his father's outraged grave, sat down upon a gap of the gray enclosure. This gap had been caused by the sweep of tempest that went up the valley at the climax of the storm. The wall, being low, had taken little harm; but the great west gable of the Abbey had been smitten, and swung on its back, as a trap-door swings upon its hinges. Thick flint structure, and time-worn mullion, massive buttress, and deep foundation, all had gone flat, and turned their fangs up, rending a chasm in the tattered earth. But this dark chasm was hidden from view, by a pile of loose rubble, and chunks of flint, that had rattled down when the gable fell, and striking the cross-wall had lodged thereon, breaking the cope in places, and hanging (with tangles of ivy, and tufts of toad-flax) over the interval of wall and ruin, as a snowdrift overhangs a ditch.

Here the young man sat down; as if any sort of place would do for him. The gap in the wall was no matter to him, but happened to suit his downcast mood, and the misery of the moment. Here he might sit, and wait, until

Mr. Penniloe had got through a job, superior to the burial-service, because no one could cut you in pieces, directly afterwards, without being hanged for it. He could see Mr. Penniloe's black stick, standing like a little Parson—for some of them are proud of such resemblance—in the great south porch of the church; and thereby he knew that he could not miss his friend. As he lifted his eyes to the ancient tower, and the black yew-tree still steadfast, and the four vanes (never of one opinion as to the direction of the wind, in anything less than half a gale), and the jackdaws come home prematurely, after digging up broad-beans, to settle their squabble about their nests; and then as he lowered his gaze to the tombstones, and the new foundation-arches, and other labours of a parish now so hateful to him—heavy depression, and crushing sense of the wrath of God against his race, fell upon his head; as the ruin behind him had fallen on its own foundations.

He felt like an old man, fain to die, when time is gone weary and empty. What was the use of wealth to him, of bodily strength, of bright ambition to make his Country proud of him, even of love of dearest friends, and wedded bliss—if such there were—and children who would honour him? All must be under one black ban of mystery insoluble; never could there be one hearty smile, one gay thought, one soft delight; but ever the view of his father's dear old figure desecrated, mangled, perhaps lectured on. He could not think twice of that, but groaned—"The Lord in Heaven be my help! The Lord deliver me from this life?"

He was all but delivered of this life—happy, or wretched —it was all but gone. For as he flung his body back, suiting the action to his agony of mind—crash went the pile of jagged flint, the hummocks of dead mortar, and the wattle of shattered ivy. He cast himself forward, just in time, as all that had carried him broke and fell, churning, and grinding, and clashing together, sending up a cloud of powdered lime.

So sudden was the rush, that his hat went with it, leaving his brown curls grimed with dust, and his head for a moment in a dazed condition, as of one who has leapt from an earthquake. He stood with his back to the wall, and the muscles of his great legs quivering, after the strain of their spring for dear life. Then scarcely yet conscious of his hair-breadth escape, he descried Mr. Penniloe coming from the porch, and hastened without thought to meet him.

"Billy-jack!" said the clergyman, smiling, yet doubtful whether he ought to smile. "They insisted on calling that child 'Billy-jack.' 'William-John' they would not hear of. I could not object, for it was too late; and there is nothing in it uncanonical. But I scarcely felt as I should have done, when I had to say—'Billy-jack, I baptise thee,' etc. I hope they did not do it to try me. Now the Devonshire mind is very deep and subtle; though generally supposed to be the simplest of the simple. But what has become of your hat, my dear boy? Surely Thyatira has had time enough to clean it."

"She cleaned it beautifully. But it was waste of time. It has gone down a hole. Come, and I will show you. I wonder my head did not go with it. What a queer place this has become!"

"A hole! What hole can there be about here?" Mr. Penniloe asked, as he followed the young man. "The downfall of the Abbey has made a heap, rather than what can be called a hole. But I declare you are right! Why, I never saw this before; and I looked along here with Haddon, not more than a week age. Don't come too near; it is safe enough for me, but you are like Neptune, a shaker of the earth. Alas for our poor ivy!"

He put on his glasses, and peered through the wall-gap, into the flint-strewn depth outside. Part of the ruins, just dislodged, had rolled into a pit, or some deep excavation; the crown of which had broken in, probably when the gable fell. The remnant of the churchyard wall was still quite sound, and evidently stood away from all that had gone on outside.

"Be thankful to God for your escape," Mr. Penniloe said, looking back at the youth. "It has indeed been a narrow one. If you had been carried down there head-foremost, even your strong frame would have been crushed like an egg-shell."

"I am not sure about that; but I don't want to try it. I think I can see a good piece of my hat; and I am not going to be done out of it. Will you be kind enough, sir, to wait, while I go round by the stile, and get in at that end? You see that it is easy to get down there; but a frightful job from this side. You won't mind waiting, will you, sir?"

"If you will take my advice," said the Curate, "you will be content to let well alone. It is the great lesson of the age. But nobody attends to it."

The young man did not attend to it; and for once Mr. Penniloe had given bad advice; though most correct in principle, and in practice too, nine times and a half out of every ten.

"Here I am, sir. Can you see me?" Sir Thomas Waldron shouted up the hole. "It is a queer place, and no mistake. Please to stop just where you are. Then you can give me notice, if you see the ground likely to cave in. Halloa! Why, I never saw anything like it! Here's a stone arch, and a tunnel beyond it, just like what you've got at the rectory, only ever so much bigger. Looks as if the old Abbey had butted up against it, until it all got blown away. If I had got a fellow down here to help me, I believe I could get into it. But all these chunks are in the way."

"My dear young friend, it will soon be dark; and we have more important things to see to. You are not at all safe down there; if the sides fell in, you would never come out alive."

"It has cost me a hat; and I won't be done. I can't go home without a hat, till dark. I am not coming up, till I know all about it. Do oblige me, sir, by having the least little bit of patience."

Mr. Penniloe smiled. The request, as coming from such a quarter, pleased him. And presently the young man began to fling up great lumps of clotted flint, as if they were marbles, right and left.

"What a volcano you are!" cried the Parson, as the youth in the crater stopped to breathe. "It is nothing but a waste of energy. The hole won't run away, my dear Tom. You had much better leave it for the proper man to-morrow."

"Don't say that. I am the proper man." How true

his words were, he had no idea. "But I hear somebody whistling. If I had only got a fellow, to keep this stuff back, I could get on like a house on fire."

It was Pike coming back from the long pool in the meadow, with a pretty little dish of trout for supper. His whistling was fine; as a fisherman's should be, for want of something better in his mouth; and he never got over the Churchyard stile, without this little air of consolation for the ghosts.

As he topped the ridge of meadow that looks down on the river, Mr. Penniloe waved his hat to him, over the breach of the churchyard wall; and he nothing loth stuck his rod into the ground, pulled off his jacket, and went down to help.

"All clear now. We can slip in like a rabbit. But it looks uncommonly black inside, and it seems to go a long way underground;" Waldron shouted up to the clergyman. "We cannot do anything, without a light."

"I'll tell you what, sir," Pike chimed in. "This passage runs right into the church, I do believe."

"That is the very thing I have been thinking;" answered Mr. Penniloe. "I have heard of a tradition to that effect. I should like to come down, and examine it."

"Not yet, sir; if you please. There is scarcely room for three. And it would be a dangerous place for you. But if you could only give us something like a candle——"

"Oh, I know!" The sage Pike suggested, with an angler's quickness. "Ask him to throw us down one of the four torches stuck up at the lych-gate. They burn like fury; and I dare say you have got a lucifer, or a Promethean."

"Not a bad idea, Pike;" answered Mr. Penniloe. "I believe that each of them will burn for half-an-hour."

Soon he returned with the driest of them, from the iron loop under the covered space; and this took fire very heartily, being made of twisted tow soaked in resin.

"I am rather big for this job;" said Sir Thomas, as the red flame sputtered in the archway, "perhaps you would like to go first, my young friend."

"Very much obliged," replied Pike drawing back; "but I don't seem to feel myself called upon to rush into the

2 F

bowels of the earth, among six centuries of ghosts. I had better stop here, perhaps, till you come back."

"Very well. At any rate hold my coat. It is bad enough; I don't want to make it worse. I shan't be long, I dare say. But I am bound to see the end of it."

"Young Waldron handed his coat to Pike, and stooping his tall head with the torch well in front of him, plunged into the dark arcade. Grim shadows flitted along the roof, as the sound of his heavy steps came back; then the torchlight vanished round a bend of wall, and nothing could either be seen or heard. Mr. Penniloe, in some anxiety, leaned over the breach in the churchyard fence, striving to see what was under his feet; while Pike mustered courage to stand in the archway—which was of roughly chiselled stone—but kept himself ready for instant flight, as he drew deep breaths of excitement.

By-and-by, the torch came quivering back, throwing flits of light along the white-flint roof; and behind it a man, shaking worse than any shadow, and whiter than any torchlit chalk.

"Great God!" He cried, staggering forth, and falling with his hand on his heart against the steep side of the pit. "As sure as there is a God in heaven, I have found my father!"

"What!" cried the Parson; "Pike, see to the torch; or you'll both be on fire."

In a moment, he ran round by way of the stile, and slid into the pit, without thinking of his legs, laying hold of some long rasps of ivy. Pike very nimbly leaped up the other side; this was not the sort of hole to throw a fly in.

"Give me the torch. You stay here, Tom. You have had enough of it." Mr. Penniloe's breath was short, because of the speed he had made of it. "It is my place now. You stop here, and get the air."

"I think it is rather my place, than of any other man upon the earth. Am I afraid of my own dear dad? Follow me, and I will show him to you."

He went with a slow step, dazed out of all wonder—as a man in a dream accepts everything—down the dark passage again, and through the ice-cold air, and the shivering fire. Then he stopped suddenly, and stooped the torch, stooping his curly head in lowliness behind it; and there, as if set down by the bearers for a rest, lay a long oaken coffin. Mr. Penniloe came to his side, and gazed. At their feet lay the good and true-hearted Colonel, or all of him left below the heaven, resting placidly, unprofaned, untouched by even the hand of time ; unsullied and honourable in his death, as in his loyal and blameless life.

The clear light fell upon the diamond of glass, (framed in the oak above his face, as was often done then for the last look of love) and it showed his white curls, and tranquil forehead, and eyelids for ever closed against all disappointment.

His son could not speak, but sobbed, and shook, with love, and reverence, and manly grief. But the clergyman, with a godly joy, and immortal faith, and heavenly hope, knelt at the foot, and lifted hands and eyes to the God of heaven.

" Behold, He hath not forsaken us ! His mercy is over all His works. And his goodness is upon the children of men."

CHAPTER XLIII.

TWO FINE LESSONS.

AT the *Old Barn* that afternoon, no sooner was young Sir Thomas gone, than remarkable things began to happen. As was observed in a previous case, few of us are yet so vast of mind, as to feel deeply, and fairly enjoy the justice of being served with our own sauce. Haply this is why sauce and justice are in Latin the self-same word. Few of us even are so candid, as to perceive when it comes to pass ; more often is a world of difference found betwixt what we gave, and what we got.

Fox was now treated by Nicie's brother, exactly as he had treated Gilham about his sister Christie. He was not remarkably rash of mind—which was ever so much better for himself and friends—yet he was quick of perception ; and when his sister came and looked at him, and said with gentle sympathy—" Oh, Jemmy, has Sir Thomas forbidden your bans? No wonder you threw his hat at him "—it was a little more than he could do, not to grin at the force of analogy.

"He is mad." He replied, with strong decision. Yet at the twinkle of her eyes, he wondered whether she held that explanation valid, in a like case, not so very long ago.

"I have made up my mind to it altogether;" he continued, with the air magnanimous. "It is useless to strive against the force of circumstances."

"Made up your mind to give up Nicie, because her brother disapproves of it?" Christie knew well enough what he meant But can girls be magnanimous?

"I should think not. How can you be so stupid? What has a brother's approval to do with it? Do you think I care twopence for fifty thousand brothers? Brothers are all very well in their way; but let them stick to their own business. A girl's heart is her own, I should hope; and her happiness depends on herself, not her brother. I call it a great piece of impudence, for a brother to interfere in such matters."

"Oh!" said Christie, and nothing more. Neither did she even smile; but went to the window, and smoothed her apron, the pretty one she wore, when she was mixing water-colours.

"You shall come and see him now;" said Jemmy, looking at the light that was dancing in her curls, but too lofty to suspect that inward laughter made them dance. "It can't hurt him now; and my opinion is that it might even do him a great deal of good. I'll soon have him ready, and I'll send his blessed mother to make another saucepanful of chicken broth. And Chris, I'll give you clear decks, honour bright."

"I am quite at a loss to understand your meaning." The mendacious Christie turned round, and fixed her bright eyes upon his most grandly; as girls often do, when they tell white lies—perhaps to see how they are swallowed.

"Very well then; that is all right. It will save a lot of trouble; and perhaps it is better to leave him alone."

"There again! You never seem to understand me, Jemmy! And of course, you don't care how much it upsets a poor patient, never to see a change of faces. Of course you are very kind; and so is Dr. Gronow; and poor Mrs.

Gilham is a most delightful person. Still, after being for all that time so desperately limited—that's not the word at all—I mean, so to some extent restricted, or if you prefer it prohibited, from—from any little change, any sort of variety of expressions, of surroundings, of in fact, society——

"Ah yes, no doubt! Of etcetera, etcetera. But go you on floundering, till I come back, and perhaps then you will know what you mean. Perhaps also you would look a little more decent with your apron off," Dr. Fox suggested, with the noble rudeness so often dealt out to sisters. "Be sure you remind him that yesterday was Leap-year's day; and then perhaps you will be able to find some one to understand you."

"If that is the case, you may be quite certain that I won't go near him."

But before very long she thought better of that. Was it just to punish one for the offences of another? With a colour like the first bud of monthly rose peeping through its sepals in the southern corner, she ran into the shrubbery —for there was nothing to call a garden—and gathered a little posy of Russian violets and wild primrose. Then she pulled her apron off, and had a good look at herself, and could not help knowing that she had not seen a lovelier thing for a long time; and if love would only multiply it by two, —and it generally does so by a thousand—the result would be something stupendous, ineffable, adorable.

Such thoughts are very bright and cheerful, full of glowing youth and kindness, young romance and contempt of earth. But the longer we plod on this earth, the deeper we stick into it; as must be when the foot grows heavy, having no *talaria*. Long enduring pain produces a like effect with lapse of years. The spring of the system loses coil, from being on perpetual strain; sad proverbs flock into the brain, instead of dancing verses.

Frank Gilham had been ploughed and harrowed, clod-crushed, drilled, and scarified by the most advanced, enlightened, and practical of all medical high-farmers. If ever Fox left him, to get a breath of air, Gronow came in to keep the screw on; and when they were both worn out, young Webber (who began to see how much he had to

learn, and what was for his highest interest) was allowed to
sit by, and do nothing. A consultation was held, whenever
the time hung heavily on their hands; and Webber would
have liked to say a word, if it could have been uttered
without a snub. Meanwhile, Frank Gilham got the worst
of it.

At last he had been allowed to leave his bed, and taste a
little of the fine Spring air, flowing down from Hagdon
Hill, and bearing first waft of the furze-bloom. Haggard
weariness and giddy lightness, and a vacant wondering
doubt (as to who or what he was, that scarcely seemed
worth puzzling out), would have proved to any one who cared
to know it, that his head had lain too long in one position, and
was not yet reconciled to the change. And yet it should have
welcomed this relief, if virtue there be in heredity, inasmuch
as this sofa came from White Post farm, and must have
comforted the head of many a sick progenitor.

The globe of thought being in this state, and the arm
of action crippled, the question was—would heart arise,
dispense with both, and have its way?

For awhile it seemed a doubtful thing; so tedious had
the conflict been, and such emptiness left behind it. The
young man, after dreams most blissful, and hopes too
golden to have any kin with gilt, was reduced to bare bones
and plastered elbows, and knees unsafe to go down upon.
But the turn of the tide of human life quivers to the
influence of heaven.

In came Christie, like a flush of health, rosy with bright
maidenhood; yet tremulous as a lily is, with gentle fear and
tenderness. Pity is akin to love—as those who know them
both, and in their larger hearts have felt them, for our smaller
sakes pronounce—but when the love is far in front, and
pauses at the check of pride; what chance has pride, if
pity comes, and takes her mistress by the hand, and whispers
—"try to comfort him?"

None can tell, who are not in the case, and those who
are know little of it, how these strange things come to
pass. But sure it is that they have their way. The
bashful, proud, light-hearted maiden, ready to make a joke
of love, and laugh at such a fantasy, was so overwhelmed
with pity, that the bashfulness forgot to blush, the pride

cast down its frightened eyes, and the levity burst into
tears. But of all these things she remembered none.

And forsooth they may well be considered doubtful, in
common with many harder facts; because the house was
turned upside down, before any more could be known of it.
There was coming, and going, and stamping of feet, horses
looking in at the door, and women calling out of it; and
such a shouting and hurrahing, not only here but all over
the village, that the Perle itself might well have stopped,
like Simöis and Scamander, to ask what the fish out of
water were doing. And it might have stopped long,
without being much wiser; so thoroughly everybody's head
was flown, and everybody's mouth filled with much more
than the biggest ears found room for.

To put it in order is a hopeless job, because all order
was gone to grit. But as concerns the *Old Barn* (whose
thatch, being used to ¦quiet eaves-droppings, had enough to
make it stand up in sheaf again)—first dashed up a young
man on horseback, (and the sympathetic nag was half mad
also) the horse knocking sparks out of the ground, as if he
had never heard of lucifers, and the man with his legs all
out of saddle, waving a thing that looked like a letter, and
shouting as if all literature were comprised in *vivâ voce*.
Now this was young Farrant, the son of the Churchwarden;
and really there was no excuse for him; for the Farrants
are a very clever race; and as yet competitive examination
had not made the sight of paper loathsome to any mind
cultivating self-respect.

" You come out, and just read this; " he shouted to the
Barn in general. " You never heard such a thing in all
your life. All the village is madder than any March hare.
I shan't tell you a word of it. You come out and read.
And if that doesn't fetch you out, you must be a clam of
oysters. If you don't believe me, come and see it for yourselves. Only you will have to get by Jakes, and he is
standing at the mouth, with his French sword drawn."

" In the name of Heaven, what the devil do you mean ? "
cried Fox, running out, and catching fire of like madness,
of all human elements the most explosive, " and this—why,
this letter is the maddest thing of all ! A man who was
bursting to knock me down, scarcely two gurgles of the

clock ago! And now, I am his beloved Jemmy! Mrs.
Gilham, do come out. Surely that chicken has been stewed
to death. Oh, Ma'am, you have some sense in you. Everybody else is gone off his head. Who can make head or tail
of this? Let me entreat you to read it, Mrs. Gilham.
Farrant, you'll be over that colt's head directly. Mrs.
Gilham, this is meant for a saner eye than mine. Your
head-piece is always full of self-possession."

Highly flattered with this tribute, the old lady put on
her spectacles, and read, slowly and decorously.

" BELOVED JEMMY,
" I am all that you called me, a hot-headed fool,
and a cad; and everything vile on the back of it. The
doctors are the finest chaps alive, because they have never
done harm to the dead. Come down at once, and put a
bar across, because Jakes must have his supper. Perlycross
folk are the best in the world, and the kindest-hearted, but
we must not lett them go in there. I am off home, for if
anybody else was to get in front of me, and tell my mother,
I should go wild, and she would be quite upsett. When
you have done all you think proper, come up and see poor
Nicie.
" From your affectionate, and very sorry,
" T. R. WALDRON."

"Now the other, Ma'am!" cried Doctor Fox. " Here is
another from the Parson. Oh come now, we shall have a
little common sense."

" MY DEAR JEMMY,
" It has pleased the Lord, who never afflicts us
without good purpose, to remove that long and very heavy
trouble from us. We have found the mortal remains of
my dear friend, untouched by any human hand, in a hollow
way leading from the Abbey to the Church. We have not
yet discovered how it happened; and I cannot stop to tell
you more, for I must go at once to Walderscourt, lest rumour
should get there before us; and Sir Thomas must not go
alone, being of rather headlong, though very noble nature.
Sergeant Jakes has been placed on guard, against any rash
curiosity. I have sent for the two Churchwardens and can

leave it safely to them and to you, to see that all is done properly. If it can be managed, without undue haste, the coffin should be placed inside the Church, and the doors locked until the morning. When that is done, barricade the entrance to the tunnel; although I am sure that the people of our parish would have too much right feeling, as well as apprehension, to attempt to make their way in, after dark. To-morrow, I trust we shall offer humble thanks to the Giver of all good, for this great mercy. I propose to hold a short special service; though I fear there is no precedent in the Prayer-book. This will take a vast weight off your mind, as well as mine, which has been sorely tried. I beg you not to lose a minute, as many people might become unduly excited.

"Most truly yours,
"PHILIP PENNILOE."

"P.S.—This relieves us also from another dark anxiety, simply explaining the downfall of the S.E. corner of the Chancel."

"It seems hard upon me; but it must be right, because the Parson has decreed it;" Dr. Fox cried, without a particle of what is now called "slavish adulation of the Church"—which scarcely stuck up for herself in those days —but by virtue of the influence which a kind and good man always gains, when he does not overstrain his rights. "I am off, Mrs. Gilham, I can trust you to see to the pair of invalids upstairs."

Then he jumped upon young Mr. Farrant's horse, and leaving him to follow at foot leisure, dashed down the hill towards Perlycross. At the four cross-roads, which are the key of the position, and have all the village and the valley in command, he found as fine a concourse perhaps as had been there since the great days of the Romans. Not a rush of dread, and doubting, and of shivering back-bones, such as had been on that hoary morning, when the sun came through the fog, and showed Churchwarden Farmer John, and Channing the clerk, and blacksmith Crang, trudging from the potato-field, full of ghastly tidings, and encountering at that very spot Sergeant Jakes, and Cornish, and the tremulous tramp of half the village, afraid of resurrection.

Instead of hurrying from the churchyard, as a haunt of ghouls and fiends, all were hastening towards it now, with deep respect reviving. The people who lived beyond the bridge, and even beyond the factory, and were much inclined by local right to sit under the Dissenting minister—himself a very good man, and working in harmony with the Curate— many of these, and even some from Priestwell, having heard of it, pushed their right to know everything, in front of those who lived close to the Church and looked through the railings every day. Farmer John Horner was there on his horse, trotting slowly up and down, as brave as a mounted policeman is, and knowing every one by name called out to him to behave himself. Moreover Walter Haddon stood at the door of the *Ivy-bush*, with his coat off, and his shirtsleeves rolled, and ready to double his fist at any man who only drank small beer, at the very first sign of tumult. But candidly speaking this was needless, powerful as the upheaval was, and hot the spirit of enquiry; for the wives of most of the men were there, and happily in an English crowd that always makes for good manners.

Fox was received with loud hurrahs, and many ran forward to shake his hand; some, who had been most black and bitter in their vile suspicions, having the manliness to beg his pardon, and abuse themselves very heartily. He forgave them with much frankness, as behoves an English-man, and with a pleasant smile at their folly, which also is nicely national. For after all, there is no other race that can give and take as we do; not by any means headlong, yet insisting upon decision—of the other side, at any rate— and thus quickening the sense of justice upon the average, in our favour

Fox, with the truly British face of one who is understood at last, but makes no fuss about it, gave up his horse at the lych-gate, and made off where he was beckoned for. Here were three great scaffold-poles and slings fixed over the entrance to the ancient under-way; and before dark all was managed well. And then a short procession, headed by the martial march of Jakes, conveyed into the venerable Church the mortal part of a just and kind man and a noble soldier, to be consigned to-morrow to a more secure, and ever tranquil, and still honoured resting-place.

This being done, the need of understanding must be satisfied. Dr. Fox, and Dr. Gronow, with the two Church-wardens, and Channing the clerk, descended the ladder into the hole, and with a couple of torches kindled went to see the cause and manner of this strange yet simple matter—a four-month mystery of darkness, henceforth as clear as daylight.

When they beheld it, they were surprised, not at the thing itself—for it could scarcely have happened otherwise, under the circumstances—but at the coincidences, which had led so many people of very keen intelligence into, as might almost be said, every track, except the right one. And this brought home to them one great lesson—"*If you wish to be sure of a thing, see it with your own good eyes.*" And another—but that comes afterwards.

The passage, dug by the Monks no doubt, led from the Abbey directly westward to the chancel of the Church, probably to enable them to carry their tapers burning, and discharge their duties there promptly and with vestments dry, in defiance of the weather. The crown, of loose flints set in mortar, was some eight feet underground, and the line it took was that adopted in all Christian burial. The grave of the late Sir Thomas Waldron was prepared, as he had wished, far away from the family vault (which had sadly undermined the Church), and towards the eastern end of the yard, as yet not much inhabited. As it chanced, the bottom lay directly along a weak, or worn-out part of the concrete arch below ; and the men who dug it said at the time that their spades had struck on something hard, which they took to be loose blocks of flint. However being satisfied with their depth, and having orders to wall the bottom, they laid on either side some nine or ten courses of brickwork, well flushed in with strong and binding mortar ; but the ends being safe and bricks running short, to save any further trouble, they omitted the cross-wall at the ends. Thus when the weight of earth cast in pressed more and more heavily upon the heavy coffin, the dome of concreted flints below collapsed, the solid oaken box dropped quietly to the bottom of the tunnel, and the dwarf brick sides having no tie across, but being well bonded together, and well-footed, fell across the vacancy into one another, forming a new arch, or more correctly a splay span-roof, in lieu of the old arch which had yielded to the strain. Thus the earth above took this new bearing, and the surface of the ground was no more disturbed than it always is by settlement.

No wonder then that in the hurried search, by men who had not been down there before, and had not heard of any brickwork at the sides, and were at that moment in a highly nervous state, not only was the grave reported empty —which of course was true enough—but no suspicion was entertained that the bottom they came to (now covered with earth) was anything else than a rough platform for the resting-place. And the two who could have told them better, being proud of their skill in foundations, had joined the builders' staff, and been sent away to distant jobs.

In the heat of foregone conclusion, and the terror created by the blacksmith's tale, and the sad condition of that faithful little *Jess*, the report had been taken as final. No further quest seemed needful; and at Squire Mockham's order, the empty space had been filled in at once, for fear of the excitement, and throng of vulgar gazers, gathering and thickening around the empty grave.

Such are the cases that make us wonder at the power of co-incidence, and the very strange fact that the less things seem to have to do with one another, the greater is their force upon the human mind, when it tries to be too logical.

Many little things, all far apart, had been fetched together by fine reasoning process, and made to converge towards a very fine error, with certainty universal.

Even that humble agent, or patient, little *Jess*—despised as a dog, by the many who have no delight in their better selves—had contributed very largely to the confluence of panic. If she could only have thrown the light of language on her woeful plight, the strongest clench to the blacksmith's tale would never have come near his pincers. For the slash that rewarded her true love fell, not from the spade of a Churchyard-robber, but from a poacher's bill-hook. This has already been intimated; and Mr. Penniloe must have learned it then; if he had simply taken time, instead of making off at five miles an hour, when Speccotty wanted to tell his tale. This should be a warning to Clergymen; for perhaps there was no other man in the parish, whose case the good parson would thus have post-poned, without prospect of higher consolation. And it does seem a little too hard upon a man, that because his mind is gone astray unawares, his soul should drop out of cultivation !

That poor little spaniel was going home sadly, to get a bit of breakfast, and come back to her duty; when tres-passing unwittingly upon the poacher's tricks, at early wink of daylight, she was taken for a minion of the Evil One, and met with a vigour which is shown too seldom, by even true sportsmen, to his emissaries. Perhaps before she quitted guard, she may have had a nip at the flowers on the grave, and dropped them back, when she failed to make sweet bones of them.

Without further words—though any number of words, if their weight were by the score, would be too few—the slowest-headed man in Perlycross might lay to his heart the second lesson, read in as mild a voice as Penniloe's, above. And without a word at all, he may be trusted to go home with it; when the job is of other folk's hands, but his own pocket.

"*Never scamp your work,*" was preached more clearly by this long trouble, and degradation of an honourable parish, than if Mr. Penniloe had stood in the pulpit, for a week of Sundays, with the mouth of King Solomon laid to his ear, and the trump of the Royal Mail upon his lips.

CHAPTER XLIV.

AND ONE STILL FINER.

IF it be sweet to watch at ease the troubles of another, how much sweeter to look back, from the vantage ground of happiness, upon one's own misfortunes ! To be able to think—" well, it was too bad ! Another week would have killed me. How I pulled through it, is more than I can tell; for everybody was against me ! And the luck—the luck kept playing leap-frog; fifty plagues all upon one another's back; and my poor little self at the bottom. Not a friend came near me; they were all so sorry, but happened to be frightfully down themselves. I assure you, my dear, if it had not been for you, and the thought of our blessed children, and perhaps my own—well, I won't say 'pluck,' but determination to go through with it; instead of arranging these flowers for dinner, you would have been wreathing them for a sadder purpose."

The lady sheds a tear, and says—" Darling Jack, see how you have made my hand shake! I have almost spoiled that truss of Hoya, and this Schubertia won't stand up. But you never said a word about it, at the time! Was that fair to me, Jack?" And the like will come to pass again, perhaps next year, perhaps next week.

But the beauty of country-life, as it then prevailed (ere the hungry hawk of Stock-exchange poised his wings above the stock-dove) was to take things gently, softly, with a cooing faith in goodness, both above us and around. Men must work; but being born (as their best friends, the horses, are), for that especial purpose, why should they make it still more sad, by dwelling upon it, at the nose-bag time? How much wiser to allow that turbulent bit of stuff, the mind, to abide at ease, and take things in, rather than cast them forth half-chewed, in the style of our present essayists?

Now this old village was the right sort of place, to do such things, without knowing it. There was no great leading intellect (with his hands returned to feet), to beat the hollow drum, and play shrill fife, and set everybody tumbling over his best friend's head. The rule of the men was to go on, according to the way in which their fathers went; talking as if they were running on in front, but sticking effectually to the old coat-tail. Which in the long run is the wisest thing to do.

They were proud of their church, when the Sunday mood was on, and their children came home to tell about it.

There she was. Let her stand; if the folk with money could support her. It was utterly impossible to get into their heads any difference betwixt the Church in the churchyard, and the one that inhabits the sky above. When a man has been hard at work all the week, let his wife be his better half on Sunday.

Nothing that ever can be said, or done, by the most

ardent "pastor," will ever produce that enthusiasm among
the tegs of his flock, which spreads so freely among the
ewes, and lambs. Mr. Penniloe would not be called a
Pastor; to him the name savoured of a cant conceit.
Neither did he call himself a *Priest;* for him it was quite
enough to be a Clergyman of the Church of England; and
to give his life to that.

Therefore, when the time came round, and the turn of
the year was fit for it, this Parson of that humbler type
was happy to finish, without fuss, the works that he had
undertaken, with a lofty confidence in the Lord, which had
come to ground too often. His faith, though fine, had
never been of that grandly abstract quality, which expects
the ravens to come down, with bread instead of bills, and
build a nest for sweet doves *gratis.* To pay every penny
that was fairly due, and shorten no man of his Saturday
wage, towards the Sunday consolation; to perceive that
business must not be treated as a purely spiritual essence;
and to know that a great many very good people drip away
(as tallow does from its own wick) from their quick flare of
promises; also to bear the brunt of all, and cast up the
toppling column, with the balance coming down on his own
chest—what wonder that he had scarcely any dark hair
left, and even the silver was inclined to say adieu?

When a man, who is getting on in years, comes out of a
long anxiety, about money, and honour, and his sense of
right, he finds even in the soft flush of, relief that a great
deal of his spring is gone. A Bachelor of Arts, when his
ticks have been paid by a groaning governor, is fit and fresh
to start again, and seldom dwells with due remorse upon
the sacrifice Vicarious. His father also, if of right paternal
spirit, soars above the unpleasant subject; leaves it to the
mother to drive home the lesson—which she feels already
to be too severe—and says, "Well, Jack, you have got
your degree; and that's more than the Squire's son can
boast of."

But the ancient M.A. of ten lustres, who has run into
debt on his own hook, and felt the hook running into him,
is in very different plight, even when he has wriggled off.
Parson Penniloe was sorely humble, his placid forehead
sadly wrinkled, and his kindly eyes uncertain how to look

at his brother men, even from the height of pulpit ; when in his tremulous throat stuck fast that stern and difficult precept—" Owe no man anything."

Even the strongest of mankind can scarcely manage to come up to that, when fortune is not with him, and his family tug the other way. The glory of the Lord may be a lofty prospect, but becomes a cloudy pillar, when the column is cast up, and will not square with cash in hand. Scarcely is it too much to say, that since the days of Abraham, it would have been hard to find a man of stronger faith than Penniloe,—except at the times when he broke down (in vice of matters physical) and proved at one break two ancient creeds—*Exceptio probat regulam ;* and *Corruptio optimi pessima.*

While he was on the balance now, as a man of the higher ropes should be, lifting the upper end of his pole, that the glory of his parish shone again, yet feeling the butt inclined to swag, by reason of the bills stuck upon it, who should come in to the audience and audit but young Sir Thomas Waldron ? This youth had thought perhaps too little of himself,—because those candid friends, his brother-boys had always spoken of his body so kindly, without a single good word for his mind—but now he was authorized, and even ordered, by universal opinion to take a much fairer view of his own value.

Nothing that ever yet came to pass has gone into words without some shift of colour, and few things even without change of form ; and so it would have been beyond all nature if the events above reported had been told with perfect accuracy even here. How much less could this be so, in the hot excitement of the time, with every man eager to excel his neighbour's narrative, and every woman burning to recall it with her own pure imagination ! What then of the woman, who had been blessed enough to enrich the world, and by the same gift ennoble it, with the hero, who at a stroke had purged the family, the parish, and the nation ?

Nevertheless he came in gently, modestly, and with some misgivings, into the room, where he had trembled, blushed, and floundered|on all fours, over the old gray Latin steps, which have broken many a knee-cap.

" If you please, sir," he said to his old tutor, who alone

had taught him anything, for at Eton he had barely
learned good manners; "my mother begs you to read this.
And we are all ashamed of our behaviour."

"No, Tom, no. You have no cause for that. Your
mother may have been a little hard at first. But she has
meant to be just throughout. The misery she has passed
through—none but herself can realise."

"You see, sir, she does not sing out about things, as most
women do; and that of course makes it ever so much worse
for her."

The young man spoke, like some deep student of
feminine nature; but his words were only those of the
good housekeeper at Walderscourt. Mr. Penniloe took
them in that light, and began to read without reply.

"Truly esteemed and valued sir. With some hesitation
of the mind I come to say that in all I have said and done,
my mind has been of the wrong intelligence most largely.
It always appears in this land of Britain, as if nobody of it
could make a mistake. But we have not in my country
such great wisdom and good fortune. Also in any other
European land of which I have the acquaintance, the
natives are wrong in their opinions sometimes.

"But this does not excuse me of my mistake. I have
been unjust to you and to all people living around my place
of dwelling. But by my dear son, and his very deep
sagacity, it has been made manifest that your good people
were considered guilty, without proper justice, of a wrong
upon my husband's memory. Also that your good church,
of which he thought so well in the course of his dear life,
has treated him not with ignominy, but with the best of
her attention, receiving him into the sacred parts, where
the Priests of our religion in the times of truth conversed.
This is to me of the holiest and most gracious consolation.

"Therefore I entreat you to accept, for the uses of so
good a building, the little sum herewith committed to your
care, which flows entirely from my own resources, and
not from the property of my dear husband, so much
engaged in the distribution of the law. When that is
disengaged, my dear son Rodrigo, with my approbation
will contribute from it the same amount for the perfection
of the matter."

2 G

" One, two, three, four, five.   And every one of them a
hundred pounds !   My dear Tom, I feel a doubt——"

Mr. Penniloe leaned back and thought.   He was never
much excited about money, except when he owed it to, or
for the Lord.

" I call it very poor amends indeed.   What would ten
times as much be, after all that you have suffered ?   And
how can you refuse it, when it is not for yourself ?   My
mother will be hurt most dreadfully, and never think well
again of the Church of England."

" Tom, you are right ; " Mr. Penniloe replied, while a
smile flitted over his conscience.   " I should indeed convey
a false impression of the character of our dear mother.
But as for the other £500—well——"

" My father's character must be considered, as well as
your good mother's."   Sir Thomas was not strong at
metaphor.   " And I am sure of one thing, sir.   If he
could have known what would happen about him, and how
beautifully every one behaved, except his own people—but
it's no use talking.   If you don't take it, I shall join the
Early Methodists.   What do you think of that, sir ?   I am
always as good as my word, you know."

" Ah !   Ah !   It may be so ; " the Curate answered
thoughtfully, returning to the mildness of exclamation from
which these troubles had driven him.   " But allow me a
little time for consideration.   Your mother's very generous
gift, I can accept without hesitation, and have no right to
do otherwise.   But as to your father's estate, I am placed
in a delicate position, by reason of my trusteeship ; and it
is possible that I might go wrong ; at any rate, I must
consult——"

" Mrs. Fox, sir, from Foxden ! "   Thyatira Muggridge
cried, with her face as red as a turkey's wattle, and throwing the door of the humble back-room as wide as if it
never could be wide enough.   For the lady was beautifully
arrayed.

" I come to consult, not to be consulted.   My confidence
in myself has been misplaced ; " said the mother of Jemmy
and Christie, after making the due salutation.   " Sir
Thomas, I beg you not to go.   You have some right to a
voice in the matter ; if as they tell me at *Old Barn*, you

have conquered your repugnance to my son, and are ready to receive him as your brother-in-law."

"Madam, I was a fool," said Tom, offering his great hand with a sheepish look. "Your son has forgiven me; and I hope that you will. Jemmy is the finest fellow ever born."

"A credit to his mother, as his mother always thought. And what is still better for himself, a happy man, in winning the affections of the sweetest girl on earth. I have seen your dear sister—what a gentle darling!"

"Nicie is very well in her way, madam. But she has a strong will of her own. Jemmy will find that out, some day. Upon the whole, I am sorry for him."

"He talks in the very same way of his sister. If young men listened to young men, none of them would ever marry. Oh, Mr. Penniloe, you can be trusted at any rate, to look at things from a higher point of view."

"I try sometimes; but it is not easy. And I generally get into scrapes, when I do. But I have one consolation. Nobody ever takes my advice."

"I mean to take it," Mrs. Fox replied, looking into his gentle eyes, with the faith which clever women feel in a nature larger than their own. "You need not suppose that I am impulsive. But I know what you are. When every one else in this stupid little place condemned my son, without hearing a word, there was one who was too noble, too good a Christian, to listen to any reason. He was right when the mother herself was wrong. For I don't mind telling you, as I have even told my son, that knowing what he is, I could not help suspecting that he—that he had something to do with it. Not that Lady Waldron had any right whatever—and it will take me a long time to forgive her, and her son is quite welcome to tell her that. What you felt yourself was quite different, Sir Thomas."

"I can't see that my mother did any harm. Why, she even suspected her own twin-brother! If you were to bear ill-will against my mother——"

"Of such little tricks I am incapable, Sir Thomas. And of course I can allow for foreigners. Even twenty years of English life cannot bring them to see things as we do. Their nature is so—well, I won't say narrow. Neither will I say 'bigoted,' although——"

"We quite understand you, my dear madam." Mr. Penniloe was shocked at his own rudeness, in thus interrupting a lady, but he knew that very little more would produce a bad breach betwixt Walderscourt and Foxden. "What a difference really does exist among people equally just and upright——"

"My dear mother is as just and upright as any Englishwoman in the world, Protestant or Catholic," the young man exclaimed, having temper on the bubble, yet not allowing it to boil against a lady. "But if his own mother condemned him, how—I can't put it into words, as I mean it —how can she be in a wax with my mother? And more than that—as it happens, Mrs. Fox, my mother starts for Spain to day, and I cannot let her go alone."

"Now the Lord must have ordered it so," thought the Parson. "What a clearance of hostile elements!" But fearing that the others might not so take it, he said only— "Ah, indeed!"

"To her native land?" asked Mrs. Fox, as a Protestant not quite unbigoted; and a woman who longed to have it out. "It seems an extraordinary thing just now. But perhaps it is a pilgrimage."

"Yes, madam, for about £500,000," answered Sir Thomas, in his youthful Tory vein, not emancipated yet from disdain of commerce; "not for the sake of the money, of course; but to do justice to the brother she had wronged. Mr. Penniloe can tell you all about it. I am not much of a hand at arithmetic."

"We won't trouble any one about that now;" the lady replied with some loftiness. "But I presume that Lady Waldron would wish to see me, before she leaves this country."

"Certainly she would if she had known that you were here. My sister had not come back yet, to tell her. She will be disappointed terribly, when she hears that you have been at Perlycross. But she is compelled to catch the Packet; and I fear that I must say 'good-bye'; mother would never forgive me, if she lost her voyage through any fault of mine."

"You see how they treat us!" said Mrs. Fox of Foxden, when the young man had made his adieu with great politeness. "I suppose you understand it, Mr. Penniloe, though your mind is so very much larger?"

The clergyman scarcely knew what to say. He was not at all quick in the ways of the world; and all feminine rush was beyond him. "We must all allow for circumstances," was his quiet platitude.

"All possible allowance I can make;" the lady replied with much self-command. "But I think there is nothing more despicable than this small county-family feeling! Is Lady Waldron not aware that I am connected with the very foremost of your Devonshire families? But because my husband is engaged in commerce, a military race may look down upon us! After all, I should like to know, what are your proudest landowners, but mere agriculturists by deputy? I never lose my temper; but it makes me laugh, when I remember that after all, they are simply dependent upon farming. Is not that what it comes to, Mr. Penniloe?"

"And a very noble occupation, madam. The first and the finest of the ways ordained by the Lord for the sustenance of mankind. Next to the care of the human soul, what vocation can be——"

"You think so. Then I tell you what I'll do, if only to let those Waldrons know how little we care for their prejudices. Everything depends upon me now, in my poor husband's sad condition. I will give my consent to my daughter's alliance—great people call it *alliance*, don't they?—with a young man, who is a mere farmer!"

"I am assured that he will make his way," Mr. Penniloe answered with some inward smile, for it is a pleasant path to follow in the track of ladies. "He gets a higher price for pigs, than either of my Churchwardens."

"What could you desire more than that? It is a proof of the highest capacity. Mr. and Mrs. Frank Gilham shall send their wedding cards to Walderscourt, with a prime young porker engraved on them. Oh, Mr. Penniloe, I am not perfect. But I have an unusual gift perhaps of largeness of mind, and common sense; and I always go against any one, who endeavours to get the whip-hand of me. And I do believe my darling Christie gets it from her mother."

"She is a most charming young lady, Mrs. Fox. What a treasure she would be in this parish! The other day, she said a thing about our Church——"

"Just like her. She is always doing that. And when she comes into her own money—but that is a low consideration. It is gratitude, my dear sir, the deepest and the noblest feeling that still survives in these latter days. Without that heroic young man's behaviour, which has partly disabled him for life, I fear, I should have neither son nor daughter. And you say that the Gilhams are of very good birth?"

"The true name is *Guillaume*, I believe. Their ancestor came with the Conqueror. Not as a rapacious noble, but in a most useful and peaceful vocation; in fact——"

"Quite enough, Mr. Penniloe. In such a case, one scorns particulars. My daughter was sure that it was so. But I doubted; although you can see it in his bearing. A more thoroughly modest young man never breathed; but I shall try to make him not afraid of me. He told my daughter that, in his opinion, I realised—but you would think me vain; and I was justly annoyed at such nonsense. However, since I have had your advice, I shall hesitate no longer."

Mrs. Fox smiled pleasantly, because her mind was quite made up, to save herself a world of useless trouble in this matter, and yet appear to take the upper hand in her surrender.

Wondering what advice he could have been supposed to give, the mild yet gallant Parson led her to the Foxden carriage, which had halted at his outer gate, and opposite the school house. Here with many a bow they parted, thinking well of one another, and hoping for the like regard. But as the gentle curate passed the mouth of the Tænarian tunnel leading to his lower realms, a great surprise befell him.

"What has happened? There is something wrong. Surely at this time of day, one ought to see the sunset through that hole," he communed with himself in wonder, for the dark arcade ran from east to west. "There must be a stoppage somewhere. I am almost sure I can see two heads. Good people, come out, whoever you may be."

"The fact of it is, sir," said Sergeant Jakes, marching out of the hole with great dignity, though his hat was white with cob-webs; "the fact of it is that this good lady hath received a sudden shock——"

"No sir, no sir. Not at all like that, sir. Only as St. Paul saith in chapter 5 of Ephesians—'this is a great mystery.'"

"It is indeed. And I must request to have it explained immediately."

Thyatira's blushes and the sparkling of her eyes made her look quite pretty, and almost as good as young again, while she turned away with a final shot from the locker of old authority.

"You ought to be ashamed, sir, according to my thinking, to be standing in this wind so long, without no hat upon your head."

"You see, sir, it is just like this," the gallant sergeant followed up, when his love was out of hearing; "time hath come for Mrs. Muggridge to be married, now or never. It is not for me to say, as a man who fears the Lord, that I think He was altogether right in the institooting of wedlock, supposing as ever He did so. But whether He did it, or whether He did not, the thing hath been so taken up by the humankind—women particular—that for a man getting on in years, 'tis the only thing respectable. Thyatira hath proven that out of the Bible, many times."

"Mr. Jakes, the proper thing is to search the Scriptures for yourself."

"So Thyatira saith. But Lord! She findeth me wrong at every text, from looking up to women so. If she holdeth by St. Paul, a quarter so much as she quoteth him, there won't be another man in Perlycross with such a home as I shall have."

"You have chosen one of the few wise virgins. Jakes, I trust that you will be blest not only with a happy home in this world, but what is a thousand-fold more important, the aid of a truly religious wife, to lead a thoroughly humble, prayerful, and consistent Christian life."

"Thank 'e, sir. Thank 'e. With the grace of God, she will; and my first prayer to the Lord in heaven will be just this—to let me live long enough for to see that young

fool of a Bob the butcher ahanging fom his own steelyard.
By reason of the idiot he hath made of his self, by marrying of that silly minx, Tamar Haddon!"

"The grace of God is boundless; and Tamar may
improve. Try to make the best of her, Mr. Jakes. She
will always look up to you, I am sure, feeling the strength
of your character, and the example of higher principles."

"She!" replied the sergeant without a blush, but after
a keen reconnoitring glance. "The likes of her doesn't
get no benefit from example. But I must not keep you,
sir, so long without your hat on."

"This is a day of many strange events," Mr. Penniloe
began to meditate, as he leaned back in his long sermon-
chair, with the shadows of the Spring night deepening.
"Lady Waldron gone, to support her brother's case in
Spain, because she had so wronged him. A thousand
pounds suddenly forthcoming, to lift us out of our affliction;
sweet Nicie left in the charge of Mrs Webber, who comes
to live at Walderscourt; Christie Fox allowed to have her
own way, as she was pretty sure to do; and now Thyatira,
Thyatira Muggridge, not content to lead a quiet, useful,
respectable, Christian, and well-paid life, but launched into
matrimony with a man of many stripes! I know not how
the school will be conducted, or my own household, if it
comes to that. Truly, when a clergyman is left without a
wife——"

"I want to come in, and the door won't open"—a clear
but impatient voice was heard—"I want to see you, before
anybody else does." And then another shake was given.

"Why, Zip, my dear child! Zip, don't be so headlong.
I thought you were learning self-command. Why, how
have you come? What is the meaning of all this?"

"Well, now they may kill me, if they like. I told
them I would hear your voice again, and then they might
skin me, if it suited them. I won't have their religion.
There is none of it inside them. You are the only one I
ever saw, that God has made with his eyes open. I like
them very well, but what are they to you? Why, they
won't let me speak as I was made! It is no good sending
me away again. Parson, you mustn't stand up like that.
Can't you see that I want to kiss you?"

"My dear little child, with all my heart. But I never saw any one half so——"

"Half so what? I don't care what, so long as I have got you round the neck," cried the child as she covered his face with kisses, drawing back every now and then, to look into his calm blue eyes with flashes of adoration. "The Lord should have made me your child, instead of that well-conducted waxy thing—look at my nails! She had better not come now."

"Alas! Have you cultivated nothing but your nails? But why did the good ladies send you home so soon? They said they would keep you until Whitsuntide."

"I got a punishment on purpose, and I let the old girls go to dinner. Then I said the Lord's Prayer, and slipped down the back stairs."

"And you plodded more than twenty miles alone! Oh Zip, what a difficult thing it will be to guide you into the ways of peace!"

"They say I talks broad a bit still sometimes, and they gives me ever so much roilying. But I'd sit up all night with a cork in my mouth, if so be, I could plaize 'e, Parson."

"You must want something better than a cork, my dear"—vexed as he was, Mr. Penniloe admired the vigorous growth and high spirit of the child—"after twenty-two miles of our up and down roads. Now go to Mrs. Muggridge, but remember one thing—if you are unkind to my little Fay, how can you expect me to be kind to you?"

"Not a very lofty way for me to put it," he reflected, while Zip was being cared for in the kitchen; "but what am I to do with that strange child? If the girl is mother to the woman, she will be none of the choir Angelic, contented with duty, and hymns of repose. If 'nature maketh nadders,' as our good people say, Zippy * hath more of sting than sugar in her bowl."

But when the present moment thrives, and life is warm and active, and those in whom we take delight are prosperous and happy, what is there why we should not smile, and keep in tune with all around, and find the flavour of the world returning to our relish? This may not be of the

* This proved too true, as may be shown hereafter.

noblest style of thinking, or of living; but he who would,
in his little way, rather help than harm his fellows, soon
finds out that it cannot be done by carping and girding at
them. By intimacy with their lower parts, and rank
insistence on them, one may for himself obtain some power,
yielded by a hateful shame. But who esteems him, who is
better for his fetid labours, who would go to him for
comfort when the world is waning, who—though in his
home he may be loveable—can love him?

Mr. Penniloe was not of those who mount mankind by
lowering it. From year to year his influence grew, as
grows a tree in the backwood age, that neither shuns nor
defies the storm. Though certain persons opposed him
still—as happens to every active man—there was not one
of them that did not think all the others wrong in doing
so. For instance Lady Waldron, when she returned with
her son from Spain, thought Mrs. Fox by no means reasonable, and Mrs. Fox thought Lady Waldron anything but
sensible, when either of them differed with the clergyman
and the other. For verily it was a harder thing to settle
all the important points concerning Nicie and Jemmy Fox,
than to come to a perfect understanding in the case of
Christie and Frank Gilham.

However the parish was pleased at last to hear that
everything had been arranged; and a mighty day it was
to be for all that pleasant neighbourhood, although no
doubt a quiet, and as every one hoped, a sober one. On
account of her father's sad condition, Christie as well as
Nicie, was to make her vows in the grand old church,
which was not wholly finished yet, because there was so
much more to do, through the fine influx of money. Cur-
rency is so called perhaps, not only because it runs away
so fast, but also because it runs together; the prefix being
omitted through our warm affection and longing for the
terms of familiarity. At any rate the Parson and the
stout Churchwardens of Perlycross had just received
another hundred pounds when the following interview
came to pass.

It was on the bank of the crystal Perle, at the place
where the Priestwell brook glides in, and a single plank
without a handrail crosses it into the meads below. Here

are some stickles of good speed, and right complexion, for the fly to float quietly into a dainty mouth, and produce a fine fry in the evening; and here, if any man rejoice not in the gentle art, yet may he find sweet comfort and release of worldly trouble, by sitting softly on the bank, and letting all the birds sing to him, and all the flowers fill the air, and all the little waves go by, as his own anxieties have gone.

Sometimes Mr. Penniloe, whenever he could spare the time, allowed his heart to go up to heaven, where his soul was waiting for it and wondering at its little cares. And so on this fair morning of the May, here he sat upon a bank of Spring, gazing at the gliding water through the mute salaam of twigs.

" Reverend, I congratulate you. Never heard of a finer hit. A solid hundred out of Gowler! Never bet with a parson, eh? I thought he knew the world too well."

A few months back and the clergyman would have risen very stiffly, and kept his distance from this joke. But now he had a genuine liking for this " Godless Gronow," and knew that his mind was the worst part of him.

" Doctor, you know that it was no bet;" he said, as he shook hands heartily. " Nevertheless I feel some doubts about accepting——"

" You can't help it. The money is not for yourself, and you rob the Church, if you refuse it. The joke of it is that I saw through the mill-stone, where that conceited fellow failed. Come now, as you are a sporting man, I'll bet you a crown that I catch a trout in this little stickle above the plank."

" Done!" cried Mr. Penniloe, forgetting his position, but observing Gronow's as he whirled his flies.

The doctor threshed heartily, and at his very best; even bending his back as he had seen Pike do, and screwing up his lips, and keeping, in a strict line with his line, his body and his mind and whole existence.

Mr. Penniloe's face wore an amiable smile, as he watched the intensity of his friend. Crowns in his private purse were few and far between, and if he should attain one by the present venture, it would simply go into the poor-box; yet such was his sympathy with human nature that he hoped against hope to see a little trout pulled out. But the willows bowed sweetly, and the wind went by, and the water flowed on, with all its clever children safe.

"Here you are, Reverend!" said the philosophic Gronow, pulling out his cart-wheel like a man; "you can't make them take you when they don't choose, can you? But I'll make them pay out for it, when they begin to rise."

"The fact of it is that you are too skilful, doctor; and you let them see so much of you that they feel it in their hearts."

"There may be truth in that. But my own idea is, that I manage to instil into my flies too keen a sense of their own dependence upon me. Now what am I to do? I must have a dish and a good dish too of trout, for this evening's supper. You know the honour and the pleasure I am to have of giving the last bachelor and maiden feast to the heroes and heroines of to-morrow, Nicie and Jemmy Fox, Christie and Frank Gilham. Their people are glad to be quit of them in the fuss, and they are too glad to be out of it. None of your imported stuff for me. Nothing is to be allowed upon the table, unless it is the produce of our own parish. A fine fore-quarter, and a ripe sirloin, my own asparagus, and lettuce, and sea-kail, and frame-potatoes in their jackets. Stewed pears and clotted cream, grapes, and a pine-apple (coming of course from Walders-court)—oh Reverend, what a good man you would be, if you only knew what is good to eat!"

"But I do. And I shall know still better by and by. I understood that I was kindly invited."

"To be sure, and one of the most important. But I must look sharp, or I shall never get the fish. By the by, you couldn't take the rod for half an hour, could you? I hear that you have been a fine hand at it."

Mr. Penniloe stood with his hand upon a burr-knot of oak, and looked at the fishing-rod. If it had been a good, homely, hard-working, and plain-living bit of stuff, such as Saint Peter might have swung upon the banks of Jordan, haply the parson might have yielded to the sweet temptation. For here within a few clicks of reel was goodly choice of many waters, various as the weather—placid glides of middle currents rippling off towards either bank, petulant swerves from bank, or bole, with a plashing and a murmur and a gurgling from below, and then a spread of quiet dimples deepening to a limpid pool. Taking all the twists and turns of river Perle and Priestwell brook, there must have been a mile of water in two flowery meadows, water bright with stickle runs, gloomy with still corners, or quivering with crafty hovers where a king of fish might dwell.

But lo, the king of fishermen, or at least the young prince was coming! The doctor caught the parson's sleeve, and his face assumed its worst expression, perhaps its usual one before he took to Church-going and fly-fishing.

"Just look! Over there, by that wild cherry-tree!" He whispered very fiercely. "I am sure it's that sneak of a Pike once more. Come into this bush, and watch him. I thought he was gone to Oxford. Why, I never saw him fishing once last week."

"Pike is no sneak, but a very honest fellow," his tutor answered warmly. "But I was obliged by a sad offence of his to stop him from handling the rod last week. He begged me to lay it on his back instead. The poor boy scarcely took a bit of food. He will never forget that punishment."

"Well he seems to be making up for it now. What luck he has, and I get none!"

Mr. Penniloe smiled as his favourite pupil crossed the Perle towards them. He was not wading—in such small waters there is no necessity for that—but stepping lightly from pile to pile and slab to slab, where the relics of an ancient weir stood above the flashing river. Whistling softly, and calmly watching every curl and ripple, he was throwing a long line up the stream, while his flies were flitting as if human genius had turned them in their posthumous condition into moths. His rod showed not a glance of light, but from spike to top-ring quivered with the vigilance of death.

While the envious Gronow watched, with bated breath and teeth set hard, two or three merry little trout were taught what they were made for; then in a soft swirl near the bank that dimpled like a maiden's cheek, an excellent fish with a yellow belly bravely made room in it for something choice. Before he had smacked his lips thoroughly, behold another fly of wondrous beauty—laced with silver, azure-pinioned, and with an exquisite curl of tail—came fluttering through the golden world so marvellous to the race below. The poor fly shuddered at the giddy gulf, then folded his wings and fell helpless. "I have thee," exclaimed the trout,—but ah! more truly the same thing said the Pike. A gallant struggle, a thrilling minute, silvery dashes, and golden rolls, and there between Dr. Gronow's feet lay upon Dr. Gronow's land a visitor he would have given half the meadow to have placed there.

"Don't touch him," said Pike, in the calmest manner; "or you'll be sure to let him in again. He will turn the pound handsomely, don't you think?"

"A cool hand, truly, this pupil of yours!" quoth the doctor to the parson. "To consult me about the weight of my own fish, and then put him in his basket! Young man, this meadow belongs to me."

"Yes, sir, I dare say; but the fish don't live altogether in the meadow. And I never heard that you preserve the Perle. Priestwell brook you do, I know. But I don't want to go there, if I might."

"I dare say. Perhaps the grapes are sour. Never mind; let us see how you have done. I find them taking rather short to-day. Why you don't mean to say you have caught all those!"

"I ought to have done better," said the modest Pike, "but I lost two very nice fish by being in too much of a hurry. That comes of being stopped from it all last week. But I see you have not been lucky yet. You are welcome to these, sir, if Mr. Penniloe does not want them. By strict right, I dare say they belong to you."

"Not one of them, Mr. Pike. But you are very generous. I hope to catch a basketful very shortly— still, it is just possible that this may not occur. I will take them provisionally, and with many thanks. Now, will you add to the obligation, by telling, if your tutor has no objection, why he put you under such an awful veto?"

"My boy, you are welcome to tell Dr. Gronow. It was only a bit of thoughtlessness, and your punishment has been severe."

"I shall never touch cobbler's wax again on Sunday. But I wanted to finish a May-fly entirely of my own pattern; and so after church I was touching up his wings, when in comes Mr. Penniloe with his London glasses on."

"And I am proud to assure you, Dr. Gronow, that the lad never tried to deceive me. I should have been deeply pained, if he had striven to conceal it."

"Well done! That speaks well for both of you. Pike, you are a straight-forward fellow. You shall have a day on my brook once a week. Is there anything more I can do for you?"

"Yes sir, unless it is too much to ask; and perhaps Mr. Penniloe would like to hear it too. Hopper and I have had many talks about it; and he says that I am super-stitious. But his plan of things is to cut for his life over everything that he can see, without stopping once to look at it. And when he has jumped over it, he has no more idea what it was, than if he had run under it. He has no faith in anything that he does not see, and he never sees much of anything."

"Ha, Master Pike. You describe it well;" said the doctor, looking at him with much interest. "Scepticism without enquiry. Reverend, that Hop-jumper is not the right stuff for a bishop."

"If you please, Dr. Gronow, we will not discuss that now," the parson replied with a glance at young Pike, which the doctor understood and heeded: "What is it, my boy, that you would ask of Dr. Gronow, after serious debate with Peckover?"

"Nothing sir, nothing. Only we would like to know, if it is not disagreeable to any one, how he could have managed from the very first to understand all about Sir Thomas Waldron, and to know that we were all making fools of ourselves. I say that he must have seen a dream, like Jacob, or have been cast into a vision, like so many other saints. But Hopper says no; if there was any inspiration, Dr. Gronow was more likely to have got it from the Devil."

"Come now, Pike, and Hopper too,—if he were here to fly my brook,—I call that very unfair of you. No, it was not you who said it; I can quite believe that. No fisher-man reviles his brother. But you should have given him

the spike, my friend. Reverend, is this all the theology
you teach? Well, there is one answer as to how I knew it,
and a very short one—the little word, *brains*."

Mr. Penniloe smiled a pleasant smile, and simply said,
"Ah!" in his accustomed tone, which everybody liked for
its sympathy and good faith. But Pike took up his rod,
and waved his flies about, and answered very gravely—
"It must be something more than that."

"No sir," said the doctor, looking down at him com-
placently, and giving a little tap to his grizzled forehead;
"it was all done here, sir—just a trifling bit of brains."

"But there never can have been such brains before;"
replied Pike with an angler's persistence. "Why everybody else was a thousand miles astray, and yet Dr. Gronow
hit the mark at once!"

"It is a little humble knack he has, sir. Just a little
gift of thinking," the owner of all this wisdom spoke as if
he were half-ashamed of it; "from his earliest days it has
been so. Nothing whatever to be proud of, and sometimes
even a trouble to him, when others require to be set right.
But how can one help it, Master Pike? There is the
power, and it must be used. Mr Penniloe will tell you
that."

"All knowledge is from above," replied the gentleman
thus appealed to; "and beyond all question it is the duty
of those who have this precious gift, to employ it for the
good of others."

"Young man; there is a moral lesson for you. When
wiser people set you right, be thankful and be humble. That
has been my practice always, though I have not found
many occasions for it."

Pike was evidently much impressed, and looked with
reverence at both his elders. "Perhaps then," he said,
with a little hesitation and the bright blush of ingenuous
youth, "I ought to set Dr. Gronow right in a little mistake
he is making."

"If such a thing be possible, of course you should," his
tutor replied with a smile of surprise; while the doctor
recovered his breath, made a bow, and said, "Sir, will you
point out my error?"

"Here it is, sir," quoth Pike, with the certainty of truth

overcoming his young diffidence, "this wire-apparatus in your brook—a very clever thing; what is the object of it?"

"My *Ichthyophylax?* A noble idea that has puzzled all the parish. A sort of a grill that only works one way. It keeps all my fish from going down to my neighbours, and yet allows theirs to come up to me; and when they come up, they can never get back. At the other end of my property, I have the same contrivance inverted, so that all the fish come down to me, but none of them can go up again. I saw the thing offered in a sporting paper, and paid a lot of money for it in London. Reverend, isn't it a grand invention? It intercepts them all, like a sluice-gate."

"Extremely ingenious, no doubt," replied the parson. "But is not it what a fair-minded person would consider rather selfish?"

"Not at all. They would like to have my fish, if they could; and so I anticipate them, and get theirs. Quite the rule of the Scriptures, Reverend."

"I think that I have read a text," said Master Pike, stroking his long chin, and not quite sure that he quoted aright; "the snare which he laid for others, in the same are his own feet taken!"

"A very fine text," replied Dr. Gronow, with one of his most sarcastic smiles; "and the special favourite of the Lord must have realized it too often. But what has that to do with my *Ichthyophylax?*"

"Nothing, sir. Only that you have set it so that it works in the wrong direction. All the fish go out, but they can't come back. And if it is so at the upper end, no wonder that you catch nothing."

"Can I ever call any man a fool again?" cried the doctor, when thoroughly convinced.

"Perhaps that disability will be no loss;" Mr. Penniloe answered quietly.

THE END.